The Velvet Rooms

SAM NORTH

SIMON &
SCHUSTER

London · New York · Sydney · Toronto

A VIACOM COMPANY

First published in Great Britain by Simon & Schuster, 2006
A Viacom Company

1 3 5 7 9 10 8 6 4 2

Simon & Schuster UK Ltd
Africa House
64–78 Kingsway
London WC2B 6AH

www.simonsays.co.uk

Simon & Schuster Australia
Sydney

A CIP catalogue record for this book is available from the British Library.

ISBN 0-7432-7634-5
EAN 9780743276344

Typeset in Garamond M Rules
Printed and bound in Great Britain by
The Bath Press, Bath

*In order of appearance, I'd like
to thank David Harsent,
Alice Kavounas-Taylor,
Jane Turnbull*

WELCOME TO THE
VELVET ROOMS

Please select the room you wish to enter.

- VELVET BALLROOM
- VELVET SANCTUARY
- VELVET SHORE
- VELVET DUNGEON

Enter Chat

Fat-armed Wife enters Velvet Ballroom

Fat-armed Wife: Hi everyone

Fat-armed Wife:

Fat-armed Wife: Hello? - tiptoe across empty dancefloor - anyone here?

Fat-armed Wife: Hey - anyone here … here .. here

Honeycake: Hi Fatarms, sorry

Fat-armed Wife: Hi Honey - why no dancing? you alone?

Honeycake: No, every1's whispering, sum went 2 Sanctuary

Fat-armed Wife: Sigh - no music

Honeycake: DanceMaster not here yet. Ur early!! - Im just at my desk

Fat-armed Wife: Just a nose round the door to look for Call Girl

Honeycake: Uhhhh?? - but what time is it for her???

Fat-armed Wife: Thought she might have been on all-nighter

Honeycake: y arnt u at work?

Fat-armed Wife: Was about to go then mail delivery - **&&^^%-%$4£$%^%!!!

Honeycake: Hnnn!? Ticket arrived?

Fat-armed Wife: Yup I'm going for real - hey - weird but true

Honeycake: u r brave

Fat-armed Wife: Wanted to drag Call Girl to the Dungeon kinda soonest

Honeycake: We allowed 2 tell folk?

Fat-armed Wife: Maybe not everyone - but tell her if you see her before me I'm lookin'

1

Honeycake: ok - Gawddd, wanna go dress up!! 'n lift a glass!! or sumthin. 2 celebrate

Fat-armed Wife: cheers Honey

Honeycake: Fatarms take my hat off 2 u, huh?

Fat-armed Wife: Thanks - I'm nervous! - bye sweetheart Honeycake

Honeycake: ~kiss~mwahh! ~ see ya later *vbs*

Fat-armed Wife: *~gone~poof!~*

In Boston, Massachusetts, Fat-armed Wife poured coffee. She liked it so thick you could stand the spoon in it. Colin stood opposite, leaning over the work surface, his arms thick and strong to hold his weight. His forefinger idly stroked the litre glass of diet Coke – two-thirds empty already. The check dressing gown was a big fall of cheap cloth, overused, imbued with his personal odour. The lines on his neck, she noticed, were as if written in black ink – four of them looping round, engraved in his skin from years of turning his head to left and right. Everyone got older at the same rate – like feathers falling, slowly, slowly – yet Colin was some way ahead of her; he was knocking forty.

She couldn't determine if he was staring at the American Airlines envelope on the counter or if he was thinking of something else and just happened to be looking down. He was frowning like a bear with a sore head. Or maybe she was putting that on him. She was nervous about the ticket for obvious reasons. She didn't want to see him too close to it. The envelope was on top of the pile; the corner where she'd torn it open was standing up, jagged. From that corner poured her lover's voice – the image jumped into her head, like in a cartoon. She stared. Yes, it was like music, the notes written in Call Girl's green italic hand in the Velvet Rooms. The words called to her alone. She took the coffee, rose to her feet and snapped the laptop shut. It was ridiculous that Colin couldn't see or hear that voice but his bear-like expression was maybe because he knew there was some-thing he wasn't picking up on. She took herself off to where the basket of jewellery waited underneath the mirror and spread out her fat fingers, flexed them, ready to carry their freight of rings. She started to lay out different ones on the counter, putting them along-side one another to judge the effect. There was an element of theatre to her job, for sure. If people admired the costumes she wore, they'd buy the costumes she sold.

She was aware of Colin's slippers scraping behind her but she couldn't see him in the mirror. She was waiting for another comment but there was silence. Then his hand arrived on her hip. She didn't answer it, just carried on plugging her fingers. She favoured silver to go with her Seiko. Besides, too much gold was ostentatious; no one wanted to put dollars into hands that looked too rich. She could load up with silver to her heart's content and still sell second-hand jeans to students.

After a while Colin's hand went from her hip – so she'd won. She imagined all married couples had a sign, a way of making the request without speaking. Well, Colin, no, she answered silently. She was late for work already. She waggled her fingers. They glittered back at her, suddenly alive with Celtic knots, coiled serpents, skulls and cross-bones.

Colin's voice sounded tired. 'With the same money we could have replaced the mower.'

It was best to agree. 'Yup.' She scooped the make-up crate, brought it near to hand. From the cleavage upwards she'd paint her-self thickly. The Real Thing shopfloor was a stage. She dressed it like one. The scene was permanently set: the most expensive items – worn by mannequins – were mounted higher up, so they could be seen but not touched. Some of them were delicate and worth thou-sands of dollars. Down below hung the more day-to-day stuff on racks. The jewellery and brooches and other curios waited in locked glass cases. Upstairs was the cheap student gear. The daily drama unfolded: her need to sell against the customer's desire to purchase. She expected people she hired to become expert at playing their parts.

Then she thought up an answer for Colin to chew on, concerning the money. 'But you know what, if this trip does what it's meant to you can have the mower and the trimmer and whatever, plus, Colin, hire the guy to do the work.'

'You know the exchange rate? It's not the time to start a business in the UK.'

'Exchange rates go up and down all over the place, let's not forget. It's ten cents less than it was, so it's heading the right way. And it doesn't hurt to go find out,' she finished.

Some minutes later she was plumping her cheekbones with blusher when the hand arrived on her hip again. It felt strangely distant and inert, that touch of her husband's, because her sexuality had been so captured by Call Girl. Also, she had in her head a map of her body that was smaller than the actual reality. She had an Irish grandmother – her ancestors had dug the canals into Lowell for the cotton factories – and she'd been stick-thin; they had the old black-and-white pictures to prove it. By the time the bloodline had reached her, it was like she'd been encased in an extra, American body, not helped by her addiction to Cape Cod potato chips. In her early twenties her weight had nudged two hundred and sixty pounds. It was practically a third less now, but still Colin's hand was way off, could only reach as far as that distant frontier, the excess of her hips.

'Maybe I should go with you,' came his voice. 'We could put Jamie across with Jill for that week.'

She kept going with the blusher although the bristles had already unloaded the colour. 'Sure,' she said. 'If you want, that would be great for me. Let me know soon, though 'cos I'd want to have you sitting next to me on the plane.' She waited, clicked the blusher shut and dropped it back in the wicker make-up bin. She remembered to breathe.

'Nah, what would I do?' he said.

She was relieved, but then just as suddenly she became frightened of her victory over him. It was her responsibility to have made him a victim. She didn't want that. There was too much she owed him. Bad luck would strike if she floated too far off in the imaginary world of the Velvet Rooms, if she became enchanted with it at no cost to herself. She should put out for Colin. She was already late for work but she turned, picked up his hand and put it back on her hip. 'Hey, big guy.'

It was an ordinary story, she thought: a fat-armed, middle-aged wife contemplates escape from a kind-of-OK marriage. In how many houses was that scenario being played out here in Somerville? On Main Street, on Broadway, on Winter Hill, in every two-family and three-family; she'd bet it was going on in practically every single one.

If they were in a soap – if they were in *Sunset Beach* – he'd lift her onto the counter and make love to her right here, on top of the ticket that was, maybe, going to carry her away. She and Colin never did things like that; it wasn't part of his vocabulary. He took his sex like meals – usually the same thing at the same time, sitting at the table properly. And she served him now, she took him upstairs and paid for her ticket. She stroked his back, his hips. Call Girl's green italic writing flowed across the ceiling of their bedroom, mocking her. She wished for the music, for the dancing in the Velvet Rooms. She wished to be taken from this life and dropped into another, in another place, another time, with Call Girl, with proper lust flowing. If that was how it was going to turn out, she'd be happy.

Fat-armed Wife enters Velvet Ballroom

Fat-armed Wife: block light in doorway - push with fat arms - struggle through - phew - big smile - wave to dancers

DanceMaster: Fatarms ~ te *abrazo*! ~ we're doing a waltz by Bernie Longham and his Big Band, 1937, called Two of You …. Your right hand on my shoulder, step, etc

Spam: ahhhhhhh fatt arrrrrrmsss

Fat-armed Wife: DanceMaster - embrace - sounds great - hello dancers - Hi Spam

Honeycake: but how do you tell a guy a thing like that ~ lol ~ someone help me out

Big Black Woman: Honeycake, give it a name ~smile~ what about ROGER??? then you can just kind of introduce him ~grin~ *"Now Jim THIS IS ROGER, say hello…"* "Hello." *"Bzzzz…"* Heh heh…

Peach: *Hi Fatarms* ☺ *how r u?*

Honeycake: ~lol at BBW~ it's not the vibrating kind *vbs* Hey Fatarms ~wink~ traveller! ~ Call Girl not here yet

Psycho-dog: whine~ lick~ hello Fatarms ~wag tail~ whasssup

Fat-armed Wife: I'm great - *vbs* - better for being here - sigh - watch this space Velvet Roomers - Dungeon calling

Spam: ahhhhhhh….

Big Black Woman: Honey why NOT??? Surely whole point is vibbb-rrr-aaa-ttt-ionnn??? Huh???

Spam: Fatarmsssss the dunnnngeooonnnnn??? For reeeeel?

Honeycake: BBW I dont like the soujnd … interferes with train of thought ~ smile~ plus I always think neighbours will hear and ask *Hey, why's she mowing the lawn at this time of night? ha ha*

Fat-armed Wife: Spam yes Velvet Dungeon here we come ...

Spam: ~lol at Honeycake~ !! ~ lawnmower!??? Groannnnnn is it that big?

Peach: *Makes me bit jelous fatarms*

DanceMaster: Fat-arms I'll have 2 go down there and oil the hinges

Honeycake: Spam put it this way I had to set up this winch over the bed and it has to be *Lowered Down To Me*. I like em big. what do u like?

Fat-armed Wife: Don't be jealous Peachy - your time will come - promise

Peach: *Fatarms u r brave or what*

Spam: Honeycake I like … welllll … I like yuung girrrlies tastingg of hunny and skkins like sillkkk of course

Fat-armed Wife: Peach thank you, brave - hope so - anxious as well tho - wish me luck - all shoulders to the wheel

Asbo enters Velvet Ballroom

Asbo: smash bottle ughhhh punch arrgg fucking dickhead wanker vomit fucking bastards shitface throw brick

Fat-armed Wife: Seen Call Girl yet anyone?

DanceMaster: Not yet

Asbo: *~gone~poof!~*

DanceMaster: *~whisper to Fat-armed Wife~* You must be safe

Peach: *Fat-armed Wife it is going 2 b alright u sure?*

Fat-armed Wife: Peach - will be all right - Call Girl will look after me - thanks for concern

Fat-armed Wife: *~whisper to DanceMaster~* Yes I will be safe - but nervous of course

Call Girl enters Velvet Ballroom

Call Girl: *… slips past bouncers … skids into Velvet Rooms… bedraggled … dirty … … breathless … knocks into dancers … Goodddd! HELP …??!!*

Fat-armed Wife: Clap - applause - hey! Whistle! Call Girl!!

DanceMaster: Here we go… All change … the music is 80s soul smooth and sexy The dance is freestyle … everyone … Hi Call Girl

Call Girl: *FAW I collapse in your fat arms - hold u tight - but have to keep running … spit dirt from mouth … knees bleeding …*

Fat-armed Wife: Call Girl my darling darling darling - hello hello hello - rise like giant boulder - roll towards you - I embrace you, hear me?! You want to dance? - cos I have news

Call Girl: *Hellllppppp!!!*

Peach: *~vbs~ hi Call Girl ☺ kiss on cheeks*

Call Girl: *~whisper to Fat-armed Wife~* *what news???! Is it what I think?*

Spam: agghhh!! Let her go everyone! My fave icon, call gurll, stumble again, stukmmbl.e for me, want to see your bruised arrrsse, show yr icon a few timmes so I grow hardddddd

Call Girl:

Call Girl:

Call Girl:

Spam: Ahhhhhhhh

Fat-armed Wife: *~whisper to Call Girl~* maybe ....

Call Girl: *someone ... !!!???? ... for God's sake, save me. Help help!!!! Pull tattered dress to hide naked breasts underneath ...*

Honeycake: oh-oh as Dustin Hoffman said in *Rain Man*

Peach: *~sits next to Psycho-dog~ Hi Psycho, my turn now to sit next to you. How's it going? Stroke stroke*

Call Girl: *~whisper to Fat-armed Wife~* *Don't tease. Have you got it ?*

Honeycake: Boss alert switching screens byeee for now

Fat-armed Wife: Haha watch out everyone Call Girl in action - ats my girl

Fat-armed Wife: *~whisper to Call Girl~* Yes, have ticket - all details here etc - ready for the Dungeon if you are? Hmmm? Later - afterwards?

Call Girl: *Don't tell him where I am ... blood at corner of my mouth ... I beg you ... clutch at them who dance ... who sit at tables drinking, as well ... don't tell him anything ... on my knees ... smeared with dirt ... please I beg you*

Psycho-dog: whine ~ pant ~ accept Peachy's strokes - ahhhh - smile ... tongue lolling ... smile smile ... mount Peachy's leg and pump hump pump ... hurrrhh

Peach: *Psycho dog no, no, down boy!!!*

Call Girl: *~whisper to Fat-armed Wife~ Whhhaaa??!! Yess!! Dungeon later yes ~kiss~ as well*

Spam: roll up, rrrrolllll uPPPPP!!!! Actionnnn Stationnsss!!!

Call Girl: *… knocks over several tables … stumbles through Velvet Rooms looking for a way out … Let go! Don't tell him where I am … stumbles, crawls, runs … let me go*

Spam: Coach leaves forrr the velvettt shorrres I reckon in ONE MINUTE!!??

Call Girl: *~gone~poof!~*

Spam: where is he thennn? Whoooo is hee? Whhatt is he

Fat-armed Wife: Anyone we know hmmm? I wonder

Biker Idiot: Peach, ur gonna dance with me?

Spam: … left standingg here, guesss whatt, holding ittty bittty piece of Call Girlll's torrn 'n stained bayyyyby doll nightdressss!!! ~sighhhhh~ Awwww, she's gone

Thruster enters Velvet Ballroom

Psycho-dog: Bark bark woof woof bark bark bark bark!!!!

Thruster: Call Girl?

Fat-armed Wife: Ahhhh Thruster - that way - point to Velvet Shore

Peach: *Hi Thruster shes gone to Velvet Shore*

Thruster: Call Girl?

Spam: Look what she founddddd - a lesserrr spotted Thruster

DanceMaster: Ah ha! *Todo el mundo,* clear the dance floor - everyone to the edge … ahem ~ points~ Thruster, she went that way to Velvet Shore

Fat-armed Wife: Big hamster-cheeks smile, hmmm? Thruster, Call Girl just left - ran fast as she could - through the dancers - glasses crashing on the ground - a table overturned - to Velvet Shore

Spam: Mind if we all follllow … with mouths opennnn …. watchingggg … ahh

Thruster: *~gone~poof!~*

Psycho-dog: Bark! Yelp! Wooooofff

Spam: uggghh … hnnnn .... ugghhh … Thruster??!! Wotta handle

Honeycake: Back again, hi everyone

Psycho-dog: Wooof woof! Bark! Peach come and watch with me. it will be good fun ~ bark!

Peach: *Psycho dog do not tease u know I wont*

Honeycake: Hey what's going down?

Spam: Honeycake call girl's goinggg down hahha hah ha … catch up catch up … call gurrrl … stumblinggg across summm boggggy moor in cybbberspace dot dot dot lifted some large stone dot dot dot and founnnnddd this MONNSSTERRRR called Thrusterrrr

Honeycake: Whaaaa!? THRUSTER??!!

Spam: u knowww himmm???

Honeycake: No jus the name ….

Spam: I KNOW - groannn -

Honeycake: whappppened?

Spam: Call Girl ran, stumbled, ran, came through in a terrrrribul state, usu7al cry of kidnap, rape! & straight 2 the Velvet Shore - nudges winks nudges winks - and so we pointed this THRUSSTERRRR - urgggg - this MAD RAPIST CUM STALKERRR *Thruster* - groannnn - to Velvet Shores also … roll up roll upppp!!! Time to goooo lookseeee. uuuu comingggg?

Thruster enters Velvet Ballroom

Honeycake: Thanks young Spam for the update. What a girl eh?

Thruster: Shes not in Velvbet Shore I just looked so where the fuck is she?

Spam: Tjhruster, handomes thruster, do theuy liee down for you and open thir longg legs and invite yor pardonable member into ther jhuingry salivfating mouthtsss

Fat-armed Wife: Thruster it means she's in private room so whisper to her - whispers will reach her wherever - unless she's locked the door in Sanctuary

Thruster: Tell me the password to her private or I'll fuck with ur site

Fat-armed Wife: mind your language - you are our guest, please remember

DanceMaster: Thruster, hombre, unwise behaviour, like she says, use the whisper box

Peach: *Leave, Thruster, please can you, we don't like this rude words, it's in The Velvet Shores not for the Ballroom* ☹ ☹

Fat-armed Wife: We like a bit of humour in here, Thruster - turning heavily - don't we everyone? - a bit of grace and charm - on the dance floor - shall we show him, DanceMaster?

Psycho-dog: Paw~ wag tail ~ Peach, cocktail and snack - here yu go - as big sorry from me ~ whine~

Thruster: She's not answering any fuckgin whisper

Psycho-dog: Woof wooff! Bark!! Bark!! Dont;' let ehte nasty man stay here or Il'l bite him

Peach: *What 4?*

Psycho-dog: 4 teasing u ~pant~

Peach: *~wipe to her lips the napkin~ sips cocktail ~ thanks Psycho-dog. What in that delicious drink? Thank you to bring it over to me. What will I owe you? That's kind of the manners we like Thruster in the ballroom*

Thruster: Fuck mannerss tell me the password 2 her private or santuary or whatever the fuck it is or I'll fuck with ur site so u wont know u exist u'll be so fucked into cyberspace u'll only ba able to look up yur own arse so givne me the fukcing passoword 2 Call Girls private room

DanceMaster: Cover your ears Peachy

Psycho-dog: Whine ~ snarl ~ growl~

Fat-armed Wife: - walks up to Thruster-thud thud thud- now look here buster - Call Girl is our favourite daughter - hear that - Isn't she everyone?

Spam: Whuppasss, whhhuppass

DanceMaster: Biker Idiot where are you? We need this guy to be thrown out … u r bouncer now

Peach: *Please Thruster we are an ok place, we don't use that bad language, except Spam ~s~ sorry Spam ~winks~*

Thruster: gimme her password or 20 of my frends cum in here evry night an smash the place up

Fat-armed Wife: Thruster go beat your meat somewhere else, hmmm, good idea?

Biker Idiot: I'm not very good at confrontation

Call Girl enters Velvet Ballroom

Call Girl: - *pushes everyone aside* - … *let me through … breathing hard … stand in front of Thruster … slick with sweat … bruised ... limping … don't, Thruster don't … it's me you want, not them*

Peach: *Call Girl, u r sure u want 2 tango with this guy?*

Fat-armed Wife: Ooof - here we go

Peach: *I don't like this*

Psycho-dog: ~whine ~ cock head ~ prick ears ~

Fat-armed Wife: everyone stand back

Spam: Whhhhhhuuuuppppasssssss!!

Thruster: Get over here On yr knees

DanceMaster: *STERN LOOK* To the Velvet Shore. Both of you

Call Girl: *My only chance is to flee - turn - trip and stumble - run and claw my way to the Velvet Shore*

Spam: Whupppassss! Coach leaving. All peeeeping Tommms this way!! Alllll abooaarddd!!!

12

Call Girl: *~gone~poof!~*

Thruster: *~gone~poof!~*

Peach: *I'm staying here, sorry everyone.* ☹

Biker Idiot: Peach do u mind if I go

Spam: *~gone~poof!~*

Peach: *Go ahead, see u later*

DanceMaster: *~gone~poof!~*

Psycho-dog: Tend the bar for me Peachy ~ pant ~

Fat-armed Wife: *gone~poof!~*

Peach: *I will b fine. U go.*

Psycho-dog: *~gone~poof!~*

Honeycake: *~gone~poof!~*

Call Girl enters Velvet Shore

Thruster enters Velvet Shore

Thruster: Get over here

Biker Idiot enters Velvet Shore

Call Girl: *Don't hurt me*

Thruster: ~smacks Call Girl's face~ I said get over here

Spam enters Velvet Shore

Fat-armed Wife enters Velvet Shore

Call Girl: *Owww …*

Thruster: ~another smack, but with a closed fist~ cum here

Psycho-dog enters Velvet Shore

Honeycake enters Velvet Shore

Call Girl: *Hold the back of my hand to my bleeding mouth … don't hurt me*

DanceMaster enters Velvet Shore

Thruster: ~grabbing ur hair, turning ur face to me~ u will do anything I want when I want

Call Girl: *Eyes plead with you … don't … you don't know how strong you are … cry a little now … face tilts up, exposed, bruised … don't hurt me .. cry some more at the pain*

Thruster: ~another blow, harder~ open yur shirt so I can c your brests

Call Girl: *Uhhh . .. whimpers … can't, my hands are shaking, can't undo the very tiny little buttons*

Thruster: Open it, I wanna c

Call Girl: *I'm trying … pulling my shirt open clumsily … trying as hard as I can*

Thruster: ~ripping the shirt off your sholders and pushign you donw~ keep yur mouth open I want to c inside yur mouth

Call Girl: *ahhhh*

Thruster: I said keep yur mouth open ~blow to the jaw~

Call Girl: *Nooohh*

Thruster: ~pushying you down to the flloor, taking both yr wrists and pinning them behind yoru back~ tell me how mch you like cock

Call Girl: *… spitting out brokenn tooth … I don't like cock, I don't*

Thruster: ~a hard slap on the face ~ tell me how much you likke cock I said

14

Call Girl: *Aggghhhh .. Don't tie my wrists so hard*

Thruster: I want yoru writst tight, Im using the matierial of yur shirt, really tights

Call Girl: *… panting … please can I have a drink of water*

Thruster: No ~standing ovr you, breathing hard~ you cant ~unpacking cock~

Call Girl: *… moving my trembling legs feebly, trying to escape … help!*

Thruster: ~ let u go, watch yr feeble attempts to get to yur feet~ Get up! ~ pull u up by yr hair and push u face against the wall~

Call Girl: *Ahhhh … whimper … moan*

Thruster: ~I kick ur legs open so yr standing splayed, redy~

Call Girl: *Don't hurt me, I beg you*

Thruster: U can beg all u like ~pull whip out of my boot~

Call Girl: *Nooohh*

Thruster: Stand still keep yur face to the wall. Let me c yur mouth, I have to c yr mouth, keep it open

Call Girl: *it's open*

Thruster: tilt your arse

Call Girl: *Can't …*

Thruster: tilt ur fucking arese

Call Girl: *what dyou mean*

Thruster: up in the air, tilt it point it up in the air

Call Girl: *like this*

Thruster: lift ur dress up over ur arse otherwise I will beat u

Call Girl: *My wrists are tied, can't can't,,,,*

Thruster: There tied behind yr back so try harder u se yr fingers pull up that bit of skirt so I can c ur thong

Call Girl: *I'm trying ~fingers moving feebly to gather and lift the flimsy fabric~ it's hard, don't hurt me, I'm trying*

Thruster: What r the bruises?

Call Girl: *Bruises? ohhh*

Thruster: There on ur buttocks there are brusise

Call Girl: *I fell over*

Thruster: ~cutting u with whip once hard~ Liar

Call Girl: *I fell over, running away*

Thruster: ~cutting u again~ harder~ keep liftng that rippeed up dress

Call Girl: *Owwww! You can see now, please don't hurt me*

Thruster: Pull ur thong ovr to one side

Call Girl: *my hands are tied*

Thruster: just do it, I want to watch u struggle. Keep ur mouth opn

Call Girl: *I'm trying … hard with my wrists tied*

Thruster: Look at me, look back at me, can u see how big I am 4 u

Call Girl: *I can't look*

Thruster: ~slicing again with whip~ look at me

Call Girl: *Owww! All right, I can see*

Thruster: What have I got in my hand?

Peach: **~whisper to Biker Idiot~** *bit lonely here. Can you come back and keep me company?*

Call Girl: *The whip*

Biker Idiot: **~whisper to Peach~** Oh … ok

Thruster: no - my othr hand

Biker Idiot: **~gone~poof!~**

Call Girl: *I can only see your donkey cock throbbing between your legs, don't hurt me with it*

Thruster: In my ohter hand

Call Girl: *Can't see, what is it?*

Thruster: switch it on can u see now or hear it

Call Girl: *what is it?*

Thruster: A big buzzing vibrating tool 2 fuck u anywhere my cock isn't fucking u

Call Girl: *Noohhh, please*

Thruster: ~walking towards you~ keep that dress held up, splay ur letgs, tilt ur arse

Call Girl: *… running, running away … desperate, scrabbling to escape … please, help me someone!!??*

Thruster: Come here

Call Girl *… stumble on my high heels … look around wildly to find a way out … gasp for breath … crying*

Thruster: ~catch u by the hair, stop u, slice the whip across the back of ur thighs~

Call Girl: *Aghhhhh!*

Thruster: ~pushing ur dress up Go on hold ur thong 2 one side 4 me, go on do it

Call Girl: *Boutnd and tied hands stretch with difficulty … and tuck finger under thong … only just …*

Thruster: pull it 2 one side

Call Girl: *got it … little strip of thong … I pull it over across my buttock*

Thruster: show me everythingm,

Call Girl: *you kick my letgs opena nd I'm splayed with my arse up*

Thruster: I can c ur hole crack

Call Girl: *and you bang my face agaisnt sth wall justs like I want it, my mouth open,*

Thruster: must aave ur mourth open otherwise I will hurt u more - whip u

Call Girl *… gasp … blinding pain in head … burning pain of whiplash,*

Thruster: get hold off yr tied wrists to use as handle 2 pull u on me

Call Girl: *tightly bound ... they hurting ... sweaty, damp thong held to one side by my finger ... mouth opne for you, because you keep on telling me ... need to go through pain, the other side~*

Thruster: Feel this

Call Girl: *What ... what is it*

Thruster: The tool

Call Girl: *Hard and vibrating against the bruised sikin of my thigh*

Thruster: Yes

Call Girl: *Like electricity, its touch ... can't stop the sudden gush of juice to my cunt*

Thruster: Going 2 fuck u hard now

Call Girl: *you catch my juicces on your wrist ... your hand ... you move the tool claoser to my cunt~*

Thruster: Going 2 push it in hard

Call Girl: *Noohhh*

Thruster: Keep ur moutht open

Call Girl: *Anything .. please.. Ahhh*

Thruster: Push the tool in ur cunt~

Call Girl: *Ahhhh*

Thruster: ~riht up 2 the hilt~

Call Girl: *...shaking, legs trembling ...*

Thruster: ~I slide it in ~ out ~ in ~ out

Call Girl: *.... hurts! Cunt won't take vibrating tool, please stop*

Thruster: ~Looking down at my swollen cock in my hand~

Call Girl: *No, too big*

Thruster: u gonna take it all

Call Girl: *You spit on the tip opf your cock and put it atgsint my arse you'r just touching slimey point of it in my cracdk and nudge forward … please, nooohhhh*

Thruster: I push it in

Call Girl: *You push it in … push … aghhh …*

Thruster: Push it

Call Girl: *My rim pops open … lets you in … holds you tight … you start moving Owww … Agaghhhh*

Thruster: ~starte my thrusting, dont care oabout ur pain

Call Girl: *Ughhh … keep going*

Thruster: ~hard and fast giobvnigt ur arse s a really good fucnking with the toole right up in yr cutnt~

Call Girl: *Ohhhh …. Yess … faster*

Thruster: really faset nadn hard

Call Girl: *That's good, thru the pain now*

Thruster: Big cock in oruit in out

Call Girl: *Yes*

Thruster: Cock pushing into you hard

Call Girl: *Uhhhnn*

Thruster: riding u fast and aherd as I can

Call Girl: *Ohhhh OHHHH push harder*

Thruster: I pushe my handa further in ur motuh,

Call Girl: *chok,e gaggg -0 urrgg - nearly theree*

Thruster: fuck with tool and with cock and with hand

Call Girl: *my open nmouth takes ur hand deep, as well as my cutn and ares full up with ur fcukionmg*

Thruster: My cock fucking yuou

Call Girl: *Gnnnnn*

Thruster: my tool fucking uoi

Call Girl: *Hnnnnn ahhhhh*

Thruster: yr mout h with my whole hand fuckingi ~ u gag ~ u choke ~ u cant breather - I will come when I kill u

Call Girl: *OHHHHHHHHHHHHHHH GNNNNNAHHHHOOHHHHH*

Thruster: adbout to comeju as welll hold on

Call Girl: *Godddd … !!!! That was fucking good*

Thruster: Now play dead and take my cum wait

Call Girl: *listen you were great. thanks v much ….*

Thruster: Wait I'm still fucking yhou play dead

Call Girl: *~tidying myself up~ I needed that ~ phew! ~ wipe brow*

Thruster: I knock u 2 the ground strangle u

Call Girl: *Sorry, I'm done here … step over Thruster's writhing body … turn to audience … bow … smile*

Thruster: fucking u hared

Fat-armed Wife: Loud clapping from here - that's my baby!!!

Call Girl: *Bye now, thanks again.*

Spam: WILD APPLAUSSSSSSSE!!!!!!!!

Call Girl: ***~whisper to Fat-armed Wife~*** *straighten dress … wipe mouth … now for the Dungeon, eh? My Treasure?*

Thruster: push u back, pin uj downs iwht ur hands behind ur back u can't move and uar dead an I'm going 2 come in ur mouth

DanceMaster: *Excelente!*

Call Girl: *Easy there tiger … patting Thruster on shoulder … you'll hurt yourself lad*

Fat-armed Wife: *~whisper to Call Girl~* yes, later on msn usual time will wake you

Call Girl: *~gone~poof!~*

Thruster:

Thruster:

Spam: Silence is goldennnnn

Fat-armed Wife: ooof… You ok Thruster?

Fat-armed Wife:

Honeycake: Ohhhhh kayyyyyy.

DanceMaster: Sorry about that Thruster. She is flighty

Thruster:

Thruster:

Psycho-dog: Yelp …. hrrrr … whimper … hrrrrrr .. whine … why he no talk?

Spam: Whuppppassss! Whupppasss!

Thruster:

Thruster: *~gone~poof!~*

Fat-armed Wife: Oof- he's gone. what about that, hmmm? Everyone?

Honeycake: Pheweeeee …

Spam: poor guyyyy

Fat-armed Wife: Are we allowed to laugh or not?

Honeycake: no definitely not allowed

Spam: teee heee

Fat-armed Wife: TEE HEE

Honeycake: **HA HA HA GUFFFAWWW**

DanceMaster: Christ u have to hand it to her

Spam: Sighhh …. Awwwww …. Showwww's overrrr, hmmmm? All aboarrdddd … Returrrn coacchhhh leaves now for Velvet Ballllroom, tired but happy, roomers go home

Fat-armed Wife: *~gone~poof!~*

Spam: *~gone~poof!~*

Honeycake: *~gone~poof!~*

DanceMaster: *~gone~poof!~*

Psycho-dog: *~gone~poof!~*

Spam enters Velvet Ballroom

Fat-armed Wife enters Velvet Ballroom

Spam: Ahhhhh … home againnnn … that poor guy - thhhhrrussstttttinngggg all he wants but nothingggg to showwww for it

Peach: *Hi Spam, hi Fat-armed Wife*

Honeycake enters Velvet Ballroom

DanceMaster enters Velvet Ballroom

Psycho-dog enters Velvet Ballroom

Fat-armed Wife: Flop down in seat - Christ - light much needed cigarette - heavy drag - gud ol' Call Girl - she sure knows how to let a guy down

Honeycake: she's kinda naughty, huh

Fat-armed Wife: Hi Peach, hi Psycho-dog … Chrissakes, it takes it out of you, watching that - llad

22

Thruster enters Velvet Ballroom

Spam: Ahhhh!!! Thruster welllll dunnnnnnnn u diddd her reeeeel good

Thruster: Where's she gone?

Thruster:

Spam: BIGGGGG PAT ON BACKK !!! u gave her a good talknikng to and sorry you were left dannnnnglinnnnggggg BUTTTT ur notttt the firsssst

Thruster: Where is she

Honeycake: SORRY Thruster

Thruster: Tell me where shes

Spam: My utterrrr smympthay 4 u thruster she's left u in the luirch and not finisehd yoo properly, sahmne on her thy husssy!

Thruster:

Spam: Call Girrrrl wherever hyu are, cummmm back and finsish hinm fofff b4 he knocks someone ofver witht that greatttt bigg thinggg!!!

Fat-armed Wife: Yes - puff - pant - as you say honeycake - Haha! ~llad~ come back Call Girl - hmmm?

Thruster:

DanceMaster: Thruster if you want to become a member it's fifty $, Full membership you have to be voted on by 2 other members and is an extra hundred but you get YOUR OWN ICON and Velvet Sanctuary and Dungeon as well for life all proceeds to charity Pueblo de los Ninos.

Fat-armed Wife: But you did well Thruster- hmmm- well done - salute

Thruster: *~gone~poof!~*

Peach: *bye Thruster*

Spam: He is a LIBRARIAN I bet or a TRAIN SPOTTERRRRR or a COMPOOOOTER GEEEEK …. Way to go Call Girl giirrrrliiee wherever you are ~ shouts ~ Cumm back and tell us a ll about tit soonestttt!

Thruster enters Velvet Ballroom

Thruster: wehre the fuck is she

Fat-armed Wife:

DanceMaster: Thruster use the whisper box to find her

Peach: *Thruster but remember please no rude words here - thank you* ☺

Fat-armed Wife: Would someone like to dance with Thruster

Peach: *sure I will*

Thruster: Fuk u all

Spam: Maybe not a librarian afterrr alllll

DanceMaster: Cover your ears Peachy

Psycho-dog: Whine ~ growl~ growwwlllllllll

Thruster:

Spam: Whuppasss

Thruster:

Thruster:

Honeycake: What's ~llad~ by the way?

Thruster:

Fat-armed Wife: Laughing like a drain

Thruster:

Thruster: *~gone~poof!~*

Spam: Looook!!! He staggers awayyy… into cyberspace … with a big loadded gunn and nowhere ot shgoot it???!!! Help!!! Watch out all girliiess!!! tun of LIBRARIAN SPERM about to spray the whole nett!!??!! Haaa hahh hahh!!!

24

Thruster fought his way out, shut down. The screensaver showed for a second, then disappeared. The fan in the hard drive switched off. The indicator lights on the keyboard died. The printer pushed through the last sheet of A4; silence grew. He commanded the clamour of her voice in his head to fade – and the pictures that went with it. He ordered her name and her icon to shrink, go away.

Like fish disappearing in the depths of a pool, they became indistinct . . . but then quickly surfaced again, clearer than ever. She'd dumped on him, there was no question. 'Bye – thanks a lot'. Humiliation ran, like fire chasing petrol, from his heart to the tips of his fingers and toes. 'Easy there tiger .. you'll hurt yourself . . .' A shiver of anger ran up his spine. His hand had been pushed down her throat, the same hand as was in front of him now – it had been as real as that. This same hand he'd pushed into that wound, the one that lived in his dreams, the ribs sticking out palely like oversized teeth, the blood slippery while his hand went in . . . She had never seen or done what he had seen and done. She had no idea.

She shouldn't have shrugged him off . . . he'd be washing his hands by now. Failure put a sour taste in his mouth. A restless night faced him, thanks to her. The carrying on of lost souls on the internet was hellish, but it had never spat him out before, not like that, not so callously. It burned in him.

In three careful movements he wiped both screens with the anti-static cloth and pushed the keyboard delicately so it rested in line with the laptop. Then he sat back, rested.

The glass partition showed his ghost: the bottle-bottom spectacles, the sideways swipe of brown across his crown, a mouth not much wider than the fleshy boxer's nose above it, his neck as thick as his head, the torso square like a trunk. In the early days he'd removed all mirrors – from in the toilets mostly. But this sheet of glass troubled him. He couldn't bring himself to break it. The picture it offered of him was thin, blurred. He leaned down to take off his shoes and his trousers so he wasn't stuck here, his ankles tied. His cock dangled uselessly under his belly. His fingers checked. Yes, stubby, empty of blood. He picked up the knife from the table, opened the blade and thought about cutting it off. No. He folded the knife, put it back.

He took the pages off the printer and shuffled through them. What had Call Girl said at the end? 'Tidying myself up. I needed that. Phew.' As he read, the words twisted in him. He felt them take root; they would begin to grow. He stood, recognising all the signs of a legitimate grievance. He needed to find her again, to exact revenge.

His shirt hung over his belly like a short skirt. He left his shoes and trousers and took the printed sheets of the conversation with Call Girl, plodding through the swing door. His cock pointed bluntly downwards, still tender with lust.

The other side of the glass partition had once been the manager's office. It was no coincidence he'd set up home in here. He was in charge now, managed himself pretty well. He smiled.

A teapot stood on the upturned packing case along with a glass dish containing teabags and sachets of semi-skimmed long-life milk. He picked up the kettle, tested its weight. Yes, enough water. He slid the button; the red light signalled. It would boil quickly.

Call Girl . . . he really did not want to be so disturbed. If he tried to hold on to her, and hurt her, his hands grasped at thin air.

The four-drawer filing cabinet invited him with its calm efficiency. He pulled open the top drawer. In here hung seven files: motor vehicle, accounts, health, British Army no. 1000345, property, correspondence, household appliances. He took out each one in turn and slipped the contents from the plastic wallets, leafed through to be reminded of what was what. Last of all he took out the heaviest, correspondence. He lifted a new plastic sleeve from the top of the cabinet and stuck a white, oblong address label in the upper right-hand corner. On it he wrote 'Call Girl'. He slipped the printed conversation into the plastic sleeve and found the appropriate alphabetical position within the file. It was becoming too fat, now, to sit comfortably. It was almost time to sort the contents, store the ones he wanted to keep in the box and start again. The drawer slid closed with a satisfying clunk.

He opened the second drawer, containing files numbered one to twelve. His fingers walked over, touching each – thoughts and memories prompted at each half-inch of movement. He counted them; the numbers were like an indrawn breath, swollen in his chest. He came to the last one, 12, and stopped motionless. On his desk – currently under preparation – was file number 14. He'd omitted the unlucky number. He let his breath go, rolled the drawer shut.

His cock was loose and empty in his hand. He walked back to the kettle and stood fiddling. His eyes glazed over as he tried to think about something else. The next meal – where would it come from? Perhaps he would eat at the Gasthaus. He wanted something solid, comforting. German sausage and root vegetables, done the way of the Ruhr peoples – everything in circles. The sausage formed in a ring, the mashed vegetables in perfect globes sitting in a pool of gravy.

Almost without knowing it, the filing cabinet was open, the transcript was in his hand and he was reading it again. Call Girl bounced right back, her power over him visceral, still thrumming in his blood. '... step over Thruster's writhing body ... turn to audience ... bow ... smile ...'

The injustice grew. He saw the words as if written in his head, '~tidying myself up~ I needed that.' It rankled. The insult was good; it worked fiercely against him. It played him exactly as she'd intended. He had fine-tuned antennae for that kind of game.

The kettle had already boiled, he realised. He'd been distracted, so hadn't noticed the crescendo of bubbling water in the still night air, followed by the descent to silence. It was mad to switch it on and then forget you'd done so. He pushed the red button again. If he'd been alert he would have avoided that fraction of unnecessary charge in the electricity bill. He must try not to behave in such an obsessive way. He should keep his mind open to circumstances around him. The wasted money was like something dropped and lost between floorboards. It made his skin crawl. He coached himself to forget.

Let it go, he murmured and dropped the teabag into the cup. He'd selected decaffeinated so it wouldn't prevent him from sleeping. He floated the teabag upwards on a boiling cauldron of water. It bobbed, its skirt full of air.

For fifteen minutes he sat in the brown chair and stared into the distance. He shut out the faint drone of the autobahn. His fingers idly trailed over the bare skin on his thighs. A light scattering of hair grew there; he wondered how many. He leaned forward, looked more closely. Some were short where the friction against his trousers wore them down. Around his knees, on the very inside of his thighs. They were all growing, and they'd continue to grow . . .

He took the pad of cloth, shook it out. The musty smell of old white spirit filled the room. Then he folded it again, as it was before, over and over until it was a thick pad a few inches in diameter. He put it down carefully and removed his shirt and socks; he was naked. He tipped the bottle of white spirit, soaked the fabric until the liquid began to dribble down his fingers. Fumes crowded his nose, mouth and eyes. He sat and cocked one ankle on his knee and wiped every inch of his foot with the astringent, powerful solvent. Next was the other foot: the sole, the toes, the ankle. He worked his way upwards in slow, broad strokes: both calves, thighs, his groin area, buttocks. The chill settled on his skin. He wiped his back and front carefully, under his arms, his neck. Then he lay on the bed and breathed. The fumes were powerful, sickening. As he lay there, the thought of flames pouring upwards from his body mingled with the idea of Call Girl's immolation. He set her hair on fire. The flesh was burned from her face. All that was left was a blackened skull.

Half an hour later he sat up, swung his feet over the side of the bed. He rode the giddiness, waited, saw it out, the familiar spin given him by inhaling the fumes.

He stood sharply, went and rinsed the teacup, put it back. He pulled on his shirt and socks again and walked down through the works. The metal stairs were silent and strong under his unshod feet. Cavernous, dusty space, long unused, travelled away from him, made him the only point of life, of interest. The stale air moved his shirt, cooled his armpits. Across the workshop floor his socks snagged on the pitted old concrete, which had been shorn of most of the machinery that it had once been its job to hold down. He pressed the button on the remote and the metal shutter lifted with its long, hollow rattle.

Outside, the night air cooled him further. He wasn't concerned at being half naked; no one could see. He breathed in the scent of broken tarmac and nettles. The sound of the autobahn was more persistent out here. In the darkened car park his '96 Ford Granada waited, the sole vehicle. He walked around it twice. The thin sodium light from the roundabout was only good enough for a vague check. There was no crimp in the panelling. Three spots on the chrome trim signalled where rust would quickly bloom if he didn't keep on it with the wax. He tried the door. It held fast, locked. All was as it should be. Sometimes he thought of this vehicle as a gallant charger. A muscular beast it would need to be, to carry his weight and bring him home.

After another turn round the car he went indoors, pushed the remote to bring down the steel shutters. He measured the solitude. How far did it extend? The nearest life was four miles away in Dorschmund.

In a single stride he crossed those four miles, giant baseball bat in hand. Bloody Germans. Don't mention the war. He raised the bat, brought it down on the town and all who dwelled within. The buildings splintered; the place was a ruin. Again and again his bat came down until the bastards and the children and the grandchildren of bastards all lay dead.

He climbed the steps. The same numbers rang in his head. The pattern of the steelwork underfoot printed the soles of his feet.

Upstairs in the office he stayed awake late into the night. He knew better than to listen to his cock's one-eyed demands. Call Girl – her outright humiliation of him – came back again and again. She insisted. It really was not his fault, because he'd done well: she'd said so herself.

What had happened, exactly? Inevitably he had to go back to the filing cabinet – avoiding his reflection in the glass partition – and take out the printed pages. He studied them, scratched the itch again. His groan sounded, small and animal-like, in the deserted building. The pages were in reverse order – the last words first – so he shuffled them the other way. His muscles tensed as he saw her icon, the show-off bust spilling out of the torn dress. He read beyond the words, he relived his authority and control over her: '... catch u by the hair ... slice the whip across the back of ur thighs ...'

She was down; he was over her . . . he turned to the next page. There – something had happened. He put his finger under the words, 'you kick my letgs opena..' He read again, 'you kick my letgs opena..'

She had told *him* what to do. Fatal. He read on, moving his finger from one word to the next. '... and you bang my face agaisnt sth wall justs like I want it, my mouth open ... gasp ... blinding pain in head ... burning pain of whiplash ... tightly bound ... they hurting ... sweaty, damp thong held to one side by my finger ... mouth opne for you ... need to go through pain ...'

Yes, it was clear, she'd taken charge. He hadn't noticed at the time because it had been everything he'd wanted to hear. He continued to read. She became more bossy and demanding. Just when he had his hand in her mouth and was pressing it in, down, into the wound of her throat, she had failed him. He read through to the end. 'Bye now, thanks again.'

It was a fast, hard brush-off. How careless that made her. It had been a cruel act – unfair, unjust, unprovoked. Shame burned anew at the gates to the citadel.

He stood, twirling his cock idly under his shirt. Then a thought occurred to him: she'd brushed him off, yes, but she'd been teasing him. He read the words once more, 'Bye now, thanks again.'

Perhaps it had only been a ruse, to draw him back.

If she had a sense of humour – if she was kidding – well, that was different. He smiled. It was possible. If so, there was a chance that her crime against him might vanish, depending on what happened next time. She was perhaps a kindred spirit. This train of thought put him more at ease. He stood, went to the fridge for a beer. It would be something to celebrate, if it turned out to be true. He held the bottle against the table top and thumped it to spring the cap. He gave a silent 'Cheers' to whoever she was in real life, and sipped.

'You have met your match,' he told her out loud. 'Lovely,' he murmured and chuckled. There was no humiliation after all – it was just the slap of a girl who is asking to be slapped right back. Next time, he'd show her that he knew how to deal with her type. There weren't many who gave him that degree of play. She was the genuine article. Excitement rose in him – this was someone who could meet his needs. He could smell it on her, that ability to play convincingly, again and again. She'd put herself in the gutter and with that final insult she'd sent a perverse invitation to him: come at me again . . . Yes.

Fat-armed Wife chuckled involuntarily. She jiggled the mouse, harassed the cursor into the bottom left-hand corner – click, turn off computer, click. The screen went blank. She rolled her chair back, stood and leaned over her desk, hand on heart. That guy Thruster must be smarting; she felt truly sorry for him. The cruel, conscience-less world of cyber sex! Smiles creased her face and she silently sent a message of congratulation – way to go, Call Girl! You played him like a fish! 'Bye now, thanks again' – priceless. 'Easy there tiger ... patting Thruster on shoulder ... you'll hurt yourself lad'. Tears pricked her eyes in appreciation of Call Girl's very existence. Ah, a good session in the Velvet Rooms! There was nothing better. Her heart was racing. Favourite people, riding their icons like wild chargers through an electric sky. Young Spam, his icon that British canned meat, gambolling about full of glee, organising what was it, a coach trip!? To the Velvet Shore . . . Ha ha.

Yes, favourite people. Real people, because of course every one of the Velvet Roomers was a real enough person underneath – but they'd all removed their bodies, their faces, their histories, their class, the accident of their voices, their wealth or poverty. They'd left those things behind. So then we can take flight, she thought, as just a voice, not an audible one, but written. It was the purest form of communication, from the inside of one head to the inside of some-one else's, and the flying was without interference, to whichever corner of the world you could find. The conversations at their best were like music in the skies: everyone a composer, everyone a listener. She blinked away tears. No one should know she was flying so high. Otherwise the balloon would burst and she'd fall.

She looked out of the window, and came back to earth. Outside was Winter Hill, Somerville, a suburb on the western side of Boston. As always. Painfully the same. Locked into its earthbound existence. One of the most densely populated areas of Massachusetts. The maple tree. The lawn sign opposite proclaiming the usual progressive Democrat for Congress. Their two cars, the Toyota and the SUV, lucky to have their own off-road parking bay. All the places they went to had lines drawn to them: school, the mall, the Burlington Ice Palace, Charles River Canoe and Kayak, The Real Thing. It was ironic that she'd chosen that name for her latest business – The Real Thing – when she'd grown to have such a struggle with this reality. It couldn't be a more different place from the Velvet Rooms. No doubt it harboured souls just like hers – perhaps in every house in every one of these ordinary streets were others trying to fly, to escape. Her own body felt like an unfamiliar carapace; what should she do with it all, slowing her down?

Her weight – 168 pounds, down from 252. Thirty-seven years old. The time she'd had, yes, those thirty-seven years, one by one, moments of elation and despair, boredom, triumph, isolation, building two businesses, love, marriage, a stepson – no children of her own yet – sometimes those moments had felt like putting on a kind of weight as well, minute by minute growing heavier the more time she added; she couldn't ever take it off.

She picked up her cigarettes and unthinkingly pushed the papers on her desk into a pile, launched herself, worked her way round to the other side to get to the door and out of here. Enough excitement, please attend to your family, she told herself. For a moment she paused in the corridor, listening. Nothing. She tiptoed down to Jamie's room and leaned in. He was fast asleep. His unknowing face was framed by a clump of unruly, mousy hair that grew as quick as grass in spring. Maybe, now he was a teenager, his dream world offered sights similar to those found in the Velvet Rooms: big breasts and six-packs and bulging groins. She turned back, went to the stairs.

One step at a time, right foot forward, she descended, still a bit drunk after those beers earlier. The banister was there; one of her fat arms grabbed it to let herself down safely. Beneath her, the stairwell looked too steep. Her small feet appeared from under the flap of the smock dress. Each time they hit the mark – reliable, thank God – although the wood was slippery. Too much drink and she'd be in danger of falling down these stairs. The treads were narrow. It was an old house; people had been smaller in those days. She and Colin had looked at a bigger Victorian house, still in Somerville, with original horsehair plastering exposed, high-end stainless steel appliances and original oak floors. They might have afforded it but couldn't bring themselves to leave their blue-collar roots so far behind. She liked to worry about money and pretend she hadn't grown two businesses so fast. They'd stick with this little two-bedroom, until . . . well, until. The area was rising fast; the upscale techies who couldn't afford neighbouring Cambridge were spilling over and bringing their money here.

The sound of the television became louder as she set sail through the kitchen. It was her sweet spot, this room, not because she did any cooking but because she'd found a booth from a diner on the internet and had it hauled here, installed it as regular kitchen seating. It was where she smoked her cigarettes, close to the extractor fan, while she made her calls and ticked off her lists, phoned her collectors and the dealers. She couldn't slide into the plump red plastic seats without expecting a waitress to come by. Except it was her husband and stepson who cooked and cleaned and scrubbed and hoovered and washed clothes and packed school bags and brought in shopping. They were back and forth between domestic appliances as if they had pieces of elastic tied to their waists. Every task sent them out, only to pull them back to engage in the machinery of more cleaning and eating, drinking – the fridge was opened and shut like the door to a brothel.

She ignored the siren call of the diner booth, spun the cigarette packet in her hand and kept going in order to sit with Colin in front of the TV.

The corridor boxed her in for a few seconds, then she was

through to the snug. Colin sat in his customary chair, knees wide apart, jeans stretched tight, check shirt covering the hump of his stomach, the one soft, clever hand resting on top of it, the big log of a remote in his other fist, ready. His slippers were crushed at the heel.

That was her husband, right there, her great big, bearded, hairy-legged, jean-jacketed, broad-beamed husband. The possession of this man was a proud achievement, one she'd told herself a woman of her weight and looks would never have. It was as if Colin had dropped from the sky, plonk, into the café opposite the shop – just a couple of panes of toughened glass and a few yards of paving between them. Like in a dream he'd walked towards her, this kind, big man; he'd seen her and not been put off by the obstacles he'd faced in his year-long, good-hearted trudge towards the altar: her disbelief, her testing of him, her insecurity. And so, with growing astonishment that he was sticking with her, admiration and love for him had grown. He'd become larger in her vision as it were, and the astonishment was crowned by a feeling of victory: whatever it was between the sexes had worked. It was precisely how little they had in common that had made him attractive to her. 'Trophy husband' – the thought had crossed her mind with the clarity of actual speech; he had been her triumph, she'd managed to win a man of her own, despite her weight.

Then, some years later, a fierce desire had been created in her by Call Girl; it had been like a wild animal suddenly let out of the stall and running riot through the town kicking up its heels. The daily, urgent sex had tapped into Fat-armed Wife like a sinuous root, fed off her very core, and grown a different kind of love which she couldn't ignore.

So should she not have married Colin but waited until she'd been confident enough to fall in love herself, rather than glory in the surprise of a man's love for her? Not yet had that path been torn from under her feet: she was going to meet Call Girl and see for real, find out . . . and if her marriage did bust up it would be her fault, a crime – she'd not answered Colin's love properly. It would be all his loss.

Certain incidents came back to her, things she often thought about: she'd used the first money she'd earned at the shop to buy him the stove so she could watch him chop wood with an axe. She'd never seen it happen yet. She'd given him the scooter he'd said he'd always wanted since he'd had one as a kid. The counter on it said six miles, only. At this rate, Jamie would be old enough to use it before his dad ever did. Both gifts had slightly missed the mark and there was always something telling about that.

Colin glanced up as she came in the room. Without a change to his expression he scratched his armpit, once. For a second, on its way back to the arm of the chair, the hand floated – it looked like he might be about to conduct a piece of music. Good with his hands – tick. She was rightly proud of that quality in him.

No greeting, then, she thought.

It was because she was going away. A little arena like . . . what, a landscape, a new geography . . . of fights and lying and cheating was between them – it had never been there before. She wanted rid of it. Soon it would be gone, one way or another. But she couldn't *not* take this journey, not now. And for sure, she couldn't tell him the real reason she was going. Therefore, this patch of boggy ground had to be slogged through.

She took her seat; it matched his and she sat in the same pose, her knees apart, her fat arms on the arms of the chair likewise. Matching husband and wife, she thought. The big Americans, a speciality breed. The difference between them was, she didn't have a beard. A bit of a moustache maybe, but . . . She blinked, smiled at herself, focused on the TV. It was always difficult to come back to earth after the Velvet Rooms. It was like having taken a flight: what was required now was to descend, land gently, return to where real humans lived.

The comfort of the seat claimed her; she was coming down. Her husband was close by. Colin. What might he have called himself, if he were a Velvet Roomer? BigStrongHusand. What kind of icon, she wondered, would she have given him if it were her choice? DanceMaster would have cooked her up something. She'd have him lean and young and unshaven, half in shadow. The strong jaw, no beard but perhaps a touch unshaven. Her one reliable fantasy was that downcast look, three-quarters on, as if her dream man were troubled by some fierce battle he had to deal with. There never was such a look in her husband's eye. He met the world with a calm gaze and sloped off at the first sign of trouble. She wanted to wave a magic wand and cast a spell, take Colin's beard away, give him burning issues deep inside, remove his blue check shirt; instead she held out for him a black leather motorcycle jacket, neat at the hips, which he shrugged into and she put a lick of dark hair across his forehead.

His beard moved as he dragged the skin on his jaw, a habit of so many beard-wearers. 'Everything OK?' she asked.

'Yes indeed.'

'Where's your beer?'

'Had it.'

'Have another with me?'

He looked at her. He knew she was excited about the trip – every minute of the day she was excited about the trip – but he had no place, no share in it. He turned down his mouth. 'Nah. Almost bedtime.'

Bedtime? Yes and no. The truth was, she'd be up again in the middle of the night. The Velvet Dungeon beckoned.

The television jumped; Colin had changed channel – but then it kept on changing, one programme after another blinked and disappeared. A rush of madness had entered the room. It was an electromagnetic disturbance, like in a Spielberg film. She glanced at Colin and saw him digging the remote out from where it had lodged between his thigh and the side of the chair. The screen stopped jumping. He thumbed it back, nonchalantly. He gave no sign of noticing that everything in the room had been flying around in circles. When he got back to his programme he rested. His absolute stillness grew, over minutes, to build in her an illogical fear. She stared at him, wondering if he'd ever move again. She wanted him to give a sign of life . . . There, he touched his nose, cocked his head sideways, still watching TV. She tried to do the same – concentrate on the TV – to break this spell. What was it on the screen? A dog, with its paw on a can of dogfood. It was an advert. The sequence was a trick: they'd put the dog's paw on the tin and filmed it taking its paw off, and then reversed the film to make it look like the dog was giving the food an approving pat. We see the trick, she told them. For God's sake leave the poor dog alone.

The Tarot cards on the coffee table caught her eye. They insisted, caught her eye again, but she'd promised not to do a reading – Call Girl disapproved. She rocked back and forth, sideways, tried to get comfortable in the chair.

An hour later they went up to bed. She changed into the usual old T-shirt and men's boxer shorts. She'd paid her dues earlier, so there was no fear of the hand on the hip or the glass of two-buck chuck. So here of all places, where it was warm and familiar, next to her husband, she wanted to be able to cast off demons of guilt and trepidation. Colin had encouraged her to make the room her own; she'd chosen the russet colours, with a deeper tone below the trim. The ceiling was a dairy cream. The bedspread had been made by Rosemary during her illness. The furniture – the maroon wardrobe, two small chairs and the chest of drawers – all came from Colin's family.

The bump of her body under the bedclothes, next to the larger bump of Colin's, was a huge engine of life, aswirl with blood and nerves, in this emperor-size bed, thirty per cent off two years ago and still being paid for, with no footboard so she could dangle her feet off the end. She wouldn't change one thing about this room.

Except – she lunged at the idea – to be in love with Call Girl, real crazy sexual love, if it turned out to hold up, to be true in real life. Also, she wanted to have a child of her own. She could have thumped her husband for having had a vasectomy. She might point at the shower and demand he wash every night. She did so herself, twice daily. Then, since she was on a roll, she changed him into a good talker, without taking away one bit from the silent repository of human understanding and acceptance that he was currently. She changed his favourite shirt from that old blue check to a decently weighted cotton in plain, brilliant white, freshly laundered each day. She had him run around with a gang of friends. She had him go to parties and get drunk. She took some of his weight off – after she'd done the same to herself – and it was like carving a snow sculpture with a hot blade, it fell that easily from his front, his hips, his thighs, face, until they were both perfect. Yes, she thought, there was a lot she'd change. Everything – she was maybe about to change every darned thing about her life.

Still he slept. She couldn't join him. She lay there, eyes wide open. Her mind wandered to the near future – tomorrow, the weekend, the week ahead, another weekend, and then Monday. She imagined taking the new three-lane I-90, heading for Logan airport, Colin beside her. It would be three hours of waiting in terminal B. They'd check in and head for the Fox Sports Sky Box and Grill if he was going to stay with her. If he went home, she'd hook up to the WiFi and visit the Velvet Rooms on the laptop. An hour later she'd board the plane alone, tighten her seat belt, suffer the lurch in the pit of her stomach at take-off; then, up there in the sky, she'd seize on the meal and the film and the magazines – anything and everything – to get through the lack of cigarettes. The time – hours and hours of it – would be like a desert; she'd just have to crawl across it, shaking, fit to scream from the nicotine withdrawal.

Then she'd be in a foreign city, London. It felt like she knew it already but it was only from the movies, mostly *Masterpiece Theater*. She tried to imagine herself in the Regent Palace Hotel, Piccadilly, Room 39. She tightened with nerves. Everything would be strange, she'd be vulnerable. She felt her stomach drop; she was always anxious travelling alone. And then the train journey northwards – if she booked the ticket more than a week in advance it would be half price; she still had to work out a way of doing that without it appearing on her credit-card receipts.

She rose as quietly as she could, so as not to disturb Colin, and went downstairs. That strange somnolence clung to everything in the house: it was as if objects slept as well, quietly standing where they had been left. The light was silvery; a magical gleam issued from the streetlights outside. She went through to the snug and lit a cigarette. Just thinking about having to go so long without one, on the plane next week, made her want to cram them in. She sat and smoked and thought about the people in the Velvet Rooms. DanceMaster, the one who'd started it all, one of her oldest virtual friends. His icon was actually a picture of a bullfighter, she suspected, but she'd never asked him; it looked like a dancer and that's all that counted. How he gently, considerately, worked to include everyone; he was truly the diplomatic and civilising influence overseeing his masterful invention. Little Psycho-dog, a long-haired terrier wearing a leather jacket, tending bar at last and proud of his new job. She wondered if he'd grow bored of the extra work, but he was shaping up well. Peach, gorgeous, busty figure floating along a beach, but in reality young and anxious for good reason and like a cartoon character who has already run off the edge of the cliff, trying to keep from falling by running hard enough, reaching hard enough for everyone. The ridiculously handsome Biker Idiot trailing after her. Honeycake, the pony princess from NYC. And Call Girl . . . When she'd first seen that green italic writing, she had literally shivered in recognition, in immediate attraction to the sound of the voice as it was written.

Would everything work out in the Velvet Dungeon? She prayed hard.

She realised she was looking at the Tarot cards again – or, rather, they were looking at her. She could believe, almost, that they'd moved silently from where they were in order to appear in her frame of vision. She pictured Call Girl sitting opposite her, tut-tutting at such superstitious nonsense. The empty space hummed with energy, filled to overflowing. You are the Questioner, she told Call Girl, I am the Diviner. Sorry, but I have to do this.

Is it a good time? she asked all the Gods. If so, send me a signal, I only want to play if it comes out right.

The cards persisted.

She stubbed out her cigarette, shifted to the edge of the chair and picked them up. She slid them out, shuffled them. To identify her Questioner she took off the ring Call Girl had sent her for Christmas last year and positioned it on top of the pack for a while. Then she cut the deck and with a smooth sweep of her hand fanned out the cards, picked the first set of ten, then the set of five. She laid them out and turned them over.

Page of Wands: loyalty, trusted friend. Yes, she agreed, underneath all the lust and love, that was Call Girl, exactly. She moved on, more confident. Three of Swords: absence, sorrow, strife, removal. She sucked in a breath, but had to continue. Card number three, goal or destiny. Four of Wands: tranquillity and contentment, romance, and pointing towards herself, the Diviner. She could agree it was what she sought, to the bottom of her heart. The fourth card, in its position to the right of the column made by the first three cards, would offer insight into the deep past. Two of Pentacles, which meant troubles, set-backs. Well, it was true they'd tried to meet once before. The fifth card was One of Cups: fulfilment, joy, family, home – she felt a twinge of guilt. Call Girl threatened her family, her restless contentment here at home. She frowned. Unless Call Girl was, as it were, part of her Velvet Rooms family – you might read it like that. She turned the next card and positioned it on its own, to the left. Future influence: the Hermit. It's not what she would have wanted. Fearful of discovery, yes, she could see that might be true, but withdrawal, loneliness? No, thank you.

She turned cards seven to ten in a row to the right-hand side, starting at the bottom. Death: sudden change or reversal, surprise event, loss, destruction, end, permanent scar on mind.

She kept calm – a change in life can be positive. The Magician: guile, trickery, willpower.

The tenth position, at the top of this column, signified the end result, the outcome of the current situation. It was the Tower.

Happiness and expectation drained away from her. The cards had called for her, they'd begged to be used, to show her . . . this? She was assaulted by an irrational fear. The room was still, dead quiet, offered no answer. The television rested, mute. Colin's chair was empty as if she'd disappeared him.

She shouldn't go to England. She must cancel the ticket. There was no question. Calamity, ruin, misery, deception.

The cards' grotesque, silent illustrations were callous and powerful, as if they might create events rather than predict them. She quickly leaned forward and messed them all up; the reading was over. She wanted to go back in time, cancel the message they were aiming to send her. She squared them, put them back in their box. Sorry, Call Girl, she thought. Superstitious nonsense, she agreed. There were tears in her eyes. The Magician blankly accused her from his illustration on the cover. She pushed him away, turned him over. The back of the packet described the contents with authority, 'The original and only authorised edition . . .' Underneath the description was the command 'BELIEVE THE CARDS'. The words swam and dissolved, before hardening again, appearing bolder and as if floating off the printed surface. Her heart threw in another beat, its rhythm was broken with shock. She scrabbled for a cigarette and lit it with shaking hands. Don't go, she told herself, don't risk it. She went and fetched a big bag of chips. Comfort food. Her mother had had the same addiction to Cape Cod potato chips; she'd died of cancer six years previously and Fat-armed Wife always found her way to memories of her, eating them.

She left the room and stalked the corridor: up and down she went, a dozen times, smoking, before wandering into the darkened kitchen. She sat in her diner booth. The Magician followed her even here: she couldn't loosen the tightness in her chest. If only she could send a message through the ether – Call Girl, do you read me, watch out, hmm? Bad reading of the cards. Be careful. Stay close, stay safe . . . will you?

How her feelings crawled in her – against her express wishes! Powerful forces were at work. It disturbed her most that she couldn't control them, put them back in their box. She couldn't stay still, not for another minute. She slid out of the booth and walked again. She switched on the lights and tried to read a lifestyle magazine, but the cheerful, well-organised pages slipped beneath her concentration; she found she was turning them, unseeing. She went back to bed, carefully inserted herself under the covers next to Colin, sick from the extra cigarettes. She would just have to lie here and cover the ground between now and two o'clock in the morning, when the time difference would allow her to phone Call Girl. She dozed, slipped between sleep and wakefulness.

The Magician came back. He stood for a while. Then, as if he had her best interests at heart, he sat on the edge of the bed, smiling in the half-dark.

Abruptly she pulled the covers from her, swung her legs over the side of the bed and sat staring at the ground, the wall, the ceiling, to try and rid herself of the vertigo. It grew worse – her head spun. She 'ooofed' and stood up. Her T-shirt floated down from her expensively lifted breasts. It was the best thing she'd ever done, to stop them looking like a couple of supermarket bags filled with water. She checked the time on the bedside clock. There wasn't too long to go. Again she went downstairs to the kitchen and sat in the booth. She lit yet another cigarette and pulled the phone close by, an automatic habit. The lists of RealThing.com auctions lay there, two or three sides, heavily scrawled over, but she wouldn't bother with them until tomorrow.

A quarter of an hour passed; she watched the minutes slip off the face of the clock.

She lit another cigarette and counted how many were left in the packet. She needed one for when she woke at four a.m., another two for when she got up, two more after breakfast. Her last packet held six. 'Thank God,' she said into the empty room. Her voice startled her.

When it was two o'clock she crept upstairs to the office and closed the door. She hooked up to the computer again and plugged in the headphones so Call Girl's voice wouldn't wake Colin. A bag of Maltesers waited alongside the screen, its opening crushed from where she'd pushed her hand in earlier. There were a few left; she popped them, one after another, quickly. She managed to avoid the internet: the siren call of that enormous sea beckoned but she went merely to msn and pulled Call Girl out of the address book so she was ready. Then she picked up the phone and dialled Call Girl's cell. Call Girl's bedroom voice came on, half asleep, murmured something incomprehensible. Fat-armed Wife knew not to ask, just to kill the expensive call straight away and wait a minute or two. She put the headphones on, so she was ready. Some minutes later, sure enough, their voices connected through the computer.

'Wake up,' whispered Fat-armed Wife.

'Nnnn, thank you so very much.' Call Girl's voice was slurred. After a while Fat-armed Wife asked, 'You still there?'

'Oh, mmm, I'm here all right.'

'Thought you might have fallen asleep on the keyboard.'

'Na.'

'I haven't slept yet. Just lay down, you know. Couldn't sleep.'

'You excited, hnn?'

'Yes.'

'Me too.'

'So we're ready, then, for the Dungeon?'

'Shall we go now?'

'OK.'

'See you there.'

'Indeed, as well.'

The image of the Tower came back, flames pouring from the top of the simple phallic structure, bodies diving out of the windows. The cruel illustration on the card mixed with the blurred footage shown on TV post 9/11. Awful, unreasonable dread filled her.

She clicked on Favourites, on the Velvet Rooms.

Call Girl enters Velvet Dungeon

Fat-armed Wife enters Velvet Dungeon

Fat-armed Wife: This is spooky

Call Girl: *Yes. Like there's cobwebs, hnnn?*

Fat-armed Wife: DanceMaster oiled the hinges but the door's still squeaky

Call Girl: *Who were the last in here, that we know of?*

Fat-armed Wife: apart from us you mean - vbs -

Call Girl: *I wasn't counting that effort*

Fat-armed Wife: Terra Firma and StripTease I think

Call Girl: *Were they before or after Timber Wolf and Dana?*

Fat-armed Wife: Earlier by a year or more

Call Girl: *Slightly different outcome, you might say, as well*

Fat-armed Wife: I'll say

Call Girl: *So you ready?*

Fat-armed Wife: Ready

Call Girl: *I'll go first then. The fair city of Hull, in Yorkshire, agreed?*

Fat-armed Wife: agreed

Call Girl: *September 16 and 17*

Fat-armed Wife: yes

Call Girl: *I've got you in one helluva English-style room at the Post House Inne for both nights, in The Old Town, cobbled streets and everything*

Fat-armed Wife: OK

Call Girl: *The Tuesday night at the Regent Palace Hotel in London, for when you get off your flight that morning, and 2 more nights, Friday and the Saturday, for when we head back down to London, two girls arm in arm.*

Fat-armed Wife: deal

Call Girl: *that is, if we both still love each other*

Fat-armed Wife: We will, we do

Call Girl: *Indeed. Your turn*

Fat-armed Wife: OK. Return ticket, flight VS007 to Heathrow, arriving early 22 September, returning Sunday 27th

Call Girl: *Hurrah, as well*

Fat-armed Wife: Catch the train up to you on the Wednesday, what time - hmmm?

Call Girl: *I'll come and meet you at the hotel at 8.30 pm how's that, gives you time to brush your teeth*

Fat-armed Wife: Do we meet in the lobby, in the room, in the street? where is the Dungeon exactly?

Call Girl: *there's a right cosy sitting room downstairs. You can't miss it, big fireplace, prints on the walls. Next to Reception. It's the only one. Always seems empty. Let's say that is our Velvet Dungeon, hnn? The neutral ground thing as well. OK?*

Fat-armed Wife: OK, that is the Dungeon. We meet there at 8.30.

Call Girl: *8.30 gives me time to go home, change a dozen times - that kind of mularky, as well. *vbs**

Fat-armed Wife: Is it done, then - waving away cobwebs down here - so can we post this???!!!! Hnnnn?

Call Girl: *I'm done*

Fat-armed Wife: Hold on - shall we have real names?

Call Girl: *God, please NO*

Fat-armed Wife: why not?

Call Girl: *if you knew my name you'd never come*

Fat-armed Wife: Don't be stooopid

Call Girl: *it's like a spell isn't it, as well.*

Fat-armed Wife: How dyu mean?

Call Girl: *What's happened for the last four years is we've made a spell, isn't it, and we ought not to break it until we meet and make a new kind of spell. And then real names are wheeled out for good or ill*

Fat-armed Wife: OK

Call Girl: *trust me*

Fat-armed Wife: haha I don't think so. what's wrong with your name?

Call Girl: *true - just you wait*

Fat-armed Wife: OK - so shall we post?

Call-Girl: *yes post*

Fat-armed Wife: happy?

Call Girl: *happy. Dungeon rules*

Fat-armed Wife: here goes

Fat-armed Wife: *~post~*

Call Girl: *Aghhhh*

Call Girl: *~post~*

~Velvet Dungeon swings shut ~ keys grind and turn ~ clunk!~ locked shut~

They went back to their phones and talked for another quarter of an hour. Fat-armed Wife sat close and whispered into the microphone while Call Girl wandered around the flat, preparing breakfast, talking out loud. Fat-armed Wife felt her eyelids grow heavy. She needed to sleep.

'Send us the flight details then, as well,' finished Call Girl, 'before you log off, so I can see it's for real.'

They gave the usual goodbyes, always reluctant, uncomfortable. Fat-armed Wife went into Outlook Express and found the details of her ticket and prepared to forward them, as requested. She had the cursor over Send, but hesitated. It was mad to fly to the other side of the Atlantic and meet someone she only knew in a chat room. How would it turn out?

There wasn't an answer; only the event would tell. And Dungeon deals weren't to be broken.

Fat-armed Wife pressed the mouse's humped back; the flight itinerary flew from the screen. She shut down, tiptoed back to bed and lay next to Colin. When she fell asleep she dreamed that he appeared, walking towards her, balancing a glass very carefully in his hands. It loomed in her dream, the red wine, a light glimmering in its sinister depth, her husband's hand round it. She could say yes to the wine and keep her marriage going, or say no and threaten its dissolution. She stretched out and took it. The glass turned into Colin's hand. The alcohol sang in her blood, made her not care, allowed her to give up. The stairs were climbed. Colin's blue jeans worked ahead of her as he rose, step by step. The hand trailing behind, attached to hers, as he led her. In bed they rolled, flesh to flesh. She knew where his hands would go, always to the same place: her expensive breasts. The dream went back and forth, like a record scratched by a DJ on the turntable. The sensation rubbed at her. The sex was perfunctory, quickly over. Her husband's breathing sounded unhappy. She pushed the dream on further – she wanted to hear his voice. Something told her she needed this man whom she so often ignored. It became urgent that he signalled he was really there, that he would save her. She forced the dream, demanded to see the end. It was like rising to the surface. She had the sense there was no light, though, merely a lightening of pressure as she swam back to her own life.

She stayed awake for ages. In the half-light, it wasn't that different from the dream.

The Magician unstuck from the card and walked; he leaned over, smiled at her.

Green-eyed Man enters Velvet Ballroom

Peach: *Green-eyed Man!? ☺☹ Huhh!??*

Green-eyed Man: Hi Peach

Peach: *this is so odd ☺☹ that u come bak?*

Green-eyed Man: can I come in?

Peach: *you got still left membership?*

Green-eyed Man: Yeah, a bit

Peach: *but I am sorry 2 do that* ☹

Green-eyed Man: It's ok, u had 2, course u did, any1 would

Peach: *Sorry anyway*

Green-eyed Man: DanceMaster still calling the shots?

Peach: *Yes with all teh dances and music*

Green-eyed Man: Sure ur ok with me here all alone?

Peach: *Yes sure*

Green-eyed Man: What u doing here all by yourself? walk over 2 you.

Peach: *I am at work, nothing doing, so might be as well waiting here*

Green-eyed Man: U mean ur waiting 4 some1?

Peach: *No just only waiting*

Green-eyed Man: want 2 dance?

Peach: *sure – stand up –* ☺

Green-eyed Man: What du fancy?

Peach: *Dunno something slow.*

Green-eyed Man: Shall I hold u? Don't mind if not

Peach: *ok*

Green-eyed Man: like this?

Peach: *Yes ok*

Green-eyed Man: So… u doing the same work?

Peach: *Yes. Did u come 2 look 4 me?*

Green-eyed Man: What time is it there?

Peach: *lunch time. Yes I'm doing the same work*

Green-eyed Man: Christ almighty. I've got 2 in the morning. Yes came 2 c if u were here still

Peach: *it's all right*

Green-eyed Man: everything still the same? squeeze

Peach: *Yes* ☹

Green-eyed Man: I came to say sorry

Peach: *~Shrug~ ... ok*

Green-eyed Man: But I really miss u and maybe I lost something

Peach: *~shrug~*

Green-eyed Man: Really miss u

Peach: *I think a lot about u, this is true*

Green-eyed Man: And I miss the Velvet Rooms. Best place on the net

Peach: *I understand*

Green-eyed Man: I wanted 2 know if we could b friends

Peach: *Dunno*

Green-eyed Man: Cos mmbrshp about 2 run out and so had 2 come back now and say sorry otherwise won't c u again

Peach: *ok*

Green-eyed Man: Had 2 put it right between us

Peach: *~ nods ~ yes*

Green-eyed Man: Thought we got on so well it would b a pity

Peach: *Yes*

Green-eyed Man: nice just us being here, slow dancing

Peach: *like old times*

Green-eyed Man: Would like 2 come again

Peach: *Sure*

Green-eyed Man: could u bear that if I came 2 visit, huh?

Peach: *I could bear that*

Green-eyed Man: I'd like it

Peach: *ok*

Green-eyed Man: I'd like it a lot

Peach: *ok*

Green-eyed Man: Holding u a bit close. Soft swaying, together

Peach: *Don't push ur luck*

Green-eyed Man: Not that, just pleased 2 b here

Peach: *ok*

Green-eyed Man: dead pleased

Peach: *Hold me then*

Green-eyed Man: Close

Peach: *Yes* ☺

Thruster enters Velvet Ballroom

Peach: *Can I know 1 thing?*

Thruster: where is Call Girl?

Green-eyed Man: course - what?

Peach: **~whisper to Green-eyed Man~** *hold on not while he's in here, wait, wait*

Thruster: tell me someone

Peach: *Thruster, Call Girl is not here*

Green-eyed Man: **~whisper to Peach~** who is this guy?

Thruster: when will she b back?

Peach: *She didn't come - no one has seen her*

Peach: **~whisper to Green-eyed Man~** *hold on*

Thruster: Is she in a private?

Green-eyed Man: **~whisper to Peach~** ok

Peach: *Her name is not on the door*

Thruster: When is she here normally?

Peach: *Can't know, any time*

Thruster: give me her phone number or addie

Peach: *I don't have this and I would not be allowed to*

Thruster: she said she was giving it to me

Peach: *Sorry*

Green-eyed Man: **~whisper to Peach~** aghhh ~vbs~ this guy's hooked, all rite

Thruster: **~gone~poof!~**

Green-eyed Man: There he goes, man with a mission

Peach: *Phew ... yes, I like as you say that, he was hooked, a good way of saying ~ it was nothing, just Call Girl u know, playing*

Green-eyed Man: Huh, ok

Peach: *~lean into the dance, look up 2 you~ I've got 2 know the truth 4 1 thing ~pleading looks~ can I ask?*

Green-eyed Man: sure go ahead

Peach: *is important 2 b honest ok*

Green-eyed Man: Ok

Peach: *did u tell any1?*

Green-eyed Man: bout what u told me?

Peach: *yes*

Green-eyed Man: not a soul. promise

Peach: *Promise u wont tell here or any other site or in real life? I start 2 cry if I think of someone knowing*

Green-eyed Man: Not a soul

Peach: *want 2 b safe and warm here*

Green-eyed Man: u are, u will b, promise

Thruster switched on the miniature TV and sat, watching. He caught moments of hilarity and glamour on satellite; they were like a type of food, they kept his mind sociable, tuned into England. The biscuits tasted metallic on his tongue; with each one he could feel his waist thicken, slow down. Two hours later he was still watching, but the German channel RDF; he watched people's mouths move without understanding much. Whatever the programme, in whichever language, these were his people, his society. They hadn't a clue about him, except as a statistical voyeur, but to him the voices were like the comforting babble at a party. The way he grazed the faces, fed off their expressions, was like staring at other guests across the room.

Every few minutes, as he sat silently at his end of this all-embracing, hectic tunnel of TV, he glanced away, imagined a glimpse of Call Girl. She was dishevelled, on the ground, already halfway to escaping. Her bust spilled from the torn white dress. Her eyes were afraid. She was about to turn and scramble away on hands and knees. She might scream, but probably he would shoulder through and get there quickly enough to stamp on the trailing hem of her dress, grab her arm and twist it behind her back, put his forearm across her windpipe and press down. He could see the resistance in her eyes slowly turn to acceptance of her predicament, replaced by proper, real, deep fear as the room turned silent, as everyone stared, not one of them moving to help her.

Somewhere – perhaps even watching her own TV and therefore connected to him via some infinitesimal transfer of electric charge – was the real Call Girl. He wondered how old she was, whether she were married or single, with or without children, what job she worked at, which continent she was on. He imagined she lived in a big city, London or New York. She'd probably be under forty, well used.

On TV a girl was scissoring her legs back and forth on a bed, her eyes closed, murmuring in an unknown language. No one was in the room with her. She threw her head to one side on the pillow, then the other. Her hands moved over her body. The picture cut to a man standing outside the house, looking up at her lighted window, smoking a cigarette in the pouring rain.

At 1.09 a.m. he switched off the television and pulled on the rest of his clothes, shod his feet. He went down through the metallic staleness of the works floor and out. The car was always a comfort. He sat in the darkened interior for a few minutes and watched the screen fog up. Then he started the motor and drove sedately into Dorschmund. He parked at the bottom of the town where the new housing had been built – mostly occupied by those whose work was connected to the army base. Under the yellow sodium lights the street curved away, up towards the older part of the town. The narrow pavement on each side was empty. When he climbed from the car, the click of the door marked him out; he felt exposed. He buttoned his heavy cashmere coat and started to walk. He passed through the modern housing estate without so much as glancing at the darkened windows. In each house people slept, eyes closed, motionless. No one would see him. CCTV hadn't been installed here.

He reached the old part of town. Here the houses leaned out of true; there was more decorative work around the windows and doors, and the roof gables hung ponderously. It had that old, severe, German charm. The cars were parked off the road and there were more Mercedes and BMWs – superior marques.

For a while he stood in the centre of the old town. No one appeared. There wasn't a thought in his head, except to poison them, fuck them, bury them, a hundred times over. He wandered the side streets, without concern as to where he would end up. His quiet, calm footsteps would sound in people's dreams.

The car waited for him, reliable as ever. He drove home carefully, settling the needle at under thirty – slow, steady progress. The entrance to the works was overgrown and the tarmac badly pitted. When he climbed from the car he stood for a while, gauged his reaction to the place. The familiar dislike ate at him.

He locked the car. As the metal shutter rattled open he ducked his head and went in. Metaphorical chains were attached to his ankles and wrists and an iron collar was locked round his neck, holding him in isolation.

Inside, he brooded. The same humiliation returned.

Call Girl.

Their joust in cyberspace – and her victory over him – meant she was under his skin, more than any person he cared to remember. There was nothing he could do about it. She'd never find him; he'd never find her. She breathed, somewhere, for real. Here, he did the same.

Towards dawn he fell asleep. The voyage took him far out. He bobbed uneasily in unconscious lands.

Spam enters Velvet Ballroom

Spiderbollocks: theyr rite in every1's face

Spam: helloooohhhh Velvet Roomers

Fat-armed Wife: Spam hurrah

FlyBoy: I agree. something sinister about aol as well - like a big brother type of thing

Spam: Fatarmmmmmsss hi

Fat-armed Wife: Spam come to Sanctuary with me?

Pluto: Yeah u feel like theyr making map of who knows who and who says what to whom and then suddenly theyre going to pull all the strings tight and catch us all

Spam: In Sanctuary - hmmmm nice to beee wantedddd … ohhh kayyy see you there

FlyBoy: what about Google I reckon they are going 2 rule the world u will only be allowed 2 exist if Google say u do

Fat-armed Wife: *~gone~poof!~*

Spam: *~gone~poof!~*

Fat-armed Wife enters Velvet Sanctuary

Spam enters Velvet Sanctuary

Fat-armed Wife: -block doorway-wag arms-struggle through-
phew - that's better - hug -

Spam: Ahnhhhh the blessingg of the Fat Arms round my so9rrry frame.

Fat-armed Wife: Spam darling man

Spam: Sanctuary … hmmmm … intrigueddd … what is it

Fat-armed Wife: I want to ask a favour

Spam: ok … goooddd yess readdy

Fat-armed Wife: Going on Monday, a week away, flying to London, my
husband knows about that bit - said I was visiting wholesalers, setting
up Real Thing UK etc - did I tell you all that?

Spam: You diddd fatarms

Fat-armed Wife: but then I have to take train north - to reach Call
Girl - and I don't want that train journey to be on my credit card - could
pay cash at kiosk but the fare is cheaper if you book in advance - like
half - so can I ask you to book it for me and I'll send you pounds when I
get there - d'you trust me for that?

Spam: Fatarmsssss of course, yes I will

Fat-armed Wife: Thank you - shake your hand warmly - don't like
involving you in my subterfuge

Spam: yunnngg man'ss hand redddy to hellpp

Fat-armed Wife: thankkkk you thankkkkk you thankkkk you

Spam: Pleasssssure. but you must tell me when and where

Fat-armed Wife: Shall I post details in an email?

Spam: Have pen handy, give it me noww, att yr service like Englisshhhh
family servant type of thinggg

Fat-armed Wife: stand by

Spam: Saluuuute!

Fat-armed Wife: arrive Tuesday Sept 22 am - spend that night in London at hotel - so need the train to Hull in York Shire - on Wednesday Sept 23

Spam: writing it down scrawllll scrawlll

Fat-armed Wife: not too early, maybe around eleven

Spam: And when coming back?

Fat-armed Wife: two nights up there so back on Friday. Call Girl with me - to put on big jewellery and do London - girls together ho ho ho

Spam: Yunngg mans hannnnnd scrrribbbling away - Friday morning return

Fat-armed Wife: yes - clean teeth again - taxi to station blah blaha balahh

Spam: Urgghhh how do I get tickets to you?

Fat-armed Wife: How about to the hotel, have them send them to the hotel in Piccadilly

Spam: name of hotel?

Fat-armed Wife: Regent Palace

Spam: addresssss and such like

Fat-armed Wife: Hold on - you are good - a saint to do this - will fetch

Spam:

Fat-armed Wife: here it is - Regent Palace Hotel Piccadilly Circus London W1F 6JG tel 020 7287 6758. That ok? Can you pay - you rich enough - hmmm?

Spam: have real grownnnn-upppp credit card and can spankkk it with help from my brother for security

Fat-armed Wife: thank you - kiss - kiss on other cheek - tug your ear - young scoundrel - sorry to ask - please forgive

Spam: Don't say a worddd - utterllly welconme deeeer Fatarms

Fat-armed Wife: you're in my conspiracy kiddo - sorry

Spam: will liftt phone and struggle with railway no problem

Fat-armed Wife: thanks thanks thanks x a million - Phew - trying not to spend so much - guilty

Spam: don't worreee

Fat-armed Wife: I do worry

Spam: Ahhhh … the kind heart of Fattt arrrmmsss

Spam logged off, pecking at the keyboard – maybe he could still learn to use all his fingers. It was never too late. He shuffled among the scraps of paper on his desk. He mustn't lose the one with the details of Fat-armed Wife's train journey. He placed it on the keyboard. He wished his hands didn't tremble so. There it was, anyway. Safe. He shut down the computer, switched it off and unplugged – he came from an era when many electrical appliances had caused houses to burn down. Then his mind wandered for a moment or two, as was its wont. His ex-wives came back to him, all standing in a row. His family home, long gone. He caught sight of his shoes – were they really the same pair, the old Grenson brogues? They'd lasted for donkey's years. How far, for how long, they'd carried him, brave servants of his progress. Well done, those shoes. He rose from the desk. Where was he? He blinked. It still seemed unlikely, even after all these years, but he was in a room at the Sharland House Accommodation Project. How far down in the world he'd come. This was council-run sheltered accommodation for seniors, a double quadrangle of flatlets with shared meals twice a day. His number was six, screwed in a chrome figure on the so-called front door. Two rooms, with a damp spot blossoming in the corner of the bedroom, plus a mini-bathroom with yet another gleaming chrome handrail fixed near the toilet and the half-bath, which had a step in it on which you sat, like the one he'd had once in a skiing chalet. He imagined buying a screwdriver and removing the handrails which sprouted from every wall, because he'd promised himself never to use them, not until the last moment, not until the heart attack or the stroke or the cancer came and got him. And it hadn't yet. He took a pace or two. God bless his new hips – not a moment of pain. Now, he had to stay alert, to book the train fare. Fat-armed Wife depended on him: he mustn't cock this up. What would he need? The credit card. A telephone. That bit of paper. A pencil. The correct number to dial. All at the same time. It was a lot to get right.

The wallet – where might it be? For weeks at a time he never saw it. After a minute or two's searching he lifted its sorry, empty carcass from last month's jacket. Next: the telephone number of the rail companies. In the old days, of course, it had been British Rail but now the various routes were owned by different companies. He had a feeling, though, that telephone bookings were all made on the same number, whatever the route. The phone waited there by the bed, but if he rang Directory Enquiries it would cost him dearly. There were directories in the common room – he should go there, stretch his legs and save himself half a guinea, practically.

It would mean he'd be seen by other residents, so he must keep up appearances. He went into the bathroom and checked for any unsightly deterioration that might have occurred. It was just as well he did: a long white hair reached from inside his nostril. It must have grown there quick as a mushroom. He pinched it hard between his fingernails and pulled. His nose smarted. Other than that he was as all-right-looking as any other seventy-four-year-old boozy aristocrat fallen on hard times, he supposed. He still had the air of a man who was getting everything he wanted, who expected the world to fall in with his wishes. Which was an illusion, needless to say. Only in cyberspace was he able to be who he wanted to be. He left the room and wandered round the quadrangle, making his way along the cloister to the cafeteria. He recognised the other oldsters but didn't offer more than a brief nod. They looked too past it to be made friends of, frankly. One fellow was parked up against the wall, motionless, as if he'd run out of fuel.

All these neighbours watching him, strangers every one – that had been the hardest thing to get used to. It had taken him a while to brave the cafeteria and the common room as he was about to do now.

He called a cheerful hello to the Portuguese chef, Carlos, who smiled across his domain of stainless steel surfaces, and wandered on through. He paused to leaf through the messed-up newspapers and magazines on the table by the entrance. He'd already read *The Times* at breakfast and the *Independent* at lunchtime but couldn't walk past a newspaper without glancing at it at least. Then he steered towards the communal pay phone.

This afternoon his visit coincided with the gaggle of women, mostly, who attended church. They were dressed in their Sunday finest; they all nodded and smiled at him in a Christian way. There was not a trace of disapproval, although he might have been expected to join them. He knew that his title – Lord Gough – had been noticed from all the Mastercard and Goldman Sachs junk mail he received. Presumably some people might think he was making it up, that he was an old conman come to grief. He enjoyed guessing at their past lives after all so he knew they must be wondering at his. One or two might become friends, he thought, if only he could take a deep breath and sign up for some of the group activities. The truth was, the Velvet Rooms was a faster, more furious, more interesting place to live. These old folk, with their churches and coach outings, doddery as all-get-out, couldn't hope to compete. On the other side of the virtual membrane he could be young and powerful; he cut the mustard over there all right . . . He wrote down the two telephone numbers, one for rail enquiries and the other for bookings. Coming, Fat-armed Wife. Your servant. He went back the way he'd come. The old gent leaning against the wall had gone. Had he died and been taken away? Maybe his only mistake had been to remain still for too long. Spam quickened his pace, breathing more heavily.

When he was back in his room he made the call. He had difficulty reading his handwriting and the number across the credit card. He moved his spectacles back and forth on his nose. Perhaps his eyesight was worse from watching the screen too much. The voice on the other end of the phone was patient with him. The tickets could only be sent to the address at which the credit card was registered. So they'd have to be sent here and then he'd forward them immediately to the hotel. There was enough time – slightly more than a week. He believed he was doing all right; everything was working.

'Done,' he murmured and put the phone down. He limped to the bed, his new hip smooth and oily in its socket, and performed the well-rehearsed turn and drop, to land with only a slight loss of control in the seat of his pants. Delirium tremens – come on, let's call it a hangover, he told himself – affected his hands as he tugged his pillows into shape. It was time for a nap. The hanky waited, folded into a neat pad; he picked it up and pressed it to his chin, just below the corners of his mouth. He felt the nerve endings tingle there as it picked up the usual trail of saliva. For a moment he fiddled with the bottles on his bedside table – had he forgotten any of his tablets? It was easy to lose track. A shiver of guilt ran down his spine at the money he'd spent on Viagra. He'd told Alma he'd needed it for liniment, prescriptions, birthday presents. He forgave himself and lay down. The late-afternoon sun streamed through the windows and heated the room. He felt as good, as replete, as fulfilled, as a cat on a window sill.

In his mind's eye he went over the phone call he'd just made on Fat-armed Wife's behalf. A reserved seat on the correct train awaited her – to deliver her to the Velvet Dungeon. He pictured his voice travelling along the telephone wires all the way to the call centre in India, where someone listened to him without knowing anything about Hull, or about England, or about trains. Yet that person had sold him a journey that someone else, on yet another, different continent, would make. It was extraordinary how everyone criss-crossed the globe these days. It was a form of bedlam, yet it all made perfect sense in terms of people's individual desires. He felt giddy. It brought tears to his eyes, to think how alone he was, and yet how plugged in, how connected. To all corners of the universe, to every soul . . .

An hour later he awoke. The giddiness immediately came back, stronger than before. It was too much. He struggled to sit up. The silence persisted. He climbed to his feet and went to his desk. The bottomless depth of the Compaq's screen stared back at him. He turned his hearing aid off to avoid interference and switched on the computer. Almost without looking he knew where the buttons were. He greeted the familiar sound, like a jet engine winding up to speed as the machine came out of its deep sleep, worked itself back to life. 'Ready for take off,' he said to himself. It was an old computer passed on to him by Alma when the hotel had upgraded – it still had a Horse and Crown compliment slip Sellotaped to the housing. It was always a little cranky but he knew its quirks and could get to where he wanted. He sat in front of the screen and picked up the keyboard, turned it upside down and shook out the crumbs. He miraculously achieved online status first time round. He cracked his knuckles, cupped his hands round his mouth and blew on them. It would take half an hour to check his favourites on eBay. He went first to peek at the latest antiquities offered by the metal detector nuts who broke into archaeological sites at night and sold public treasure trove illegally. Then he checked that his bid was still in front on the second-hand *Plants and Flowers Encyclopaedia*. It made him curse; he'd probably overpaid. The 1935 gold fob watch supposedly taken from an Italian soldier in the war, so the vendor had claimed, was way past his pathetically optimistic early bid: twenty-two people had already trampled all over him in just one day, which was a bit insulting. Next he went for a quick trawl around old poultry equipment and out-of-date hand tools. The steel they'd used back in the old days was of a much better quality. Next he visited poshtotty.com to see if StableGirl was there, but he'd confused his world clock, and the time difference meant she wasn't online, so he quickly lost interest and went to Poolsidechat.com instead and found Tart-with-a-Fart in her office in Oklahoma. She was always good for a laugh at this time of day. Before he knew it, he'd orbited the world twice, he'd adventured with the brave and the bold in cyberspace and he was exhausted, his eyes pricking with soreness. None the less there was still the Velvet Rooms – it was always best to go in later, heading towards midnight, Eastern Standard Time. He clipped his finger-nails – dry and brittle as potato crisps – before he went back, walking on just two fingers, to tell Fat-armed Wife he had the train tickets, they were on the way.

Thruster enters Velvet Ballroom

Fat-armed Wife: Everyone this is the best thing - thank you all - vbs - it is like the best gift - just that you are all HERE - if the plane explodes I will have died happy??!!

Thruster: *~whisper to Call Girl ~* come here

Call Girl: *~whisper to Thruster~ Hi Thruster … we're in the middle of something can it wait … but jaunty smile … good to see you*

DanceMaster: it is our pleasure Fatarms

Fat-armed Wife: oh no - check watch - running out of time everyone

Thruster: *~whisper to Call Girl~* ~smile~ I kno how 2 play u, I know what u r, what u do, I can handle u ~ light smack ~

Fat-Armed Wife: And DanceMaster thanks most of all for that speech - the best things anyone's ever said - my god - I clasp you all tight - and say it again DanceMaster, I wish I could write all this down, remember it somehow - thank you everyone I love you all

Call Girl: *~whisper to Thruster~ ducking neatly to avoid 'light smack' - hur hur - not the time nor the place Thruster … this is kindofa party … just wait ok*

DanceMaster: I propose a toast. Charge your glasses please

Peach: *You must tell us Fatarms everything that happen*

Psycho-dog: ~scurrying round to fill glasses - pant pant, bark bark

DanceMaster: To Fat-armed Wife, to Call Girl, and to the Velvet Dungeon. Salud!!!

Honeycake: Cheers!

Oldermom: GO FOR IT

Spam: Sannnnn johhhh varrrrrrr bottoommmms upppppp

Thruster: *~whisper to Call Girl~* a party uh?? hand slips around yopur waist ~

Fat-armed Wife: -still breathless from dance with DanceMaster- drink and cigarette in hand - sip - puff - cheers - and yes Peach we will come and tell what happens, straight away

Call Girl: *We will Peach*

Fat-armed Wife: OH GOD - now I have to go - flight beckons

Biker Idiot: knock em dead

Big Black Woman: yeah go for it

Fat-armed Wife: *~whisper to Call Girl~* bye bye I kjiss you gotta go

Call Girl: *~whisper to Fat-armed Wife~ come to me sweetheart, crossing fingers for your flight right now, hurry hurry to me*

Fat-armed Wife: Bye everyone wish me luck - yes on my way to Velvet Dungeon - gorgeous thanks for your help - bye!!! - wave my fat hands - waggle my fat fingers wearing all my ten fat rings!!! WAVE!!!!

DanceMaster: Everyone give a thunderus handclap for Fatarms, she is off to the Velvet Dungeon for the deepest, darkest, most dangerous sensations available! We stand and applaud.

Psycho-dog: bark! Bark! Yelp! Yelp! WAG TAIL LOTS

Call Girl: *~whisper to Fat-armed Wife~ Safe journey, Treasure, come quickly … I wait for you … kiss …. Hurry!*

Spam: not going to say bye fatarms … too much hi and bye in here - ughhh no more - but will say bon voyage.

Oldermom: Bye fatarms and good luck

Fat-armed Wife: Gotta go- last call for boarding- I send love to my dear friends. NO I don't send it I throw it, yes by the bucketful. Both hands! Love to all velvet roomers. Love! Love! Byee!

Nerdy Uncle: Bye then

Fat-armed Wife: *~gone~poof!~*

Call Girl: *unpicking Thruster's hand from around my waist ... errrr ... Thruster let me introduce you to few people ... this is Peach who is a Baptist from Barbados*

Thruster: *~whisper to Call Girl~* stroking your arm ~ feather light touch ~ listen to me I know ur teasiong

Call Girl: *deftly stepping aside to avoid inappropriate seduction technique by Thruster ... And may I introduce Spam ... one helluva successful young charmer here in the Velvet Rooms, as well*

Thruster: *~whisper to Call Girl~* my han d in ur hair - twisting ~ I know yur wet for me now

Honeycake: Oh-oh! as Dustin Hoffman used to say in *Rain Man*

Call Girl: *here we are at a party Thruster, in public, polite smiles, hmmm? And where do you come from Thruster, eh?*

DanceMaster: Maybe the band has stopped, no? I think so

Spam: Thruster whennn yurr a memberrr we can givve yuuu an iconnnn - wotttt aboutttt an ennoirmous chest and rippped jerkinn knind offfff thingggg???!!!

Thruster: *~whisper to Call Girl~* admit it ur wet 4 me

Call Girl: *wet for you????!! YUKKK!*

Thruster: Ok I don't care about wispers either, I pull the hair off your neck an bite u there. Shivers of pain run up and donw ur spine

Spam: ~patting gud old THRUSTER on the sholder, Lett meme hlep you thruster, the delgihtful Call Girrllll only ever puts out once, its a *ONCE* in a lifffetiimme experience

Call Girl: *SHIVERS OF PAIN !!???* URRR??? *... looking at Thruster's red face and bloodshot eyes - oh deary me, looks like I have another stalker, fellow Velvet Roomers*

Peach: *~wave at lovely candlelit interior~ Thruster you like the dancefloor? And there's plenty more, something 4 everyone, there is the Sanctuary. Shall I show u round?*

DanceMaster: Dios mío! ~saunter to Thruster - offer him free drink no less … Call Girl's well known habits, eh!? I understand it will be frustrating ~wink~ but tke heart my friend … we're in the middle of the party so perhaps u can join us … plenty more dancers on the floor

Thruster: Call Girl I press my thumb just on the side of ur neck - against the nerve you feel that, hmmmm?

Call Girl: *Pushing aside Thruster's grubby thumb … Errr no …. Don't feel that at all do you feel this … Oops sorry touched the tip of my burning cigarette on your hand … very sorry … Peachy … kind of you to offer to show Thruster around … Thruster take that guided tour with Peachy why don't you*

Thruster: ~I will fuck u so hard, cum here ~ put my hand around yur nmeck and draw you twards me ~

Honeycake: Oh-oh, as Rabbit used to say in *Looney Tunes*

Call Girl: *Tripping over Thruster's smelly feet … ughhh … sorry .. didn't see you there … what was ur name again … thruster or buster?*

Peach: *Thruster this is smokers' corner, see the nice little red velvet sofa, Dance Master watches the dancers often here. Where next …*

Thruster: Com e hjere

Call Girl: *You all right Buster? You look a bit red in the face - r u in pain?*

Thruster: Stand blocking yur way and unclasp leather belt, stand legs apart ~ cum here u bitch

Call Girl: *Buster maybe you ought to stop writhing around on the floor and stand up*

Thruster: ~coming clsoer~ not wise ~ pull leather belt clear, buckle swings in my hadn

Call Girl: *Put your silly boy scout buckle away Buster, as well*

Thruster: ~grabbign Call Girl by the hair~ You met ur match I can play harder than u

Spam: TELL HIM Call Girrrrl!!!??? Y doncha telllll himmm??! Pleeeze!?

Call Girl: *Thruster I'd just like to point out that you haven't got me by the hair at all, I'm standing here surrounded by close friends, perfectly happy and content, drink in hand … ciggie poised yaknow, while you bump into all the walls LIKE THE MAD FUCKING DOG YOU ARE*

Spam: Call Girl can we TELL THRUSTER - TELLLL HIMMM - goohh onnn, PLEEEEZ!!

Thruster: Say goodbye to ur fguckgtin velvet erooms. I cn brng enogh frnds hnere to sswamp theis place and fuk all of u

Call Girl: *Buster you have scrambled egg on your chin*

Thruster: u r good but I'm better … cum here ~twisting hard~ open ur mouth wide cos its gonna needs 2 be 2 fit muy cock in it

Spam: Pleeeeeeze cannn I

Thruster: I push past all yur teasoing I know wat ur game is and now I bounce u out of that teasing, u hear me - grabbing ur arm and twisting

Call Girl: *Oh cor blimey look at that puddle - Buster's wet himself he's so excited*

Thruster: I twist yr arm … hard … furhter, harider, so u go down on the lfoor and beg me fore mercy~ I don't take this crap from anyone ~massive blow to your face~ opne ur mouth, im gonnna fuck it so hard you gag and choke

Call Girl: *~whacking Thruster so fucking hard that he stops dead in his tracks … and clutches his face in shock … Now listen here, dickhead … I've tried to be nice about this but ur not listening … I told you back in Poolies … but I'm going to tell it to you one more time now and you'd better dbelieve it … I only ever go with a guy ***once!!*****

Spam: nowwwwwww?

Call Girl: *go ahead Spam*

Spam: thank yuuuuu …..!!!!!!

Thruster: I push my hand into your mouth that just had my cock in it, open your mouth wide

Call Girl: *May as well - he doesn't listen to lil ol me*

Honeycake: oh oh as Dustin Hoffman says again

Spam: Wipe SWEATY palms on trouseerrrrss - ahem - Thrusterrrrr Call Girl is a mannnn in reeeeal life

Call Girl:

Call Girl: *Thruster???*

Thruster:

Spam: you fucked a mann … hnnnn?? go home and weeeeeep ….

Call Girl: *How do you do Thruster … manly handshake, as well*

Thruster: Cun t

Spam: … Thruster, thatsss the poinnt, gedddtt? not a cunttt at all??!! A prickkkkk he's a blohhhhhke … ahhhh!!!

Call Girl: *all MAN*

Thruster:

Call Girl: *hombre uomo herrr guy bloke male!!*

Thruster:

Call Girl: *I'm a bi CD/T, slim/slender, long legs, sometimes corseted waist (30") but sorry not full nipples, can be sub or dom, play as male or play as female with boybits strapped up for Gummiklinik style acts and with own private equipped playroom with fetish as you might have noticed for double fantasy kidnap/rape role play but basically up for whatever fun is going on, as well, with men or women*

Thruster:

Peach: *Think I might log off 4 a bit. sorry every1*

Call Girl: *So Buster who are YOU in real life … I'd like to know … just so I can CROSS TO THE OTHER SIDE OF THE STREET ha ha*

Psycho-dog: come on Thruster, chill, this is a cool site

Peach: *~gone~poof!~*

DanceMaster: errrrr … music, anyone? Dancing?

Call Girl: *Buster we run a munch every month, friendly atmosphere, partners and admirers welcome, in scene-aware bar. Wanna come along?*

Thruster:

Biker Idiot: *~whisper to Peach~* Awww, Peachy, I was here, come back

Call Girl: *Plus - !!!??? go to Rogerzone.com and I'm RentBoy, go to slingbacks.co.uk and I'm Daisydoes. Much cheaper as well. Fifty dollars here … expensive huh? … to keep cheap tarts out of the site … hee hee*

Peach enters Velvet Ballroom

Spam: Hez still heree, bitt of a shokk in cyberland scenario, silence is goldennnn eh thrusterrr?//

Psycho-dog: … whine … pant … why he no talkkk??

Jetman enters Velvet Ballroom

Jetman: Hi every1. 50 dollars, this place betta b gud!!??

Peach: *Hi Jetman we have a bit got a situation here*

DanceMaster: Thruster, I extend the hand of friendship. Would you like the complimentary alcoholic beverage now? No harm done I hope. Call Girl is male. The Velvet Rooms welcomes all voyagers in cyberspace who behave with good humour

Peach: *Jetman?*

Psycho-dog: lick lips … sure, free drink … bark, whine

Thruster:

Jetman: Oh ok sorry - wot situation

Peach: *don't worry, welcome, I'll look after u*

DanceMaster: Ladies and gentlemen, shall we dance?

Thruster:

DanceMaster: Thruster, would you like first choice of partner

68

Jetman: Wha's happening?

Peach: *Jetman U want to go on a tour, I can show you around?*

Thruster: I AM THE SHADOW ON THE WALL

Call Girl: *Ooo-errrr*

Jetman: Ok

Peach: **~whispers to Jetman~** *c u in first in The Sanctuary 2 start I can take you there because im full member. Type yr name in the sanctuary box*

Jetman: **~whispers to Peach~** Hey this is great,m what a welcome, thnks v much

Peach: *C u in a minute everyone, just showing Jetman around* ☺

Jetman: Hold on, haven't introduced myself, Hi Thruster, hi Call Girl, hi Fat-armed Wife, hi MadBadMotherFucker, hi Psycho-dog, hi DanceMaster, hi Spam

Spam: ~ beggggs ~ no more hi and bye

Peach: **~gone~poof!~**

Thruster: I AM THE FACE AT THE WINDOW

Call Girl: *Oh my word*

Jetman: **~gone~poof!~**

Call Girl: *HE IS THE BOGEY IN MY NOSE*

Spam: And Call Girl's nott evennn a YUNGGG boyyyy, Thruster, he's hundredds of years OLDDD

Call Girl: *fifty-five isn't old by the way Spam … But I am balding it's true and I got a septic ear from my earring at the moment as well and smoker's breath*

Spam: HE ISSS THE WILLLY IN THE BOTTOMMM hee hee

Call Girl: *lol at Spam!!!!*

Spam: yeeee hahhhh!! Lol at Call Girl

Thruster: don't believe you

Call Girl: *I AM A GREAT BIG DONKEY COCK*

Thruster: crap

Call Girl: *Show him the pics Spam*

Spam: Thrusterrrrr, urrrr not a memmmber bu cannn I invite uuuu to the messagee boaorddsss? There are picccturesss of usss, you can have a lokk at Callll Gurrrll, just checckkk the messaggge boards box top right of screen

Call Girl: *This is me … wave cheerily … Hiya Thruster*

Thruster: I AM THE FOOTSTEP ON THE STAIRS

Thruster: *~gone~poof!~*

T hruster was motionless. Not one thing stirred around him. Yet sweat broke from his skin as if he'd pumped weights for an hour. The insult had worked his system.

Slowly, the situation settled, dripped through the levels of consciousness. Call Girl was male.

He undressed, stood naked and palely luminescent in the semi-dark. He wiped his arms, shoulders and neck with baby oil. He checked his teeth, gripping each one between thumb and forefinger and testing it, back and forth. The incisors were immovable. A third molar tweaked with slight pain. The abrasive edge of a damaged crown still exercised his tongue. He squeezed the roll of fat round his middle and dressed again.

A minute later he fetched the photographs from the printer. He swept a space clear on the surface of the desk. The truth stared up at him. Call Girl was a man. The crooked, smiling mouth and unshaven chin. The face thin, sallow and chiselled by time and drink and drugs, probably. The lines from the nose to the corners of the mouth were deeply engraved. The surface of the skin looked rough, pitted, under the make-up. The eyes were small and dark and spoke of excitement. The whole was framed by an unkempt mass of curly hair. Tattoos covered much of his torso and his arms and part of his neck. Underneath the tattoos coursed startling sinews, like a map of strength, but there was only slight muscle bulk. He would be wiry but lack real power. His nipples, eyebrows and nose were pierced. Thruster grazed over the details, reading the signs, storing detail.

That person, there in the picture, had written those words, taken him in. Those hands had typed out the lies, posted them. Thruster had swallowed them. He bit on that, chewed it; his skin crawled.

The second photograph had been taken outside a nightclub. Call Girl was leaning against the side of a taxi, cigarette held at a jaunty angle, wearing a silver chain-mail top and a gold lamé miniskirt. His hair was presumably hidden underneath the blond wig. One thin, muscular leg in mesh stockings was folded across the other, poking daintily from under the miniskirt. The workman's boots looked outsize and clumsy in contrast. His mouth was open; he was laughing. On the door of the taxi a name and a phone number could be partly deciphered, written in a circle. Thruster leaned closer to see if he could read it . . . Maybe.

The last picture showed a stretch of beach under a grey, cold sky. Call Girl stood naked, arms outstretched as if about to catch someone running towards him. Needle tracks could be seen on the insides of his elbows and the same tattoos covered his torso. His hair was curly and dark and tousled and he wasn't wearing make-up. The skin on his face had been coarsened by acne, yes. The small dark eyes looked hardbitten, unashamed and full of glee.

It was as different as you could get from the image Call Girl had conjured for himself on the Velvet Shore as an abused girl, on the run. Thruster rose to his feet, stood for a whole minute, before sitting again to pore over one particular picture – of Call Girl leaning against the taxi. He found the picture file in the computer and zoomed the picture bigger. He could read 'Star Cars' and some of the numbers printed on the side of the vehicle – one or two were illegible and others invisible behind Call Girl's legs. He wrote down what he could and looked at it closely. It would be a UK telephone number, not a US one – he could tell from the make of car. So it would begin with a 0 and the second number would be a 1. The third was either a three or an eight, he couldn't tell which. He wrote down both versions and painstakingly listed all the possible permutations. Even though it was the middle of the night he called them up, one by one, dialling them through the computer.

On the fourth try a Yorkshire accent answered, 'Star Cars'.

'Hello. I just wanted to know where your offices are.'

'We're in the old part of town.'

'Which town is that?'

'We're in Hull. Where are you?'

Thruster didn't reply.

'Hello?'

He put the phone down. Hull. That was a surprise – he had expected it to be one of the major cities – but it might or might not be Call Girl's home town. He looked at the photographs again. The one on the beach, that counted. It made it more likely. Hull was on the coast. He put the man in the photograph behind the name 'Call Girl' and tried it for size.

It was like a door opening. The mask had been torn away from a face. Reality had poked a stick through.

Hull.

He took the plastic-covered wire basket that functioned as an in-tray. The stiff-backed manilla envelope waited there. He recognised his father's influence in the style of handwriting – in the way a circle was drawn round the number 14 on the front of it. A crawling sensation moved over his scalp. He shook out the contents. Four months previously his random placing of a forefinger on the mileage grid at the back of the large-scale AA road atlas had given him either Exeter or Durham; he'd chosen Exeter. After two weekends spent in a B-and-B in the Heavitree area he'd settled on someone who, he'd subsequently found out, worked for the cathedral. One Michael Hughes of Orchard Close. In front of him now were photographs of Michael Hughes and his wife and the interior of their house. The best picture showed him bowed against a cold wind, a tuft of hair standing up in the middle of a bald crown, a puffa jacket bulking out his shoulders. There was also a collection of mail which Thruster had taken from his porch, a hand-drawn map and photographs of a section of curved road close to the cathedral, with high, blank walls, not overlooked from any direction.

Now he took a fresh, clean stiff-backed envelope from the drawer and took the same indelible marker as always. On it he wrote the number 13 in a circle. He gathered together all of Mr Michael Hughes of 2 Orchard Close, Exeter, and put him in the envelope. It was the equivalent of having trapped him – as he walked, bowed into the wind, that tuft of hair standing up – of having caught him gently in both hands as you would a frightened mouse, but then dropping to one knee and letting him go unharmed. He would scurry away up the high-walled, windowless alley and escape.

Right now, as Thruster peeled the sticky backing from the flap of the envelope and sealed it, he could imagine Michael Hughes's sleep suddenly disturbed in Exeter. He'd sense the rush of freedom, the threat lifted from over him, and sit up in his bed . . .

He filed envelope 13 in the second drawer of the filing cabinet and returned to his desk. He took the empty envelope, number 14, formerly occupied by Mr Hughes, and examined it. The seams had been stretched out of shape slightly and showed signs of wear. A corner was damaged. Yet it was serviceable. He scooped up Call Girl – the pictures, the transcripts, all of it – and slotted him into the envelope. The flap he left open. There was more work. Hull.

Asbo enters Velvet Ballroom

Asbo: Kick and spit and stamp throw brick through window scream and shout inject drugs snatch bag

Asbo:

Asbo: Run across knocked down by car scream in agony punch and kick fucking stupid driver and limp off smash up bus stop

Asbo: hello?

Asbo: *~gone~poof!~*

Fat-armed Wife tried to shake herself clear of cyberspace; the party writing itself into the Velvet Rooms lived on in her head. When she dared to look up it was like a stage set had been assembled around her and it was a play she was in. She was the star of the show. The flats dropped around her had been painted to look like Boston's Logan airport, terminal B. The lights were up full. The props were in place. Television monitors hung from the ceiling relaying departure and arrival times. The American Food Court jostled for customers with Burger King Expressway and Gourmet Bean. It was faultless. No one could deny the designer had done a great job. But it felt like she hadn't rehearsed and didn't know the words. She clicked the laptop shut and slotted it into its case.

And for real, it was no smoking. She automatically checked the Art Deco cigarette lighter which hung on a cord round her neck; even though it was there, safe and sound, the panic rose in her breast. Her throat was still burning from the four she'd smoked in a row outside the terminal building before gritting her teeth and walking in. The penalty for that intake of nicotine had been Colin's leaving; she'd had to check in on her own. She took the other half of the Valium tablet and closed her eyes, tried to tune herself out of the need. She was about to take a flight – the direction, the arc of the rainbow, was towards Call Girl. She rocked back and forth with nerves and prepared to stand. Let the signs and the instructions be her guide. Flight 108, American Airlines, 7.05 p.m. departure, gate B33. The friendly uniformity of the airport lounge welcomed her. Every step of her journey was looked after. It was a process that people went through in their thousands every minute of the day and night. They were like burgers – everyone put in a box and flown out, millions a day. None the less, it would be a long flight in a metal tube, thirty thousand feet up in the air at five hundred miles an hour with no cigarettes – stupid *not* to panic. She clutched onto the prospect of meeting Call Girl: that was the pot of gold at the end of the rainbow; he drew her onwards. He occupied a room in her head, a place of its own, where she always went. Now she was following the rainbow to its source – her love for Call Girl was imbued with every colour – and it would carry her safely in a great circle arc over the Atlantic; all she needed to do was put one foot in front of the other and she'd find . . . what? Treasure? She didn't know. Suddenly it came back to her: he was calling her that now, it was his new pet name for her, Treasure.

A straggle of people were making their way; she was one of the last. She slung the computer over her shoulder, picked up hand luggage and duty-free. Thus burdened she made her way to the gate and submitted to another search. Security was exhausting but a comfort. No danger would be allowed to pass. She sat down, waited some more. Her hands trembled already; she talked to them as if they were a pair of friends.

The blurred, vibating voice of the tannoy asked the rearmost passengers to board the aircraft. Other people rose to their feet and the impetus lifted her also. The laptop and the handbag bumped against her legs – she felt like she was being hosed onto the plane, or swallowed. She gave her best smile to the heavily made-up stewardesses; she felt sorry for them, having to be so polite and friendly to a sweating, nervous, stressed-out smoker facing hours of punishment: it would be, for her, like being asked to cross a desert without water. As she barged and huffed and puffed down the plane she scanned the numbers. It would be an aisle seat – she'd insisted on that because she did need to spill over the sides.

Here – 19c – she'd arrived. She pushed her stuff into the over-head locker. So much work was exhausting. She carried too much weight – in the metaphorical sense of the word as well. Even the rings on her fingers felt heavy, and they caught in the laptop case which she was stuffing in. Her whole life was too much; a secret life as well as a normal one. Everything was too small, too constrained, for her to fit. 'Didn't anyone tell chair manufacturers that we're all over one hundred and eighty pounds?' she asked a neighbour. She squeezed into her seat and hid a packet of Marlborough in the pocket in front of her, teased it so she could see the red flip-top. Would it help to know they were within reach? She pushed them out of sight and brought them out again. Her neighbours might be worried she was going to smoke in the plane's toilet. She reached up to the locker and put them in the side pocket of the computer bag, then sat back down. The sweat trickled down her arms. She was up again immediately to help someone close their overhead locker; it was nothing to her, with her strong arms, to squeeze it shut.

Soon they'd be asked to switch off phones, so she unpacked her cell and dialled home to say goodbye. As she slotted the earpiece under her hair she heard the familiar chirrup: a text message had arrived. She killed the call; she wanted to read the message first. 'A deep kiss on yr mouth and a suck on both yr breasts and prayers fr the safety of yr flight.' From Call Girl. She murmured under her breath, smiling. She was only a flight, plus a day and a night and a day, from meeting him eye to eye, flesh to flesh. She bounced the text back, 'About 2 take off in flying bomb prayer and all kisses gratefully received.' She wanted to pick him up, plonk him in the seat next to her.

She smiled at the thought. That would put the cat among the pigeons: six foot one of cross-dressing British bi-sexual in American Airlines Economy Class. Ha ha! Next, she went to call home, but when the tone came it was obviously wrong – this was a UK telephone, from the tune. She glanced at the screen. Somehow she'd become tangled up with the text message and had dialled Call Girl by mistake.

'Fat arms?' came his voice. 'What's up?'

'Hey,' she said, 'my phone just called you on its own.'

'You must be nigh on at the gate, are you?'

'You kidding? I'm on the plane.' She rocked back and forth in her seat. Her eyes glazed over. It was as if her surroundings had disappeared and all she could see was Call Girl's icon, his green italic script. His voice was alive in her head. Lust for him swept through her – it was because she was near to the risk of dying that the urge to fuck him was so strong.

'Are you there?' she asked.

'I am, my darling.'

'No, I mean are you really there? Do you exist? Are you for real?'

'Yes, sweetheart. Look here I am, pinching myself, real skin, real blood in my veins, Treasure, as well, and a heart beating for your arrival.'

'You still all OK that I'm coming?' She coughed, squeezed her eyes shut. She didn't want to cry.

'Yes! What about you?'

'Sure, yes.' She held on tight to the seat in front of her, as if she might be carried away.

'I will not back out again. Never worry about that, will you? I won't do that, I promise you.'

'Dungeon rules.'

'Dungeon rules, certainly. I am right here. All I will do is clean up the flat, go to work, go to bed, wait for you. With Buttons on me lap, as well. 'Til you arrive.'

'Sure we can't do real names now?'

There was a pause. 'Hmmmm . . .'

'Not if you don't want, then.'

'Like I say, names are like a weird magic, you know? Not sure, Treasure. When we see each other, when we meet? That's the time for it, isn't it?'

'For God's sake, the mystery's killing me.'

'Actually, me name's Roger Goering Hitler Bush.'

'OK, OK. When we meet.'

'Will be all right, won't it? If you don't object.'

'Just feel a bit nervous, I guess.' She wiped away tears. 'But this is on my cell, it's costing a fortune and I'm on the plane – phones not allowed.'

'Come quickly, then.'

'At five hundred miles an hour or whatever,' she said. 'Stay right where you are, don't move.'

'Signal when you land, hm?'

'Yes, yes I will.' She remembered the cards. Flames poured from the top of the Tower. The Three Swords lined up, threatening. 'And . . .'

'And what, my fat arms?'

'Stay dead safe, you hear?'

'I will.'

'No car journeys.'

'OK.'

'Don't cross a road in the dark.'

'No.'

'Don't eat any old seafood sandwiches left over in the fridge. Hmm?'

'No. I'm just going to wait here for you. And I'll smoke for both us.'

'Heck, wish you could!' she murmured. 'Bye, then. Bye.'

'Bye for now.'

The line went dead. The voice disappeared. Instead, the nylony, furred surface of the airline seat, and the sprung trap of the pocket containing the magazines, and the miraculous, cylindrical tube in which she and her fellow passengers sat, and the stretch of wing outside the porthole – all this came back. Numerous frowns were aimed at her from those who worried that her cell phone might interfere with the plane's instruments. She switched off and smiled and nodded at the young mother a couple of rows ahead who was throwing the worst looks. She pushed back in the seat, wrestled with the buckle, then settled and closed her eyes. She breathed in her neighbours; she needed to guess whether or not they'd be OK. She didn't want to be stuck with an unwanted conversation. She wished she might reach into thin air, through the membrane, and pluck the Velvet Rooms from cyberspace, unpack Call Girl, DanceMaster, Spam, Peach and Honeycake and arrange them in the seats next to her. She wondered: if that had been how they'd first met, on a plane, would she have guessed that a passionate love was possible with Call Girl? Would she have seen beyond his black-and-orange hair and his skin all marked by acne and his being fifty-five years old? And just because Psycho-dog was Cypriot and so looked like an Arab, wore shirts and ties made of manmade fibres in mis-matching colours, would she think he had a bomb strapped to his chest?

She'd probably have put on the blindfold and gone to sleep or used the headphones and the little TV screen to ward them off. How polluted that makes our judgement, she thought. She felt tears burning behind her closed eyes. The Velvet Rooms was a heavenly place; they all lived there happily. She put them away again, one by one. Peach, we will pay your membership, don't worry. Honeycake, he will ask you to marry him, it won't be a weekend thing for ever. DanceMaster, you are allowed to talk about yourself, you don't just work the Velvet Rooms, you are our friend and we want to share your confidences. Spam, you will live for a few more years yet. Big Black Woman, trust us, show yourself, put your picture in the members' gallery. Velvet Roomers, you are fine people, you belong, you are beloved, whoever you are. With such fervent messages she placed each of them on the dancefloor, set them moving gracefully, then pushed them through the membrane and into cyberspace where they belonged.

A picture of Jamie sprang to mind, with his mouth open. Mentally, she sent him an apology for being so far away. She wondered if men felt the same when they had to travel for work. Her husband and stepson were tethered at a distance. She sent an apology to Colin: sorry for spending all this money.

Soon the call for seat belts was made; the business of the flight began. The phone was in the seat pocket, switched off. The computer nestled in its carry case in the overhead locker. These tools were waiting for her, ready for her arrival. The plane began to roll backwards. Fat-armed Wife welcomed the slight undulation: the pulse of the journey had started. Outside, the wing flexed gingerly up and down; it was impossibly slender for the work it would shortly be asked to do. She felt her arm jogged by her neighbour's searching for his seat belt.

Here we go, she thought. To the Dungeon. The craving for real sexual congress with Call Girl opened in her a familiar, restless, unstoppable hunger.

When the jet powered down the runway she gritted her teeth and started to count. She brought to mind the first time she and Call Girl had kissed.

Just imagine my hand. Call Girl had had blue writing, back then.

Your hand? she'd posted back.

Yes, my hand. Just by itself. Don't think about what it's attached to, not woman or a man, just someone, anonymous.

OK. Your hand.

Look - the fingers, the skin creased at the knuckles, across the palms. The nails painted. A ring on the third finger. Can you see?

Yes.

Take it in yours.

It's warm. Dry.

The fingers are long and thin and older than yours. You can hear my voice.

I'm holding it, I know it's yours. I can hear you. I feel good. I'm holding your hand.

No one else's hand can come close.

No.

Turn it over. See the back of my hand resting against your palm. Not moving, just resting there. As if it belongs to you.

OK, I can see.

Now it moves, it encloses yours.

I like this. We're holding hands.

Now we move, yes, like a dance, and the tip of one finger moves over your wrist.

I'm watching.

Along your forearm. The touch reaches the inside of your elbow. Stays there just for a while. Feather light.

I'm nervous.

Do you want it to move higher?

Yes.

The tip of that finger moves over your upper arm . . . just the lightest touch . . . and across your shoulder blade . . . and to the base of your neck.

I want to see you.

But your eyes are closed, Precious. The touch moves up your neck, and caresses the side of your face.

Yes. Feels like kindness.

The fingernails are painted pink. Does that matter?

No.

The fingertip moves slowly to the very corner of your mouth.

Ohhh, that tickles.

Is your mouth ready? Is it open just a bit? Is it still, motionless? As the touch moves across your bottom lip.

Yes. Tingling.

Does your mouth care about anything except this, except for what will happen next?

No.

The touch is lifted, it's gone. There's nothing there.

Sudden emptiness now.

Do you feel hunger?

Yes.

My mouth is moving towards yours. You don't see it but you know it's coming closer. Do you wish it, darling? Our lips to touch?

Yes.

My lips touch yours, open

Yes, open

There was a bump; the jet took off. Fat-armed Wife opened her eyes to see the ground falling away.

Call Girl's first kiss.

She could always find that memory, at will. She could remember what she had been wearing at the time, the weather, the date and day. Now, four years later, she'd come to know this man's heart as well as her own. The Velvet Dungeon was prepared and ready, petals scattered at the door.

The jet's engines rose in pitch. She walked her rainbow, traversed the sky.

Jetman enters Velvet Ballroom

Soft-boiled egg: I want you to grow in my hand

Peach: clap of hand~jump down and up~ Jetman! Hi!

Jetman: Hi every1

ChuckerUpper: divine intervention or what??!! Yuck

Peach: u look handsome Jetman?

Jetman: Hi Peachy u wanna dance?

Maneater: Laura, you in Scotland or here in USA?

Soft-boiled egg: Hi Jetman

Peach: ~step in Jetman's arms~ yes please

Oldermom: ~helping Laura to her feet~ Poor darling ~vbs~

Peach: Maneater, do you want to meet this Jetman, he's a marine?

Maneater: Hi Laura

Laura: Maneater, I'm in Glasgow, Scotland

Maneater: how d'you do Jetman … staggering a bit … pleased to meet you, any friend of Peachy's a friend of mine … stumbling around dance floor… no good at dancing … drunk as usual … Let's see, who's doing what to whom … … sneeze, wipe nose

Laura: Phew it's hot in here

ChuckerUpper: Is that true, a marine?

Maneater: ~lurch ~ lift glass ~ Heard you Scots Girls are GIB … cheers to that

Laura: Thanks Maneater, time to let the Scottish girl in me out to play ~lol~

Jetman: Pleased 2 make yr aquaintance ~salutging army style~

Maneater: Marines ??!!! Strewth!! Come down under, ever?

Peach: ~hanging proudly off Jetman's broad shoulders~ He's new to the Velvet Rooms. *winks*. I told him about all of us

82

Oldermom: Maneater, well done. Fight that fire. I got beaten up in madaboutchat. com

Jetman: And I like all I hear, my kind of place, hope no one minds if I come often, now Ive found Peachy

Laura: Maneater, nice cheeks

Maneater: thanks. Fun to be had up your kilt, I bet

Spam: Wheree yuuu from, Jetttyman?

Big Dick: So ~winks~ Scots lasses are known for bieng wild?

Peach: *me and Psycho-dog r going 2 sponsor Jetman* ☺

Laura: ignore Big Dick everyone

Jetman: Spam, I'm kinda an anywehere type of guy, anywhere they tell me to go for tours of doooty - what bout u

Spam: Im from uk, jettyman, yunnngg 'n hunnngry from the old country, thatts me, you evverr bin to deeer ol blighty Jettttyman?

Peachy: *~standing prettily for every1~ I told him about Green-eyed Man and he still wants 2 go out with me*

Jetman: Greeneye d man is nin the past so I'm not gonna worry about him

Soft-boiled Egg: sorry every1 gotta go

Jetman: Yes Spam to Aldershot, Wiltshire, visit with my unit, love those English girls

Soft-boiled egg: *~gone~poof!~*

Oldermom: and I take your dick in my mouth, the whole of it, and work the back of my throat on the top of your fat hard cock

Spam: Jetttyman it's the yummy American gurrrlllls that make the best lovers, me in myh laiirrrr wakiting for luverrllly yankkeee flowers to bee pickked

Peach: *Oldermom??!! Please not here*

Oldermom: sorry everyone, was meant to be a whisper, got carried away

Biker Idiot: *VERY STERN LOOK* Oldermom I see you … stride over to your hiding place ... come on, both of you - pull back table and chairs - please, up you get - adjust yourselves - the Velvet Shore is the place for that kind of thing … hands on hips .. off you go

Oldermom: Sorry

Peach: *Well done Biker Idiot u r the bouncer now all right*

ChuckerUpper: Hey, where did the porn suddenly come from Oldermom?

Biker Idiot: thanks Peach ~ vbs ~

Peach: *~turning away, thankful to Jetman's strong arms~ Spam Jetman's a Baptist like me ~smile~ aren't you honey?*

Jetman: Sure am

Thruster enters The Velvet Ballroom

Biker Idiot: ~emerging once more from gloom~ Thruster?? ~music halts and dancers stop moving~ U are not welcome here

Thruster:

Biker Idiot: Thruster?

Thruster:

Spam: Silenss is goldennnn Thrusterr, uve switched everyhone offf like wee are all ur sexx toyyys. R U not going to talkkkkl at all?

Thruster:

Spam: Thruster is wayyytingg for Call Girl, me thinks … yesss. Whnen she doess come Thruster, hmmm, lets yuu and I takke herr poorrr brrruised aresssse to the barr for drinkkkies, watch herr ssemmen-stainnedd hands shakkingg~ and she willl tell uss what she's been up to, what neew gamme

Thruster: *~click here to see picture~*

Spam: Prayee Thruster, what is thisss? A pretty boat? The Spurn??? Hnnn???

Biker Idiot: ~holding meaningless photo aloft~ anyone put us out of our misery? Ehhhh???

Peach: *It's a strange look ship, why do you send us this ship Thruster*

Thruster:

Spam: Thruster???!! You iz looking for more bruuses, for more arssee, more cunnilinnnngusss, for morre titttiees held for youuu to splurge overrr, eh Thrusterrr? But nohhh!!! Instead man's boooolllllocks swingggg in ffornt of yurrr facee!! HHHA HHHHHAAAA HAAAAA!!!!!!!!!!!!

Thruster:

Spam: Thruster if u like I showww yuuu my pinkk bottttty fresssh from famous Englishh puliccc shcooll and lean over so you can take out that thinggg and playyyyyy????

Thruster:

Peach: *Jetman, this is the guy I was telling you about. Thruster, what's the point??? Please???*

Thruster: **~gone~poof~**

T hruster sifted through the contents of envelope 14. He examined the photograph of Call Girl leaning against the taxi, cross-dressed in gold miniskirt and silver-chain-mail top.

He put the bullet through the chain mail, explosively hard, into Call Girl's heart. The barrel warmed his hands. He saw the shock drag the expression on Call Girl's face. He opened up the abyss and pushed him in and felt the familiar lunge in his groin.

He cast an eye over the green italic writing.

Thruster: u gonna take it all

Call Girl: *You spit on the tip opf your cock and put it atgsint my arse you'r just touching slimey point of it in my cracdk and nudge forward ... please, nooohhhh*

Thruster: I push it in

Call Girl: *You push it in … push … aghhh …*

Thruster: Push it

His eye wandered elsewhere on the printed pages. He'd sliced Call Girl with a whip – she'd felt that. He read the exchange where she'd dumped him. She'd finished and left him hanging; she'd laughed at him. Behind her mask was this man . . . He sifted through and read the last few words of the conversation: 'wave cheerily ... Hiya Thruster'.

The insult fluttered in his chest. The same sweat sprang from his neck, forehead.

Afterwards he tried to meditate but it was impossible. Call Girl had stirred him, pushed him to some place beyond sleep. He couldn't leave it alone. He set off on a tour of the empty works, switching on lights as he went. A pigeon was trapped under the skylight, beating effortfully at his approach. He stood by the door to the old rest room, which hung off its hinges. The drum kit waited silently. He wandered over to the derelict troop carrier and touched its side. Mostly, he just gathered the space inside him, breathed in and out.

The idea of finding Call Girl in Hull hardened still further; its focus in his mind became pin-sharp.

He couldn't have said how but he found himself back with the drum kit. This had previously been the workers' rest room; the kitchenette had been ripped out but there was a decent level floor, still with red and blue lino tiles. He went and flipped the broken switch and the strip light winked a half dozen times, then came on.

In the sudden white light glittered the highly polished black and chrome Mirage. Sandbags were piled against the bass drum to stop it moving. He gathered the lightest pair of sticks from the holster and straddled the stool and beat out a steady four–four – with not one fancy riff or even a break in the boom-boom. He kept going, waiting for his shoulders to loosen, drop in their sockets. The sticks balanced almost by themselves. He picked up the pace and began to find the quarters of beats, filling them with snare or bass or high-hat. He coached his body to become more still – to help concentration and to hypnotise himself, take himself back to that moment. His chin turned sideways as he listened for music and searched for the pictures in his head. He remembered his visits to the Shippe Inn, in Fore Street, Yarminster. The door always snagged on the carpet. Sally Fitzpatrick always asked him to close it. She smiled, recognised him. He'd sat and ordered his meal and watched her move among the other customers. He'd eaten the food she served him. He'd had to stop himself talking to her about her father, Jonathan. On his first visit, Sally had been twelve years old. Now she was nineteen. How her life had changed. Might she have gone to university if her father had lived? To keep quiet, he had to keep his mouth full. She came more often to his table than to others because she knew he'd leave a big tip. He always sensed the ghost of his victim, felt the heat of his anger and resentment, the wild animal buried in his heart. Here was his daughter; but she was unknowing. He'd wipe his knife on his fork, sip the last of the gravy, pay the bill. As he left he always said, 'Cheerio. Until next time . . .' She gave that slight wave and the same smile.

Without knowing it he'd found his way into a drum solo from a track on the U2 album and now he was getting there; his limbs found their separate ways, disengaged but listening to each other. He unleashed riffs, went wild for ten sets of four and more before finding his way back, marking the return with that emphatic cymbal, before running off again. The sweat began to pour down his face, his arms. His torso dampened under his shirt. He spiked the pace, hurried it beyond where it should go and kept going for twenty more hard minutes: he was alone with his fluent, hard percussion. It was fitness, it was strength, it was work.

'Buster'. Call Girl's joke name for him sprang into his head and he stopped abruptly. The silence was like an alarm, louder than anything in his head.

Nothing sounded except the wrong done to him.

He chucked the sticks back in the holster, switched off the light and headed back upstairs to the office. He undressed and stood naked. He examined every inch of his right forearm. There was always an itch here, night and day. His nails scored at it, over and over. There wasn't a bite mark; no rash coloured the skin. Why should it itch, this forearm? It wasn't logical.

There were deposits of dirt in the corners of his toenails, he noticed. He took the penknife from his pocket and opened the spike, used it to dig. He kept at it until every fragment was gone.

He checked his pulse.

These events, in the dead of night, followed a well-worn track; things done before. A list was made, as always; his handwriting crawled slowly across the paper, making neat capitals. Yet he must try and sleep, if only for a few minutes.

Later, in darkness, he lay on his back, one thick arm across his chest and the other to one side, palm upwards, apparently summoning a reluctant guest. Behind the lids his eyes rolled; he was dreaming of that wound, his hands entering it, as if dipped in a basin, immediately soaked in blood. The ribs stuck out, matching the teeth, both white smeared with red. His hand moved to find the source of the bleeding, to pinch it shut. The sound of breathing, sterterous, uncertain.

He half woke, and the sound of the breathing – his own – moved him seamlessly from the dream to a familiar memory, except that now it was coloured with the bright veracity of a dream conjured in darkness. It was a different place, a different time: a section of broken wall, the roof timbers hanging in midair, a tiled floor strewn with rubble, the smell of burning, his own constant movement and effort – that breathing. As suddenly as a switch turned on, out of nowhere, the enemy stood in front of him. All his hurry, his panic, stopped dead. The man's uniform was wrong. A crushed pack of cigarettes peeped out of his rolled-up sleeve. Multiple whorls of dark hair crawled on his neck; tufts sprouted from under the T-shirt he wore. A grunt burst from him as he tried to move quickly enough but in response there was the immediate buck of the weapon in Thruster's hands. Then came the puff of the uniform jacket as – only an arm's length away – the round went into the man's chest and he staggered backwards. The disturbance created by the bullet was a sharp tug inwards at the cloth, then a slight blow outwards, as if a small animal had turned tail and run into the man's heart. The barrel of the gun had become warmer in his hand. Agony arrived on the man's face as he lay on his back. Death opened its abyss in front of him. Thruster watched as the stranger was pushed in. Terror shone in his eyes as he fell. There was certain, absolute knowledge that there was no coming out of this. After a minute or two, the headlong fall bottomed out: the man's expression slowed, emptied.

Excitement had spread in Thruster quickly and virulently. It startled him. This death, this yawning of deep nothingness, he himself had created – it caused in him an intense, masculine excitement.

He rose from the bed. The undersides of his knees caught on the raw, abrasive wood of the pallets the mattress rested on. He stood, dragged the mattress a few inches away from the wall; the chafed edges of the wood were covered. Within days the mattress would creep back and he'd have to do it again.

He turned his attention to the trunk. He raised the lid, stared. He counted the value, the measure of his achievement. Twelve so far. It was worth more than any numbers lined up on his bank statement, NatWest sort code 30-90-10, account number 7566455. This was work that had been done for nothing so cheap as money.

For ages he breathed in the ghosts of numbers 1 to 12. He'd worked hard, conscientiously, to achieve them. It was only right to be able to remind himself of past success. Yet he admitted he had a problem with hoarding. He would constantly maintain his files, he would visit and re-visit the scenes of his crimes, the collection of photographs grew and grew, but it was never enough. He always had to work towards a higher score. The count would continue. It gave him vertigo to think of how high it might go. He swallowed, shut the lid. Number 13 omitted, because it would bring bad luck. Number 14 . . .

His mind wandered, lost focus, it was like drunkenness.

The seat-belt lights went off; Fat-armed Wife immediately unbuckled, stood up. She tried not to hyperventilate but the effort cost her and it made her feel sick. She bullied her way out of the plane as quickly as she could and rushed through customs and immigration, out of the arrivals hall and through the sliding glass doors fronting the terminal – all this as if the airport were engulfed in flames and she was blindly trying to save her life. Of course, the type of air she needed was the lungful that carried that first belt of nicotine; it was the only thing that made it possible to survive. She stood at the side of the road, her bags dropped any old how, as she turned in circles and tamed her shaking fingers in order to put them to work at the packet, at the vintage lighter that dangled on its leather cord round her neck. She mumbled incoherently, tripping the cigarette from between her lips: she watched it roll, clean and slim and white, at her feet, and without shame she picked it up and threw it back in her mouth. She was ready with the lighter, stood the flame against the tip and breathed in hard; at last the suffocation left her. She had survived, she'd escaped. She coughed wretchedly like the victim of a house fire.

Two more cigarettes were smoked to the nub before she could stop shaking. Her luggage was scattered around her feet; she arranged it neatly and checked nothing was missing. Fears assailed her. She was alone in a strange country, the air chill and wet, the strange grubbiness of this foreign country which she remembered from previous visits, the sound and movement of others, so much more closely packed in than back home, and all of them confident and certain of who they were and where they were going. Without thinking, blindfolded, these strangers knew their way into London, and she didn't have the courage to ask for help. It was left to her to try and navigate the impossible sprawl of the map. She was an overweight, overdramatic American who wore too many rings and who was still foolish enough occasionally to put glitter in her hair for parties, on a nonsensical journey to throw herself at someone she'd never met. There was no rainbow. She wanted her husband, of whom she was proud to the very bottom of her heart. She wanted her stepson, Jamie . . . the way he sometimes bumped into her as if she were a piece of furniture inexplicably moved from one spot to another. She told herself not to stand and think, not to remember, not to let her thoughts twist together until they constricted her, but instead do something – anything.

She commandeered a trolley and loaded her pile; then she set off to find a train into the centre of town. The Regent Palace Hotel, Piccadilly Circus. The Real Thing UK – a potential new business. This was the reality, the grain of things. Her body heavy, corporal. The shoes itching at her feet. The stickiness of the blouse against her skin. These were things that could not be questioned; she could touch them. She told herself to hang on.

Honeycake enters Velvet Ballroom

Peach: *Hi Honey*

Honeycake: Hi Peachy

Peach: *Only us here*

Honeycake: Ahh that's ok

Peach: *So shall we dance?*

Honeycake: A pleasure. Hand on your shoulder, other hand laced to yours, step sideways one, backwards two

Peach: *Not ur usual time to be here*

Honeycake: wanted to see if there was any news of Velvet Dungeoners

Peach: *No news is good news. The plane must have landed*

Honeycake: We all hold our breath

Peach: *She is brave*

Honeycake: they've known each other four years, they'll be all right

Peach: *what about if they do not like each other? Then it is gone wrong, it is a waste*

Honeycake: I guess

Peach: *I am anxious with both of them*

Honeycake: Me too Peachy

Peach: *She is alone in London*

Honeycake: yeah but that's ok, she's sensible, she's not 18

Peach: *We should pray for them*

Honeycake: ok. And dance for them and wait

Peach: *Yes*

Honeycake: Send good thoughts

Peach: *Yes. Christ, guys are difficult huh*

Honeycake: ~sigh~ yooo bet

Peach: *Glad you came*

Honeycake: - lean on Peachy - yeah me too

Call Girl wore gold sandals left over from the summer's toga party, jogging bottoms and a '50s housecoat tied around his torso. Last night's make-up was smudged on his old, male face. He turned the music up loud and started cleaning with a vengeance. The loo, basin and bath were scrubbed. He cleaned the toilet-roll holder. He polished the bathroom light switch. With Abba crying out at full volume he went at the mirror with the Windolene. He could see himself behind the back-and-forth of his own arm – and underneath the day-old make-up his skin showed its fifty-five years, he thought. It had seen a few goings-on. Yet he refused to slow down or stop. He was going to leap into his grave still a twenty-one-year-old. He wielded the bathroom mousse and cursed the white specks on the glass. They were like crushed insects on a windscreen: every single one clung on. He creamed the sink and slaved with the cloth to make the chrome taps shine.

Abba stopped; the silence carried him away from his task. He went and sat and smoked and wondered what on earth it would be like to meet Fat-armed Wife. She was in London, carrying a charge of love, the chance of love . . . The only thing that might frustrate them was this last hurdle, coming up fast now: the sight of each other, the precise, unequivocal effect of a real human presence, the chemical foment. If they overcame it, would they want to make a life together in reality? If so, would she live here in the UK or would he go over there?

From his sweet spot on the sofa Buttons watched intently. His little terrier eyes were bright with questions, the fronds of hair that hung over his eyes trembling as always, as if he were in a permanent panic. Call Girl picked him up and settled him on his lap, soothed him. 'It'll be all right,' he crooned. 'All OK, it'll pan out somehow, one way or the other.'

He went and stood on the little balcony. People below scurried for their cars, carrying shopping. Everyone was on their way some-where, making for their hearts' desires if possible. He found himself remembering other lost loves – only two of them, but they still lived in him as bright and as important as they had ever been. He shook his head. Nothing could be known for certain, but this was maybe a last chance, given he was fifty-five years old. He went back inside and paced around the flat, marvelling at what was going on. They were at the very doorway of the Velvet Dungeon . . . Nerves crowded the tips of his fingers.

He slung a compilation album on the CD player and continued to work. He bleached the grouting between the tiles. He threw away everything except toothpaste, toothbrush, flannel, soap, shaving cream and razors. He trotted down to the little Nissan Micra and drove to B&Q, ducked in to buy some khaki paint. He drove back home, changed into rags and painted over the graffiti that covered the bath-room walls. Each stroke brushed the dense, creamy colour over the scribbles and drawings and messages of eight years' worth of bath-sharing lovers, both male and female. He kissed each one goodbye, tucked them in the past, affectionately . . . Yes, plenty of goings-on.

By five o'clock in the afternoon he was kneeling at his chest of drawers, working feverishly. Next to him was a black bin bag. He picked up armfuls of useless stuff which he hadn't worn for ages and put them in the bag. He kept only the items he actually used.

Likewise he turfed out shoes, hats, tipped up jewellery boxes – all of it could go; he wouldn't have room to take it all to America. He started to pull the rings from his fingers but then stopped. Three of them he would keep. They had magic; they had kept him.

The landing outside the flat was crowded with black plastic bags tied at the neck; he toiled up and down the concrete stairs and drove everything down to the charity shop. In minutes it was gone. As he drove back, a kind of purification of the soul descended on him. He felt lighter; it was more likely that he and Fat-armed Wife were going to fly. Back at the flat he loaded up the CD multi-player and rehearsed handing in his notice at work.

The dressing-table mirror offered him a different person, he thought, as he wiped off last night's residue of mascara with a cotton-wool swab. The tattoos on his thin, scarred body were written on him for life, but he could find space for a new American one no doubt. His real face appeared, wipe by wipe. The eyes were smaller and less charismatic without make-up, yet they were alive enough and charged with years of high and low living.

For an hour he lay on the bed, thinking of everything that had happened, ever, in his life. Then he rose quickly and wrapped his robe round him. Everything seemed bigger. There was more space. It felt luxurious, clean. He sat in the newly decorated living room, nauseous at the smell. He smoked cigarettes, which helped. Fat Phil would arrive soon.

The sun lowered over his concrete balcony. In his mind's eye he made pictures of Fat-armed Wife in London. He walked her about, had her smile, laugh. He brought her to stand in front of him.

'Tiredness kills' the road sign told him. 'Take a break.' Thruster obeyed – in almost every respect he was a responsible citizen – and stopped at the Moto services on the A63. He went into the self-service restaurant and ate bacon and eggs, anonymous among other travellers. His jaw moved mechanically. He queued at the shop to buy what anyone else might buy: a takeaway coffee to refresh his thermos, a comedy tape, screenwash. The angling this way and that of his front wheels as he negotiated the petrol forecourt was no different. The closed-circuit television cameras let him go, didn't notice.

At eleven fifteen he was looking through the windscreen at the picturesque fish-and-ale town of Hull. His right ankle tweaked with pain from maintaining position on the accelerator pedal for so long. He wriggled it every few minutes, laid it on its side, then raised it again, moved it forwards and back in the footwell of the car.

The town of Hull had offered no resistance. It had simply allowed him to drive in.

He parked in the town centre and poured coffee from the thermos. It was too hot to drink so he stood it in the cup holder. He re-sealed the lid of the thermos and inserted it in the cylindrical holder stitched to the side of his rucksack. He settled the street map on the steering wheel and used the Granada's compass to ascertain north. He marked with a black point the position he was in now, then lined up the map correctly and looked through the windscreen. The townsfolk went about their daily business. There weren't that many of them – 148,000-odd.

Thruster's look glazed over. An hour and a half passed, and he found himself in a café, sitting alone, with nothing in front of him. His rucksack was on the seat opposite, like a stuffed dummy of a companion. Inside was the laptop; it always made him feel uncomfortably exposed, carrying it around. He ordered a cup of tea and a cake.

Afterwards he meandered through the cobbled streets of the Old Town and visited the harbour. He stood for some moments looking at the *Spurn*. There it was, a lighthouse fixed to the deck of a boat, which had once – according to the tourist information sign – done sterling service warning ships of danger in the Humber estuary. He walked down the steep gangways and steps to the deck of the last sidewinder trawler to come out of Hull, the *Arctic Corsair*, and wandered aimlessly. He dropped the rucksack to the ground and perched for a while on a winch-housing next to the lifeboats. He took out the photographs of Call Girl and looked through them, briefly. He gazed over the water at the buildings crowding the opposite shore. This evening he would investigate the list of nightclubs and bars and the so-called 'munch' which he'd culled from the internet. They were over there somewhere. Mentally he called to them: offer up your secrets. He'd smell the opportunity when it came.

More hours had passed; he found himself in his Granada again, the steering wheel gripped in his hand. He was in an underground car park. The key fob was between his teeth.

For a while he drove around, over Drypool Bridge and back via Myton Bridge, familiarising himself with the layout of streets. When the sun started to slide faster towards the horizon he drove back down the A365 for a couple of miles before executing a U-turn and parking in a lay-by overlooking the town. His army training allowed him to register its topography in a certain way; he sought its strong and weak areas, its hidden tucks and folds.

In his mind's eye he put himself among the stones and bricks piled one on top of the other with such precision, beauty and purpose to make the town of Hull. He ran fast as light along the cables that charged the town with electricity to bring it all manner of convenience and entertainment. He rumbled along the railway to the heart of the town. He occupied each and every slab which made up the pavements leading to the front doors of every resident. In this way might he find Call Girl. He checked his watch. Five thirty p.m. He took out his thermos again. The coffee was cool now. He lifted it to his lips and swallowed.

Thruster enters Velvet Ballroom

Spam: Like tiny spider I tippppytooeee towardsssss u BigggBlackkWomannnn .... Wanna dance I whisssppper verrrry softleee hoping she might hearrrrr

Thruster:

Big Black Woman: Spam iz ur yung body sweaty?

Peach: ~whisper to DanceMaster~ *Do we say nothing to Thruster? is that what is happenign?*

Spam: Yesssssslipppppperrrry with sssweatttt, yunnngg stonnng tttorrrsooo gllleaammming, slickkkk as helllll

Thruster:

DanceMaster: *~whisper to Peach~* Yes. It is all agreed. If none of us talk to him he will go.

Big Black Woman: Hmmmm, I'm dancin wit u, then, Spam ……

Thruster:

Spam: Hah hah Ahhhhh can we look forward to tales of the deeppesstt fassstessst pennnetrations with exxxplossive insemm-inn-ation

Peach: *please don't turn rude Spam*

Spam: sorry Peachy

Big Black Woman: Spam u cumin wit me or wot?

Spam: Sorrreee Biggg Blackkk Womannn jusss cumming … now tell me where u gonna putttt urr hands hmmm?

Thruster:

Big Black Woman: *~gone~poof!~*

Spam: Biggg Blackkk One, r u there? - wave arms maddly - am I dancing on my ownnnn?

Thruster:

Spam: AM I ON MY FUUUCKIN OWNNN HERE Biggg Blacckck Wommannn OR WHAT? why are weeee waittttting?

Thruster:

Big Black Woman: *~whisper to Spam~* Hey I'm on the Shore, where r u? Spamhead?

Thruster: *~gone~poof!~*

Call Girl bouffed the pillows against the headboard, laid his colourful torso against them and tucked the blankets round his hips so his legs were a neat tube under the covers. He patted his thigh. 'Come on, you,' he called to Buttons. 'Hup.' The little dog, waiting his turn down below, made the impressive leap onto the bed and scouted for a comfortable place, his short tail wagging. He made a spot for himself and settled. 'There,' said Call Girl. 'We've everything we need, no?'

'Nohhhh, not *quite*. Beer would fill a little gap, y'know?' Fat Phil patted his tummy.

'Go on, then, and one for me as well.'

Fat Phil stood up off the laundry basket, which rose a couple of inches in relief. He went and fetched two cans, popped one for Call Girl and handed it over.

'How 'bout you on the bed, so we can see you?' suggested Call Girl.

'Right y'are.' Fat Phil was about to heave himself on board but then stopped. 'Hold on – ciggies.' He scouted for the packet of Silk Cut and the lighter. He found a clean saucer for an ashtray.

'And the phone the phone the phone as well.' Call Girl pointed to it, on the chair. Thus fully equipped Fat Phil could settle himself at the other end. He chucked the phone to Call Girl, took a cigarette and tossed the packet after it, pushing the saucer into a dent in the bedding between them. They faced each other and sipped from their cans. 'Now we're set. Cheers.'

'Cheers.'

'Smoking in bed – hope the alarm's working, if we set the mattress on fire.' Fat Phil pointed at the ceiling.

Call Girl aped surprise. 'Is that what it is, a smoke alarm?'

'Aye.'

They sat and chatted and smoked. Fat Phil checked his watch. 'Where is she tonight?'

'Dinner at someone's. To do with the business. You know.'

'What is the business, then?'

'There's two, no less. An old one and a new one.'

'What's the new one?'

'She buys, like, whole bales of old clothes. Imagine – container lorries full of worn-out jeans. The idea is, she says, that the farm boys from Idaho want to buy stuff from Hollywood stars, and the Hollywood stars want to buy from the farm boys. She puts herself in the middle, you know, with her website and her shop. No, two shops now, as well.'

'What's the old business?'

'Clever stuff, 'n' all. Biotechnology. There's the Human Genome Project. All this software – a whole ocean of the stuff – dumped in the public domain and all these companies who might want to use it. She provides the training, teaches companies how to make use of the software, like a how-to for using the human genome what-not. She kicked it off but sold it and bought a house and started the new one.'

'Is she rich, then?'

'Richer than you or me, chum. But don't hold it against her. She doesn't feel like a rich one. Was poor before, which makes all the difference.'

'But she's married.'

'Yes, with stepson in tow. So that's how the whole trip doth look to her husband. "Hey, I've got to get hold of the UK business, expand over there" is how she managed to swing it. After a week or two of fights and sulkings, I do believe, as well.'

'Ah. She lied to her old man.'

'Well . . . not told the whole truth. For the first time, apparently. None too comfortable about it. Neither of us. But no other way of reaching the Velvet Dungeon. Y'know, might as well find out what's in the apple cart, before upsetting it.'

'Indeed.'

'Helped that it's her own money, not as if she has to beg from him, she's an independently meaned woman, she is, true.'

Shortly after midnight the phone sang its tune. 'This is her,' said Call Girl and thumbed to answer. 'Hello, you.'

The worried voice of Fat-armed Wife sounded far away. 'This is still an international call, from my cell phone, even though I'm in your country—'

Call Girl interrupted, 'It's only about a hundred pound a minute,

Treasure, gimme the number of the hotel and your room number and I'll ring you back. Quick then.'

'020 7287 6758.'

Call Girl repeated the number, looking at Fat Phil, coaching him to remember it.

'Room thirty-nine. Uggghhh.' The line went dead.

He dialled, and sure enough, like magic, he was answered by something called the Regent Palace Hotel. 'The nutty woman in room thirty-nine, please.'

'I beg your pardon?'

'I was saying can I talk to the mad lady in room thirty-nine?'

'Thirty-nine?'

'That's it.'

'D'you have a name please?'

'Fat-armed Wife.' Call Girl winked at Fat Phil.

'I beg your pardon?'

'The name of the character I wish to talk to . . . is . . . Fat-armed Wife.'

'I'm sorry, I need the name of the guest before I can put you through.'

'Tell you what, I am not teasing. If you dial her room and mention that name, Fat-armed Wife, she'll beg, I tell you, to have me put through, as well.'

There was a pause, then a click. 'Hello?' Fat-armed Wife sounded anxious.

'Gotcha.'

Her voice came running down the line at him, 'At last, you are there . . . save me . . . what am I doing? . . . this is crazy . . .'

Fat-armed Wife plumped down on the bed, sucked on a cigarette. Everything was strange – the bed covers, the bathroom in the little cupboard, the hordes of people outside. She could hear them in the street. So many were drunk. She was frightened.

'Hold your horses. You just got back?' asked Call Girl.

'Yes. Saw my suitcase in this strange hotel room and began to panic. You know, because this is where I leave the tracks. Tomorrow, when I take the train, I'm off the schedule, it's secrets and lies, and I don't know what to think.'

'My Treasure, my Fat Arms . . .'

'You're there, you're really there, aren't you? We're in the same country?'

'Yes, I'm here, Fat Phil is here as well, as it happens.'

'Hullo, Fat Phil.'

'She says hullo,' reported Call Girl and held the handset up. 'Say hullo back, Phil.'

'Hullo,' called Fat Phil. Buttons unhooked his nose from his tail to look up.

'You hear that?' asked Call Girl into the phone.

'Yes, I heard.' She sounded calmer.

'And Buttons is here, aren't you, Buttons?'

'Hullo, Buttons.'

'He's wagging his tail for you. What d'you wear for the dinner, then?'

'The print dress, leopardskin shoes, full make-up. The cab ride! The suspension is so hard. It's like driving in some old truck, yet the guy was telling me it was brand-new and cost . . . I can't remember what it cost.'

'You're living the high life, then, taxis.'

'Yes. What about you?'

'More like the low life. Fat Phil and myself have taken a calm stroll through the town's salubrious quarter this evening, you know, as well.'

'I can imagine.'

'And then we lay abed, chit-chatting, waiting for your call.'

'I'm nervous.'

'Me too, yes. Bag of nerves. Nest of snakes. Cleaned the place from top to bottom. Cleaned out my whole life. Painted all the walls. Fat Phil's eyes popped, like, when he came round. Could not believe it. But . . .'

'But what?'

'Don't say it's nerves, it's excitement.'

'OK. Excitement.'

'All right, then.'

'Can you wait for a moment, while I undress and clean my teeth? I want you to see me into bed.'

'Treasure, shall we slip to the Velvet Rooms? Is that an idea?'

'You're right. 'Course. In five minutes?'

'See you there.'

Fat-armed Wife shed her dress and shoes and underwear and went to the shower cubicle. When she pulled the door open it banged against the toilet. Everything in Britain was so cramped. There was hardly an inch to walk round the sides of the bed, even. She stepped under the dribble of hot water for a minute to wash the cigarette smoke out of her hair. Her head felt more clear, straight. She had to take responsibility for this lie she was telling Colin. Own up to it. Shoulder it. Carry it. She shivered, hurried to wrap herself in a towel, and used the other one to pat herself dry. She brushed her teeth, feeling the kick of the cigarettes and wine in the back of her throat. She was in a foreign country, alone.

Yet not alone. The Velvet Rooms were just the other side of the membrane. It took only a few seconds to push through.

Fat-armed Wife enters Velvet Ballroom

Fat-armed Wife: Stagger in - wave arms widly - bit drunk from night out in LONDON - phew! Hello everyone

DanceMaster: ~ sweeping bow ~ Fat Arms!

Call Girl: *WAVE … I'm here already, ducks*

Spam: Hurrahhhh and three cheers for the Dungeonnersss

Honeycake: Hi Fat Arms, incredible, u r nearly there

Fat-armed Wife: hi Honey - hi Spam, DanceMaster

Peach: *Hi Fat Arms we r all realy excited*

DanceMaster: Velvet Roomers I give you Fat-armed Wife and Call Girl. A round of applause … On the gramophone is Abba's 'SOS'.

Fat-armed Wife: twirl - thud thud thud

Call Girl: *clap clap clap*

Fat-armed Wife: Get down low to kinda twist - ooof

Call Girl: *look at her go*

Fat-armed Wife: My love - hold out hands

Spam: appppplausssssse!!!

Honeycake: Clap clap *vbs*

Peach: *I smile at u both kiss u both*

Call Girl: *take your hand, tug you towards the Velvet Shore … brb Roomers … come on, Fat Arms*

Psycho-dog: woof wag tail bark bark

Call Girl: *~gone~poof!~*

Fat-armed Wife: *~gone~poof!~*

Spam: Awwwww, they've gone

DanceMaster: NO FOLLOWING, SPAM! LEAVE THEM ALONE

Call Girl enters Velvet Shore

Call Girl:

Fat-armed Wife enters Velvet Shore

Call Girl: *Darling*

Fat-armed Wife: Ahhh … bliss

Call Girl: *You tired?*

Fat-armed Wife: Bit.

Call Girl: *Rest in my arms*

Fat-armed Wife: Yes. Peace and love found there.

Call Girl: *And lust.*

Fat-armed Wife: Yes. What you wearing, your old guy's nightshirt?

Call Girl: *No. Dressing gown, Treasure*

Fat-armed Wife: hook my leg around yours - I'm wearing a nightie

Call Girl: *hmmm, nice vintage robe, I bet*

Fat-armed Wife: Like the way you've started calling me Treasure

Call Girl: *Well you are*

Fat-armed Wife: Where's Fat Phil?

Call Girl: *next door in the bedroom with the music system, bless him*

Fat-armed Wife: Ahhh

Call Girl: *Would Madam like the menu?*

Fat-armed Wife: Ahhhh, the menu

Call Girl: *What would Madam like this evening?*

Fat-armed Wife: Can we have my train? Since I'm on one tomorrow

Call Girl: *The train it is, then - dedum dedum. It's a dead old train, as well. Rickety rackety. V. cold weather outside. Like, not much more than a walking pace. Like the old movies.*

Fat-armed Wife: Yes, the train a long, thick line drawn against the white of the snow - darn cold - the heating is working overtime - so deathly cold outside - too hot inside

Call Girl: *We're crossing the Siberian steppes ... see out the window?*

Fat-armed Wife: it's dark - have to cup my hands to the glass to see beyond my reflection - just the snow seen by the light thrown from the carriage

Call Girl: *What shall I be, what would Madam like?*

Fat-armed Wife: You are a big old dirty old soldier in rough uniform

Call Girl: *and yourself, as well?*

Fat-armed Wife: I am a little itty-bitty Russian schoolgirl - thin and beautiful

Call Girl: *Ahhh …. perfect*

Fat-armed Wife: but I've borrowed my father's clothes - dressed as a boy to try and pass unnoticed

Call Girl: *Looking at you pretty hard … thinking maybe you're a girl … I think you might be a girl … and even if you're not, you'll do anyway … I don't care … big old rough soldier like me … been in prisoner of war camps, seen everything, done everything, don't care what I stick my cock in*

Fat-armed Wife: The clothes are rough against my skin - itchy, uncomfortable, hot - but dare not take off the heavy wool jacket - even though it's so coarse and rough against my girlish breasts

Call Girl: *Ahhh … my cock stirring in its lair … have not seen naked flesh of girl or boy for a long time. Have been too caught up in the killing, in the war, in the desperate hunger and death …*

Fat-armed Wife: *I've been separated from my parents - was torn from* their arms when they were arrested but I escaped - and I'm heading for the big city - on the run. Christ knows what awaits me there in these God-forsaken times

Call Girl: *Looking at you more often now because I'm sure you're a girl wearing boy's clothes… catching your eye*

Fat-armed Wife: Looking at you - scared because you are big and dirty - soiled in battle, I reckon

Call Girl: *I've been in action not long ago … blood … grime*

Fat-armed Wife: oh - frightened - don't want to be taken - have only had one lover - and he a young boy, careful and tender

Call Girl: *I've noticed the look in your eye … You're frightened of me. I think you might be a girl*

Fat-armed Wife: squirm in my seat - try and avoid your eye

Call Girl: *you're pressing against the cold glass, to look outside*

Fat-armed Wife: It's dark, but I can see the snow just rolling past - shown in the grimy light from the window. Then I turn and look at you, and you have moved closer - you all - you big dirty soldiers - three of you now????!!! God I hope you leave me alone

Call Girl: *Move quickly ... suddenly clamp my big dirty hand on your thigh, keep it there, squeeze hard*

Fat-armed Wife: oh no - please - what do you want?

Call Girl: *Have you got any food, anything to eat, tucked away in those pockets?*

Fat-armed Wife: No

Call Girl: *I'm hungry*

Fat-armed Wife: So am I - there will be food soon - at the next stop

Call Girl: *Where I just came from, men are eating other men who died in battle*

Fat-armed Wife: sorry, I haven't got anything

Call Girl: *grip your leg harder ... hmm feels like a girl's leg ... Are you sure you've got nothing I want?*

Fat-armed Wife: Please let me go

Call Girl: *I don't think you're a boy*

Fat-armed Wife: Yes I am

Call Girl: *Squeeze your thigh under the rough cloth ... doesn't matter anyway*

Fat-armed Wife: I'm a boy

Call Girl: *kneading your thigh ... that's OK ... my hand moves higher, towards your groin ...*

Fat-armed Wife: please stop. My father will pay you money

Call Girl: *your father?*

Fat-armed Wife: Yes

Call Girl: *Where is your father? Is he here? I don't see him ... I don't see anyone who can help.*

106

Fat-armed Wife: please be kind - please be nice

Call Girl: *I seize front of your uniform and tear it open*

Fat-armed Wife: Ahhh … no …

Call Girl: *what are those, then? All three soldiers staring … breasts full and young and proud, as well*

Fat-armed Wife: Frozen in terror

Call Girl: *Breasts - Young girl's breasts - nipples out hard - all of us can see what you are … what can be done with you*

Fat-armed Wife: the train lurching - trying to pull uniform closed over breasts - please - but can't, you are too strong - leave me alone I beg you

Call Girl: *staring at those breasts … the other two soldiers stand up, to see better*

Fat-armed Wife: the train jolts, squeals - the lights flicker on and off - no please

Call Girl: *The cloth of the uniform bunched in my fists as I hold you down*

Fat-armed Wife: please don't

Call Girl: *I am hungry*

Fat-armed Wife: whimper - stare beseechingly - let me go

Call Girl: *No. We are too hungry. D'you think we would be doing this if it wasn't for the war? It has turned us into animals*

Fat-armed Wife: what … ohhhhh

Call Girl: *all three of us in this carriage … brutalised … you only have one choice*

Fat-armed Wife: What - don't know what you mean - shake - squirm in seat

Call Girl: *You know what I'm talking about. All of us crowd round you in your corner, hold you down … you can feel their hands too … finding buttons, buckles*

Fat-armed Wife: DON'T - scream over the racket of the train's

whistle - what choice? what do you mean? - help - the train
sways - shudders

Call Girl: *All of us stare … there are three of us and one of you.
Hmmm? Look, the others are unlacing their boots … and we promise to
agree to whoever you say goes where*

Fat-armed Wife: begin to weep … looking up at you … don't hurt me…

Call Girl: *lower my mouth to your breast .. take its sweet promise …*

Fat-armed Wife: cry softly - rest my hand on your shoulder

In New York, Honeycake slept among her cushions in her loft apartment. In Nova Scotia Psycho-dog stared resolutely, almost all night, at cable TV. In England Spam tugged the lid off the laundry basket and fished around for a shirt that might be clean enough to wear. In Colombia DanceMaster was driven into town in the Mercedes, the sun painting the windshield with golden light. Peach was bitterly cold, her heart an empty cavern of yearning, while she darned sheets. Big Black Woman clung to her lover while he walked her round the room on all fours. Call Girl was at work, delivering mail as if this were any other day. Fat-armed Wife took the train from King's Cross to Hull.

If viewed from far enough away – the world a seething mass of particles so tiny that they became in effect constructs of energy, of electrical charge, of signals on the move – all the Velvet Roomers put together were an infinitesimally small proportion of what was going on, of the signalling, the waving, the desire, yet for each of them they were the centre of the universe – it was arranged for them, against them, around them. Their desires, whether negatively or positively charged, like gravity pulled them always, as quickly as any obstructions would allow, in the one direction, towards their satisfaction and accomplishment. Call Girl and Fat-armed Wife were going to meet, for real. The thoughts of all the Roomers were with them.

Fat-armed Wife jammed the hotel's elevator doors open – it took all her strength to lever them back – so that a family had time to run and squeeze in with her. She grinned at them; words flew from her loud, American mouth as they descended. She had good things to say about everybody and everything and many wishes for a good day's sightseeing for them in London, even before they'd reached the ground floor; their friendly smiles came back at her.

Outside the lift a porter came with a trolley to take the bags to the desk, and her luck held: the train tickets had arrived at the last minute. Spam's spidery handwriting wove across the old second-hand envelope Sellotaped together. The address of the hotel had been very carefully written. The word 'PRIVATE' was printed in the top left-hand corner. A task well done. He'd come through, just as he'd said he would. For a moment, yesterday, she'd thought she was going to have to buy new, expensive tickets.

Outside the sunlight squinted onto the crowded streets. Everything was grey and old. British people were smaller, quieter, more clever, she thought.

At King's Cross station she stood with her big arms aching under the information board, watching the trains march across in orange letters, chain-smoking and guarding her bags with her stout legs.

On the train, they soon eclipsed walking speed; moments later they were travelling faster than the taxi, reaching a hundred and twenty miles an hour. There was no going back. As each station went past she felt she was like Spiderman – she'd watched the movies with Jamie – firing the sticky stuff from her wrists, attaching it to the next station, and swooping towards it. Catch it, drop down for a quick smoke on the platform, and then on to the next. Meanwhile the texts from Call Girl shook her phone lightly in her lap; she snatched at each one. She could picture his green writing. That voice would at last come alive against the black-as-night darkness in the Velvet Dungeon.

Time slipped by; the train carried them effortlessly. Her seat was by the window and shadows fluttered over her. The train was taking her to a future which would be very different. By this evening she'd have his real name like a magic talisman, she'd have looked him in the eye, talked non-stop, face to face, touched him for real – made love? Would it ruin her life or make it? She couldn't know; all she was certain of was that the gap between them – in the Velvet Rooms – had become wafer-thin and then had disappeared altogether; they'd moved into one another, through each other's skins. To meet was all that could happen next. If it was a disappointment, or if it meant too much for her to carry on her life as it stood now – whichever – that was something she'd have to face.

Guilt flooded her. Colin knew nothing of this. It was a separate life from the one she led with him. She pictured him at home: in her mind he stood by the railing as she came out the other side of the airport. He had his hands on his hips. It was how he always welcomed her home – no outward show of affection, just the hands on the hips, signalling . . . what? She wasn't sure.

The Ridings of Yorkshire opened their landscapes; it was a grand sky to swoop through, towards the east coast.

The Victorian-built station of Hull surprised her with its elegance and cleanliness; somehow she'd expected it would be degraded and industrial. It was six o'clock in the evening and still sunny, but the chill, damp air refreshed her after the cramped train carriage. It blew between her arms and body, around her legs. She huffed and puffed on two life-saving cigarettes, which made her calmer, more ready. Then she struggled along the platform, up the stairs and across the bridge. Outside the station the low, warm sunlight struck her; she thanked it gratefully. She headed for the taxi queue. One driver caught her eye: he had a big belly, and his feet turned out like a ballet-dancer's. His shirt hung loose over his belt. His hair was oiled back, a clutch of it around his neck, thinner on top. He was standing with a placard in the crook of his elbow, smoking, and as people walked past they were smiling, talking to him. When she was close enough she was astonished to read on his placard the handwritten words 'Fat-armed Wife'. People murmured as she went up to the beer-bellied driver and identified herself: 'That's me.' Laughter and whoops of approval accompanied her during the few steps to the taxi. She showed off her arms for all and sundry. She could hear her voice become louder; as always, she enjoyed an audience. Someone asked for a photograph and so she lined up next to the taxi driver.

She fetched out her own camera and had them take a photograph for her, too. The late-in-the-day, golden autumn sunshine and this surprise welcome made her spirits soar – she thanked Call Girl for that generous touch. Was there no greater blessing, she wondered, than an unexpected kindness to a lone traveller?

The taxi was an elderly diesel saloon; inside she was nearly overcome with the scent of air freshener and stale cigarettes. The driver had an enormous stomach and was difficult to understand; he seemed to hold all his words together in his mouth, jumble them up together and kind of aim them out the back of his throat, but she recognised it as a more extreme version of Call Girl's accent and so it delighted her. She felt brave enough to admit she couldn't understand a word, even though her lover spoke the same way. The man chuckled; he wasn't offended. By the end of the ride they were friends. He gave her a card with his cell phone written on it so she could be sure to hire him if she needed to move around town.

The Post House was a traditional English inn, exactly as she'd hoped. The walls were of metres-thick stone and the ceilings low, set across every which way by heavy black timbers chipped and scarred with use. She could imagine the horse-drawn carriages flying into the yard at the back, the mail carried to the next carriage, the passengers, tired and bedraggled, taking their soup in front of a huge, roaring fire, the hems of the women's dresses all soaked in mud, the talk of kings and queens and my liege this and sir that. She'd seen it all on *Masterpiece Theater*. This was Old England all right.

As soon as she'd checked in at Reception she went to look for the Velvet Dungeon. A few minutes later, looking to left and right, and she found it, recognising Call Girl's description: a small sitting room with a disproportionately large open fireplace occupied by flowers at this time of year, two leather sofas facing each other, a low table between them. The pictures on the wall were of old fishing vessels from the past – sepia photographs. The carpet was a deep burgundy, soft underfoot. Dark wooden panelling was fixed on each wall, waist high. This was it; where they would see each other for the first time. She paused for a while, looking in. A cleaner pushed a Hoover back and forth, but didn't notice her. For we are all slaves in the Velvet Dungeon, she remembered; yes. The cleaner was young with dark hair tied back at the neck and pale skin. She looked tired. Her gaze didn't shift from the carpet in front of the Hoover. Fat-armed Wife expected her to stop and greet her but of course she herself was just a guest like anyone else, someone for this woman to clean round, the tide of humanity bringing its load of grit and dust in here. She went further in, stood in the middle and turned round twice, trying to picture what it would be like, what would happen as a result of meeting Call Girl, in here, at 8.30 p.m. She had to pinch herself: she was standing in the Velvet Dungeon.

The cleaner slaved away, back and forth with the Hoover. DanceMaster had said that the here and now, on earth, was like being in a dungeon: we are all imprisoned, we have to work, we are slaves. We all are punished. We toil in our small, dark, place. Yet there are sensations and pleasures available there which don't exist in the Velvet Rooms. So we will have a dungeon of our own, he'd suggested, where such pleasures and sensations can be made available – a Velvet Dungeon. It would be like a wormhole for Velvet Roomers to travel through the membrane and touch reality: for that time, and in that place, the Velvet Rooms would be created on Earth. Roomers could swoop like angels from above, momentarily, reveal their true selves under tightly controlled conditions, and return safely.

Terra Firma and StripTease had been the first to go in. The Dungeon was identified as a motel room in Texas. The deal had stipulated no real names, one and a half hours, no penetrative sex but a little fooling around allowed. However Terra Firma had been driven there by his wife, who'd apparently accepted this new development in his Velvet Rooms obsession. It had been her duty to park outside and wait for him to finish but when she saw StripTease emerge from the motel room, she'd attacked her – pulled her hair and kicked and bitten – Terra Firma hadn't been a strong enough specimen to pull his wife off. Also, she'd taken StripTease's car registration number and filed a police complaint claiming she was a prostitute.

The cleaner turned a handle on the Hoover to pull in the cord.

Then she stood and wiped her brow with her wrist. Fat-armed Wife resisted the urge to apologise to her. She turned and left the room, smiling at the old guy waiting with her luggage. 'Great hotel!' she exclaimed. They carried on, took the stairs.

Her room was in the roof. A small, square window overlooked the street. A quilted counterpane covered a pine bed. A vase of flowers cheered up the bedside unit.

When she held out the tip to the older man carrying her bag he refused to take it. She couldn't stop smiling. This was England, this was Hull, where Call Girl lived. She was here, at last. The journey hadn't just been from London, today; it had taken four years to arrive at this point, travelling hard and fast, on a rollercoaster in real life and through many sexual adventures with Call Girl in cyberspace . . . She sat on the bed. A woman of thirty-seven, 168 pounds. She'd started her own training business and had sold it but kept options and a seat on the board. She ran two vintage clothes and collectibles stores and an internet site. She was married, with a stepson. She was in a strange town in a foreign land, in secret. Was it sad, desperate? She begged for that not to be true.

She scrabbled for her phone, texted him. 'Here. Will shower and change. Ready for 8.30. xxx.'

Honeycake enters Velvet Ballroom

DanceMaster: Honeycake can I invite you to perform for us the Alegrías?

Honeycake: Sure DanceMaster, if I knew what the eff it was

DanceMaster: It is an old Spanish Gypsy dance. The most pure, the most refined. You must mimic the movements of the bullfight. It is done by a woman alone

Honeycake: sure I'll do that me ol' DM - sauntering through dancers to take centre stage - the what was it called?

DanceMaster: the Alegrías - your hands are very important

Honeycake: My hands - yeah I have the fastest slipperiest hands in the west, ask Jim when they slide up and down his pole

Peach: *please Honeycake I don't want to think of Jim's pole ~ shy smile*

DanceMaster: Honeycake attend - lift needle onto old 78 vinyl

Honeycake: Jim's pole could hold up a tent on a windy day let me tell you

DanceMaster: Honeycake, start poised, feet slightly apart, with both your hands as if they hold the matador's red cape. Your hand a bit higher. Sí, that's it. Hang on - swing round … nowww … go

Honeycake: watch me everyone

Psycho-dog: ~wag tail ~ ahhhh, sight for sore eyes

DanceMaster: We have one and a half hours to go, before they meet.

At seven p.m., Call Girl waited in gorgeous, silent splendour, six inches taller than his natural height: three gained from the heels and a further three inches from the coiffeur. He had bathed and primped and pampered. Julie had come and dressed him and helped with make-up. The flat was sparkling clean. The walls wore their bright new colours. All the photographs were down. Drawers and cupboards were sorted and tidy. He stood first in one doorway, then in another. He sat carefully in the lounge, then in the bedroom. He checked that his headband was straight. He leaned over the balcony for a while, smoking a cigarette, careful not to spoil his lipstick nor spill ash on his lime-green '50s American housewife's dress – a parody of her Velvet Room name which Fat-armed Wife would enjoy, he hoped.

Three steady, patient knocks sounded at the front door of the flat. Instantly Buttons trotted through from the bedroom, yapping furiously. Call Girl picked him up. He wasn't expecting anyone. He went, Buttons under one arm, and unclipped the Yale to see who it was.

A stranger stood there: belted cashmere overcoat, thick glasses, a square face, carrying a briefcase. Call Girl had never seen such a bizarre creature in his life. The hair looked as stiff as a helmet; anyone could tuck a finger under that side-parting and simply lift the whole thing off. Perhaps too much hairspray had been used or the hair never washed. He could easily guess: this was another Man of God. Sure enough the figure started using that very reasonable voice, 'I've come a long way . . .'

'No, thanks,' Call Girl put in quickly and shut the door in his face. 'Not today!' he shouted at the closed door. Buttons wriggled in his arms, kept up his high-pitched barking for another full minute.

Quietness returned. Call Girl wandered around the flat. He straightened a picture. He went and compared his wristwatch to the clock on the kitchen wall. He pictured Fat-armed Wife at the hotel, and excitement squirmed in him – the possibility of true, grown-up, erotic love with a big woman. He texted her, 'We r 1 breaths distance apart.'

Silently he offered a prayer: that he would take her; that she would take him. What they had together – what they thought had happened between them – was already incredible. Let it go further, he demanded. He felt breathless and old and sat down for a while.

The unlikely, inoffensive knock came again at the door. Buttons's barking made it impossible to ignore. He went to open up and – no surprise – he faced the same thickset, belted, bottle-glass-spectacled, concrete block of a man as before. It was funny. Call Girl was quick to speak first, 'I'm all right, as it happens, with hell and damnation.'

'I am not a religious extremist or a salesman.'

'Oh. What are you, then?' Call Girl waited. Nothing could spoil his mood.

'If I could come in for five minutes, we could resolve the dispute between us in a reasonable way,' came the stranger's voice.

Call Girl couldn't remember any dispute. 'I don't think so, chum,' he said and went to shut the door but the man had his foot in the way; the door thumped six inches short and jarred Call Girl's hand. 'What dispute?' he asked.

'When we met before—' began the figure, standing squat and

dreary in the concrete stairwell, pushing the heavy, steel-rimmed glasses up the bridge of his nose.

Call Girl immediately interrupted, 'There was no dispute between us, I just didn't want you in my place.'

'Not that dispute.'

'What, then?'

'We have met before.'

'I don't think so, mate. Now, if you don't mind, I'm going to give you a little push, just so's you get the message.' Call Girl shoved the man in the chest. He had the impression of blank, iron strength – it was like trying to move a small building – but the other man's foot momentarily shifted from between the door and the jamb; it gave Call Girl time to slam the door shut. He shouted, 'The *dispewte* between us is now resolved!' He stared at the door. What was all that about? He listened for the sound of footsteps, the familiar tread, tread, tread of someone going back down the concrete stairs, but it didn't come. This fella, thought Call Girl, must still be waiting out there, or else he had dead soft shoes.

He went back to wandering the flat, but couldn't help listening for his odd visitor. Nothing. Silence reigned.

He went and lay on the bed, staring at the ceiling, his hands folded behind his head. He imagined that he was on a beach some-where on the eastern coast of the United States. His wife was a large, successful American woman with her own business. He himself had work of some sort. The sun beat down. Their skin was hot to the touch, oily. He could hear waves breaking on the shore. He missed England, aye, but . . .

The clock crawled, minute by minute, towards eight thirty and his rendezvous with Fat-armed Wife. The little Nissan waited down-stairs to take him into town.

He jumped with shock at the sudden noise. The front door had burst. It was as if a syringe of adrenalin had been emptied into his veins. Someone was in the flat. His first thought was that it must be that strange guy. What was going on? His heart beat wildly and immediately he was shaking. Buttons leaped from the bed and started a furious yapping, darting back and forth across the carpet, turning

116

in circles. He himself dashed across and threw the bedroom door shut – catching a glimpse of whoever it was – and drew the flimsy little silver bolt across and stood there frozen, heart hammering, one foot jammed against the bottom of the door to help keep it shut, listening to footsteps.

When he'd been chased into that kebab shop last year he'd shouted and screamed, 'Get off me, you bastards, you fucking piss-heads, go back to your mummy and daddy because the police are already on their way.' When he was shoved in the back when standing at the gents' urinal that time, he'd gone into a rage and had been shouting and screaming even as they'd torn into him. When he was punched through the window of his car he'd shouted insults it seemed like for miles, all the way round the harbour, even though it meant he'd been pulled out and set upon. But he didn't know how to read this situation, he couldn't imagine what the man wanted. He racked his brains to try and remember meeting him, what the dispute was. Somehow, he couldn't bring himself to act, say anything. He stayed dead quiet; he leaned against the door, watched the handle and listened. Then he gripped the handle, ready to open up. Was it the same guy? And if so, what did he want? Slowly the usual anger and feeling of injustice rose in him.

'Fucckkkkk offffff!' he shouted through the door. In a moment he was going to do what he always did: walk towards the fear, run towards it, embrace it even as it entered his stomach, its sickness as familiar to him as old shoes. There had been many a time – in drag or with his arm round a man – when he'd faced up to the shouted 'Oi!', the snigger behind his back, the sound of footsteps matching his own increase in speed, but usually it was outside his front door; how dare *anyone* come into his home right now, just when he shouldn't be interrupted? For whatever reason?

He still couldn't bring himself to open the bedroom door and find out what the man was doing. He shouted at the top of his voice, 'Go away and leave me alone unless you want your head pulled off your shoulders and fed to my *dog*.' Buttons panted his tiny breaths, miniature teeth as sharp as needles, looking up at him.

The phone – he could pretend to call the police. If so, he had to pluck up the courage to make a dash for the living room. But who was it out there? It must be that man. He'd understand better if it were skinheads from the estate or addicts after his stash. They knew he wouldn't call the police.

He pushed down on the handle, got ready to run. At the worst, he'd be covered in blood and minus a few possessions and cash. Fat-armed Wife would take him to hospital; they'd come back and recover here. He looked around for something he could use as a weapon. It was pointless because he couldn't hit a soul – there wasn't a violent bone in his body – but he knew he could *look* desperate and mad and that was enough to put some people off. He picked up a candlestick made of welded scrap metal and hefted it. Now . . . Was it the right moment? God only knew. He shifted from foot to foot; the candlestick was too heavy. His whole body shook uncontrollably with rage and fear. This goddamn flat that he'd cleaned and painted . . . 'Fuck off you wanker! . . . I'm coming out there to kill you!' It didn't sound convincing.

He stopped shouting so he might listen. There was something going on around the front door. That gave him easy access to the lounge and the telephone. He kicked off his high heels and dashed through in his stockings, brandishing the candlestick. Buttons ran under his feet, yapping his ear-splitting barks. He had a brief impression of the man's back, the belted overcoat, as the man leaned over the damaged door, propped it shut.

The next instant he was through to the lounge, holding his heart; he dropped the candlestick and picked up the phone. Yes, it was the stranger. The unknown dispute . . . they'd met before? 'I'm calling the fucking cops!' he shouted in triumph and lifted the receiver to his ear.

There was no dial tone. Where was his mobile? He couldn't see it.

If the phone lines had been cut . . . Suddenly it was more serious. The planning, the intent, was ominous. He turned, headed out onto the balcony – passers-by below might hear his shouts for help. He wasn't that keen on the police, anyway – in fact, the last thing he wanted in his flat was the police. None the less, he needed

118

help. His hand shook so much he could hardly press down on the aluminium handle. It took all his weight before the glass door opened.

Outside it was dusk and he shivered the instant the cool evening air touched his bare arms. He leaned over the edge and drew a breath to shout at the top of his voice but then a hand was glued over his mouth pressing hard; the man pulled him backwards into the lounge, before letting him go and shutting the glass door.

Call Girl stumbled, swung round. Panic was like a continual electric shock through his system. The man stood, here in the flat, the tail end of the telephone wire sticking out of his coat pocket. He'd kicked the front door in. *Why?* The spectacles were a thick, distorting mask across his face. That hair was like a helmet glued to his skull. The collection of nose, mouth and eyes occupied less of the surface area than it should, which gave him a bloated look, although he wasn't fat, just solid. The fawn overcoat was tightly belted round that hard, drum-like body. What was the briefcase for?

The intruder glanced at the computer on the table, then moved around the room. At his feet yapped Buttons, scurrying in circles. Brave dog, thought Call Girl.

Their eyes met. There was no shift in the man's expression. 'Now we have to wait for a little while,' he said politely.

Call Girl shuffled awkwardly. His heart and lungs were convulsed with fear; he couldn't breathe or shout, unlike Buttons who yapped on and on and darted at the stranger's ankles comically. He, Call Girl, should be as brave . . . he made a dash for the door but the stranger sidestepped, blocked him. He tried to kick his way through. Without shoes on, the physical contact was sickening; it was like stubbing his toe against a gatepost. He felt weak as a piece of straw. He flailed at the man's chest but made no impression, not a dent in the intruder's unknown purpose. He was caught and held like a child as he tried to force his way past and his arm was taken and twisted until he stopped struggling.

After a moment, the man let go of him. 'Sit down,' he said and pointed at the settee along the back wall.

Call Girl stood with his weight on one leg, the other shaking uncontrollably. 'No, I will not,' he shouted. 'Get out, whoever you are.' He was beginning to wheeze; he would need his inhaler soon. He turned to Buttons, still yapping and buzzing from one hiding place to another, claws scrabbling on the slippery parquet flooring. 'Buttons, KILL!'

'I'll sit down myself, then.' The man swivelled the chair away from the desk, eased into it. He unbuttoned his coat.

'Who on fucking earth are you?' screamed Call Girl and stamped his foot. 'What do you want?' The man's unblinking eyes, murky behind thick lenses, regarded him steadily. There was nothing in there that Call Girl could read. They were incurious, like those of someone watching television.

'I'm Thruster.'

Fat-armed Wife hung two blouses in the wardrobe with the sticky door. She laid out her slacks in the chest and bundled underwear in the topmost, right-hand drawer. The classy vintage nightdress went under the pillow. These were feather pillows, she noted as she handled them. The hotel went up a notch in her estimation. She took care with the gift she'd brought for Call Girl, making sure it was wrapped properly; with a flourish she stuck the cheerful bow on the corner. She knew he'd like it.

The make-up bag should be in the en suite bathroom, where there was better light. As she went through, a picture of her dressing table at home jumped into her head. Colin would be sleeping in that bedroom by himself. He'd turn off the clock radio at the mains, so she'd have to re-set it. He'd watch twice as much sport as usual on TV. He'd not return any phone calls. She felt a pang of guilt which she quickly ran past.

She arranged her washing things on the glass shelf under the bathroom mirror: toothpaste, electric toothbrush and charger, floss, ladyshave, deodorant, shampoo and conditioner – each of the familiar items called out to her how strange was this adventure, that she was far from home. She put the washbag in the little pine cupboard, and caught sight of herself in the mirror. Her face was OK. The more weight she'd lost, the more a kind of heavy beauty had come to her – a bit late in life but all the more enjoyed for that. The chocolate-brown eyes were good and fierce, like two points of electricity to plug into. The rosebud lips didn't look like they could smile as widely as they did. Neat white teeth – her favourite feature apart from her cleavage. If only her breasts had a proper tiny waist to sit on instead of this more solid, masculine kind of trunk. The eponymous fat arms she could do without. She waved them, plucked at their unchanging heaviness and strength. Fat-armed Wife, in a hotel room in Hull, in the UK . . .

Strangeness crept over her again. She ran cold water into the sink until there was enough to plunge her hands in and splash the face that stared back at her in the mirror. That was better. She patted the skin dry and brushed her teeth. She put a last touch to her make-up, smoothed her dress. Should she wear all the rings? Yes. Perhaps the glitter in her hair was too young, too dramatic, for some people's tastes; but not for his. She was unlikely ever to upstage him in dress-ing up. She sprayed on more.

They were calming, these small tasks. The stillness, the quiet, was welcome. It was almost time to go down.

'Thruster?'

'Yes. I am Thruster.'

Call Girl frowned. 'You what?'

'Maybe you don't remember.' Thruster took a sheet of A4 paper from the briefcase and read from it. 'Call Girl. Pushes everyone aside. Let me through. Breathing hard. Stand in front of Thruster.' He looked up. 'Hmmm? That's me.' He blinked, watched for Call Girl's reaction. There was nothing, just a stare. So he read again, 'Don't, Thruster don't. It's me you want not them.' He lowered the paper and looked steadily across at him. 'Well, here I am.'

Call Girl was jaw-droppingly, head-shakingly, stupidly aston-ished. Thruster was here. He stood, staring in disbelief. 'You found me.'

'Yes.'

'How?' The situation made his skin crawl with disbelief.

The silence was broken by a familiar ring tone. It was Call Girl's mobile, he recognised it, but the sound came from Thruster's pocket. Sure enough, Thruster took it out – *his* phone. It sang repeatedly like a trapped bird.

'Can I?' asked Call Girl.

'No.' Thruster killed the call, then looked more carefully at the phone, slid the back off and removed the battery and the sim card. He put them in separate pockets of his overcoat. Then he sat back comfortably.

Some moments later Call Girl tried to find a way out of this silence. 'Ummm, what are we waiting for? I mean, have you come here expecting me to say sorry? Is that it?'

There was no answer.

'This is real life, my friend,' went on Call Girl. 'In the Velvet Rooms, it's like a game, you know? It's always handy to distinguish between the two. That's not to say it's not my fault, like I say, as well. I owe you an apology, no question.'

'I know.'

'That other place, in there,' he said, pointing at the computer, 'isn't real life. So it's not a real insult.'

'Everything is real life.'

'Well, that's true in a way, I suppose, yes.' There was a pause. 'Tell you what,' he said, 'I've got to go out in a minute, but what about a cuppa first?'

'Thank you.'

'And maybe a can of Stella, as well, eh? Or something stronger? We're within our rights.'

'A cup of tea. Thank you.'

Call Girl went to the kitchen. Close behind him trod Thruster, so he dared not run for it. Buttons sauntered into the kitchen, looked at him questioningly. He'd stopped barking, was behaving as if this man was any other guest. Call Girl checked the clock and groaned inwardly; it was fast approaching eight thirty. This was mad. The kettle clicked off, and he filled the two cups. How could he get this over quicker?

'Tea's up.'

'Thank you.' Thruster gave a little nod and an indication that they were going back to the lounge. When they were seated, Call Girl tried again. 'I am sorry, you know, I really am. It's good, your coming here, because it's taught me that what happened between us was more than a bit of fun. I don't know . . . I love that place, the Velvet Rooms. I love the way it's always teaching you something about people. And this, your turning up, is one of those things. Hey, you're right, it's all real life. We hit the mark, you and I. We did. Without doubt. But then I had you down as just one of those brief touches in cyberspace – no less strong and vibrant for all that. You know what I mean?'

Thruster leaned back, rested an ankle on his knee and nursed his tea. 'Yes, I know what you mean,' he said automatically. 'All part of life's rich pattern. But, offence was taken.'

Both men waited. Call Girl tried to shake off the strangeness: tonight the Velvet Rooms had poured into life: Fat-armed Wife was waiting in the Velvet Dungeon; Thruster had bullied his way though.

How different he and Thruster both were, come to that, from the characters they'd chosen to represent them in the Velvet Rooms. He should be a thin, frightened girl with a bruised elfin face and large breasts, lying as if just thrown to the floor, looking back over her shoulder, pitiful and pleading, the white party dress torn right to the hip, unlikely bust spilling out, whereas in real life, here, he was a scawny, asthmatic middle-aged man. Thruster wasn't a full member and so didn't have an icon, but the name he'd chosen gave the impression of a rippling masculine torso, model good looks; yet this side of the membrane he was coarse-grained, ugly, bespectacled.

His watch gave him twenty-five past. He'd be late. Fat-armed Wife would be wondering what had happened. He wished he could shout to her, Hang on, I've just got to get this idiot out of the way first.

'I was going to ask,' said Call Girl, 'can I have your name and address, and a telephone number as well, because I think we should stay in touch, you and I.'

Still nothing came from Thruster.

'Ah well, the night's entertainment calls. What d'you think, shall we be on our way?' he asked. 'Can I give you a lift somewhere?'

Thruster stared blankly, sipped his tea. Buttons slumped sideways on the wooden floor, rested his head. The silence wore out Call Girl's nerves. He could see his hands trembling. He felt the adrenalin, the fear, interfering with his heart. The smell of the new paint made for a light, chemical sickness in the air.

Thruster dipped into his briefcase and took out more sheets of A4 paper. He fidgeted, assembled them into one sheaf. Call Girl had to stifle a groan of disappointment. The time slipped past eight thirty.

Fat-armed Wife checked the phone again. The signal was strong enough: four bars. There was plenty of battery. 'Come on, you!' she chastised, her voice loud and very American in this strange British hotel. She grimaced, glanced at her watch.

Ten minutes later, she went to the mirror and refreshed her make-up.

The phone remained silent.

She sat on the bed and checked it yet again. The miniature screen was empty of messages, text or voice. She frowned. The service provider was Vodafone, loud and clear. The time in the top right corner moved silently to the next minute. She called him again – straight to answering machine. She texted twice more: just a question mark. She checked the hotel phone by the bed. Yes, there was a dial tone. She pressed nine and when a voice answered she asked if the phone system was functioning correctly. The man assured her it was. She tried his number again – straight to answering service. She dropped the handset back on the rest. Suddenly all these lines of communication – cell phones, land lines, emails – entangled her; it was too much and yet nothing at all, no sign.

For the second time she went downstairs and checked the Velvet Dungeon. It was empty. The leather sofas yawned heavily. The piles of magazines had been mussed up and two empty glasses stood on the table. The room spoke of the absence of the people who'd taken those drinks. She lingered for a few minutes. The pictures showed people working on the decks of old-fashioned vessels. It looked so tough, their life. She remembered the cleaner – where was she now? She looked down at her phone. Its screen was coldly empty. Voices sounded in the Reception area. She felt uncomfortable and worried; she returned to the privacy of her room.

Suddenly she was utterly alone. She could hear a muffled television – from the next-door room, she supposed. Her own TV offered its silent screen welcoming her as a guest to the Post House Inne. She put the phone on the charger, just for the sake of it. 'Where *are* you?' she murmured. Her voice sounded isolated, wrong. 'Where have you gone?' The words hung in the air. She imagined a speech bubble with the questions written in it. The voice that should answer – the voice that had accompanied her whole journey here, that had listened and talked back to her for four years – had gone.

Was he standing outside the hotel, trying to summon up the courage to come in? She opened the old-fashioned sash window and leaned over the sill to look into the darkening street; she felt like she was on the edge of an abyss, peering over. Nothing there except the lighted shop fronts, vehicle headlights. She shivered, stepped back.

Half an hour later she was lying motionless on the bed; a cold dread had locked her into a state of panic, of disbelief. What had gone wrong? Once before he'd backed away from meeting her, but before they'd made any effort actually to reach each other. She knew that if he wanted to pull out, he'd tell her; he wouldn't just let her suffer. It wasn't his way, to be mysterious and difficult. He was lots of things – he was capricious, he changed his mind at the drop of a hat, he soared and he fell, he faced in numerous directions all at once – but he never, ever went quiet.

Both phones were silent. The television next door had been switched off; there was only the noise of the street outside: the odd laugh, the click of high heels, the squeal of a lorry's brakes. Her eye was caught by the pile of books on the chest of drawers. Wilbur Smith, Desmond Bagley and the Bible – nothing she might read.

Perhaps there'd been an accident . . . in which case what should she do? She'd search, walk the streets, find him in a pool of blood. She'd breathe the life back into him. It would make the newspapers – 'Fat-armed Wife Saves Life of Virtual Lover'.

An ancient dread surfaced: Call Girl didn't exist. He was a sales manager for a second-hand car firm. Or he was a spotty teenage boy; he and his friends had been laughing at her for years, and never more so than now, all of them drinking cans of beer and laughing, having stuck her in this hotel room in Hull. Look, they'd point out, she even brought us a gift. The photographs, the family background, even that he lived here in the town of Hull – all of it had been made up.

She'd asked more than once for his real name. She could hear his replies now, 'Real names, hmmm . . .' He'd talked about it being a spell that shouldn't be broken, not until they met. She heard again the sucking in of his breath as he answered, 'Not sure, Treasure.'

She sat up sharply, held her breath and clutched her stomach, fearing she might actually be sick. Love was famously blind. Lust had led her astray. The room held her tightly. She could doubt she herself existed. What was true? What was real? What had *happened*?

Her eye was caught by a slight movement: a mouse slowly made its way from behind the chest of drawers and along the wall. Its gait was unhurried, private. The panic fluttered in her; she fought the impulse to scream. The last she saw of it was a wriggle of its tail as it disappeared into the skirting board.

Fat-armed Wife let her breath go. She stood up. Dizziness assailed her. Tears sprang to her eyes. She wished she were in the Velvet Rooms – from sheer force of desire she would pass through the membrane and become an invisible, electronic signal in the mad scribble of everything. It had worked between them, in there. He had existed, he was for real, there. She breathed twice, hand on chest.

Spam enters Velvet Ballroom

DanceMaster: No dancing at the moment Spam but we are playing poker while we wait

Spam: Wherrrree are they RIGHTTT NOWWW I wonder it's ten at night here

Peach: *Hi Spam*

Spam: Hi Roommmmmerrrsss just had to come in and check again

DanceMaster: we wait we wait

Honeycake: Hi Spam

Spam: Ahhh Honeycake dooooo youooo dwellll amongg urrr cussshions in urrrrr ny appartmentttt

Psycho-dog: pant pant lick nose pant drool

Honeycake: ~lol at Spam~ sure me and my cushions … ya know how it is .. the one thing that separates men from women, huh … is cushions

Spam: Sooo trooo …

Honeycake: I think they are at a restaurant ten o clock so just lifting coffee cups to lips

Psycho-dog: wine, pant, there are candles on all the tables

DanceMaster: Pretty girls and handsome men serve them food

Spam: Ahhhh andd musiccc playyyyying soffffftly.

Honeycake: she#s wearing a great vintage gown of course

Peach: *What he is wearing?? The same ha ha*

DanceMaster: I think they are walking in moonlight

Spam: yes why nott alongggg the harbour wall … hannnddd in hannnddd … lights twinnnkllinnnnggg on the boats as they bobbb in the waterrrr

Honeycake: is it good weather in UK Spam?

Spam: yes big harvessttt moon heh heh

Sweetpea: Oh yeah I bet

Spam: Allll rightttt then it's raining

Sweetpea: GAwddd ~ thumps keyboard ~ I wanna know!!??

'Treasure, help me.' Call Girl sent this imaginary message to Fat-armed Wife but there could be no reply. He willed her to know what was happening to him, to be able to imagine, to reach him.

'What happened next was that you "unpicked" my hand – as you put it – when I slipped it round your waist.' Thruster stood, walked over to the bound and blindfolded Call Girl, who flinched at his touch.

'Go on then,' said Thruster. 'Try and "unpick" my hand like you said.'

'You're dead right, I can't,' replied Call Girl, 'due to the fact you've tied my hands behind my back. I was wrong to say that. You're too strong altogether, as it turns out.'

'So it was careless to say you could.'

'I was wrong, definitely. Learned my lesson now, all right.'

'Do you remember what happened next?'

'I don't, no.'

Thruster took a moment to read from the transcript. 'You stepped to one side to avoid what you called my "inappropriate seduction technique".'

'Right.' Call Girl stood, hypnotised, waiting.

'Go on.'

'Nah, it's all right.'

'Oh, I see. OK. You can't, hmmm? Deftly step aside?'

'No.' Call Girl's voice croaked. He tried again. 'No.'

'Sit down, then.'

Call Girl felt the seat of the swivel chair against the back of his knees. He sat.

'Is my thumb grubby?' asked Thruster.

Call Girl was already repeating, 'No, no,' even before he felt the ball of Thruster's thumb touch his neck. 'No, it's not,' said Call Girl. If he played it out like this, agreeing with Thruster, it would end; Thruster would have what he wanted. 'It's not grubby at all,' repeated Call Girl. 'It's dead clean as it happens. I can feel that, all right.'

'Pushing aside Thruster's grubby thumb,' said Thruster.

'I was wrong to say that, as well.'

'And this is when you strike me, swear at me,' said Thruster.

Call Girl waited for a while, breathing in the silence. 'Plainly I'm not going to do so,' he said. Perhaps a minute passed. Instinct told him it was nearly over; he only needed to get to the end. 'Sorry, OK?'

'Hmmm?' said Thruster.

'I wouldn't dream of trying to hit you or swear at you.'

'I see.'

'I'm sorry for what happened. Really. Very sorry. 'Cept it didn't really happen, chum. It wasn't real life.'

'Everything is—'

'Yeah, I know, everything is real life.' His frustration had shown through. He didn't dare move. It might be that he'd escaped lightly. 'Sorry,' he repeated, and listened hard for what would happen next. He heard the rustle of the paper. He had a vision of what it would be like inside Thruster's head: seething with people, all suffering, punished, humiliated, like in those pictures of Dante's Hell, and all this so Thruster could climb above his own humiliation.

'Should I go home and weep?' asked Thruster.

'You've not one reason to weep,' replied Call Girl with certainty. 'And I'm glad we sorted this out. If you want to call it a day, let's just stay here and we can celebrate.' His mouth dried. He waited. 'We could go for a couple of beers?'

There wasn't a sound except the click of Buttons's claws on the parquet floor. The truth was, Buttons was too used to seeing all sorts of things to worry about this. Call Girl sat and waited, and listened to Thruster's footsteps leaving the room. He couldn't make out what was happening but could only think Thruster was ransacking the place. He heard drawers tunnelling in and out. Kitchen cupboards were opened and shut. The tap was run in the sink. He sat, sweating and breathless and uncomfortable and blind. Longer and longer . . . He couldn't think what was taking this long. If Thruster wanted to go, why didn't he just leave?

Eventually the footsteps grew louder and Thruster came back into the living room. Call Girl felt the knot of the blindfold untied. The first thing he saw was Buttons, who started a renewed attack of shrill barking, darting back and forth, looking from Thruster's face to his feet, his ears folding and unfolding. On the floor was a bulky overnight bag: Call Girl recognised it as his own. It was half full. What was in there? He stared at the bag as Thruster shrugged into his overcoat again and tied the belt, then squatted on his heels and held out the back of his hand for Buttons to sniff. Buttons stopped barking and approached, sniffed the hand tentatively, growling, and veered away. Moments later he returned and Thruster stroked him for a while, smoothing the hair on his head which made his eyes bulge. Then he picked the dog up and pushed him into the bag. The zip closed shut.

'No!' shouted Call Girl. It came out as an inhuman cry. The bag moved and the dog whined from within. Call Girl felt every beat of the dog's fear and bewilderment as his own.

'If you do as I say, you won't have to worry about your dog. We just need to get out of this cleanly, now.'

Thruster straightened, adjusted his cuffs in the overcoat and came over to Call Girl, swivelled him in the chair until he faced the computer. He heard the penknife opened and the cord was cut from his wrists. 'Thank you,' he heard himself say. It sounded ridiculous. He felt the stranger's stubby fingers spread out on his shoulder. He watched as Thruster stabbed at the keyboard and the screen came to life. The cursor was set to find the internet; very quickly they stood together at the entrance to the Velvet Rooms.

'Give me your password,' said Thruster.

Call Girl knew it was pointless to lie. 'Spank.'

Thruster typed it in. Call Girl stood there, just the same as ever, in her cheap, flimsy, torn white dress, sprawled on the floor, her bust spilling out. All the times that he'd flown this character like a kite in

130

cyberspace, to attract adventure and fun-and-games, had come to this: someone else taking her as easily as that.

Immediately, Thruster swivelled the chair to face away from the computer. Call Girl couldn't see what was being written in his name. He heard some keystrokes, and then a period of silence followed. A few more keystrokes, and then the absence of noise as the computer closed down.

Call Girl was politely encouraged out of the chair, turned and pointed at the door. The bag was moving. He sent out a prayer: Buttons, you will be all right, God willing. Out of the corner of his eye he saw Thruster pick up the briefcase, then the overnight bag. Call Girl felt a hand at the small of his back and he was guided forward. He stumbled into the corridor; and, glancing into the kitchen, he saw that the washing-up had been done, everything put away. He was escorted to the front door. Buttons whined from inside the bag.

The splintered door frame had been more or less repaired. The broken wood had been glued and nailed back in place.

He was turned ninety degrees and stood facing the wall; the electricity and gas meters were only inches away. He heard the chink of keys. His own? His vision swam with tears. End this now, he begged. Thruster was on his way out, surely? He, Call Girl, would be told to keep his mouth shut or else. The dog would be kept as a hostage against calling the police. There would be the flurry of blows, the rain of kicks when he was down, then the door opening, and himself locked in, no doubt, to stop him following. Then Thruster's footsteps on the stairs, followed by the quiet after the storm. He would limp back to the sitting room and wait for news of his dog. He'd reach Fat-armed Wife. He called out to her, silently, It's all right, not to worry. Soon, soon now.

The blows didn't come. Instead he was pushed over the threshold, out of the flat. The sides of the bag moved comically. Call Girl was too shocked to say anything. Why was he being taken as well? Why would Thruster risk being seen?

'I need to take you with me . . . for a certain distance,' said Thruster. 'If you behave, your dog will survive. If you don't, it won't.'

The hand on his shoulder controlled him. The handrail was a chill bar of iron in his hand. Thruster's footsteps echoed in the footwell as they went down side by side, like husband and wife.

Thruster asked evenly, unexcited, 'Is that your own place?'

'Yes,' answered Call Girl.

'You own it?'

'No, housing association.'

'But it's a lifetime lease?'

'Long as you pay the rent, sort of it is, yeah.'

'Probably got a right to buy on that, I would guess.' Thruster pushed heavily, impelling Call Girl down the stairs.

He tried to assimilate the new shock as it kicked in: this situation hadn't ended where he'd thought it was going to. The flat had been made to look as if he'd left on his own account. Where was he being taken? A sinister new depth opened up. Why would Thruster risk discovery outside the relative safety of the flat? Call Girl decided he'd have to fight; it wouldn't be the first time.

One flight down, Thruster paused. Call Girl heard voices. Who was it? Someone, other residents. When they were close enough to see him, he'd scratch and kick and bite and scream . . . The voices became louder – his luck held. He wondered if it was anyone he knew.

Seconds later the voices stopped: there was silence. Thruster continued. It was too late. No one there? Then, on the next flight down, Call Girl saw them after all: a young couple, silent because they were folded in an embrace, kissing. The man was in a shell suit, she in a short dress in shiny aquamarine, the hem stretched across the backs of her bare thighs. They looked sly, a bit drunk. Call Girl knew his moment was here – this would be his escape. Thruster's arm tightened round his neck as they went down, step by step. Call Girl's throat constricted; he was caught in the ridiculous, polite, charade. He tried to take a lungful of air but it was as though someone had zipped up his chest – everything was packed tight, he couldn't breathe, he could only suck hard; his lungs were like wooden blocks.

As they passed, the young man barely spared them a glance; he was concentrating on his girl. In his hand was a key. He fitted it in the lock; the door opened and they went in. Call Girl stumbled, turned into Thruster's embrace and tried to kick, stubbing his toes on Thruster's shins, at the same time clawing at the bag to try and reach Buttons, but his wrists were easily held and folded back by the impenetrable, solid weight of Thruster. He was still under Thruster's arm; he was walked forwards, fighting for breath. As if from a long way off he heard Thruster's murmuring voice. He dragged hard at non-existent air; only tiny, rough sips were possible. He didn't have his inhaler. He was ashamed, frightened – and felt stupid with his bare feet, stockings and '50s housewife frock, the hairband, the make-up. It inferred he wasn't real, that he was a toy, disposable. He was swung through 180 degrees to face the next flight of stairs, and the next . . . His vision blurred; the ground beneath his feet lost focus.

Outside, the autumn night air fanned through his dress easily. He blinked, searched the windows of other flats, looking for light, for someone watching, but saw nothing, no one. The landscaped grass sloped tidily away on three sides of the car park.

They threaded through the vehicles parked in three ranks between the blocks of flats. His own Nissan Micra waited there, a sanctuary, a means of escape if only he could reach it.

He locked his knees, began to haul back – someone would see, call the police – but he was dragged onwards.

They stopped by a Ford Granada, an old-fashioned one like they used to have in cop shows. It gleamed under the yellow sodium lights. Thruster put down the bag and the briefcase to free one hand; he was manipulating the keys. Instinct told Call Girl, don't get in the car.

Thruster moved his grip from Call Girl's shoulder and wound his hand in his hair instead. The tight pain in Call Girl's scalp returned. He was aware of a shadow, a movement, as the boot lid rose slowly. Then came a steady, slow push against the back of his head, downwards; a sharp pain bit into his thigh as he was rolled into it. Asthma strangled him as he fought to untangle himself, fight his way out. A rush of air blew against his face as the lid slammed shut; darkness was immediate.

He couldn't see. His hands pressed against the back, the lid, the sides, he was tightly enclosed, couldn't even turn over. It was like being buried alive. Panic burst from him, but the cry at the back of his throat stayed there, the terror and the asthma wouldn't let it out.

He clamped his eyes shut and inhaled – out through the mouth, in through the nose . . . repeat. The struggle for breath put those other crises – missing the rendezvous with Fat-armed Wife, and the abduction of Buttons – at a terrible distance, as if it were never going to be anything to do with him, ever again. His legs were curled up, unable to straighten. The boot lid was inches from his face. His elbows banged uncomfortably as he scrabbled to find some way of escape. At the back of his mind he began to pray, Our Father, which art in Heaven . . . He couldn't remember the rest and so kept repeating those words, begging for there to be a God nearby.

Sweetpea: Christ, I know what they're doing! They're fucking each others brains out!!

Peach: ~ *sigh* ~ *sweetpea, language*

Spam: Ahhhh hope so … limbbbs entwinnned, sheeeets thrownnn offfff

Psycho-dog: whine … shagged out 'n sweaty … pant

Honeycake: lighting up the ol' post-coitals no doubt ~puff puff~

Spam: Ahhhhh …. Orrrrrrgassssmmmms a plenty on all sides I betttttt

Sweetpea: woop wooop wooop - waving fist - woop

Peach: *It is a bit odd, now*

Spam: Noohh … no newsss is goodd news

Fat-armed Wife visited the bathroom and lifted the toilet lid. In the water floated something. She thought at first it was another mouse, as if a plague were afflicting her, but it wasn't. She fished it out with the tips of her fingers. It was a bat, drowned. This appearance of small animals everywhere, like a signal, a message which she couldn't quite decipher . . . Cruelty and inhumanity surrounded her. She unfolded the precious creature's wing. It was delicate, like a piece of thinnest latex, but immensely strong. The long, conical ears were even flimsier. She caught sight of its pinprick eyes and screwed-up monkey face. The poor little creature. She folded it in tissue and laid it carefully in the waste bin.

Tears came; she couldn't stop them. She shivered; her jaw trembled. She looked in the mirror and wiped her big face with her hands. 'Christ,' she murmured. Without thinking she halfway undressed, then put her clothes back on again. She needed help. The nice man at the desk, he would know what to do. She rehearsed what she would say but stopped abruptly. Again, she fought to pull herself together. There would be some rational, ordinary explanation which would be made clear to her very soon. It was her duty to find out what it was. It occurred to her to log onto the Velvet Rooms to see if he was there. The laptop waited; she unzipped the case, took it out. Near the hole where the mouse had disappeared was a double socket. She unwrapped the converter and assembled the mains line. Gingerly, she plugged it in, sat the machine down, opened it and positioned her cell phone next to the IR port. At that point she hesititated. As soon as she went in, anyone who knew her would ask questions, demand to know how it was going. She couldn't bear the humiliation. She'd click on 'trial' and use a new name. What to call herself? Anything would do . . . Sitting here, rocking back and forth in the foreign hotel room, overweight, shapeless, hopeless . . .

Blob enters Velvet Ballroom

Peach: *Hi Blob. Welcome! Enjoy your trial.*

Top Dick: go on sweet pea I dare you

Blob:

Peach: *Blob you ok? You need anyone to show you around?*

Blob:

Blob:

DanceMaster: Hi Blob, welcome. May I ask, do you like to dance?

Peach: *Blob?*

Blob:

Peach: *~whisper to Blob~ Just checking ur ok?* ☺

Blob: *~gone~poof!~*

Fat-armed Wife picked up the hotel phone; it burred in her ear, willing. What would she say? That Call Girl was missing . . . had had an accident or been mugged. But without a real name and an address the police would laugh at her or think she was a time-waster or a drunk. She put the phone down again. She'd go to the police station; there was no other way of making herself understood, of showing how serious this was. She was an American citizen; that would help. She made sure of her passport. She remembered she still had the phone number of the helpful cab driver and dug in her purse to find it. Star Cars. She used her cell to dial.

It would be a twenty-minute wait, he advised her.

Meanwhile she changed clothes, and tore the zipper on her pants stumbling to the bathroom again. Even in such an emergency she felt a lurch of shame at how ridiculous she looked: great big face, brown hair like a forest sprouting from her scalp, eyes like currants buried in her cheeks, too much make-up, too many rings on her fingers. She flapped her hands and exclaimed, 'Ohhhh.'

The police, what would they think? Yet she had to go.

She sat, clamped her hands between her knees and rocked back and forth. Call Girl? Somewhere in this town, in this very small town in which she sat right now, far from home, was Call Girl. Or maybe not; who else might he be?

She flinched in panic and wiped every trace of make-up from her face. It would be important to give the right impression.

The phone bleeped and she snatched it up. The taxi was here. She took her keys, her purse and her coat, but then she was paralysed for a moment, homesick and stupid and overweight, imagining that when she opened the door – like in a fairy story – it would reveal the upstairs of her own home, the brown carpet and the cream walls marked by Jamie's careless coming and going, the fabric of the house around her like cupped hands, embracing and warm.

No. It didn't.

She found her way down the two narrow staircases separated by a landing which sloped: you could roll marbles here. Downstairs, all was quiet. She had to check the Velvet Dungeon again. It was empty, dead still, the outsize fireplace gaping. The drinks had been cleared away and the magazines tidied into a pile. And yet it was full of possibility, like a theatre before the audience has arrived. She checked her watch: almost midnight. She pushed her way through the lobby. The outside door was fastened with a simple Yale latch – she had the key so she could come back in at will.

Outside waited the same taxi, the same driver. She wiped her eyes, climbed into the back seat.

'What can I do you for?' asked the driver.

'Can you take me to the nearest police station, please?' She begged him not to ask why. She kept the phone in her hand. Every few seconds she stared at the screen, waiting.

'It's not going to rain, anyhow,' he said eventually.

'No, I don't think it will.'

A shameful silence grew in the murmuring car.

'I thought earlier it was going to,' went on the driver, 'and then it was like someone rubbed the clouds out of the picture.'

'Yes, I know.'

The tone of the engine had risen in pitch – he was going faster for her. She was ashamed to need his help, to be alone, to face up to such a ridiculous thing. His shoulder, the back of his neck, was a burly, fat presence in the front seat. He was a native, he knew every road in this town. It was likely he'd have taken Call Girl home from some club or other, in the past. She was bursting to ask him for help but courage deserted her. She remembered that he'd held up the sign at the train station. Had Call Girl been one of those people watching, laughing at her? If that were true, the gesture took on a different colour: it hadn't been kindness; it had been cruelty.

'Sometimes I think God picked up a stone and here we all were, wriggling around underneath,' said the driver, miming with one hand. 'You know?'

'Yes. That's true.'

A few minutes later the cab slowed, drew up to the kerb. 'Just here, look.'

'Thank you.' She hurried to pay him.

'Keep my number, let me know if I can be any help, OK?'

She stood on the sidewalk and smoked a cigarette quickly, facing a grey stone building, one storey high but with a basement, she noticed as she passed underneath the covered porch. There were heavy bars across the windows below ground level – they must be the cells. It made her blood run cold to think of who might be lurking down there.

The door buzzed, she pressed and walked through. She was held for a moment in a small glass lobby and she was aware of the officer at the desk checking her over. Then another buzzer sounded and she was let in. Her legs went suddenly weak, as if the power had been switched off between heart and head and her whole system was about to crash. She headed for the counter; beneath it was a glass-fronted display illuminated by strip lights, showing 'Wanted' posters. It was as if these faces were for sale; it was the business of this shop. They could find you a good criminal just like an estate agent could find you a house.

She reached the desk. A female officer greeted her – WPC Townsend. She had a lick of blonde hair held behind her ear and kept off her forehead with Bobby pins. Her hands had short fingers, the nails bitten down. She wore a strange, ill-fitting uniform which made her look more like a school janitor than a police officer, but Fat-armed Wife knew they were like this in England. It was almost comic. She blurted out, 'I'm an American tourist here.'

'And how can I help?'

'This is going to sound mad but I think something's happened to my friend who lives here in Hull.'

'What do you think has happened?'

'He's gone missing.'

'Right.' WPC Townsend fetched a slip of paper and a pen and slid them across the counter. 'First things first. We must know who you are, yourself. Just the boxes at the top, I'll do the rest.' Fat-armed Wife began to write quickly. 'You're visiting from the States?' she asked as Fat-armed Wife bent to her task.

'Yes.'

'And why d'you think your friend has gone missing?'

'We were due to meet up but he didn't show. I'm pretty sure he's been taken ill, or had a car wreck, or something that means he can't get to the phone, anyway.' Fat-armed Wife completed the form and handed it back. 'Can I smoke, please?' She was shaking.

'Go ahead. Take this seat here . . . Sit down. And tell me what happened – start from the beginning.'

'This friend and I have been real close for nearly four years.'

'Can I take the friend's name?'

Dread filled her but she took her courage in both hands and told the truth. 'I don't know his real name. I know him because we share the same chat room, you know, on the internet?' She felt all the warning signs.

'You met him in a chat room.'

'Yes.'

'What's the name of the chat room?'

'The Velvet Rooms.'

'The Velvet Rooms?'

'Yes.' She saw a corner of the officer's lips begin to curl in a smile.

'That's where you used to meet him.'

'Yes.'

'But you don't have a name.'

'I've always used his chat-room name, because, you know, that's what you do. But I've spoken to this man practically every day for the last four years. He said I'd never marry him if I knew his real name, because it's so awful,' she said simply.

'What is his chat-room name?'

'Call Girl.'

'Call Girl?'

'Yes.'

'He's a man and—'

'Yes,' said Fat-armed Wife impatiently. 'He's a man but he's . . . Well, he clowns around, you know. He's kind of bi-sexual. He called – calls – himself Call Girl to have guys coming on to him. Other places he calls himself other names. He's playful like that.'

'And he lives here in Hull?'

'Yes.'

'Whereabouts?'

'I don't know.'

'You're here to visit from the States and you don't know where he lives?'

'No.'

'So you've travelled all this way . . .'

She nodded dumbly. 'I know. It sounds bad. But I want you to know I'm a rational, sane individual. I run my own business – two businesses – I'm effective, successful. But yes, I did fly halfway round the world' – she waved her cigarette – 'without knowing his real name or address. All I can say is that we trust each other.' She trembled with all that was going wrong.

'I see. Perhaps give me a description, then.'

'He's around . . . er . . . He's tall, six-one? He's in his mid-fifties, slim build. He's asthmatic. He has pierced ears. He used to have a stud in his nose and through his eyelid and navel but not any more. He has lots of tattoos. He often has dyed hair. Orange and black usually. He sometimes dresses in women's clothes. There can't be many like him.'

'Madam, this isn't a joke?'

'No! I swear to you.' Fat-armed Wife felt lost.

'All right. Let's carry on.'

Suddenly she had no choice but to burst into tears. 'I don't know any more. He was meant to come to the hotel at 8.30 but he never came.'

'That's all you can tell me?'

'I waited in my hotel room for him. We'd texted, spoken . . . I've got those texts still on my phone. Everything was fine and then suddenly . . . nothing. Which has never, ever happened before. I texted, I called – he has the number of my hotel as well as my cell.'

'A real hotel?'

'Yes, the Post Inne, here in Hull.'

'I know.'

'He didn't call and he didn't call and I waited and waited and then I checked the message boards.'

'Real message boards?'

'No, the ones in the Velvet Rooms. I went and checked but there was nothing.' She heard three or four people murmuring, and a cup of tea arrived. The kindness made her feel like a child. She held her breath, afraid of more tears. WPC Townsend picked up the form she'd been filling in. 'But you say you were in contact with him by phone. We can get a name and address if you have his number.'

'It's 07747 862768.'

'OK. For now I'll log it in here as a potential missing person. Known as Call Girl, male caucasian, mid-fifties, occasional cross-dresser, Sid Vicious look-alike. Do you have a picture of . . . him?'

'No. At least, I got some on my computer back at the hotel. I can email you one when I get back.' The distress in her voice made the policewoman blink; Fat-armed Wife saw the kindness there, a reaction. She clung to it. 'Please will you help?'

'Yes, I will. Leave it with me. In just a moment or two we can get the name from his phone.' She lifted the scrap of paper that she'd written the number on. 'And probably an address as well.'

A frown crossed the officer's face and she put a hand on Fat-armed Wife's shoulder. Her voice softened, dropped in volume. 'Stay for a bit. Drink your tea. I'll be back in a minute, OK?'

Tears poured down Fat-armed Wife's face at the kindness – and the cup of tea was just what she might expect, in England. She drank it and smoked another two cigarettes while she listened to the policewoman making her calls. Every few seconds she checked her phone.

The policewoman came back. 'D'you know what I mean when I say the phone is pay-as-you-go? There's no name attached, no contract, you just buy a top-up card in the newsagents or wherever. D'you have the same thing in the States?'

'Sure, yes. I know.'

'So we can't trace it. Which means there's nothing much we can do now except circulate details. And wait. You know, if he works as a postman and he doesn't turn up for work tomorrow . . .'

Fat-armed Wife nodded dumbly, exhausted and weak and feeling stupid, childish, needy.

'Are you here tomorrow?'

'Yes.'

'Well, let's see what happens. Hopefully . . . well, I'm sure he'll turn up. Would you like me to drive you back to your hotel?'

'Thank you.' What else could she do? She rose unsteadily to her feet. Maybe Call Girl would even now be waiting for her in the Velvet Dungeon, dressed to the nines, eyes merry with excitement, ready to explain what had happened. She needed to hurry back.

Outside, on the sidewalk, she waited for the car. She lit a cigarette and checked her phone. Nothing.

Wet-stretched-t-shirt enters Velvet Ballroom

Psycho-dog: wipe down the bar ... again ... pant

Wet-stretched-t-shirt: hi everyone what's the dance?

Honeycake: **sigh** what time is it over there in UK?

Psycho-dog: Hi Wet-stretched. Pick up the odd glass, wash it - we're all waiting for the dungeoners - no sign - yawn

Psycho-dog: Dunno bout you West Coast Roomers, but it's eleven

142

here - yawn ~ slump on bar, head on forearms *growl* - which means three in the morning over there

Spam: Efffinnnggg SLOWWWWW dance Wet Stretched and by the way everyone agrees we alll spend too much time saying hi and bye and how are u itssss terrrrible and borrrring letsss say NO MORE hi and bye and NO MORE how are yous … let's say theyre nottt allowwwedddd

DanceMaster: Hi wet t-shirt, we dance the Mento, popular native dance of Jamaica

Wet-stretched-t-shirt: Ohj, ok, never heard of it

DanceMaster: it sort of resembles Rumba but played very slow tempo, like a dead-footed shuffle, everyone tired out

Wet-stretched-t-shirt: And we still waiting for Call Girl and Fat-Armed Wife to report?

Psycho-dog: Yup ~ pant, whine ~ lift head to stare at doorway ~ cock head sideways *whine* ~

Wet-stretched-t-shirt: hi there Spam

Peach: *Maybe they are having too much a good time and can't come to tell us*

Wet-stretched-t-shirt: oops, said hiya 2 u Spam, sorry

DanceMaster: Velvet Roomers keep dancing Spam you dance with Wet-stretched-t-shirt?

Spam: Would love to hold hand outttt to leaddd wet t-shirt onto the floorrrr 'n lead her assstrayyy hnnnn…!!??? But eyelidddddss clossssssingggg zzzzz

Wet-stretched-t-shirt: Spam prop me up just one last dance

Spam: Sorrrrry folks gotta go …. not shhhhure I can last … Will check in tomorroowww …. See what happened

Wet-stretched-t-shirt: Bye Spam

Honeycake: Spam Sweet dreams

Spam: *~gone~poof!~*

DanceMaster: Good night Spam

Honeycake: *Call Girl, Fatarms!!???* come back please, tell us what the efff's happening, tell your old roomer friends WHAT'S GOING ON??

Psycho-dog: Wherever they are … listless wipe of optics with cloth … whatever they do … we wait for them * it's like some Tennessee Williams play ~ curl up in basket ~ groan ~ gotta sleep, bye everyone

DanceMaster: Stroke Psycho-dog good night

Wet-stretched-t-shirt: Night Psycho

Peach: *Bye Psycho-dog *kiss**

Psycho-dog: *~gone~poof!~*

Eagle-eye: Hubby's back, I gotta go too

DanceMaster: Bye Eagle-eye

Honeycake: Everyone's going

Eagle-eye: *~gone~poof!~*

DanceMaster: stay someone. We should be awake and dancing until they come back. Who's with me for a dance marathon?

Honeycake: Dunno … might not be for ages

DanceMaster: Awww go on Honeycake *propping you up* dance with me all night

Honeycake: Ok count me in

Peach: *And me*

DanceMaster: we start slowly with the Shim Sham

Peach: *shim what?*

DanceMaster: The soft shoe shuffle from Harlem's Old Cotton Club

Honeycake: Never hurrrrd of it

DanceMaster: How about the Truckin - listen to this

Peach: *yeahhh, the Truckin*

Honeycake: The Truckin yes

DanceMaster: shuffle shuffle, shake a finger above my head

Peach: *shuffle shuffle, finger above my head*

Honeycake: Finger above my head, shuffle shuffle

DanceMaster: Three of us, that will do

Fat-armed Wife was ashamed to be seen climbing out of the squad car and being escorted, head down, across the road, the policewoman's arm round her shoulders. Next to the slight build of the other woman she knew she'd look funny – the rolling walk on the squat legs, the high heels making her buttocks stand up optimistically. She couldn't fit the key into the lock, unable to see properly through a blur of tears. Call Girl would be there, in the Dungeon itself. This was a delay, a bad dream . . . WPC Townsend took over. Fat-armed Wife nodded dumbly at the other woman's insistence that she be all right, that she look after herself. Yes, she would, she agreed, thank you. This was kindness piled on more kindness – it dug the well of pity deeper, made it harder to climb out.

The night-time somnolence of the reception hall accused her: it had all gone wrong. She hurried to the Velvet Dungeon – she prayed that Call Girl would be there, leaning back on the sofa, smiling, rising to his feet to tell her what had happened . . . She would sit, too, they would lean towards each other, talking animatedly, in bursts of relief and amazement . . .

The Velvet Dungeon was empty. The pictures looked out steadily from the walls. The fireplace yawned, a mysterious depth opening towards the night sky.

A dungeon. She wished DanceMaster had chosen a less sinister name for the bubble of real life he'd created in the Velvet Rooms. She shivered. She saw his words write across the gorgeous design in the Velvet Sanctuary: 'because it's real life, it's where we all are slaves'.

Upstairs . . . Her footfalls thudded anxiously; she held the key ready, turned it; she was in. The door shut behind her. The TV offered its silent welcome as before. She sat down, fumbled a new cigarette, sucked down more smoke. The room was the same: the chest of drawers, the wardrobe with the sticky door, the pine bed, the skirting board along which the mouse had run.

She phoned the police, emailed them a photograph of Call Girl from her computer. To have done something constructive made her feel better. What to do next? Search the town, walk every inch until she found Call Girl? It was three o'clock in the morning and she was scared of the streets outside, in the dark. She lay down on the bed – couldn't begin to undress – but even to think of sleep was impossible. Half an hour later she was pacing up and down. Dread and anger and fear mixed in her: he didn't exist, not as she knew him. Instead he was that car salesman or the spotty teenager. He and his friends had been laughing at her for years, never more so than now. He was callous and cold and clever. He had sent photographs of someone else so his real looks wouldn't be revealed. His friends slapped each other's backs as they leaned over the computer screen at work or at home – look at that poor fat-armed housewife stuck in a hotel room in Hull. Perhaps they laughed at her from the safety of a different town, or a different country, even. She plonked herself down on the bed.

An unknown amount of time passed; she awoke to find herself in this strange hotel, a pool of saliva wetting the pillow – she'd slept after all but it had altered nothing. She checked her watch: five o'clock. She undressed and brushed her teeth and pulled on a night-dress and climbed into bed properly; she hoped all these formalities would help. Instead, her worst fears came back. The Tarot cards had warned her: the Magician grinning . . . She remembered a story in the papers of a woman who'd had an internet relationship with a man for years; he'd told her he had a sick wife and a paralysed child. She'd tracked him down and found his wife was perfectly all right and he had three healthy children; he'd made it all up to win her sympathy.

She sat bolt upright. How stupid of her to believe Call Girl was a real person. He didn't exist. She was merely the office joke. It was a cruel act.

The next moment she knew it couldn't be true: no one could

maintain such a pretence for so long. She wasn't a cyberspace virgin, she'd seen all the tricks, she saw the plays as they went down. She turned on her side, ordered sleep to come – here, now – and take her away. It didn't. Instead, pictures of the terrible fate that Call Girl might have suffered floated in her imagination. He'd had a car crash on the way to the Dungeon. Or he'd walked and been mugged – a boot thudded into his ribs as he lay on the ground. A burglar with a knife . . . A sex crime committed by a former lover . . . He was bound and gagged on the floor . . . dead . . . partially clothed, dumped by a railway line and covered with a thin scattering of earth and leaves. A child took another step forward, crouched on one knee, discovered the body.

Anything might have happened, or not. The point was she didn't know. She smoked a cigarette down to the filter while the first signs of dawn illuminated the window and turned it, minute by minute, into the open eye of the room. It looked onto a town which kept its secrets. She checked her tickets and read again what she already knew: discount fares meant she couldn't change the time of her return journey unless she paid again. So it would be more expensive to run away. In any case, she should have the courage of her convictions – she must walk the streets and look for Call Girl.

Who else cared about him? His friends and family, where he worked? Fat Phil, for instance, Tricia, Sall, George. These were friends who'd often cropped up in his adventures. They would be her best allies, if she could find them. As she dressed in fresh clothes she set herself to remembering his family – she knew all their first names but not the surname. She'd walk the streets and bring knowledge of his disappearance to as many people who would listen. She would find out which post office he worked at – there couldn't be that many. People would help her. So the make-up went onto the big face, the expensive bust was lifted into its brassiere, chunky jewellery made her ears seem more delicate, the oversize hips and thick legs were draped in a sensible black dress with loose sleeves to cover her famously fat arms. The normal, everyday person was assembled before her eyes in just half an hour. She brushed powder onto her chest to disguise the coarseness of her skin and tied the usual gaily coloured chiffon scarf round her neck. She was ready – a good-looking, larger woman.

She went downstairs to sit at her designated table in the breakfast room. She ate fruit and cereal and asked for the coffee to be made stronger. Anyone looking at her might have wondered at her glazed expression, the automatic hurrying through the meal, her spin through the pages of the newspaper, at first quick and hopeful, then disappointed. After breakfast she went up to her room and prepared to go out. Plans circled in her head: post offices, gay clubs, the police station again. She picked up her handbag and a light waterproof because she knew that in England it always rained, even when the sky was bright blue as it was now. After she'd checked her make-up one last time she went downstairs.

She measured her pace as she went past the the Velvet Dungeon. Of course she had to glance in – and she was shocked to see a child standing in front of the fireplace, staring out at her like a ghost, dressed in a maroon dress and a hat. They didn't look like clothes you might have bought from a regular store. The thought leapt at her that this was her own child, conceived with Call Girl, visiting from the future. She stumbled on, disconcerted.

She braved the reception area, managed to walk past the new arrivals gathered around the desk. She approached the swing door; the light flared into the darkened interior from the street outside. She pushed the door an inch and the noise suddenly arrived – of cars and buses and the footsteps of passers-by. Her heart hammered suddenly; she could almost hear it. She paused, waited for the panic to die down. She hadn't reckoned on how frightened she'd be. She promised herself a cigarette and managed to wander around for half an hour aimlessly, seeking courage, hoping it would come. In the end, however, she couldn't carry on. Grief obscured her resolve. She went back to the hotel and stood in the lobby, wondering what to do. She sought out the Velvet Dungeon, the room with the big fireplace with its spray of flowers. Both the child who'd stood there earlier and the flowers had gone.

For a few minutes she waited here, hoping the fear would pass. She felt self-conscious and went to the ladies' in order to lock the door against the curious attention of other guests.

From there she went back up the stairs to her room. The fear and humiliation brought alive again the worst scenario and so she ran over the broken ground of last night – Call Girl didn't exist, never had, not really. The gang of car salesmen took turns, they were all laughing. The spotty teenagers couldn't care less. She leafed through a pile of women's magazines which she found on the bedside table. Hunger drove her to order room service. She phoned home; at this time of day there'd be no one there but she wanted to leave a message to say that everything was all right. Every now and again she logged onto the Velvet Rooms, always signing in under 'trial' and as Blob, so only allowed a few minutes at a time. Blob – yes, she felt that low, and without shape, useless. She only checked who was there and visited the message board. She didn't reveal herself to anyone. She didn't respond to any greeting.

There was no sign of Call Girl.

For an hour during the afternoon she slept. When she awoke she watched television. It was cricket: an incomprehensible game.

Twice that evening she tried to go downstairs for dinner, maybe even leave the hotel. Both times she failed. She returned upstairs. A dream came to her: of the burning tower, the long, desperate fall past the windows to the pavement . . . She awoke with the certain knowledge that Call Girl didn't exist, he was a hoax. Hull was probably a name he'd picked out of a hat. She was stranded.

She had the idea of finding a telephone number for Kenny's – the club he went to most often – and if she found it, she promised herself she'd go there in a cab. There was a local phone directory downstairs: she searched carefully under K.

Nothing.

A space opened in her head. She'd been made a fool of, well and truly. It hurt.

Back up in her room, the television claimed her. It was a kind of anaesthetic. She was in trouble.

At midnight she awoke suddenly, surprised to have slept again. She called home to say she was having a good time in London. It took all the strength in her big fat arms, to hold up this lie for Colin. She had to struggle to remember what she'd told him – it seemed a lifetime ago that she'd fought off all his arguments and caught the flight. She kept to the straight and narrow by merely describing the hotel at which she'd stayed in London.

When she fell asleep this time she dreamed of Colin and Jamie. Her two lives circled each other, occluded centres of emotion and love and fear and guilt whose edges bumped into one another and mixed.

The next morning she couldn't go through with the performance of breakfast in the dining room. Instead she called for room service.

An hour later she managed to leave the hotel – for her own sake she had to, to stay sane – but she could only make one enquiry, at a post office, before the feeling of futility grew too strong. She went back to the hotel and drank everything from the mini-bar until she was in a stupor. She'd smoked sixty cigarettes – her duty-free was busted almost to death. Under her assumed name, Blob, she visited the Velvet Rooms and wandered there for no more than a minute or two each time, more sad and lost than she had ever been, because it occurred to her that Call Girl might be doing the same: coming back under an assumed name to avoid her. She telephoned hospitals, more post offices, the police again and again. Without a name to give them she was treated as a mad woman. She wanted to run home, but even if she went to London it would be the same: she'd be hanging around waiting for her flight. She was better off here where she had a room.

On Friday she could start the journey home. The time of departure was engraved on her memory; the moment hurried towards her and was shaming in its own right because she undertook this return trip empty-handed, weighed down by the absence of Call Girl. He was meant to have accompanied her – he'd been going to show her some of London's sights and he would have escorted her to the airport. She packed her bag and moved one foot in front of the other. She paid the hotel bill in cash and tore up the receipt.

The train journey wound her backwards. It was dispiriting. She bitterly resented the overnight stay in London which kept her from the sanctuary of home. It was a lost time in an enormous, sprawling no man's land. To return to the Regent Palace Hotel was a painful irony: when she'd left, she'd been full of courage and optimism and love . . .

Call Girl enters Velvet Ballroom

Call Girl: *Help anyhone there*

Peach: *CALL GIRL???? IS THAT U!!???>>>* ☺☺

Psycho-dog: Bark bark bark!!! Pant pant!!!! - Rush up and wag tail like mad!!!! ~ ready with champagne cocktail ~ welcome back Call Girl long time no see ~ wipe bar ~ very big smile ~ bark ~ smile ~ bark

Spam: CAlllll Gurrrrlllllllll ???? Christ have we been waiting whatttt happppennneddd?

Call Girl: *FOR REAL THIS TIME please help I m kidnapped IT WAS THRUSTER*

Honeycake: Call Girl hiya!! Tell us what happened in the Dungeon, we were all worried as all hell

Call Girl: *No joke non joke no joke don't know where I am b ut trapt its dark and done't know what time its dark but no daylight THRUSTER CAME*

Psycho-dog: Furious bark *** bark bark *** Call Girl **** whine whine lick lick —— hnnnnn???

Call Girl: *FIND THRUSTER I AM WHEREVE HE IS No sound either cant hear anything no cars or voices just silence and*

DanceMaster: ALL DANCING STOPS … hang on everyone … Call Girl … where are you?

Call Girl: *No listen 4 REAL 4 real u must all listen its 4 real Dancemaster I don't know where I am can't remember A THING but help find me … maybe I was drugged I can't remember except Thruster somehow coming*

Peach: *ohhh .. Call Girl if u r teasing??? You sound different r u teasing?*

Call Girl:

Call Girl:

Call Girl: *thisis not a jo*

DanceMaster: Call Girl tell us everything you can

Call Girl: *~gone~poof!~*

Psycho-dog: uhhh? whine ** where she gone? *** pant *** stare at door **whine… whine…

Peach: *Maybe she wasn't teasing??? Was that real?*

DanceMaster: Has anyone else talked to her before?

Spam: Peach, she was teasinnnnnggg, must have beeen, she alwayyyys teases

Psycho-dog: whimper *** cock head on one side***whine***sniff at door*** what happened?

Thruster bought a kilo of venison and carried it back, vulgar and heavy and sweet-scented in its supermarket bag. In the large Tupperware box he mixed the ingredients: vinegar, wine, water, onions, celery, carrots, pepper, cloves, bay leaves, sugar and salt. He poured this mixture into the plastic bag with the meat. He tied a knot in the top and hung it from a nail outside, high up so that no animal could reach it.

Every so often, over the next two days, he would take down the bag and squeeze it, tip it from side to side, shift the contents.

He drove to the garage on the outskirts of Stinhalstadt and put the tokens in the slot for the steam cleaner. He gave the car a thorough going over, including the engine block, the upholstery and the carpets, especially in the boot. Back at the works he lifted the steel shutter and drove the car inside. He nudged it onto the old Finkbeiner hydraulic ramp so he could lift it off the ground. He switched on the pressure washer. He stepped down into the well underneath and sent the powerful jet into the treads of the tyres and into every nook and cranny of the vehicle's underside. Then he lowered the hydraulic rig and drove the car back out.

On the third day, he unhooked the bag of venison from the nail and brought it inside. He took out the meat and poured the marinade back into the Tupperware box. He rubbed flour into the surface of the meat and browned it in shallow oil, frying it in the grill pan of the Baby Belling two-ring camping gas cooker. He added half the marinade and sealed the dish with foil, then put it in the oven. There was enough for two people.

At intervals during the next three hours he went back to add more marinade. He poured off the dripping to make gravy. When it was done he poured the gravy over the meat and ate it straight from the dish, cutting off slices with his sharp, small penknife. During this time of preparation, he needed to eat a lot.

From: DanceMaster@thevelvetrooms.com

To: mjwal127@aol.com

Fatarms where are you? Call Girl posted. His actual words something like 'For real this time, help I am kidnapped by Thruster.' BUT – you? Where are you, what happened? Come back and see us whatever it is, good or bad. We are very worried not to hear. With respect and love, DanceMaster. Please come soon. WE ARE GOING MAD WORRYING.

Asbo enters Velvet Ballroom

Peach: *Asbo have u seen them?*

Asbo: fuck shittting fucking hell hit head against wall wreck bus stop piss in street

Peach: *Asbo tell us if you've seen FAW and CG we r all frightened*

Asbo: *~gone~poof!~*

Fat-armed Wife flew back to America in a state of numb shock. She pulled her lap belt tight, gripped the arms of the seat and took off into the sun, back in time, to her real life.

Colin and Jamie were waiting for her in Logan's arrivals lounge as she'd known they would be. She was in tears the instant she saw them. Colin, with the tips of his fingers tucked into his jeans pockets, gazed at her over everyone's head; Jamie restlessly cruised nearby until he ran for her. The connection between them snapped tight – as she pulled her wheeled case, fumbling for cigarettes. Colin's face fell, he was concerned that she looked upset. He asked what was wrong but she dug in tight and managed to stutter that she needed to keep going, reach the outside so she might smoke – which was true, yes. Silently she begged his forgiveness.

Once she was home she went up and had a bath and changed clothes. She took a bottle of wine to the office upstairs.

It was with some dread that she approached her computer. It looked like a sinister machine, now.

She checked her emails. DanceMaster's name leapt at her; she opened it first. He reported that Call Girl had posted into the Velvet Rooms. She felt the answer just within reach; her desperate need to know was about to be soothed.

The next few words made her heart sink. Call Girl had written 'Kidnapped by Thruster'. She cursed. More fake, made-up, fucking stories about kidnap! There was nothing beyond. She'd made all that effort to turn it into something real and it had been like grasping at thin air. He was a fraud. He was heartless, to have tempted her all the way over there. It hurt cruelly. She read the email over and over, 'His actual words something like "For real this time, help I am kidnapped by Thruster." BUT – you? Where are you, what happened?'

She had to turn away from all this, to save herself. She deleted the email. The Velvet Rooms was in her list of favourites; she went there immediately and struck it off: click, delete. She made a promise that she would never visit any chat room again. Grow up, she told herself. Concentrate on real people, on real events, on family, on work. She'd blog on dailykos.com again; she'd go back to her progressive politics. She called Teresa and caught up on the shop. She visited therealthing.com and worked hard. Ten minutes passed in a blur.

She'd put down two glasses of wine already. She began to smart, badly. She'd been conned by Call Girl. She needed help. She Googled 'internet stalking' and began looking for what she should do. 'Report the incident to the system administrator of both your ISP and the ISP of the stalker or harasser.' She made notes. She ordered a book from Amazon, *Cyberstalking: Harassment in the Internet Age and How to Protect Your Family*.

When she went downstairs again the alcohol was singing in her head. She did the stairs in the same old way, as if with a limp, one forearm on the banister, leaning sideways. She checked each step – small neat shoe safe dangling ready, then down, transfer of weight, other shoe catches up, then tilt again, carefully send the other one. At the bottom she called, 'Coming, yes.' She arrived in the kitchen, blinked. It would soon be time for dinner. She couldn't remember the last time she'd cooked but now it was what she would do: keep her feet on the ground, put food on the table, give time to the people who actually existed. She went to the fridge and found some steak and began to peel potatoes and wash the beans.

Her husband's face floated in front of her, incredulous. 'What you doing?'

'Dinner.'

'It's all done. Can't you smell it? We got ribs, house recipe, your favourite, plus salads.'

She nodded. Of course, this was the special welcome-home dinner. No wonder the surprised look. She was behaving oddly, still exhausted and anxious from having clawed at so much thin air during the last few days. The Velvet Dungeon had proved to be an empty, dank, foul-smelling, deserted place. Quite rightly she'd abandoned it for ever.

Colin stood over the ribs he'd made. Fat-armed Wife slid into the diner booth. In front of her were a knife and fork and a place mat. She'd chosen the tableware from the Sears catalogue. She watched her husband lift the ribs, move them across, put them on his son's plate. The back of his hand was hairy. In the hair nestled the wristwatch she'd given him as a third wedding anniversary gift. Jamie sat with his legs sideways and chewed with his mouth open. She didn't want to tick him off for it. He'd learn by himself. Let there be no more 'Do this' and 'Don't do that' in such a very difficult world, she thought. God grant her the patience to get through this.

Jamie was saying something. She looked at him and saw his mouth moving. What was it? A friend's dog was missing. She blinked at the word 'missing'. She felt qualified to give advice: walk the streets, ask everyone, find that dog, for God's sake. He was looking for her response but she couldn't say anything, she didn't trust that more tears wouldn't come.

Her husband and stepson were so familiar. Everything had been seen and done a million times: she'd sat here until her presence was imprinted, she'd worn out this linoleum with her heavy tread, over and over. She tried to hang on to this feeling of belonging. She put her hands on the table and looked at them. They were her flesh and blood. With Colin she'd made a marriage and they were looking after Jamie, the son he'd had with his former wife. Literally, they'd grown the boy in their home, with the food they'd put in his belly. Now look at him, she thought. He came up to her chin and was still eating. Next he would go to bed and sleep. Tomorrow he'd go to school. She was proud of him. Yet, with everything that had happened, she couldn't touch her husband and stepson and they couldn't reach her. It was as if they were sitting on different planets, far away from one another.

She picked up a rib, chewed it. All her body – fat arms and all – floated; it was just a servant, like a battery: she was meant to keep it charged up but it was failing, the energy was seeping out of her.

She stopped chewing.

Was she a virtual teenager, inexperienced, cut loose in an electronic storm of love, trying to shrug off a virtual boyfriend who'd never in fact existed? Or was she a thirty-seven-year-old stepmother and wife and owner of a training business and a vintage clothes shop sitting at the dinner table, trying hard for her family? She just had to plod on.

Afterwards she put her knife and fork together, cleared the plates. She went to the freezer for ice-cream, talking all the while about the shop. She risked a look at Colin as she put a bowl of ice-cream in front of him. His beard moved. The blue shone brightly in his shirt, the same blue as in his eyes. When she sat down he asked if anything was wrong. She shook her head. The mouthful of ice-cream couldn't be dealt with. She let it melt to nothing, waited for the crisis to pass. She held her husband's gaze. What's wrong? he was asking. She longed to tell him.

She cleared the ice-cream bowls almost before Colin and Jamie had had a chance to finish. She opened the dishwasher and started to load stuff in. 'Whoah,' said Colin, in wonder.

'Colin, the door won't close.' She pointed at the dishwasher. He scraped his chair back and came over. He had to take almost everything out and load it again properly. She burned with frustration. She'd thought she'd been doing well.

She clicked the kettle on, poured Jamie a tumbler of juice.

Yet what if Call Girl had existed, for real? It had been the sound of his voice: she'd heard it first in his writing, before she'd known he wasn't a girl. To hear a voice in the written word – it was the purest form of intimacy, like music that could be heard only by the two people concerned. It had moved through her immediately; it had found every nerve ending and stayed there, for years, reliably. Surely that couldn't be a trick?

Her eyes smoked. She shifted in her seat, stared glassily at her husband and son, eyes shining unnaturally, brilliant with unshed tears.

Colin dropped his spoon with a thunk and said, 'Honey, you are going to have to tell us what's wrong. I'm not sure I've got another guess left in me.'

She drew a breath, opened her mouth . . . and came close to telling him the truth but shied away. 'Just pleased to be back with you guys. Look at you both, hmm?' She squeezed Jamie's hand.

'Doesn't look much like pleased.'

'It's more than pleased. It's like . . . everything, to be here, to have you both. It's always worth going away, just to come back.'

The four walls moved like they were on rollers, crowded in on her from all sides. She was trapped.

Jetman enters Velvet Ballroom

Jetman: Hi everyhone

Peach: *Jetman!* ☺ ☹ ☹ ☺ *~ run to you ~ sorry Biker but I have warned you*

Jetman: Hi Peach great to c u

Biker Idiot: ass ok ~ shrug ~

Jetman: any1 wanna dance with me

Biker Idiot: Jetman remember we have music but no dancing until Fat-armed Wife returns

Jetman: oh yeah **sigh** but what about Call Girl

Spam: Call Girl is a dirty word if she has mucked about with Fatarms

Peach: *Missed my Jetman ~ *sad smile* ~ Goddd! ~stand at tiptoe and lean against you*

Spam: sorry, greetings Jetman.

Peach: *Jetman ~ take your arm ~ thank god u came*

Jetman: salute Spam: @ttenshun!! Y no spam writing

Biker Idiot: Kinda grim how much we miss her

Spam: At ease soldier ~ we're all grieving missing Fatarms. And Call Girl a prankster. Can't write funny any more

Jetman: Ahhh, noooo ,,, please Spam u r the best at spam writing go on do it.

Peach: *lol at my jetman*

Spam: Jettyman here goes, I am in my studdennntt digs, comppleeeete with gurlllls behinnnd evry doorway waitttting for mullttttiplle pennetrationss and getting tiedd and spanked for being baddd while givvving handjobbs to muchhh ollddder guysss … ***sigh ** doesn't have the same ring to it withouttt gufffawww of Fatarms …. Shake fisttt at heavennnns … where is she???

Jetman: Thanks Spam. where u peachy?

Peach: *at work*

Jetman: u alone?

Peach: *Yes, alone*

Jetman: squeeze your waist - you wanna go 2 the Shore?

Peach: *~blush prettily~ sweetheart?! What do you suggest here?*

Biker Idiot: we just want happy Velvet Rooms back

Jetman: just testing didn't want Spam to dance with u

Peach: *no, it's ok, I don't mind*

Jetman: *~whisper to Peach~* maybe u can invite me to the Sanctuary 4 a while so we lose the traffic

Peach: *~whisper to Jetman~ No, someone in there and the door locked*

Jetman: *~whisper to Peach~* Who's in there

Peach: *~whisper to Jetman~ There's a rule not to say, so ... better not*

Jetman: *~whisper to Peach~* But if ur a full member u know, right

Peach: *~whisper to Jetman~ Not necessarily only if they tell you*

Jetman: *~whisper to Peach~* it's call girl right and dancemaster mayb

Peach: *~whisper to Jetman~ No ... *big frown* sigh*

Jetman: *~whisper to Peach~* whgat dyu mean big frown sigh

Peach: *~whisper to Jetman~ Honey I'd better not say, d'you mind?*

Jetman: *~whisper to Peach~* don't worry. wish I was full member

Biker Idiot: Hey is everhyone whispering am I all by myself?

Peach: *~whisper to Jetman~ my soldier u will b. 1 more week and the sponsors. I am one sponsor ~vbs and touch~*

Jetman: Hey guys anyone want 2 sponsor me, Jetman, 4 full membershoip?

Peach: *Spam, will u sign up my Jetman ~ smile, lean up to my handsome soldier~*

Spam: yesss, will doooo

Peach: *hurray ~ my hand against your chest ~ that's 2 sponsors. Honey you sure you may afford it?*

Jetman: yeah sure

Peach: *it's so lot of money*

Jetman: Ur worth it

Peach: *~blush prettily~ glad u think so* ☺

Jetman: shall we go 2 the shore maybe to avoid this traffic

Peach: *You??!! ~little push at Jetman's chest~ you don't give up ~vbs~ it's not bad, how it is now between us, is it?*

Jetman: Remember I'm a marine, wer trained 2 invade…

Peach: *Invade!? ~gasp~ darling?!*

Jetman: Honey shall we?

Peach: *I never know anyone have such effect ~hand holds heart~ how do u do it?*

Jetman: cum here 'n dance

Peach: *~smile~ no dancing until they turn up, we all agreed*

Jetman: ~ closer ~ wanna whisper somethin in your ear

Peach: *~enter with your embrace~ what?*

Jetman: ready?

Peach: *~holding on tight~ yes ….*

Jetman: Lean downs to ur ear

Peach: *~gasp~ wriggle~ that will be delicious*

Jetman: ready

Peach: *Yes*

Jetman: ***~whisper to Peach~*** I luv you

Peach: *Sweetheart??!!!!*

Jetman: I mean it

Spam: Heyyy, we allllll wanted to hearrr what that was

Peach: *~ trembles~*

Biker Idiot: Leave da lickle luv birds alone!!

Jetman: Peach can we go 2 the Shore or sumwhere e so we don't have 2 keep on doing the whisper thing or can u make a private room?

Peach: *Ok*

Jetman: Ur the member

Peach: **~whisper to Jetman~** *I make a private room*

Jetman: Ok

Peach: *see u in Bliss*

Jetman: **~gone~poof!~**

Peach: **~gone~poof!~**

Jetman enters Bliss

Peach enters Bliss

Peach: *I can't believe you gave me three magic words ...!!??*

Jetman: Yes

Peach: *I am so lucky*

Jetman: Im the guy whose lucky

Peach: *Jetman ...*

Jetman: What???

Peach: *u won't say those words unless u did mean them?*

Jetman: course not

Peach: *I am so happy, u don't know how happy I am, but don't think ... we can't dance without knowing FAW and CG are safe*

Jetman: Come here

Peach: *~smiling prettily~ you are going to hold me*

Jetman: ~ take you in my arms~ yes

Peach: *Is there music here*

Jetman: course

Peach: *but we don't dance*

Jetman: No, just touch

Peach: *~turn my face 2 urs~ Jetman?*

Jetman: What

Peach: *How tall r u?*

Jetman: six-one

Peach: *so ~turn my face up 2 urs~ do u want 2 kiss me?*

Jetman: ~tuch ur lips with my fingers~ what a beauty

Peach: *kiss me Jetman, touch ur lips to mine*

Jetman: I kiss u

Peach: *that feels good, very soft and dubious ...*

Jetman: Push my tongue between ur teeth

Peach: *Hold on, hold on, wait ~ beat hand to chest~*

Jetman: Pull u tight against me

Peach: *~Put both my hands to your broad chest~ hold on*

Jetman: Sorry, just want u

Peach: *I know, me 2 ~breath hard~*

Jetman: maybe just need 2 talk about something else so exictied u know, otherwise will jump u, want 2 take things really slow

Peach: *~smile~ you need 2 talk of something else?*

Jetman: ~wipe brow~ sure do

Peach: *Let's talk of how you are raised, your mom anmd dad*

Jetman: No tell me about what's happening in the sacncutary. What is that gossip u couldn't tell me?

Peach: *Are you teasing*

Jetman: No, big thick cock in my trousers need 2 think about something else

Peach: *U!!!!!!??? R???!!! Terrible!!!?? I am sorry I am difficult and stiff, cant stop but think of where they've gone and what might have happened*

Jetman: tell me about Call Girl

Peach: *What about her?*

Jetman: Him u mean

Peach: *in here she's a her*

Jetman: oh yes of course is she a good friend of urs?

Peach: *Yes, she is ~rest my head against your chest~ Tell me if u believe in marriage*

Jetman: why are people keeping quiet?

Peach: *I can't darling, with the trust in me, they went to the Velvet Dungeon and Fat-armed Wife hasn't come back yet and Call Girl has come twice but says only that she is kidnapped which is like her usual joke but she is meant to report seriously on the Dungeon. So everyone is worried. But I might have 2 b thrown out if I talk with it 2 you. Is that ok?*

Jetman: What is the Dungeon?

Peach: *when ur a member u will know ~ look up in ur eyes ~ have you married b4?*

Jetman: Never

Peach: *~ tighten my arms around you ~ and do you like the children*

Jetman: Yeah I want lots of children. What does everyone think, what does Fatarmed wife think?

Peach: *She's got a stepson herself and she says I ought to have lots of children.*

Jetman: No I meant what does she think of Call Girl?

Peach: *Handsome man ~ squeeze my hand through the hair at the back of the neck ~ pick me up u know how I like that*

Jetman: squeeze u gently ... and lift ~ hugghhh ~ u kick ur feet in the air

Peach: *I love that ... oh ... higher*

Jetman: Yes higher in the air ~ u squeel an kick ur legs

Peach: *I smile down 2 ur sunburned face touch my lips to yours but not too much, want 2 wait for u and 2 want u*

Jetman: Will u tell DanceMaster I will help if anyone needs help? Remembger I am a marine

Peach: *I will tell him, yes! ~ my hand to the back of your neck ~ look in ur beautiful eyes~ do u kiss me now*

Jetman: *~whisper to DanceMaster~* Hey, remember if u need help I am a marine

Jetman: Do u want 2 kiss me?

~Auto-reply~ I'm sorry, the recipient you have chosen ~ *DanceMaster* ~ is not available.

Peach: *yes*

Jetman: don't want 2 hurry you

Peach: *I am ready, you said high in the air - the sky is around me and the sand is under our feet and the ocean is in our ears - so I am happy and ready*

Jetman: That soundsx like were on the Velvet Shore, sand and ocean

Peach: *I am nearly ready 4 the Shore, I want ur kiss, a deep kiss*

Jetman: Frightend that if I kiss u it will make me 2 excited ~ put u down on sand, look in2 ur eyes~ dont want 2 spoil it

Peach: *~shake my head, long dark curly hair falls on my shoulders, over my breasts ~ u don't spoil it*

164

Jetman: Holding you ~ I' glad tha u want me, huh

Peach: *~trembling in your grip and look in your eyes ~*

Jetman: r u ready

Peach: *Ohhh ...*

Jetman: we could go to the Shore?

Peach: *hand on your chest ~I'd love 2 but*

Jetman: but what darling Peachy lets go all the way

Peach: *not yet, nearly but not yet ~lean against you, raise my face to be kissed*

Jetman: watch out, u r going to make me cum

Peach: *Stop it ... !! You !!*

Jetman: Sorrry - big thick cock pressed against u

Peach: *we will go soon 2 the Velvet Shores - just need u 2 know me a bit ...
and me know u ... when ur a member ...*

Jetman: Straight after I am a member I'll come looking for u

Peach: *Ur not bored with me honey???*

Jetman: u r jokoing

Peach: *~slip hand in your shirt~ don't want that you ... be bored of me*

Jetman: ***~whisper to Bra-less~*** Hi babe, u playing?

Jetman: Never, u hear

Peach: *It's just that a lot of guys don't want ... u know*

Jetman: I only want u

Bra-less: ***~whisper to Jetman~*** Hey, whered you suddenly cum from,
handsum???!!

Peach: *Sorry don't want 2 be insecure but need 2 know what you are like as a
person and want you 2 know what I am*

Jetman: Sure

Peach: *I went 2 far and fast with Green-eyed Man and it hurt when it was wrong*

Jetman: *~whisper to Bra-less~* just scrolled thru list of names and wanted 2 fuick urs

Peach: *Forgive me? Loads I want 2 tell u, need 2 tell u, but have 2 be sure of u first darling man*

Jetman: Nothing 2 forgive

Bra-less: *~whisper to Jetman~* Uh-huh? Wonder why, hahaha, leaning forward in tight low-cut shirt insy winsy buttons straining

Peach: *Stay with me, handsome soldier – until this bad patch is over in the Velvet Rooms*

Jetman: *~whisper to Bra-less~* What cup size r u?

Bra-less: *~whisper to Jetman~* 36D

Jetman: My gun sure is loaded and is going to stay loaded at your service mam

Peach: *You!!!!?/ What are ur duties today ~sitting on ur lap~ do you have 2 work?*

Jetman: *~whisper to Bra-less~* Cum here

Jetman: Oh the normal u know - drill then firearms then exercise planning which will be sometime soon

Peach: *what kind of exercise?*

Bra-less: *~whisper to Jetman~* Tell u what, let's cut the crap and straight to Shore I'm horny as hell - u a member?

Jetman: u know, like mock operation, somewhere in the world, don't know where yet, might even be real ops ~ tour of dooty

Peach: *How come u don't know?*

Jetman: they dont tell u til last minute where they send u

Peach: *well ~my arm around ur broad shoulders ~ don't get hurt, hurry back to my arms ok*

Jetman: *~whisper to Bra-less~* Go to redlightdistrict.com right now and u r my toy

Jetman: Sure honey

Bra-less: *~whisper to Jetman~* Oooh I like a real masterful kinda guy ~ saunter off ~ backward look ~ hmmmm

Peach: *Jetman honey, I wish u know how I like the three words u gave*

Jetman: What three words

Peach: *Don't tease!!!??? But I can't say them back 2 u almost only although I want 2, because I have 2 better know u*

Jetman: *~whisper to Bra-less~* I will have my hand around ur throat and watch ur mojth open while my cock thrust in u nd u will cum just as last breath leaves ur body and I will cum as u go dead quiet and still under my thrusting cock

Bra-less: *~whisper to Jetman~* hnnnmmm … start to go wet … knees weak

Jetman: *~whisper to Bra-less~* go to redligthdistrict.com now

Jetman: Honey I gotta go now

Peach: *Go??? Huh?!* ☹ ☹

Jetman: Aggghhhh sorry - something come up, tell u later

Peach: *hurry back… ~ kiss you ~ my sweet love, can I tell u b4 u go that u r the best that is happened 2 me and I will tell truthfully about myself. Always.*

Jetman: *~gone~poof!~*

Peach:

Peach:

DanceMaster lifted the bow from the violin; the note hung in the room and he heard it out. There was no vibration quite so raw, so perfectly designed to interfere with the human ear, as a deeply cut flourish from the violin. He wished to send it into the ether, into cyberspace, for all the Velvet Roomers to hear, so sad and plaintive as they all were at the moment. He chased its last reverberations until the room was silent, and put down the instrument gently, trying to preserve the mood. He waxed the bow and released the tension before putting it back in the case; then he rested the cloth over the bridge and fastened it shut. No one except María would come in here without his permission, and she knew that she must only Hoover the floor and clean the windows – never must she move or touch anything.

He ran both hands through his hair, teased his brow with cool forefingers. It was stressful, this business with Fat-armed Wife, but he knew he was right, he just needed to check. He might as well get it over with.

He rolled out of the room, slowed the left-hand wheel to make the turn. Since his accident the ground floor of the family home had been adapted for his sole use. The stairs that led up from the hallway might as well be a vertical precipice whereas they'd once been his to do with as he'd wished; up and down he'd flown, thoughtlessly privileged. A hundred times as a child he'd slid down the polished mahogany banisters. Now, on the first floor, his two elder brothers' bedrooms had been converted into a new kitchen and dining room for the rest of the family. They had left home; he'd remained behind. This door had previously been used only by servants as they trotted back and forth carrying meals or cleaning gear and linen. He'd converted part of it into the office from which he ran his charity, El Pueblo de los Niños.

María was staring into her screen. How much of the world's population, now, he wondered, spent its time staring into the bottomless, vacant gaze of a computer's eye, during working hours? She turned and gave him her gay smile. 'Como estás?'

'Bien, gracias. Y . . . María?'

'Señor?'

'Pues, quiero mirar los pagados de los Velvet Rooms, por favor. Solamente dos particulares. Creo que una nueva, que se llama Blob, es tambien Fat-armed Wife.'

'Ahora, quieres?'

'Por favor. Es un poco . . . Soy disconcertado. Es malas noticias, tal vez.'

'Blob?'

'Sí.'

'Y Fat-armed Wife.'

'También.'

'Espera un poco.'

María switched screens, hummed and hahed. She went back and forth from printer to computer. A minute or two later she put two sheets of paper in front of him. On each was a blue cross. These marked the payment lines for Blob, a new temporary member of the Velvet Rooms, and Fat-armed Wife. It gave their real names and their credit-card details. He scrutinised the numbers, carrying the memory of one to compare it with the other.

When he was eighteen, before the accident, he'd been the Colombian junior champion at ballroom dancing. Afterwards, when he'd set up the Velvet Rooms and it had become a success, he was amazed to receive money. He, who needed for nothing, whose family were so extraordinarily wealthy, found himself with more and more of the stuff, and he'd offered the regulars life membership for nothing. They'd refused; they wanted to 'keep him going', as they'd put it. He didn't want to tell them of his fortune, so instead he'd diverted the income to his charity for street children and felt happy again to take money for what was his hobby – no, the love of his life, the charity which allowed children in Bogotá to crawl out of the drains, even if they'd murdered and thieved, and find a bed for the night.

He already knew the answer, of course, but it might be possible they were different people, merely shared a surname. Now he could see that the initial was the same, it was the same bank, the same address, identical card numbers. Blob and Fat-armed Wife were one and the same. She was paying twice, in order to come in disguise.

DanceMaster enters Velvet Ballroom

DanceMaster: Blob?

Psycho-dog: Ah - wag of tail - DanceMaster - drink for you - woof

Blob: Hello DanceMaster

DanceMaster: Psycho no thanks. Blob may I invite you to the Velvet Sanctuary

Blob: Ok

Psycho-dog: Very good - polish bar, pant cheerfully - here if you need me

DanceMaster: I will go first, unlock the door

Blob: Ok

DanceMaster: *~gone~poof!~*

Blob: *~gone~poof!~*

DanceMaster enters Velvet Sanctuary

Blob enters Velvet Sanctuary

DanceMaster: Fat-armed Wife it's you

Blob: knew you would find me

DanceMaster: my darling friend what went wrong ??

Blob: He didn't show

Dance Master: I don't believe it. What was the last he said?

Blob: I went there - thousands of miles - plane and taxis and trains - I went all the way there - texts back and forth - he was happy I was happy - Dungeon rules, everything OK - time set for him to come to the hotel at 8.30 pm. THEN - suddenly - like a switch thrown - no answer to phone, texts, no message in the Velvet Rooms, nothing. Blank

170

DanceMaster: something HAS happened have you seen his posts

Blob: YES but do you believe them?

DanceMaster: Tell what happened, when he didn't show?

Blob: went mad – went to the police – searched the town, called hospitals, the places he might work, nothing – and I had no name – he'd refused to tell me his name. I thought about that a lot – why not? He said because it was a silly name but is it a trick? Still don't know – why else would he let me come all that way without telling me his name??? – lost confidence – utterly – breakdown – felt stupid, yes – cheap flight meant I had to wait there – imagine – couldn't run back home – stupidest time ever I thought – is he ill, was he mugged or hurt or what?? But the WORST was to get your email and see the word kidnap etc, he must be up to all his old tricks and I am dead sure he is still playing around, that he is a fake, BUT dot dot dot

DanceMaster: So so sorry

Blob: still can't help worrying ... is he a fake or not, is he teasing or not?

DanceMaster: We all thought maybe it was a joke the two of you were playing

Blob: No - on my life - this is real. When I came home, tail so firmly between my legs - you can imagine - and saw your email, I told myself I would never ever come to the Velvet Rooms again, but couldn't help it, had to see if he was back in here. Came as Blob so I wouldn't have to tell anyone. I went to the Dungeon for him, for the sake of God it was miles, by plane and train and cab - and then just everything stops. Can you imagine how stupid I felt? Yes I thought it was a trick bujt maybe it's not, not at least a trick by HIM. Am I right? I don't know any more. maybe I am stupid and empty after all and about to be tricked for the second time

DanceMaster: My darling darling darling friend of course you are not stupid, not empty, not a victim. You are Fat-armed Wife, our best creature.

Blob: these visits he makes to the Velvet Rooms - you have seen

DanceMaster: Yes

Blob: Is that him - for real? Do you think? Or is it Thruster? Or – is Call Girl Thruster as well? With two computers?

DanceMaster: I do not know

Blob: how many times have you seen him?

DanceMaster: only once but there are three times we know about

Blob: It's a big empty hole, huge empty hole. Will I ever fill it? I don't know. I beg whatever God there is, DON'T LET HIM BE A FAKE - I can't work or do anything properly - don't sleep, nothing - without any kind of action I can take and no sign of Thruster to ask him about it

DanceMaster: he did sound more real ... It is more desperate, his language, not like normal Call Girl. Fatarms, my darling darling darling Fatarms, i can tell you, it is odd because it is the same, as if nothing had happened - it is like denial - when we asked him about Dungeon it was like he did not read the question, as if we are not there and the question is not said, he just talked about Thruster and about kidnap - but more desperate and clumsy - saying it is for real.

Blob: How do we find out? Police think it is a stupid game. I say it is him but not him, they say well when it is him let us know

DanceMaster: I am sorry, keep with us Fatarms, come back as yourself, do not mind what everyone says, knows, does. We are on your side

Fat-armed Wife held her hair back; swapped the receiver to the other ear. 'Hello?' She thumped too hard down on the chair and felt something break.

'Can you hear me?' It was a woman's voice.

'Yes.'

'This is Police Constable Townsend calling from Hull in the United Kingdom.'

'Yes? Hello!' The voice came flooding back to her: the kindness of the cup of tea, the counter at the police station with its glass cabinet showing the faces and the crimes of those Most Wanted ...

'I wanted to let you know that we have a report of a missing person who matches the details given by you on 24 September.'

'What is it? What report?'

'A man named Jonathan Sowerbutts was reported missing yesterday from flat 16, Shelton Heights.'

'Sowerbutts?'

'Yes.'

Fat-armed Wife remembered his voice during that phone call: 'Actually, me name's Roger Goering Hitler Bush.'

'That's his name?' she asked.

'Yes. Caucasian, six foot one, dark hair, aged fifty-five, thin build, asthmatic, a well-known cross-dresser and bi-sexual, and worked as a postman. Which exactly fits your description.'

'Someone else reported him missing?'

'Yes, Philip Masters.'

Suddenly the phone handset was slippery – sweat had sprung from both her hands. 'So he is missing, something did happen.'

'He didn't turn up for work for a week. There was no answer on his phone or at his door. Philip Masters called us because he thought he might be with you. When he learned of your report, we forced entry into 16 Shelton Heights. We found that a bag had been packed – clothes, wash things, et cetera. His passport had gone. He had a dog, apparently, and the dog wasn't there, nor was its lead, nor its food bowl. No one knows where he is but there's every sign that he's gone away. Although the door had been broken into and repaired, several times. I thought you'd like to know and perhaps you could call and let me know if you are in touch with him.'

'Sowerbutts is his name?'

'Yes, Sowerbutts.'

'Thank you. Thanks. Very much. Jonathan?'

'Yes.'

Fat-armed Wife finished the conversation and repeated his name over and over: Jonathan Sowerbutts. It had really happened. She was no longer an idiot, a victim. Jonathan Sowerbutts was the victim. She remembered that she'd asked him what was wrong with his name; he'd answered, 'Just you wait.'

Her grief segued halfway to laughter. Sowerbutts?!!! Jamie appeared at the door to the office and asked what was so funny. She hurried from her seat, bumping the table, knocking over the lamp-stand. She went and held him tight, wiping the tears from her face. Sowerbutts? She was in love with someone called Jonathan Sowerbutts, for Christ's sake.

From: DanceMaster@thevelvetrooms.com

To: Honeycake@thevelvetrooms.com

Try and remember. We cannot get its name without a description, what type of boat and where it is registered. What was the thing sticking up from the deck, if it wasn't a funnel? D'you have any idea in what country the picture was taken? Where did it look like?

Call Girl enters Velvet Ballroom

Call Girl: *tell them Thruster Thruster Thruster does everyone understand Thruster came for real and there was a car and a jouirney don't' know how long but some time and I can hear nothingk so must not be in a tonw but somewhere deserted there are footsteps of onlhyone person and they sound like theye are in a big echoing building but never a door slamming the room has block walls like odl industrial unit anyone there???*

Oldermom: Yes I am here Call Girl I am here writing this down Thruster you said

Call Girl: *tell everyone Thruster came forced me on there was the drive, a long way nd must come soon I am getting weaker is there anything has anyone found out anything if thrusters comes here get him, must know who he is, where he is because I am with him*

Oldermom: You are a missing person, you are reported missing

Call Girl: *only a min*

174

Call Girl: *~gone~poof!~*

Oldermom:

Oldermom:

From: BigBlackWoman@thevelvetrooms.com

To: DanceMaster@thevelvetrooms.com

THRUSTER HERE. Posting nothin unless he's whispering. Come see.

Honeycake woke quickly – still groping for what it was that had caused her to rise from sleep. Then she got it – she was sure that just now, in her dream, she'd remembered the name of the boat in the picture that Thruster had posted. It had been given to her, dead flat certain, as plain as if written on a piece of paper, but she couldn't see it any more. It made her disoriented.

The name of the boat in the photograph . . . She was trying so hard to reach back into sleep that she'd hardly registered her surroundings. She was in her own bed, so it wasn't the weekend. The curtains that separated the sleeping area from the rest of the loft apartment were drawn. There was no sound – often the elevator coming up from the floor below woke her, rattling its cage in the shaft, but not this time. She checked her watch: a quarter to five in the morning. She swung her legs over the side of the bed and sat, head in hands. She was thirsty from smoking too much, standing shamefully outside work with other tobacco exiles.

Her dream had been of a broken window. It was necessary to mend it. The measurement was taken for the glass to be cut to the right size – however the tape was applied not to the window frame but across her icon in the Velvet Rooms. And then had come the realisation . . . the boat that Thruster had posted in was called . . . what? It was separate from the idea of the glass and the measurement, it was different, it had come in sideways.

Her nerves snapped tight as it came to her: *The Spurn.*

She saw again the short, stubby vessel with the strange thing sticking up out of its deck. Like an old child's toy put together with parts of other toys.

The Spurn. What did it mean? She was already reaching into the internet, hurrying to Google it, find out anything she could. *The Spurn* – the name had its cruel, heartless association: the spurned lover, Thruster . . . maybe that was why.

Within minutes she'd made the link. *The Spurn* was permanently moored in Hull, *Call Girl's home town.* Thruster had posted it as a clue – he'd given them a nudge to say he knew where Call Girl lived, and that he was going after him.

Reality took hold of Honeycake. This wasn't any kind of game, after all. This was Thruster's revenge. The extravagance of it struck Honeycake so hard that she actually whimpered, 'No . . .' The pitiful, animal cry sounded in the empty loft.

RipeCherry enters Velvet Ballroom

RipeCherry: Hiya every1, heard this was a good place from Liks2SuckOnU

RipeCherry: u guys whispring?

RipeCherry: ~ sort of twirl in middle of empty dance floor ~ Stranger in town, anyone gonna dance with me?

RipeCherry: Hello?

RipeCherry: Thruster is kindofa promising name after all …

RipeCherry: Fat-armed Wife and Thruster, u guys whispring? Wanna tell me what's going on here?

RipeCherry: sigh - guess it's not going to be a good night

RipeCherry:

RipeCherry:

RipeCherry:

RipeCherry: ~little pout~ I was told this was a good place. Here I am all alone, no one 2 dance with…

Fat-armed Wife: *~whisper to RipeCherry~* sorry to be rude but I can't chat at the moment

RipeCherry: *~whisper to Fat-armed Wife~* Hmmm, u enjoying Thruster r u? I don't mind just watching

Fat-armed Wife: *~whisper to RipeCherry~* not enjoying Thruster not whispering, just watching and waiting. Sorry, apologise on behalf of Velvet Ballroom - please come back another time.

RipeCherry: ok u guys, if no one's going to dance

RipeCherry:

RipeCherry: *~gone~poof!~*

Thruster logged off, shut down – the keys offered their well-designed, pleasurable resistance. His touch found its way quickly but with numerous mistakes. The mouse scuttled to his precise directions. He blinked: the screensaver showed for a second. The brief surge of power flushed all light from the screen and it went blank. The indicator lights died on the keyboard. The fan in the hard drive blew for a while longer and then switched off; silence grew.

In Thruster's head, the clamour of voices faded. The names and the icons shrank like fish disappearing in the depths of a pool. In three well-rehearsed, careful movements he wiped both screens with the anti-static cloth and pushed the keyboard delicately so it rested in line with the laptop; his forefingers found the corners and adjusted them fractionally. His latest ride into battle, his camouflage, his intelligence network, his ops room, all were contained in these slim tablets of black and silver plastic.

He spent some minutes cutting extracts from local and national newspapers. The new scissors had ten-inch blades which made the edges neat, straight. He printed the pages he'd saved from the Velvet Rooms. The resulting documents were filed in envelope 14.

Within an hour his attention wandered and he fired up the machines again: he found himself going back. The crime page of the *Hull Echo*'s website hadn't changed its entry. Call Girl's page on www.missing.org.uk had two additional sightings and an hysterical plea for information from someone called Lady Godiva. He dipped into the Velvet Rooms briefly.

This was his circuit; he went round it obsessively, checking for post.

By the time he'd crawled to a halt it was dark outside – the diodes said 2 a.m. He switched off the desk light; night entered the room in a blink. He welcomed it as he sat there waiting for more content to arrive. He closed his eyes and mentally turned in a circle, like radar, checking what was near him, all the circumstances, in every direction, so that he might identify the blip, the sign of something approaching. The enemy knew his position – they had their hands on him, in effect. He himself had given them his shape, his purpose, his electronic shadow. And yet he was dead safe. He opened his eyes again and his sight had adjusted; he could see that the clock threw a pale green cast of light over his hand as it lay there on the desk.

He undressed, his body becoming palely luminescent. He charged the pad of cotton with white spirit and wiped his body carefully from top to toe, ending around his nose and mouth and neck. For an hour he wandered here and there, breathed the fumes.

His cock stirred uneasily, nodding, trying to wake up. Powerful urges competed in him – to receive satisfaction, maintain his position; they galloped like wild horses. His exact centre – the point around which, if you stuck a metaphorical pin in there, he would balance and float evenly as if weightless – was the seat of these impulses, the stabling, as it were, for the wild horses; it was here that they always returned.

Suddenly the night was too big, loose, unformed. He switched on the desk lamp again, and stood. The loose floorboard flexed under his weight. The tips of his fingers were planted on the desk top; he could sense minuscule particles of lime dust. He wiped the surface with a cloth. Simple domestic tasks tethered him closer to happiness.

He moved to the glass partition but didn't touch it – it would be cold on the other side. The oil-fired radiator was on its autumn setting, 5, warm enough to sit at his desk in a T-shirt. He told himself to brave the cold and generate some adrenalin, so he went through and took a draught of cold air, shivered as it hit him. It was as if he'd jumped into a swimming pool, it clothed his forearms in goose pimples and made the hairs stand up. He switched the lights on and walked slowly across, breathing deeply. He went and sat next to the kettle and tea station. The wooden trunk was there. It snagged his eye. The quietness took him further into listening . . . He got to his feet and approached, softly. It was painted a dusty, faded blue, apart from where the middle strut had at some time in its long history been torn off, revealing the bare wood and grey primer underneath. The missing strut also interrupted the name that had been stencilled in heavy black capitals across the lid: CAPT. J. DARLING. Its corners had been chafed to the bare wood. Here and there were fragments of shipping bills, telling of the trunk's journey some fifty years ago – mostly around the Baltic and the Mediterranean. He'd replaced the hinges himself. They were of brass; they didn't match the black hasp and loop that fixed the trunk shut. The padlock was steel; he'd bought that also.

He kneeled down, listened closely. He could hear shallow breathing, interrupted by the sound of swallowing. Afterwards there came a slight grating in the throat. The breathing deepened. The lid moved; it lifted just a fraction, before dropping back. Then came a strange rattling sound. He realised it was Call Girl's teeth; his victim was shivering.

Thruster stood, swayed slightly. Not long to go.

He made the familiar tour of the wrong spots in his physique. He massaged the pad of flesh on his hips, feeling its mass, whether it had grown more or less, looking for the pelvic bone. He folded his hands under his arms, felt how loose his breasts were. He held his paunch, kneaded it, testing for the power and strength underneath. It was there, a solid bank of muscle, an unbroken wall of it as thick as a fist, yet hidden by these six inches of flab, top to bottom. His arms were strong as any man could want. His legs also – powerful, thick and short. He held his buttocks, the softest, worst part, as if all the fluid weakness in his body had run down here and gathered in a couple of watery sacs. He cupped his genitals, teased the whole group into a jumbled handful. He shivered, then took a deep breath and squatted. He defecated neatly into the plastic bag, sealed and stored it.

He lay on his back. The chill wooden floor caught his nerves for one second before his skin acclimatised. He curled his hands to his jaw, as if ready to defend himself in a boxing match. He lifted his ankles off the ground just an inch and felt the muscle board in his stomach grip tight and his thighs tighten. He brought his torso up and twisted it sideways and counted, one, and let himself back down. Up again, two . . . He fixed his gaze on the same point as always in the ceiling, where the hook had been driven into the beam, and kept counting: ten, eleven . . . He began to speed up. The floor was hard under his back as he ground through the sit-ups, curling then straightening time after time. His face stiffened as he approached two hundred and fifty. He hissed through his teeth and counted out loud. At two hundred and ninety his face was staring, grim with effort. His insides were tearing. At three hundred and five his stomach would be commanded no more; he stopped. His gaze loosened from its hook in the ceiling. He turned on his stomach and flexed his back the opposite way to loosen the pain, then rested, to recover his breath.

The press-ups took more resolve. The numbers were lower. The action looked vaguely obscene.

Call Girl enters Velvet Ballroom

Call Girl: *Can anyone do snaything*

Peach: *Call Girl ????? Tell us where u arrr*

Psycho-dog: *~whisper to Fat-armed Wife~* CG is here

Call Girl: *plese please find me help me*

Peach: *CAll Girl Fatarms is here somewhere hold on*

Fat-armed Wife enters Velvet Ballroom

Fat-armed Wife: Call Girl what happened?

Call Girl: *Only hav a fw seconds dont know wher this is*

Fat-armed Wife: what's the name of your dog

Call Girl: *Buttons please help*

Fat-armed Wife: Darling darling - how, tell us how to help

Call Girl:

Fat-armed Wife: who's there with you? where are you?

Call Girl:

Fat-armed Wife: tell me the name of your niece with spina bifida

Call Girl:

Fat-armed Wife: can't you type? Try and tell us

Call Girl: *my jobs a*

Fat-armed Wife: You there? Is that you? Can you not post - just say yes or no

Call Girl: *~gone~poof!~*

From: mjwal127@aol.com

To: DanceMaster@thevelvetrooms.com

He knew dog's name but then didn't answer niece's name. Call me call me call me xx

Fat-armed Wife swung into the warehouse and switched on all the lights. She could hear nothing except her own breath as she went down on hands and knees and began to sort through the bales from the rag yards. She hadn't done this kind of work for two years but she had to be doing something, anything, as long as it took her away from the computer screen and the phone. She needed to escape from the tyranny of the situation, its grip over her heart and mind. She rubbed her arm forcefully back and forth against her hip. The psoriasis had come back: she had patches of rough, itchy skin on the insides of her wrists and round her eyes. The hum of the strip lights accused her; she couldn't go home, not in this state. Harder and harder she worked: cheap stuff for the students in one pile, ready for the first-floor rails. Classier goods for the ground floor. Anything exceptional for the store in the Copley Mall or for auction on the website. Washing pile, ironing pile, throwaway pile. The clothing blurred in her hands. She hardly saw what she was doing; all she could think about was the merry-go-round of Velvet Rooms, police, Call Girl, Thruster, the *Spurn*, the Velvet Rooms again. She could practically walk around Call Girl's apartment standing ominously empty, clean. The missing bag and items taken were listed in the police report. She could imagine the terrier, Buttons. He knew what had happened, maybe. She begged for him to be found and to provide some clue. She saw in her mind's eye Call Girl's handwriting appearing in the Ballroom – the music of the voice was different and the mis-spellings were uncharacteristic but maybe that wasn't surprising given the circumstances. Thruster would be nearby; Call Girl might have only seconds to touch the keys, very quietly, with fingers she'd never seen, but which had touched her so . . . She cried with frustration, blinded by the fog of events.

She breathed, to prevent panic. It helped to think about what was in front of her, what was real – the here and now. She dragged forward another bag, opened it. She wished never to stop working, never to see another human being, until Call Girl was safe and they were the other side of this grief and fear. She surveyed her piles, the backlog of other bags, the ironing board standing there. The little shop she'd started, after selling the first business, had turned into this, three floors of vintage clothing and bric-a-brac plus internet auction site. She had become well known among collectors. She was running like mad just to keep up. But it had all become meaningless suddenly. She dug deep in the bag. You never knew what you were going to get. She kept going, worked as fast as she could to give herself a feeling of progress at *anything* . . .

Asbo enters Velvet Ballroom

Asbo: Fucking fucking fucking hell. Kick bollocks tear up paving stone throw bottle pissinthebusstop

Oldermom: hiya Asbo everyones in the Sanctuary and the door's locked.

Asbo: throwbrickatdoor sod them kickdoor bastards let me in headbutt door you bastards punch door whats going on headbutt kick punch tear off door handle

Peach hunched down against the cold. It had entered her heart; she could feel its icy fingers reaching in. She wanted to cry. She pulled the wool over her head, curled up tighter. Underneath the mattress was stone; on all sides the wooden walls were damp and swollen from the wet air that swamped Hebei province for four months of the year. Her stomach gnawed with hunger. She could hear the men talking. They had been up all night playing cards and Cho-min. They gambled more money in one night than was paid to her and her half-sister all year. She squeezed her eyes shut and fought the twin aches of hunger and cold, moment by moment. She could not look forward to any more sleep now. Two hours was good – a weapon given by exhaustion against hunger and cold, obliterating them for that short time. Sleep was the same as happiness; she only longed for dreams which were similar to the conscious, unalloyed excitement and adventure and travel she enjoyed in cyberspace. Except that, even in the Velvet Rooms, cruelty had reared its head. Jetman would help stop it. He was a Marine.

If only she could go to work earlier. Each moment was in the way, between herself and Jetman. She could remember when she'd felt the same about Green-eyed Man, and how quickly that had gone, what a betrayal it had been. She must steel herself for the same; and to make it hurt less this time she would show her true self before going with him. She must be sure.

An hour later, daylight stole into the room and the voices had gone. She could see the clump of black hair in the cot opposite: her sister. She whispered, 'Mu?' but there was no reply. Her sister was lucky: she slept five or six hours. Yet she was unlucky in other respects. She had the men to take care of and that was not a good deal. There had been no happiness beyond the age of twelve for Mu – she did not have the protection Peach had.

An hour later she was dressed and sipping at a bowl of thin, hot soup, finding the rice floating in it. She tried to imagine where Jetman might be right now. He wasn't allowed to tell her, for security reasons. She pictured him as like the Western troops she'd seen on TV. How tall he would be. How strong. He was capable. Upstanding. Honour was his watchword. He seemed almost childlike in his simple goodness.

The movement of her body and the hot liquid fought against the cold, and the weak winter sun helped – it was warmer to sit on the bench outside and watch the men bicycle to work. One or two waved and smiled; among the many intent, downcast faces these few smiling people stood out like a chosen race of great beauty, mysteriously blessed with happiness. Peach thought maybe they were all a bit stupid in the head, and she was careful not to encourage anyone to stop and speak. They certainly knew better than to do so.

After she had pulled up water and washed, she bound her head in a scarf ready for work. An hour after the men and the other women she walked the mile and a half to the Hushan Tangali Ceramics Co. Each step of the way was towards Jetman.

184

Her uncle's car was in its usual place. The giant, grinding-down power of the factory was at work. Sometimes she thought of it not so much as a factory in which 800,000 pieces of hygiene porcelain were made, but as a place where the clay dust moved like a river and wore out the hands and lungs and minds of its human workforce; it rubbed away at men and women slowly but surely until they could not walk or stand or answer their own names but only lie ill or become old and worn down.

Inside, she welcomed the warmth: thank God for that. She climbed the long wooden stairs which always seemed like they might lean over and fall; she trod close to the wall because there was no banister. She pushed the plastic curtain aside and passed into a greater density of noise – the ceramic mill and tunnel kiln were just the other side of this blockwork wall, hastily constructed when the old one fell down. She watched her feet make prints in the dust. Ahead of her was her uncle's office but she did not go as far as there. She turned into her cubby-hole: the metal-armed bench with its familiar slab of wood split and worn, squared up to the desk with the Tandy word processor. The gateway to the Velvet Rooms, and to Jetman. Its weedy old wires were coated in sticky dust. In a redundant kiln insulation box lay a pile of invoices and orders to be sorted, added up, translated into English. A certificate on the wall told her this company was named Municipal Civilisation Unit by the Municipal Party Committee. For sixteen hours she would travel the world, and marvel at the lives of others, and search for Call Girl, and Thruster.

Spam couldn't log off, either; he'd become attached to the Velvet Rooms by an electronic umbilical cord. He stared into the site's gorgeous, painted design. The Ballroom. Its surface was wafer thin, contained within the grubby plastic box of the computer monitor, but the light it emitted and the signals it carried had a blind, conscienceless reach and power. He dabbed the folded napkin at the corner of his mouth; blinked. His eyes were weeping from too much time spent travelling through the screen.

It had no longer seemed appropriate to play at being Spam. A peculiar honesty had taken over the Velvet Roomers; it was because of this crisis. He wished to be himself. But what could be done? Fat-armed Wife was trying to reach into – through – the vastness of the internet in order to find Thruster, but if he didn't want to be found then it was as if she was plunging her hand into a barrel of sand in a bid to find a single, individual grain.

He rose to his feet; a little wave of giddiness took him. He wished for a small pistol, and a sight of the enemy, that he might shoot.

Peach enters Velvet Ballroom

Peach: *Jetman darling ~come for peck of kiss~ glad u r here already* ☺

Jetman: Hi Peach

Lesley: I am a yoga instructor in NY. You?

DanceMaster: Peach welcome

Peach: *How is the situation Dance Master?*

DanceMaster: I am meeting Fatamrs in the Sanctuary later and will email everyone afterwards

Jetman: what situation

DanceMaster: *Atención!* Change partners. This dance is for Peach and Jetman.

Peach: *I thought we weren't dancing until they came back*

DanceMaster: Fat-armed Wife is back, and now we dance like fighters, like matadors. We dance to increase our courage, to warm our blood, to signal our allegiance. And so it is the Bamba, old Mexican air from Veracruz. For you Peach and Jetman, and for Fat-armed Wife and Call Girl. Two lovers throw a sash to the floor. They tie it into a knot with their dancing feet.

Finger-of-Fun: Yoga instructor does that mean u can bend over backwards?

Peach: *DanceMaster, then yes we dance, thank you. And hi Spam ~vbs~ how are you?*

Lesley: ~s~ and sideways as well ~lol~

Finger-of-fun: ~lol~ having fun thinking of you bending forwards ~wink~

Spam: Urgghhh … Peachy … anxious … cant sleep

Jetman: thank u a dance of our own. Peach? ready?

Peach: *Spam!? Be brave*

Spam: Yes. Will. r uuu bearing up?

Peach: *Spam just walked on the beach and stopped with coconut milk, now at work ~ sigh ~ and all right in Jetman's arms ~ what could a girl want for more ~ moving softly ~ vbs ~ kiss Jetman~ sure I'm redy*

Lesley: ~grin~ i'll show you what I can do - yoga means I am elastigirl

Finger-of-fun: hmmmm … can you wrap your legs round the back of your neck?

Peach: *Thank you for the dance DanceMaster*

Lesley: have to warm up a bit first ~s~ before they wrap right around

Jetman: ~smile at Peach~ kiss

Finger-of-fun: ~lmao~ tell me what I have to do … to warm you up

Jetman: So lets Bamba

Lesley: first tell me a bit about yourself

DanceMaster: And thanks for your message on message board Jetman. Welcome to membership

Finger-of-fun: Ok. I'm male, 28, a high school teacher

Peachy: *See Jetman darling, everyone loves you*

Lesley: male?!!???!!!

Jetman: Thank u DM. Meant what I said, so … u know

Finger-of-fun: Sure, male. That bad news?

Lesley: You need a fucking blow-up doll … to wank over … u prick … take your slimy cock and stuff it up ur own arse …….

Spam: Oooooopps Finger of funnnnn

Finger-of-fun: *~gone~poof~*

Peach: *DM Jetman's a Marine you know* ☺

Jetman: *~whisper to Peach~* Can we go 2 the Sanctuary?

Spam: *~whisper to Lesley~* didn't know that Finger didn't know yuuuu … hah hahh YOUUU are my faaavourit lesbian

Peach: *~whisper to Jetman~ Of course. What's up, ,my sweetheart?*

Lesley: good riddance to him

Jetman: just 2 look around … my first time

Peach: *Sure c u there*

Peach: *~gone~poof!~*

Jetman: *~gone~poof!~*

Jetman enters Velvet Sanctuary

Peach enters Velvet Sanctuary

Jetman: Hey this is it - nice

Peach: *You like it?*

Jetman: How du lock the door

Peach: *top right of the screen, see*

~door locked~

Jetman: Thats great huh

~door unlocked~

188

Peach: *Yeah it's clever*

Jetman: think whats been said and done in here

Peach: *yeah lots*

Jetman: I really am a full member

Peach: *Welcome ~ hug~ kiss~*

Jetman: and u know what?

Peach: *what*

Jetman: thinkn I might be able to help

Peach: *help what?*

Jetman: about what you told me, I have an idea

From: mjwall@aol.com

To: DanceMaster@thevelvetrooms.com

Jetman has had a v good idea, he says why not create a character to lure Thruster, someone like Call Girl, so we can tempt him and maybe find out who he is, where he lives, come and I'll tell you more

Colin's voice floated up. 'Darlinnng?'

'Yup, up here.' She cursed under her breath – she was in the lowest, bleakest place she'd ever been. She scraped her wrists against her sides. The psoriasis had spread over the heels of her hands and up her forearms. It itched viciously. Round her eyes it had turned puffy; she looked as if she'd been in a fight. She swapped windows on the computer. She couldn't cope with an interruption now. She had been crying; no one should see her like this. 'What is it?' she called.

'Close your eyes before we show you.' Their voices were closer.

He'd said 'we', which meant Jamie was with him. She felt a pang of guilt: she'd been spending every minute at her desk, sucked back into the Velvet Rooms. It was easier to go mad here. She could stay logged on the whole time and think she was doing something useful. 'OK,' she called, rolling back her chair. They must have bought her a gift.

There came the sound of their last few footsteps and she did as she'd been told and closed her swollen, itchy eyes and held her hands up to hide them as well. Her appearance was so awful. She felt Jamie arrive next to her; his hand was on her shoulder. 'Shall I stand up?' she asked.

'No.'

She heard the excited, nasal tone of his voice; he had his usual autumn cold. 'What is it?' she asked.

'Keep still.' Colin was close now, just in front and above her. 'Eyes shut,' he warned.

'They are.'

'OK, just sit back, leave a bit of space . . . OK there you go.'

Fat-armed Wife opened her eyes. A big chocolate-coloured kitten was sitting on her lap; it stared up at her and its gaze met hers before it jumped off, took two steps and lay sideways, flipped its tail up and down. She looked at Jamie; he was alive with excitement, watching her. Colin asked, 'What d'you think?'

'It's absolutely gorgeous.' She was dumbstruck by its beauty. She cooed at it, stroked it, felt the bones beneath the soft fur. Life itself electrified its narrow frame . . . She picked it up. 'What's its name?'

'We wanted you to give it one.'

'Oh, OK.'

She swung the kitten round to look in its keen young face. 'What shall we call you, hmmm?' She asked Jamie, 'Is it a boy kitten or a girl?'

'A boy,' replied Jamie.

'He's beautiful isn't he?' She looked into the clear, amber eyes of this little creature, which began paddling the air, trying to escape again. She couldn't think . . . What kind of name? 'Let's call him Jonathan,' she said.

'That's a human name.'

'Yeah, but I like it because it's not cute. I don't want to call him Fluffles or . . . whatever.'

'Oh, OK, Jonathan. If you say so.'

Colin watched for her reaction. Obediently she kissed Jonathan; felt his body twist sharply. She set him down. Immediately he ran across the office and climbed up the shelving unit, then he disentangled himself, fled back again, pausing to bat at the forest of computer cables under the desk. He stood, looking at each of them in turn while keeping half an eye on the disturbed flex. He glanced swiftly at the ceiling; a dozen other sights caught his attention in quick succession.

'He's incredible,' she said, heaving herself to her feet. 'Where d'you find him?'

Jamie smiled. 'Rescue centre,' he said. There was pride in his voice; he knew she'd approve of that.

'How old is he?'

'Four months. Jonathan . . .?' Jamie tried out the name. 'Jonathan?' He clicked his fingers. 'D'you like him?' he asked her, smiling.

'He's gorgeous. I'm not sure what I've done to deserve my own kitten.'

She told herself to take a break from the computer. Jamie and Colin were trying so hard for her and they couldn't know what was wrong – and how much it had gone wrong. She went over, held out her hand; the kitten stared briefly into her eyes and then galloped – as if his life depended on it – across the room, swerving to avoid Jamie and then towards the door to the stairs, which thankfully Colin had shut.

'Jonathan!' called Jamie. A second later the kitten tore back; it was difficult to keep an eye on him. He stopped dead, his front paws up against the radiator; he was entranced. Colin's arm was round her shoulder. Jamie watched her, still. Their kindness brought to mind the hand on her shoulder and the cup of tea brought by WPC Townsend in Hull, and this new, vital energy of the kitten suddenly injected into the office was a criticism of her: she was tired and lacked any idea of how to move forward. She was desperate. It was so frustrating when the police told her how many people went missing in England, many of them never found. There was no crime evident. It had been a mistake to tell them that Call Girl had always pretended to be chased, kidnapped, anyway.

The psoriasis crawled up her arms, it had infected her eyes. She was in trouble. Perhaps she should take the truth by the scruff of the neck and tell her family everything: Thruster, Call Girl, the police, the Velvet Rooms. Was it too big a secret to keep, now? She was avoiding her husband and her stepson; she was smoking and drinking more. She looked a mess. She wanted to bang the table with her fist, move this awful suspicion forward, achieve a result. Call Girl was missing, they had identified his attacker. Thruster had posted the picture of the *Spurn* in Hull – he had been telling them what he was doing all along. Yet there was nothing she could do. She was powerless. She scratched her arms, turned her blasted eyes on her husband.

'Colin?'

'Mmm?'

'I think, to get better, I might have to move to a motel for a while.'

'What on earth is it in a motel that's going to make you better? We thought the doctor was going to do that. We even thought the kitten might do it.'

She flapped at the air. 'I have to get away from the stress of home. I want to go and . . . stop. Escape. Do nothing. I can't bear anyone even to see me like this. Will you grant me permission to stay in a motel for a bit?' She tried not to be angry.

'No.'

Fat-armed Wife enters Velvet Sanctuary

Fat-armed Wife: *~whisper to DanceMaster~* I'm here

DanceMaster: *~whisper to Fat-armed Wife~* Coming

DanceMaster enters Velvet Sanctuary

Fat-armed Wife: lock the door?

DanceMaster: Yes

~door locked~

Fat-armed Wife: you got my email

DanceMaster: yes

Fat-armed Wife: What d'you think

DanceMaster: It might work

Fat-armed Wife: OK

DanceMaster: We can make our own or it's quicker off the shelf

Fat-armed Wife: what have you got on the shelf

DanceMaster: Like Call Girl as much as possible?

Fat-armed Wife: Same but different

DanceMaster: What about . . . I've got LickMeHere, what about her

Fat-armed Wife: Bit too funny, good humoured. Want to have edge of suffering sort of. Might be important, masochism etc.

Fat-armed Wife: You still there?

DanceMaster: hold on

Fat-armed Wife:

Fat-armed Wife:

DanceMaster: I present for you, Bruised Ass

Fat-armed Wife: More like it, I think, similar kind of white panty hose thing going on with her as with Call Girl

DanceMaster: Hold on

Fat-armed Wife:

Fat-armed Wife:

DanceMaster: What d'you think of this one?

Fat-armed Wife: She's better again, she's the one, who last used her?

DanceMaster: Spam used her once a few months ago. He brought her back. It was a joke he said.

Fat-armed Wife: Can I do this???

DanceMaster: Try, there is no harm

Fat-armed Wife: ok

DanceMaster: maybe practise first?

Fat-armed Wife: now?

DanceMaster: yes go and choose your font and colour etc, general style and come back in ten minutes and practise

Fat-armed Wife: I will have to come in through Ballroom

DanceMaster: that's ok

Fat-armed Wife: how do I explain sudden full membership?

DanceMaster: you are an old member from years ago. No one will question it

Fat-armed Wife: seriously important no one knows

DanceMaster: Of course not. La sepultura de mi mamá etc

Fat-armed Wife: not even members

DanceMaster: understand

Fat-armed Wife: Will it work? After all, he's told us it's him, he will be expecting something - all along he is laughing at us Velvet Roomers

DanceMaster: You can only try. There is nothing to lose. If u want someone else can do it for you maybe without your emotion and involvement

Fat-armed Wife: No, I want to do it. And if anything happens, if you want to test me for any reason, ask the name of my new kitten and I will answer Jonathan.

DanceMaster: Now you frighten me

Fat-armed Wife: I'm frightened

DanceMaster: Jonathan. Your kitten. ok

Fat-armed Wife: am I mad? Is this all a dream?

DanceMaster: No

Fat-armed Wife: ten minutes to set up Wet Lysette's membership, then I'll come back

DanceMaster: what's your password

Fat-armed Wife: the name backwards ettesyltew

DanceMaster: ok

Fat-armed Wife: Thank you. She'll do the job - tuck her under my arm - time to practice

DanceMaster: I'll wait here

Fat-armed Wife: You know what, I still have the gift I took for Call Girl to England, all wrapped up, a 20s sequinned minidress in deep red, and I want to give it to him. My hand to his hand, my eye to his eye, my smile to his smile. But going mad because scared I won't ever do it. And my eyes are worse. Doc says infected ecxma.

DanceMaster: Fatarms. You are a daughter of the Velvet Rooms. We are all here - the Velvet Rooms love you. Always tell us how to help. Where. What. When.

Fat-armed Wife: I kiss you. DanceMaster you are the all-seeing all-hearing God of the Velvet Rooms. Bless you.

DanceMaster: *salud!* at your service

Fat-armed Wife: *~gone~poof!~*

DanceMaster:

DanceMaster:

Wet Lysette enters Velvet Sanctuary

Wet Lysette: How's this?

DanceMaster: I think it's good. Different and extrovert. What you call a show-off, hmmm? Maybe red is aggressive. Should it be pink? And lots of stars and flourishes and winks etc

Wet Lysette: **more like this?/!!** vbs** wink

DanceMaster: Yes, more sub to his dom, is better

Wet Lysette: *** The name sounds tough kinda trailer trash**8??!! ### kinda ball-breaker type ???88####''' should it be like that?

DanceMaster: I think you should be more like … hmmm … lying back on cushions … chocolates and flowers … more like your cat

Wet Lysette: ###//// YES WILL BE A CAT *** Makes it easier for me to remember how to be ///#### miaowwww ***** clean whiskers *** purrrr

DanceMaster: Exactly that is great

Wet Lysette: I am scared

DanceMaster: Stay calm, my darling Fatarms. You will be OK

Fat-armed Wife was awake, fully dressed, lying on a strange bed in the Killarney Motel on the outskirts of town. It was dark; she'd drawn the feather-light maroon drapes across the windows and now tried to shut out the sound of the traffic on the expressway. The bedding was boiled clean. She wondered who'd slept here last night, and the nights before that. All the goings-on – she could imagine. Yet with each person checking out the slate was wiped clean: the linen changed, the towels replaced, the place wiped down and Hoovered – so easily did the crimes and passions of the previous guests disappear.

Back home Colin slept, no doubt. She could almost see him in the darkness of their bedroom, the beard not much distinguishable from the kitten who would be lying snug against his head. Colin had this poise, when he slept, a pointing of the nose and mouth as if a stream of air, moving just above him, had to be caught. She always had to resist the impulse to prod him and stop the snoring.

The events in England ran constantly through her mind. She put her hands to her face and tried not to panic. One of the reasons she'd wanted to move to the motel was so that the pulse of wakefulness, of fear, wouldn't transfer to Colin and Jamie. If she'd stayed home, they'd all have gone mad.

She and Colin were both, she thought – the skins they were in – like envelopes into which their characters had been slipped, before being posted to this reality. Colin had always been comfortable in his, whereas there had been a mix-up with hers: she'd minded about being overweight, it had been a false start. It wasn't until she'd lost eighty pounds and had two successful businesses to her name that she'd managed to grow out of the low self-esteem.

Here, in this strange new room, she wasn't getting any sleep – the bed was comfortable enough although if she sat on either side her knees practically touched the wall – but it was a relief not to have Colin and Jamie witness her blasted, swollen eyes and her constant policing of the Velvet Rooms. She could take her antibiotics and stare into the depthless vastness of her computer without interruption or fear of judgement. She could be anonymous, awake, ill, obsessive, mad, all in private.

She checked her watch. It was almost a surprise that the darkness allowed her to move through it because it had thickened and coalesced around her, with this ongoing panic which had settled so uneasily in her breast, making it difficult to breathe. She clung to the cheap familiarity of the motel room: the way the hard nylon carpet crept a foot up the sides of the walls, the protruding heads of the screws that fitted the identikit panelled walls and ceilings disguised with plastic nubs, the ultra-light plastic wood fittings. She wondered if her mother could see – from a swing-seat on heaven's porch, she liked to think – how her life had been suddenly gripped by this unreal, electronically induced fear, and what advice she might give.

She wanted more corn chips. She sat up, rising on the crest of a fresh wave of panic, and tugged down her sleeves. The cloth tickled against her raw forearms. She rubbed them back and forth against her sides. The pain was mixed with gratification at answering the intense itch. She stood up off the bed; three sideways steps allowed her the space to turn and sit in the little area before the bathroom, where her laptop waited on a vanity table. She switched on the lights to banish her fear, try and bring some dull, harsh sanity into the room. She slid onto the stool, leaned an elbow on the unfamiliar surface. For a while she dabbed her swollen eyes, looking at them in the mirror. The skin was infected, weeping. She looked like a monster.

She found her comfort zone by tugging towards her the ashtray, lighting a cigarette.

What had happened since her trip to England, really? As she sat smoking, she rehearsed the sequence of events over and over; and as if she were a director making a film she altered the story to see how the logic worked. Her role stayed the same – her character, dialogue and circumstances did not change – but the other actors swapped masks, became terrifying and then benign in turn. The Velvet Roomers were a family of voices buoying up her mission to find out what had happened to Call Girl – and then they dissolved into cyber-darkness, disappearing behind icons, into nothing. She lit another cigarette, sucked it down. A headache started its gentle insistence in her brow. She was going to play Wet Lysette as if she were the cat, Jonathan. She imagined it was a mask she had to wear like in the musical; if she kept this in mind her behaviour – how she wrote the part – would be consistent.

She imagined Thruster approaching her: he reached out and pulled off her mask, saw her face underneath . . . The breath hissed from her body; nerves made her stand, stub out her cigarette. She must have courage.

Wet Lysette enters Velvet Ballroom

Peach: *Hi Wet Lysette. Welcome!*

Top Dick: go on sweetpea I dare you

Wet Lysette: ** hi all *** don't mind me, roomers ### I'll just curl up in this corner

DanceMaster: ~whisper to Wet Lysette~ Well done. I am here if you need me.

Finger-of-fun: Did you know Dell pick up old puters … almost for free …?

Nerdy Uncle: Finger youu'll be fine with that Dell for years

Sweetpea: Hmmmm … you dare me … ok then … saunter over … Nerdy Uncle, I heard you got the biggest cock in the whole Velvet Rooms

Peach: *Wet Lysette I have not met you before. Where do you come from?*

FlyBoy: my laptop ws 2900 frm dell the dvd player screwed up but hey they sent me a new 1, no questions asked

Wet Lysette: ~~smile at Peach ~~ honey I used to come here years ago *** purrr *** had loadsa fun !!???*** just lookin in 2 c how u guys r ???~~#*** mebbe hang round *** c sum old friends **

Nerdy Uncle: Sweetpea no thanks I'm nmot that type repeat not interested. I am dancing with Flyboy and Finger

Top Dick: ~whisper to Sweetpea~ Go onnnnn!!! Don't take no for an answer just grab his cock in ur hands, I dare you

Finger-of-Fun: I donated my old puter tho' to women's shelters, sent it off to someone in need.

Peach: *Great. Wet Lysette welcome back*

Sweetpea: U sure bout that Nerdy Uncle? ~ stroke the front of yr pants with my forefinger ~ looking out for a rise ~ big grin ~ and I got Top Dick's cock in my other hand

DanceMaster: *STERN LOOK* what's going on over there?

FlyBoy: Just ignore Sweetpea Nerdy Uncle. I got my puter hooked up 2 my tv now - use the surround sound on the puter 2 play the audio

Wet Lysette: thanks peach *** wipe whiskers *** purrr ** I'm

happy just waiting here for a bit if that's ok ~~~ grin
~~~

Nerdy Uncle: Sweetpea leave me alone

Sweetpea: - lean forward - put tip of tongue to end of Nerdy Uncle's giant cock - if I do this to both of u, will both of u do it 2 me?

Peach: *Sure wet lysette ~ ☺ just shout if u want 2 know anything* ☺

Nerdy Uncle: hated dell never could get thru, tthats why I changed

Sweetpea: Ahbhhh … so turned on by Nerdy Uncle's dirty talk. say dell again

Spam: My commmputerrs a donnnkey, it's so old and slowww, a righttt donnnkey

Nerdy Uncle: Sweetpea please leave me alone I am asking politely

Sweetpea: I have both ur cocks in my hands and begin to stroke both shafts holding my mouth against one and then the other and hey Nerdy Uncle's is definitely biggest

Top Dick: Hey, great, a threesome

Nerdy Uncle: ~ sigh ~ does anyone want to do Microsoft versus Apple?

Spam: Hoorayyy someone behaving badleeeee

Nerdy Uncle: it's not funny I'm trying to have a conversation. Dance Master?

Big Black Woman: I wouldn't touch that thing if I were you honey

Sweetpea: Nerdy Uncle I wipe tons of saliva around your glans … gently move hand on ur shaft, hold tip against my open wet mouth

Nerdy Uncle: Guys … stop it

DanceMaster: *VERY STERN LOOK* off 2 the Velvet Shore Sweetpea and Top Dick

Nerdy Uncle: I was told when I paid my FULL LIFE MEMBERSHIP that this sought of thing was confined to the Velvet Shores

Sweetpea: - take Nerdy Uncle's shaft in mouth - can't talk -work mouth on2 shaft - hardly fit it all in -

Top Dick: Sweetpea, don't forget me, work my cock as well baby

Sweetpea: can't help myself - slide wet hand up and down on shaft - sink wide open mouth on glans of Nerdy Uncle's giant cock

Nerdy Uncle: Hey!!

DanceMaster: *VERY STERN LOOK* sweetpea go to the Shore

Big Black Woman: rather u than me honey, I ain't no nodding dog

Sweetpea: - bury your cock in my mouth - gasp - cup your balls in my hand - pump your shaft with my hand

Big Black Woman: OH MY WORD

Nerdy Uncle: Can we get back to talking about Dell puters soon?

DanceMaster: Where is our bouncer? Biker Idiot, are you there?

Fat-armed Wife blew her nose, then held still. There was the sound of a car pulling into the motel. Another customer. Drunk, she guessed, from the squawk of the gearbox as whoever it was tried to park. She lit another cigarette and pulled the ashtray an inch closer. This was her comfort, over and over. She watched her hand shake, then a shiver ran along her nerves and she had to roll around the room. She paused for a while at the door, listening. She walked some more, trying to compose herself. She sat down and called WPC Townsend, who wasn't there; it wasn't her shift. She left a message. As she finished, she realised the footsteps were close to her room.

A moment later the noise of the TV became louder next door and she lost track of the footsteps. Then came a knock at her door. Someone . . . for one minute she got it in her head that it would be Call Girl but she opened the door to find Colin in his habitual pose: fingers tucked into his jeans pockets, slumped on one leg. She left the door open and went and sat on the bed.

Colin stepped into the room and closed the door behind him. He lifted a thumb and forefinger, pinched the end of his nose, then quickly cleaned out one nostril in a well-practised turn. 'When are you coming home?'

'Not yet.'

'Christ, you're in some state these days. What's happening?'

'Nothing.'

'Come on.'

'No, it's nothing.'

'What is it? Work?'

'No.'

'So what's up?'

'Not sure. Just seems cold outside, real cold, you know, heartless place.'

'Oh, so this is a general state-of-the-world type of thing.'

'I guess.'

'You're depressed.'

She shrugged. 'Maybe.'

'Why d'you think it's a heartless place? There's plenty of folk doing all they can for everyone. Look at you, for one.'

'I know, but sometimes . . .' Fat-armed Wife swept the tears from her cheeks. 'It's unfair. There's a whole load of cruelty out there, and coldness and . . .'

'Well, you know what they say: all it takes for evil to triumph is good people doing nothing about it.'

'I know.'

'You been watching too much TV.'

'No.'

'What brought this on, then?'

'Nothing . . . much.' Her body heaved, sobs burst out even as she tried to swallow them, she sank back on the bed and covered her sore face with her hands; she had to get rid of the cigarette or she'd set her hair alight again; she chucked it into the ashtray.

'Hey, hey.' Colin came further into this foreign territory and sloped over to her side. 'Come on, tell me. What is it, honey? Hmmm? What is it?'

She shook her head. 'Nothing, just . . . general feeling of the . . .

the world turning, you know, so many people, so far away . . . and life cruel . . .'

'Not all of it's cruel. There's a load of us out here having kindness and love and—'

'I know, I know.' She couldn't tell him.

'OK?'

'Will be.' She sniffed, and dug in her sleeve for the tissue. She blew her nose. She wondered if the people in the next-door rooms were listening.

Colin suddenly leaned away and looked at her as if she'd said something odd. He nudged forward, and then said with certainty, 'You're seeing someone else.'

A laugh escaped her; she could look him in the eye because it was much worse than that. She had a whole secret life, not anything as simple as an affair, she wanted to shout in his face, a whole spare fucking life! In the Velvet Rooms, somewhere he didn't even know existed. She'd tried to run away but it had sucked her back, charged her with this Herculean task of finding Call Girl among the billions of electronic signals each second.

Colin's slab of a face broke into a smile to match her laughter. 'What, then? Twice this week you've gone mad for no reason. Now you've . . . kind of removed yourself, and I'm sure as hell not clever enough to see why. You might as well tell me straight out it's the early menopause and I'll have my balls cut off and throw Jamie out into the snow and we can become old people and die.'

'Colin, Colin.' She pushed him, like they were kids in a playground.

'What?' He pushed her back.

She shoved him harder. 'You're my husband, you dope. I'm not having an early menopause. I'm not having an affair. I'm just having a bit of an anxiety crisis, OK?' She picked up her cigarette.

'Can I go home and watch the game highlights while you're having your crisis?'

''Course, go ahead.'

'Come with me.'

'No.'

'Come home.'

She felt all her heart strings loosen. 'I can't.'

His hand was like a soft crab as it lifted suddenly to touch his chest, then drag at his beard, then it went to her shoulder. He gave her one last rub on the back and left. The security light sensed his heat and switched on, showing him all spare and slow and unwanted, as he went to the car.

DanceMaster enters Velvet Sanctuary

Spam enters Velvet Sanctuary

Jetman enters Velvet Sanctuary

Honeycake enters Velvet Sanctuary

Big Black Woman enters Velvet Sanctuary

Sweetpea enters Velvet Sanctuary

Wet-stretched-t-shirt enters Velvet Sanctuary

Peach enters Velvet Sanctuary

Fat-armed Wife enters Velvet Sanctuary

Fat-armed Wife: thanks for coming everyone

Big Black Woman: You with your sisters. Say it out loud.

Fat-armed Wife: All of you, need all to know, now - what's going on. I must ask for your help - shall I just splurge?

Honeycake: Have no fear darling. Splurge all u want

Fat-armed Wife: We have this question, where, who, what is Thruster -

and Jetman had the idea of creating another Call Girl, someone similar, to tempt him – nod and thanks to Jetman – so DanceMaster agreed and fellow Roomers he gave me a new icon, something Thruster would go for, so I became like a lure - a honeytrap - I became Wet Lysette

Spam: fatarms - Wet Lysette ??? !!! that is you???!!!

Fat-armed Wife: Yes - tried to make her similar to Call Girl - trailer trash type of gurrlie, torn white dress, damaged goods - so I would tempt Thruster I thought, and I kept it secret from you all because I thought it would be easy for one of you to give it away

Peach: *Oh ... worried ... I am scared*

Spam: Sorrry I crept up on Wet Lysette didn't I .. .that was yuuuu!!???
Blushhhhh ….

Fat-armed Wife: Don't worry Spam, sorry I didn't answer, but … so you know now I have been waiting, as Wet Lysette, just waiting for Thruster - it is like going fishing - yes I am the lure - but nothing, haven't found him.Have to sleep sometimes., so please can you all spend more time in the Velvet Rooms - and call me - like you do already - just the same but more. Especially other time zones. If Thruster is in Velvet Rooms call or text or email or Skype or IM exchange, whatever, tell me. And be nice to him. Keep him writing back.

Thruster enters Velvet Ballroom

Pluto: Mainly progressive rock

Thruster: Hi everyone

FlyBoy: So you kinda like to think a bit when you listen to music

DanceMaster: Hi Thruster

Peach: *Thruster I wave to you from the dance floor - doing a foxtrot - Psycho-dog and me panting and red in the face! How you doing?*

Pluto: Sure.

Thruster: any1 want to dandce?

DanceMaster: ~stops the music~ All change partners please

Wet Lysette enters Velvet Ballroom

Spam: Thrusterrr! ~yunnng man's embrace~ welcome. Fasssst and furrrriusss in the Velvet Ballroomm

FlyBoy: I want to keep dancing with Pluto, we're talking music n stuff

Thruster: anyone dance with me?

Psycho-dog: Lurved dancing with you Fatarms thank you ~pant pant ~ back to my bar now ~ bark

Thruster: *~whisper to Wet Lysette~* Hi u gotta nice icon

DanceMaster: Flyboy carry on with Pluto

Peach: *Likewise Psycho-dog. Thruster, u want 2 dance with me?* ☺

DanceMaster: I will dance with you Thruster

Wet Lysette: *~whisper to Thruster~* Thanxx ~ grin ~ like it myself

Thruster: hey I luv it whnen girls fight over me

DanceMaster: Hmmmm how do we sort this out now?

Peach: *I will dance with him DanceMaster*

DanceMaster: Thruster you ok with Peach?

Thruster: *~whisper to Wet Lysette~* You wanna play?

FlyBoy: Pluto you got broadband?

Peach: *Thruster ~stroll 2 u ~ don't tease me. Where r u in real life?*

Thruster: takeing luvly Peach in my arms ~ I am at work

Wet Lysette: *~whisper to Thruster~* Hnnn ... stretch ... yawn ... play??

Peach: *ahhh ... step in2 yr embrace ~ hi handsome* ☺

Pluto: yeah, got the aol package for my sins

206

Psycho-dog: drinks anyone ?? wag of tail

Thruster: Peach u look peachy urself grin and whre r u?

DanceMaster: Big Black Woman will u dance?

Thruster: *~whisper to Wet Lysette~* go 2 the Shore where I will fuck u like uve never been fucked b4

Peach: *At my factory*

FlyBoy: Yeah man! Clogging up the net bastards

Big Black Woman: DanceMaster dis an unexpected hona

Wet Lysette: *~whisper to Thruster~* *** I like a man who knows where he's going ~purr~ ***

Thruster: Peach the 1 yr family own?

DanceMaster: the pleasure is all mine. A woman as light on her feet as you

Peach: *yes*

Thruster: *~whisper to Wet Lysette~* Go to the shore … push .. grab your hair and pull

Big Black Woman: heh heh heh - ur no mean foot-shuffler yeself

Thruster: and what r u meant to b doing if u weren't dancing w me, wats ur job exactly?

Pluto: and I hate all the bright colours on aol home

Wet Lysette: *~whisper to Thruster~* Hmmmm **** fast worker ~~~ huh?!! ### sigh %$£^ ~ wink??!! ~vbs~~

DanceMaster: we haven't danced in a lonnnng while

Peach: *I translate into English all orders and invoices and letters*

Thruster: *~whisper to Wet Lysette~* Go ther now

FlyBoy: sounds like you ought 2 cancel your subscription

Wet Lysette: *~gone~poof!~*

Pluto: tried to cancel - tried like mad - but can you heck

Flyboy: Call to put in a new order and they answer on the first ring. Call to try 'n cancel and it takes hours and hours

Thruster: *~gone~poof!~*

Wet Lysette enters Velvet Shore

Thruster enters Velvet Shore

Thruster: hey that's better no traffic

Wet Lysette: *** ~ smile ~

Thruster: Never been in here be4

Wet Lysette: ** huh ** !!??? ** NO?? ***

Thruster: No one ever invited me

Wet Lysette: **8 !! surprised ^ ^ ^ you're a handsum guy

Thruster: u like a handsome guy?

Wet Lysette: ~~** no actually ~~ purrrr ** handsome guys r 4 beginners *** I like it real 'n ugly ^ ^ ^

Thruster: You play?

Wet Lysette: ** I kinda have my scene, u know??! **~~wink~~** but it might b a bit tough 4 u

Thruster: What du play then?

Wet Lysette: ** depends what you mean by play hmmm? *** smile **

Thruster: what u into?

Wet Lysette: I don't need to bother you with what im into ~~grin~~

Thruster: you can bother me

208

Wet Lysette: thanks ~sigh~ lie back on cushions ~ mebbe one day huh??****** when I know u 4 real *** purrrr

Thruster: cum here and I tell you what I want

Wet Lysette: no offence but that's all play acting *** Huhh???~~ and I like my men 4 real

Thruster: cum here

Wet Lysette: ** smile ** u got the right idea ~~ not take no for an answer ~~~ grin ~~ what d'yu look like?!!** 4 real???

Thruster: I'm six one, rugby player type

Wet Lysettte: ~smiles~ nice, like a good-sized man

Thruster: U?

Wet Lysette: *** hhmmmm ** purrr *** 4 real I am five six, brown hair curly to the shoulders, not slim. 34DD !!!??? ***

Thruster: like the sound of those ds.

Wet Lysette: *** sigh *** like the sound of u *** !!!?? bvt now tell me what you really look like??? ~~Grin~~

Thruster: I said what I look like

Wet Lysette: *** & the next thing is you ask for me to come closer - hmnmm - that true? ~smile~

Thruster: less talk from u. Cum here

Wet Lysette: *** 'n tell me what u want ??? what u like *** ??????

Thruster: want 2 take u 2 the edge and then push u over

Wet Lysette: *** purrrr *** clean whiskers *** hmmmm *** WELL *** in that case I can play - more than u might think - don't choose my icon just for fun *** VBS ***

Thruster: I like ur icon

Wet Lysette: ~~ I like that you like it ~~

Thruster: cum here

Wet Lysette: ~take step towards you~ here I am then

Thruster: closer

Wet Lysette: ~slight parting of the lips~ this close enough?

Thruster: ~winding my hand in your hari~ for now

Wet Lysette: *** tilt head up, look into your eyes - u don't have to be good-looking in fact I prefer ugly men in real life ~~smile~~ r u? ***

Thruster: yes, ugly

Wet Lysette: But strong - hmm? - touch your hand in my hair - or not? *** smile***

Thruster: I am strong

Wet Lysette: *** In real life tho - serious look - ??/ ***

Thruster: yesin real lifke, I am strong

Wet Lysette: Need to know how strong u r in real life - slight shift away, hand on your chest ~~ grin ~~~

Thruster: bench press 180, straight lift 240 pounds ~pull you closer~ brick shithouse territory, me.

Wet Lysette: *** hey ~~ u got a photograph you can post? ~~grin~~**

Thruster: no

Wet Lysette: *** y not? *** coy smile ** u can see mine on members board

Thruster: Open yuur moruth

Wet Lysette: want picture of u first - parting lips - please

Thruster: look at me ~screwing your head back, my hand on your throat~

Wet Lysette: ** hey *** du get it ** that's my play *** purrrr

*** its gotta b real *** I've grown outta fantasy ** What's ur name, what do you do for a job?

Thruster: put my thumb to your mouth - push it in

Wet Lysette: *** hnnn **++I take your thumb into my mouth, suck it ~ soft smile into ur eyes~

Thruster: you want to know my name

Wet Lysette: **** hnnn ** want this 4 real *** that's my play *** tell ur name and where u r ~ soft smile ~~

Thruster: *~gone~poof!~*

Wet Lysette:

Wet Lysette:

Wet Lysette: *~whisper to DanceMaster~* He's gone, lost him

DanceMaster: *~whisper to Wet Lysette~* come and tell me

Wet Lysette *~gone~poof!~*

Fat-armed Wife was shaking. Her hands sweated. He'd been that close – at her fingertips – and she'd panicked; she'd been too obvious, too easy?

Minutes later, after two more cigarettes and having called DanceMaster, she went back in again. Then she thought that if she found him it might look desperate, like she was chasing him, so she closed down the computer and told herself to give it a day or two, play a bit more hard to get.

When she stood, there she was in the motel bedroom mirror. Her eyes were responding to treatment; she didn't look so much as if she'd been in a fight. She was losing weight.

She lay on the bed, thinking. It felt odd to be so utterly safe, alone in a motel in Massachusetts, when in another sense she felt as if she were facing terrible danger. She closed her eyes and commanded herself to relax. In the blackness behind her eyelids she went back over what had happened. He had come at her. She had fumbled, lost her confidence. He'd invited her to the Shore and she'd accepted too easily. In the Shore it had begun to work; away from other traffic she could play the game better. But had she pushed too hard for his name? She hoped and prayed that he'd come back for more. She wanted to shout to Call Girl, Coming to get you!

She summoned her gallery of photographs of him and pored over them. She listened for his voice, saw the green italic writing in the sky. The countless dots were sprinkled between words like fairy dust. He flew towards her, all mischief. If they were to fall in love for real and marry, he'd said, she'd have to whisper fantasies in his ear, beat him up and work him with tools as if he were a broken-down old boiler. All right, she'd agreed.

As she skidded on the shallowest surface of sleep she saw his face close up – the kindness and the fun but the casual, greedy callousness also, the admission and enjoyment of what he was and the insistence that as many other people as possible enjoy that. The face grinned mischievously, small black eyes alive in a thin, acne-scarred face, a knotted, energetic body covered in garish tattoos and dressed whether as man or woman. She smiled and a conversation started – the love thing fed on the words that batted back and forth between them and grew an inch larger, before she reached out, in the flood of jest and joust, to lay a hand against his cheek but instead it dipped in water, she felt the chill wet shock and saw with dismay the face instantly dissolve into ripples, a patch of light and shadow. The breath lunged in her, it was panic, she woke again.

The motel room came back, arranged itself around her. But nothing held it down, none of it was real; the terror of depthless space and meaninglessness sent her rolling around behind her squeezed-shut eyes like a drunk, calling for something or someone to hold onto so that she might find herself.

Wet Lysette enters Velvet Ballroom

FlyBoy: urgghhh hate all the ads and boxes and all that shit just want my porn straight up

Wet Lysette: *** hi y'all!! **

Big Black Woman: Hi Wet Lysette

Psycho-dog: *** bark!! ** Anyone requires refreshments? ~ behind the bar polishing glasses~ pant pant

DanceMaster: Take my hand BBW. Ready everyone? The music is Albéniz. The suite *España*

Pluto: yeah death to all ads and pop-ups and spam fucking death to all of it. Leave us alone you fuckers just give us girls girls girls I don't need all this Viagra and cock-busting machinery

Thruster: *~ whisper to Wet Lysette~* I was waiting 4 u. Come to Shore

Wet Lysette: *~gone~poof!~*

Wet Lysette enters Velvet Shore

Wet Lysette: *** WELL WELL WELL *** smile *** hello stranger

Thruster: Im a member now

Wet Lysette: *** so I see, if ur using the Shore u must b ** purrrr

Thruster: Yes

Wet Lysette: Congratulations - welcome ~~smile~~

Thruster: Cum here

Wet Lysette: ***Not this again??/!!!***

Thruster: cum here

Wet Lysette: *** extend claws *** miaooowww *** NO!!!

Thruster: ~ grab your hair, pull you

Wet Lysette: No u dont

Thruster: what d'you mean?

Wet Lysette: don't like wanking ... doesn't work anymore ... yawn ... has to b real sex 4 it to work *** SIGH *** wish it wernt true but ... !!!??? some of us girls like our fantasies 4 real

Thruster: R u 4 real?

Wet Lysette: can u phone me?

Thruster: what is ur game? don't fucke with me

Wet Lysettte: Guys who answer my needs ar ehard to find *** wink ***

Thruster: I'll fuck u to death

Wet Lysette: *** ahhhh ** if only *** vbs ~~shift slightly ~ smile ~ most guys run a mile when its real

Thruster: I never run

Wet Lysette: post a photo now then ~smile~ call me, huh ??? you got a wife ??? can u travel???

Thruster: no photo no names no call

Wet Lysette: yawn ~ stretch back on cushions ~ purrrrr ~ open my legs a bit so u c my stockings ~ I am the best fuck ~~ grin ~~

Thruster: u 4 real?

Wet Lysette: ~groan~ yes ~ *** Goddd. are you ugly? hope so ~ stretch ~ purrrr

Thruster: open ur mouth

Wet Lysette: *** NO *** wink ***

Wet Lysette: *~gone~poof!~*

Thruster:

214

Thruster:

Thruster: *~ gone ~ poof!~*

Thruster stood in front of the glass wall, used it as a vague mirror. He fetched the can of foam and the razor, and shaved his chest. As the blade circled one nipple he pulled it, affectionately called it Jetman. He crooned sweet nothings – his smile broke into a laugh. It was like washing a baby's head. When he came to the left nipple he named it Thruster and soothed that one as well. He drew the blade round each equally carefully. When he'd finished, both Jetman and Thruster were clean and hairless and weighted with muscle; his torso was creamy, glowing, the skin toughened with white spirit.

He switched the music on loud and stripped for a weights session. Thruster and Jetman, both characters were contained in this one body. He had sixteen pounds in each hand. As he lifted the right one he hissed, 'Thruster'; as the left came up he grunted, 'Jetman'. He said the names over and over; it built up a rhythm, a purpose: Thruster, right, Jetman, left . . . He went faster, kept going.

Then he slumped. He waited until the sweat had oozed from him. He was virtually motionless. Images hung in his head: the cars he'd had. The Renault at the bottom of the quarry. The lists he'd made, all neatly filed.

He fetched the square green plastic box which contained his first-aid kit, unclipped its fancifully designed lid and picked out the roll of sticking plaster. He cut two strips, then pushed the box aside to give himself space. At first he tried a Biro but the ink transferred only weakly onto the skin-coloured surface. A minute's rummaging in the drawer brought him a permanent marker; he hoped it still worked. He took one strip of plaster and tried to smooth out the kink but as soon as his fingers lifted, it humped unhelpfully. He bent it back the other way, rolled it firmly until it lay flat. He took the permanent marker and wrote 'Thruster', filling the strip from left to right and top to bottom. Then he unstuck the backing and positioned it above the Mac's screen, in the centre of the plastic housing. He pressed down firmly and it sat there, a sign.

Next he took the second piece of plaster and went through the same ritual of flattening, smoothing. He took the permanent marker and wrote 'Jetman' across its full width and height. He popped the laptop open and stuck the plaster in the same position, above the screen, in the middle, on the plastic housing. He tested whether the lid would shut; it did; he could push through the soft resistance until he heard the click. He opened it again, moved its thin, hard, intelligent body to line up with the keyboard of the Mac. Both computers were labelled: this would minimise any chance of an error. He could play both at the same time without losing track.

Wet Lysette enters Velvet Ballroom

Spam: So then yuuu got someone new to annoy

Wet Lysette: *** Hi y'all ***

DanceMaster: *~whisper to Wet Lysette~* WARNING He's in the Dungeon

Filthy UK: see it's good isn't it? *WEG*

Tease: ~laughing at Filthy~ wellllllllll, yes, it is, have fun ha ha ~s~ hi wet lysette

Wet Lysette: *~whisper to DanceMaster~* ALONE ??

Jetman enters Velvet Ballroom

Peach enters Velvet Ballroom

Sweetpea: Hi Wet Lysette welcome

DanceMaster*: ~whisper to Wet Lysette~* Yes in the Dungeon alone

Spam: Hi Fatarms.

216

Wet Lysette: *~whisper to Spam~* careful!!!??? you posted hi fatarms - I am Wet Lysette

Spam: *~whisper to Wet Lysette~* Chrissttttt ~ thump fist against own head ~ sorrrrrry

Tease: Hi Hi Hi Hi Hi

Spam: Grrrrrrrr!! ~staring wild eyed at screeen~ grrrrr!!!!

Filthy UK ~giggling at Spam~ it's no bad thing to be polite, what else canya say?

Tease: Hmmmm, what about saying … fukc you!! Is that better than hello? ~laugh~

Filthy UK: Heyyy, you saying fcuk yu to little mee?? ~lol~

Jetman: Hi all

Peach: *Hi Velvet Roomers*

Wet Lysette: *~whisper to DanceMaster~* He's waiting for me

FilthyUK: Hey, Peach and Jetman, congratulations

DanceMaster: *~whisper to Wet Lysette~* I think so yes

Peach: *~smiles shyly~ thanks*

Thruster: *~whisper to Wet Lysette~* You want a real face a rfeal name a real cock to fuck u cum in here … guess wehre

Tease: congrats 4 wot?

Wet Lysette: *~whisper to Thruster~* *** U what?!! Hello by the way *** purrrr **** always believe in good manners

Peach: *Jetman and I are going out, aren't we sweetheart?*

Thruster: *~whisper to Wet Lysette~* fuck good manners cum to the Dungeon if u want t a real face and a real name and a real stranger 2 fuck u . cum in here u know what its for u know the Dungeon rules THIS IS 4 REAL

Wet Lysette: *~whisper to DanceMaster~* He wants me to go in

Tease: ok, congratulations, right on man

Wet Lysette: *~whisper to Thruster~* *** 4 real huh? *** don't tease me now *** a girl likes to know where she stands *** serious look ***

Jetman: we are sweethearts, troubled times broght us together

Fat-armed Wife: *~whisper to Jetman~* Your idea is working. Right now.

DanceMaster: *~whisper to Wet Lysette~* Don't go in, not yet. Let us think about this. He has jumped ahead of us.

Spam: Arrrrrr luvverrly

Jetman: *~whisper to Fat-armed Wife~* hey. Great. Well done.

Peach: *we are not lovers yet but just dating, until we get to know each other better.*

Thruster: *~whisper to Wet Lysette~* Come to dungeon right now or offer closes

Peach: *And everyone is swooning at sight of my Jetman?!!! ~falling into the arms of my handsome guy~ Jetman, sweetheart!? ~sigh~ so good to feel your strong arms around me*

Jetman: my honey~holding Peachy tight~

Wet Lysette: *~whisper to Thruster~* this is 4 real 4 real?

Peach: *~whisper to Wet Lysette~ see you're there Fatarms and we send all our love ~anxious ~ you be safe ~ good luck ~ kiss~*

Thruster: *~whisper to Wet Lysette~* u r the 1 who wanted it real so I am going to give it 2 u real so cum right now if u have the guts to fuck a stranger 4 real

Wet Lysette: *~whispers to Peach~* thanks Peach … and to Jetman

Peach: *~whisper to Wet Lysette~ yes ~smiles~ he's a good soldier huh?*

Wet Lysette: *~whisper to Thruster~* *** the guts, huh? $$%*{@WELL …. ~ mayb now we're talking ~~

Wet Lysette: *~whisper to DanceMaster~* what shall I do

DanceMaster: *~whisper to Wet Lysette~* Just make a deal in there.

can u handle it? Means u will have photo or name or meeting place

Spam: run my finger frommm the corrnerrrr of your gorgeous lips down your long neck to restte my lippps there at the base of yourr lovely neccke and cupp one fulll breast warrmm inn my hand ... ahhhh ... u r the best

Wet Lysette: *~whisper to Thruster~* *** coming in *** u better b good 4 this @@ ^ &% no time wasters ~

Liks2suckonU: come on, handsome Spam, stop showing off

Spam: sorrry ~picking uppp SuckonU from the floor~ cumm onnn hunny bunnnnny

Liks2suckonU: *~whisper to Spam~* Lets go to the shore, hmmnnn ???

Spam: *~whisper to Liks2suckonU~* Hold onnnn, sweetheart gurrrlie, gotta keepp my eyee onnn something here ~light spanke~

Thruster: *~whispers to Wet Lysette~* what u waiting 4? is the dungeon too scary 4 u?

Liks2suckonU: *~whisper to Spam~* whadddya mean ~groan~ u know when u toufche my necke that's just something that's gotta carrry on

Wet Lysette: *~whisper to Thruster~* *** no. like to be a bit scared ~~~ ***

Spam: *~whisper to Liks2suckonU~* Seriuss now ~heavy smackkk!~ go make an omelette

Thruster: *~whisper to Wet Lysette~* ur not brave enough after all

DanceMaster: *~whisper to Wet Lysette~* Get photo, name, number, addie

Thruster: *~whisper to Wet Lysette~* It's now or never

Wet Lysette: *~gone~poof!~*

Wet Lysette enters Velvet Dungeon

Wet Lysette: *** I am serious***

Thruster: In Brussels, the President Nord Hotel, room 19, the 23rd of November

Wet Lysette: *** you are quick off the mark ???? need photo first***

Thruster: you heard. This is ur so called Velvet Dungon. You b in that room on that night @ 8.30 pm.

Wet Lysette: *** I'm in NYC not possible ~ ***

Thruster: I don't care where u r

Wet Lysette: ** ~ it has to be America those are the rules~ ***

Thruster: I make the rules. Write it down the President Nord Hotel Brussels, Boulevard Adolphe Max 107, 1000 Brussels, 23 November 8.30 pm, room 19. You are behind that door when I open it

Wet Lysette: ~~post photograph ??? what's your name? *** what kind of address is that?~~

Thruster: a Brussels address

Wet Lysette: It has to be America

Thruster: Good bye

Wet Lysette: I can't afford to go all that way

Thruster: u can

Wet Lysette: That's not fair

Thruster: u want this more than me

Wet Lysette: America

Thruster: No

Wet Lysette: Yes

Thruster: NO.

Wet Lysette: Send me a pic of you

Thruster: no

Wet Lysette: what name is the room under?

Thruster: Room 19 is the name of the room

Wet Lysette: Send me a photograph and then it's only maybe

Thruster: The President Nord Hotel Brussels Boulevard Adolphe Max 107 1000 Brussels 23 November 8.30 pm, room 19.

Thruster: *~post~*

Thruster: *~gone~poof!~*

Wet Lysette:

Wet Lysette:

Wet Lysette: *~whisper to DanceMaster~* He's gone. I've got to post or not

DanceMaster: *~whisper to Wet Lysette~* Did you get picture or name?

Wet Lysette: *~post~*

~Velvet Dungeon swings shut ~ keys grind and turn ~ clunk!~ locked shut~

F at-armed Wife stood, swaying. Thruster had snapped, bitten hard, only just under the surface of cyberspace. He was about to burst through. He'd squared up to her so quickly it had taken her breath away.

She transferred the details to the note pages at the back of the Filofax. A real time, a real place, an unknown person. Far away.

She spoke to DanceMaster, Psycho-dog and Honeycake on the phone.

Hours later she rose and went to her bag and pulled out her diary. She leafed through it. November 23 was a Friday, a half-moon.

Three hundred and twenty-four days of the year would have gone, forty-two would be left. Christopher Columbus discovered Puerto Rico on this day in 1493.

Tears ran freely down her cheeks. She smeared them into her Max Factor with the back of her hand. She took a pencil and on the line at the bottom wrote '8.30 p.m.' in neat letters. Then, on the same page, with feathery touches of her pencil, there appeared a tousle-haired girl in a torn white dress crawling away from an unseen attacker, her bust exposed, her mouth an O of fright.

DanceMaster enters Velvet Sanctuary

Spam enters Velvet Sanctuary

Honeycake enters Velvet Sanctuary

Big Black Woman enters Velvet Sanctuary

Psycho-dog enters Velvet Sanctuary

Wet-stretched-t-shirt enters Velvet Sanctuary

Peach enters Velvet Sanctuary

Fat-armed Wife enters Velvet Sanctuary

DanceMaster: lock the door

Peach: *Can Jetman come in?*

~door locked~

Fat-armed Wife: thanks everyone for coming

Peach: *Fat-armed Wife can Jetman be here? Don't mind if you say no*

Peach: **~whisper to Jetman~** *come and join us*

~door unlocked~

Fat-armed Wife: Yes of course he can come in if he wants, we are only here because of him, it was his idea

Peach: *sorry*

Jetman enters Velvet Sanctuary

~door locked~

Fat-armed Wife: thank you Velvet Roomers for coming

Fat-armed Wife: The news is that he nibbled - and nibbled again - and now he has bitten hard

Spam: Saw you go into the Dungeon

Peach: *I don't like this.* ☹

Honeycake: what happened?

Fat-armed Wife: yes went to Dungeon

Big Black Woman: that is a big bite to chew on

Peach: *I am frightened and don't like it*

Wet-stretched-t-shirt: did u post a deal?

Fat-armed Wife: yes

Honeycake: Oh oh

Spam: Where, when is it?

Fat-armed Wife: President Nord Hotel, Boulevard Adolphe Max 107, 1000 Brussels, Europe, 23 November, 8.30 in the evening

Spam: Brussellllllsssss???

Big Black Woman: We can call the cops now, we need the full team, we need armaments and two way radios

Fat-armed Wife: Exactly I called the UK police and they will be there

Honeycake: this is incredible

Spam: Thruster is on the hook and dos not know it??!!!

Honeycake: ~ arm around Fatarms ~ way to go, sister ~ squeeze ~ we're with you all the way.

Fat-armed Wife: But you guys are my ears and eyes. Tell me everything you see and hear. Everything. I will co-ordinate

Peach: *Is this 4 real, u r not joking?*

Fat-armed Wife: Peach 4 real we have him. We will find Call Girl.

Thruster booked a hotel room in Isestrasse, Hamburg, for 18 to 23 November. He checked his new email account: disclosure67@hotmail.com. He downloaded the site map of Zaventem, the Brussels airport, and studied the layout of Terminal B. He printed the list of incoming flights and checked the arrival times from America, whatever the airline, whichever city.

He broke for lunch and drew towards him the foil-wrapped package, still warm. He unfolded it carefully to avoid spillage. The aroma of lamb shank suddenly escaped. His mouth flooded with saliva. In the package were the leftovers of four portions of other men's food – a jumbled collection of bones, clean and dry at one end, the remaining hunks of meat gathered conveniently at the other. It was one of the reasons he liked lamb shank. It felt like a club when you picked it up, and he took a carnivorous satisfaction in eating with his hands. There was still plenty of meat on these – when soldiers were drunk they ate carelessly and more was left. He picked up each bone in turn and gnawed until all meat and gristle was gone. He folded the silver paper over and over, until it was a small square. Then he squashed it, rolled it between his hands to turn it into a dense, silver ball before aiming it at the waste-bin: it went in with a pleasing thunk.

During the afternoon he drew up a map of future events, marking out the boundaries of cause and effect, of things that might or might not happen. In the green boxes he wrote the actions of others; in the red boxes he answered with his tasks, his reactions.

When this was done he found his camera and emptied its memory, checked it was functioning correctly. His pleasure would be merely to photograph and store whatever happened. His favourite was a picture of himself standing with his hands pushed in his coat pockets, the police tape at his waist, anonymous but at the very front of the mass, worldwide audience for his crimes.

The camera was empty, ready for the airport. Envelope 14 would be bulging. Never before had he enjoyed the luxury of giving himself away, of in effect being caught – and to record it happening, close up, because it was all virtual, unreal – and so here he was, free to go about his work, see the police summoned from England, paint the psoriasis across Fat-arms's eyes and up her arms, send the Velvet Rooms into panic . . .

None the less he was anxious. It was this kind of obsessive psychotic behaviour that would lead to his future arrest. The thought of it – the boot raised to his front door, the swarm of police and press, his wrists cuffed behind his back – rose to the back of his throat, nudged his reflexes.

Call Girl enters Velvet Ballroom

Call Girl: *it's ok everhyone*

Fat-armed Wife: Call Girl

Call Girl: *we had lamb shank. I was given the left-overws but it was enoujgh*

Fat-armed Wife: tell me the name of your niece with spina bifida

Call Girl: *Don't worry it is better now for me. I am on the mend. Tracey is her name by the way*

Fat-armed Wife: what's her nickname? tell me her nickname - forgive me - I have to know this is you for real

Call Girl: *Thrusters ok. Hes fed me and clothed me. Don't worry any more*

Fat-armed Wife: what was your name for me - tell me that - Call Girl??? Your pet name for me?

Call Girl: *he was justg a bit harsh to begin with*

Fat-armed Wife: you are not Call Girl - what have you done with Call Girl?

Call Girl: *We have become lovers Thruster and me*

Fat-armed Wife: just tell us, how did you get Call Girl's password? what have you done with Call Girl?

Call Girl: *tell everyone it's ok. I'm happy*

Fat-armed Wife: please have mercy - show kindness to us. How did you get Call Girl's password? Where is Call Girl?

Call Girl: *~gone~poof!~*

Fat-armed Wife:

Fat-armed Wife:

DanceMaster enters Velvet Sanctuary

Spam enters Velvet Sanctuary

Honeycake enters Velvet Sanctuary

Big Black Woman enters Velvet Sanctuary

Psycho-dog enters Velvet Sanctuary

Peach enters Velvet Sanctuary

Fat-armed Wife enters Velvet Sanctuary

Jetman enters Velvet Sanctuary

Fat-armed Wife: Roomers re 23 yes - the case is transferred to jurisdiction of Europol which is international body co-ordinating all European police forces

Honeycake: they will help?

Fat-armed Wife: Yes and I am sure now it isn't Call Girl but someone using her password - the music is all wrong, and whoever it is can't answer the questions. it is not Call Girl and never was. In grief, in mourning, because where is he?

Big Black Woman: honey I AGREE that puts us right back on the starting block don't it

DanceMaster: FAW, there is a small chance this is all some big game and Thruster and Call Girl are the same person?

Fat-armed Wife: No never - could never be. Four years? We knew him, DM

DanceMaster: We have the police, we have the trap, we will find out.

Fat-armed Wife: but - all us girls - can we still try and entertain Thruster? If he hits on you can we all try and get a name or where he lives or what his job is or a picture - anything that will help - don't give him any letup - the more stuff the better

Honeycake: He hit on me once … urgh … ran away … but I can go back 'n pick him up, I'll try

Fat-armed Wife: I will carry on as Wet Lysette - but shaking badly sometimes now - not sure I can keep from breakdown

Spam: Ladies good luck don't let pannic or nerves skeww ur deft tuch, … plenty of jiggery pokery and not too many questions?? Get him drunnk on sexy scenes

DanceMaster: Fatarms is it best if you carry on with police or should I?

Fat-armed Wife: I will

DanceMaster: I have emails for everyone unless anyone's changed addie? Except you Jetman, I haven't got your e

Jetman: disclosure67@hotmail.com

Peach: *I dont like this. Is it for real?*

Fat-armed Wife: sorry Peachy … yes

Jetman: Peachy, I'm here, I'm your soldier

Peach: *Hang off Jetman's neck*

Fat-armed Wife: I want to tell Thruster face to face: see, we are more clever, more brave, more everything than you

Jetman: salute Fat armed wfie

Fat-armed Wife: But I am very scared. That is not Call Girl, I am sure now it is not. So where is he? Thruster knows. Thruster has his password

DanceMaster: There have been three relationships and one marriage from Velvet Rooms in six years but this is the first manhunt

Spam: strange goings on indeeed, my fellow adventrureerrrs.

Honeycake: Peach no one can hurt us over the wires, no one can reach us, touch us, not 4 real - and when it is real on the 23 the police will b there, tell us who is Thruster, and what happened

Spam: Fingers and toes crossed, fellow Roomers. Gather round.

DanceMaster: My darling Fatarms, I can see you shaking. I can see you lighting cigarettes

Fat-armed Wife: No, eating them

Spam enters Velvet Sanctuary

Fat-armed Wife enters Velvet Sanctuary

Fat-armed Wife: Thanks Spam

Spam: thattt's okkk what is it

Fat-armed Wife: first u must make a hundred per cent promise

Spam: Huh?? What?

Fat-armed Wife: not to tell anyone what I am about to ask. You can refuse to do it but you mustn't tell one soul what I said

Spam: OK

Fat-armed Wife: you promise?

Spam: I promise

Fat-armed Wife: I have a 1920s sequinned dress - was going to give it to Call Girl - took it with me - sat there in hotel room with it all wrapped up - it's worth a thousand dollars believe it or not. Can I sell it and have the buyer put the money in your account?

Spam: A thousannnd dollllllarsss??? What kind of dress is thatt?

Fat-armed Wife: it's the real thing, vintage 1920s - the sequins make it valuable

Spam: Ok

Fat-armed Wife: I have sold it to a collector and if u agree she will transfer the money to your account today electronically

Spam: very kind of you I'm sure

Fat-armed Wife: and then you can buy me an air fare

Spam: Hnnnnh?

Fat-armed Wife: I can't use my credit card - Colin found my motel. He is checking the accounts and he might stop me going - even with cash he will see the amount leave the account - and I have to just run and then tell him afterwards - it's the only way - joint accounts - grrrrr.

Spam: where are you going FAW?

Fat-armed Wife: Soon as I'm gone he'll check credit cards and phone all travel agencies and so I thought I could do it like this

Spam: go where, do what?

Fat-armed Wife: Fly to Brussels on 22 November arriving morning of 23

Spam: fatarms

Fat-armed Wife: Don't worry

Spam: the police are going to handle it

Fat-armed Wife: It's fine for me to go

Spam: OR . . . I think they are nottt goinggggg to helppppp at alll??? Am I right?

Fat-armed Wife: I'll be fine I can handle going

Spam: Will you walk into the lions mouthhh FAW? WITHOUT POLICE?

Fat-armed Wife: It was my mistake to tell them about Call Girl - and how he played - what he did in here - they don't believe us - wouldn't help unless a crime is committed, I said a crime is being committed

Spam: Fatarmsssss ... this is a chat room not nypd bluuuuee

Fat-armed Wife: will you do it for me - this fare?

Spam: You mustn't go

Fat-armed Wife: will not be in Dungeon alone, will hire someone to be with me

Spam: it is like I am handing you a loaded revolver.

Fat-armed Wife: that's ok I can ask someone else or pay in cash on the day and Colin won't notice until it is too late - just means I have to answer to him

Spam: You are hiring someone?

Fat-armed Wife: Yes

Spam: Who?

Fat-armed Wife: don't know yet but I will

Spam: Fatarms … Don't do this

Fat-armed Wife: I can pick up the paper ticket at the airport - all I need is your account details for the electronic transfer

Spam: can't do it forrrr you my deeearrr darrrlinnng Fatarms NOTTT SAFE

Fat-armed Wife: I am not yunggggg interrrnetttt virginnnn - I am solid Fat-armed Wife and sensible owner of The Real Thing - not superwoman but not able to do nothing. Will hire help.

Spam: Hmmmmmmmm

Fat-armed Wife: you made your promise not to tell anyone

Spam: yes. I did.

Fat-armed wife: I am going to telephone you. Hold on.

The next morning Spam rose from his bed at the Sharland House Accommodation Project. Fat-armed Wife still lived in his head from the night before. He could think only of her.

His feet arrived on the rug strategically positioned so he wouldn't have to touch the linoleum floor. God bless his new hips – not a moment of pain, even if he was still blue with cold first thing in the morning. Fat-armed Wife would be asleep on the other side of the Atlantic. Her sleep would be troubled, restless. Poor old Fatarms, he thought. He checked the dial on the electric wall heater – it was full on, as he'd thought; there was no reason for it to be different from the last time he'd looked. Was everyone else in this building as cold as he? He already had on a thermal vest and leggings; thereafter he pulled on two shirts and a jacket and tie, the usual trousers and two pairs of socks.

The hair-dryer was plugged in, ready for duty. He switched it on and slipped the roaring nozzle up his front, between vest and shirt.

The hot air blew comfortingly out at the neck. He moved the hairdryer to layers two and three and repeated the performance – with some difficulty – behind his back. Finally he poked it up each sleeve before switching it off and attending to the buttons at collar and cuff, and knotting the tie at his neck to seal in the heat. It gave his circulation a head start.

He took the handwritten details of the flight required by Fat-armed Wife and made sure of his wallet before leaving for the cafeteria, where he stopped for an emergency draught of hot coffee. Then he shrugged into his overcoat and negotiated the icy pavement. He walked into town; it helped maintain his body heat. Down the hill he proceeded more gingerly. Any fall in this cold weather could be fatal. He checked his balance at the cash machine on the High Street. She'd said the money would be there already. He peered through the cloud of his breath at the blurry screen, and sure enough it was. The figures made him jump. How events moved under you, carrying you along, he thought. It was part of the miracle of the modern age. He got his card back and wandered around until he found a travel agent. It was a relief to sit down at last and talk to someone young and good-looking and have them talk back as if one were important. The inevitable computer terminal was there to be consulted.

The fare required by Fat-armed Wife was substantially less than the amount of extra money in his account and it crossed his mind to use the extra to buy a ticket of his own. He ought to go as well. Someone ought to. As many as possible. DanceMaster, Honeycake, Big Black Woman, Psycho-dog – they should all go, so that she wasn't in the Dungeon alone. But he was bound by his promise. And she had promised, in her turn, to hire someone.

'I beg your pardon, sir?'

He realised he'd been saying all this out loud. 'Nothing,' he mumbled, blushing. 'Racehorses,' he explained. 'Kempton Park.' He ground to a halt. He put his credit card down on the counter; it gave a satisfying click. He slid it across. It felt as though he were taking part in a crime.

*

Trying to think back over too many years of indolent and useless life, but believe that may be the first promise I've broken. So sorry.

Jetman enters Velvet Ballroom

Poo: I'm a floater … heh heh

Peach: *~waving~ over here darling Jetman*

Jetman: Hi Peach good 2 c u

Terra Firma: Hey Poo, I had a girlfriend called Boo. She frightened the life out of me *canned laughter*

Tease: lol at Terra Firma

Terra Firma: Tease would I fall in love with a girl like you?

Jetman: hi everyone else as waell

Tease: Ummmm … I doubt it *s* Why d'you ask?

Peach: *~hand on Jetman's shoulder~ Want to stay here or go some other place ~ more private? ~shy smile~*

Terra Firma: Cos I wanna, I wanna fall in love ~drops on one knee~

Tease: Stop that, it hurts, making me laugh so bad, what is love ho ho ho

Jetman: **~whisper to Peach~** Velevet Shore?

Terra Firma: First time I heard a woman tell me 'stop that it hurts' since the beerfest in Munich where I kinda slipped out and by mistake went back in the wrong hole

Peach: **~whisper to Jetman~** *ok… *wink* see you there ~little sashay of hips~ is this ok?*

Tease: who said it was the wrong hole? ~ cheeeeeesy smile~ mebbe it was the right one after all ~lol~ hah hah hah

233

Jetman: *~gone~poof!~*

Terra Firma: OH MY WORD HEH HEH HEH

Peach: *~gone~poof!~*

Jetman enters Velvet Shore

Peach enters Velvet Shore

Jetman: Ahhh - at lastt!

Peach: *~sidles over, leans against u~ were alone*

Jetman: ~lifting ur chin to see ur face better ~ this is it

Peach: *You want me 2 sit or lie down ~smile~ my brave soldier?*

Jetman: yes - lie down

Peach: *~lying down ~ ok ~ and tell me what did everyone else say?*

Jetman: Honeycake can go because DanceMaster is paying the fare

Peach: *U will meet Honeycake!! U sure ur not going 2 change me 4 her ;~) wink ~*

Jetman: No never

Peach: *when u meet her 4 real u might like her better*

Jetman: Im waiting 4 u

Peach: *Is big black woman going*

Jetman: No she cant

Peach: *oh*

Jetman: oh what

Peach: *I am afraid ... ☹ know u r brave but still afraid*

Jetman: I am a soldier

Peach: *I know but what r u all going 2 do?*

Jetman: bravery not required there are three of us we r going because she is going

Peach: *My soldier*

Jetman: what6

Peach: *~sitting in velvet-covered chaise longue, taking you in my arms ~ u r brave. This is kind of happiness but unhappiness u know? Love but fear at same time*

Jetman: yes it is

Peach: *b careful all of u, b really really careful*

I will be careful, thought Thruster; I have many eyes and ears.

On 20 November he moved into the rented room at 76 Isestrasse, Hamburg. He slipped the euros from his wallet, counted them and then compared the sum to the list of costs he'd estimated for the journey. He unpacked the new pay-as-you-go mobile from its box, plugged it into its charger and switched it on. Smoothing out the instructions leaflet, he dialled the network and followed the electronic voice's instructions. He glanced from the window and pictured the microwaves finding the local aerial. When the phone was investigated it would be thought Jetman came from Hamburg.

He had with him the roll of sticking plaster and indelible marker he'd used for the computers. He cut off a strip, stuck it across the bottom of the keypad, avoiding the mouthpiece. On it he wrote 'Jet'. He logged in its directory the Brussels airport flight information number, 0900 7 0000, as well as the mobile numbers of DanceMaster, Psycho-dog, Honeycake and Fat-armed Wife, including international code. He texted all of them and settled down to wait for the answering messages to come back in. Each one, as he received it, made him smile. He wrote down their answers neatly.

The camera, too, he checked obsessively, to make sure it worked.

The photographs would add to the record of his crime. He didn't rule out talking to one or other of the Velvet Roomers as they arrived and recording their voices but he guessed he might easily not. Should not.

He pored over the airport terminal plan. Arrivals were on level 2. He identified the transit area, the bars and restaurants, the airline lounges and the transit systems. Brussels was not an airport he knew; he'd chosen it for the very good reason that the partial collapse of the newly built terminal building meant that the CCTV system wasn't working. He checked the timetable again, knowing what he would find: on the afternoon of 22 November DanceMaster would fly in via Miami. Honeycake arrived from New York that evening, and Psycho-dog also during the evening. Lastly, flight SN8002 would arrive at 08.35 on 23 November; on it would be the last and – as far as he was concerned – the most important of them: Fat-armed Wife. Can you hear me, he whispered to her. I am the ghost looking over your shoulder, breathing down your neck, unseen . . .

He had taken her away from her husband and son and pushed her into a motel room. He'd infected her eyes. He'd stripped her of sleep. All this he would see, for real.

He buttoned his coat round him and went for a walk. Everyone he passed, he might guess, had their wives and husbands or partners, their children, their pets. The mechanism worked for them. They rose, ate and drank, went to work, came back to watch TV, slept again. The women were mounted, the men seeded them. It was as automatic as cows in a field. Yet none of it worked for him. The trigger was broken. He was on the outside, walking this unfamiliar street, his footsteps no more than a whisper on the cold paving stones. There was none like him in any of these houses. There was only a few of his type in the whole of Europe. They were all hidden, forced to occupy a private world which touched the normal reality of most people in only the most tenuous ways – passing in the stairwell or lobby of an apartment block, money crossing from one hand to another to pay for goods, or driving past in the street. When they were caught they appeared like monsters, always unearthed where they were least expected. The headlines when such unhealthy appetites were exposed to the glare of public scrutiny caused a lurch in the collective stomach of society.

He was certain that one day he would be caught. The machinery of justice would grind him up. It was enough to stop him walking. He had to breathe, untie the knots in his nervous system.

If he were caught now, he might conjure all his victims, sit them metaphorically at his last supper, and ask which one had unwittingly betrayed him, left the vital clue that had led the police to his door? It might happen at any time. Yes, his victims were his family, in a way. They'd been chosen at random but he'd never abandoned them subsequently. Most frequent – every few months – was the trip he made to stay at the Shippe Inn, in Fore Street, Yarminster. If he took four meals at the bar he could expect at least two of them to be served by Sally Fitzpatrick. She never asked why he was there, what he was doing. Somewhere in the back of her mind, he thought, she must know he was there only to see her. It was his duty – a duty he took pleasure in. She was almost his daughter in a way.

Back at 76 Isestrasse he checked the weather bulletin. It predicted high pressure of 1028 milllibars and no cloud cover, so it would remain cold, with little wind. Their trap – their Dungeon – would snap shut, but on thin air, on nothing. He'd be leaving Brussels just as they were expecting him to arrive.

He sifted out the photographs. DanceMaster was in a wheelchair, so there'd be no problem recognising him. His photograph from the members' gallery showed a slight, intense young man, dressed formally in a soft, unstructured suit.

Psycho-dog was swarthier, older, perhaps forty. He had a thick beard and wounded dark eyes. His bottom lip was snagged downwards in one corner as if a fisherman's fly had caught there and the line had been pulled. He also wore a suit and tie, but conventional in style.

Honeycake's picture showed a girl in her twenties with streaked blonde hair. Her bust spilled out of a bikini, the cleavage offering a deep, vertical smile. There were dents in her flesh on each side of her waist. Her hips ballooned. She looked pleased and happy and extrovert, the picture catching her in the middle of an exclamation. He guessed that she'd talk a lot, eat greedily, watch films and read books that made her laugh or cry.

There were two photographs of Fat-armed Wife: one was from the members' gallery and was the same as her icon: bear-like she walked from the sea, hair plastered to her skull, her large frame accentuated by the black swimming costume, a blurred smile on her face. It was an extraordinary picture – as she'd said herself, she looked like a monster from the deep. The second photograph was the one she'd emailed to everyone only a few hours ago. She looked very different; she'd lost weight over the last five years. It was a good-quality, posed shot taken from a magazine article. The hair was a rich brown, the face heavy and smiling. Her eyes were small and dark and twinkled merrily above the high cheekbones. She looked similar to a young, darker Bette Midler. Underneath the picture some print was visible. He leaned closer to read it. In bold type the magazine had asked 'What is it?' In lighter, smaller text came the answer: 'It's The Real Thing, a treasure trove of vintage collectibles – not only fabulous clothes but glass vases, quirky art-deco lamps and antique jewellery.'

He stuck the Roomers' pictures in a row on a piece of A4 paper, making his own gallery. Under each one he wrote the flight number and arrival time.

Call Girl enters Velvet Ballroom

Call Girl: *Hi everyone*

FlyBoy: Click on downloads and I'll give you my number

Fat-armed Wife: Call Girl, my darling - sorry sorry sorry I have been a cow

Call Girl: *Eh*

Peach: *Big Black Woman I agree*

Fat-armed Wife: I didn't believe it was you because I was jealous - upset - disappointed. I am sorry - do you forgive me?

238

Big Black Woman: Sure Peach, you shake your bosom, I'll shake my bosom - lol

Call Girl: *Do u mean it?*

Fat-armed Wife: can we kiss and make up?

Peach: *Yours are bigger than mine - bump - ooops* ☺

Call Girl: *If this isn't a trick hten fine*

Big Black Woman: And they shure as hell cost more - haha

Pluto: FlyBoy I'm in, ready

Fat-armed Wife: No, not a trick. Now I bet you are waiting for handsome Thruster, hmm?

Call Girl: *He will be back soon*

Big Black Woman: And that's the only reason they still bounce hahhaha

Fat-armed Wife: you expecting him?

Call Girl: *he has 2 put up with me … like husband and wife now except he does the cooking*

FlyBoy: ok you'll find it at onetruevoice.com

Fat-armed Wife: sorry I was such a bitch

Call Girl: *Hi Finger-of-Fun. Thats ok fatarmedwife I understand*

Big Black Woman: Peach I'm not usually into any girl on girl thang - but always gud to c anuther darkie in here

Finger-of-Fun: Hi Call Girl

Fat-armed Wife: where r u at the moment Call Girl?

Call Girl: *fatarmedwife Im at home and u?*

FlyBoy: my reg is 5676-9846-3264-4528

Fat-armed Wife: yeah, same - boring old home in Minneapolis

Call Girl: *Have u moved house then?*

Fat-armed Wife: last week - yes I did. How's your cat by the way

Call Girl: *u mean my dog*

Fat-armed Wife: Sorry, I mean dog - yes - how is your dog?

Peach: **~whisper to Fat-armed Wife~** *Tell me if u need help*

Call Girl: *fine took him to have his nails clipped*

Fat-armed Wife: did he refuse to go into vets as usual?

Call Girl: *Finger-of-fun what u doin?*

Fat-armed Wife: did he refuse to go into the vets? haha

Finger-of-fun: I'm hiding at work that's what

Fat-armed Wife: I know he hates injections

Call Girl: *hiding what from?*

Fat-armed Wife: remind me of your vet's place you go to, wasn't it that place on the tv?

Finger-of-fun: hiding in marketing so my boss doesn't fetch me off my lunch hour

Call Girl: *Yeah thats right*

Fat-armed Wife: it's that's with an apostrophe

Call Girl: *sorry in a hurry*

Fat-armed Wife: no, I'm sorry, sorry

Call Girl: *Maybe hurry is wrong word - just naxious for my master, Thruster 2 arrive*

Finger-of-fun: Your Thruster is it now heh heh

Call Girl: *~grin~ yeah, sure is wot I want an need*

Fat-armed Wife: **~whisper to Call Girl~** listen - will be able to forgive you - I hope - but I have to go and lick wounds. remember you were my best love in cyberspace and never will I forget you or leave you out, not in a million years - you must know how important you are to me?

Finger-of-fun: How old is Thruster?

Call Girl: *Kind of forty or so Don't know don't care*

Finger-of-fun: tall etc?

Call Girl: *yes powerful build and tall*

Finger-of-fun: Ahhh

Call Girl: *~whisper to Fat-armed Wife~ That's ok I hope u get better soon and we can b friends again*

Fat-armed Wife: *~whisper to Finger-of-fun~* Ask for Call Girl's birthday

Finger-of-fun: Call Girl how old r u?

Call Girl: *fifty-five*

Fat-armed Wife: *~whisper to Finger-of-fun~* no, not how old, ask him what day his birthday is

Finger-of-fun: Call Girl when is your birthday?

Call Girl: *I'm a virgo*

Fat-armed Wife: *~whisper to Finger-of-fun~* say not just the sign, what exact day

Finger-of-fun: what day tho?

Call Girl: *Finger is someone telling u 2 aksd these questions?*

Finger-of-fun: no

Call Girl: *sigh ~ it used 2 b strainghtforweard in here*

Fat-armed Wife: I agree it did

Call Girl: *Fat-armed Wife you only just said sorry and called a new truce*

Fat-armed Wife: tell me the nickname of your sister's child with spina bifida

Call Girl: *not a truce then*

Fat-armed Wife: I can **SEE** you Thruster

At around two o'clock in the morning, Fat-armed Wife rose from her motel bed and wrapped the big green dressing gown around her. The cheap drawer slid out so easily it practically fell from the chest. She fetched the Tarot cards from behind her underwear.

The silence ticked away. There was fluff on the carpet; it acted kind of like Velcro and held onto every thread of fibre and dust.

She sat on the end of the bed and placed the pack of cards on the chest of drawers, clearing the surface of clutter. She lifted the necklace from her neck: on it hung the gold cross Call Girl had bought for her. She kissed the cards lightly, touching the cross against them. Whichever way the cards fell, they would point at her – she was both questioner and diviner. She cut them and shuffled, and eased herself into a more comfortable position. Then she paused, looked around the room. The lampshades on the wall glowed fiercely and the pale brown scorch marks made by the hot bulbs seemed to move, flow over their surface. The TV waited silently on its stand, the red dot of the stand-by light unblinking, like a warning: stop. She shuffled again, to break the spell.

'My question is,' she murmured, 'is Call Girl still alive?' She turned the first card.

It was the Fool: delirium, frenzy, unrestrained excess. Something new. Excitement. That meant yes? She saw it as yes. She turned the second card. Four of Swords: exile, certainly – Call Girl was not where he was meant to be.

Card number three, her eventual destiny or the best that could be hoped for, was – she almost closed her eyes as she turned it over. It was the World: completion, perfection – the strongest, most favourable card. And yes, she did have the world. DanceMaster, Psycho-dog, Honeycake, Peach, Spam, all of them were gathered around; from all points on the globe they converged on this problem, faced it with her. It had been amazing. Suddenly she felt courageous and determined. She could achieve anything with her fellow Roomers at her side, that card answering her.

She hardly dared go on but she had to complete this now. Next was seven of Pentacles: hard work, progress, growth. Yes, in the past, that was what had happened. She'd grown her life with Call

Girl. It had been a virtual life, but it had occupied every inch of interior space. They had worked hard, given each other time. They had built something.

The fifth card was ten of Swords. She blinked and hissed at it, rocked back and forth. All the courage given her by the World drained away. She looked for any different sense that could be attached to it, but without doubt it meant pain, trouble, tears . . . She put the pack down and stared at it. The eventual outcome was starred so well . . . You can do it, she told herself. She stood up, had to walk around for a bit. Two paces in each direction and she'd explored every corner of the room. She went outside and smoked a cigarette, looking at the foliage that crept over the kerb and invaded the pavement of the car park. There was one lone sodium light illuminating this end of the Killarney Motel. The way the roots of those weeds worked their way into the tiniest little fracture in the surface, made it bigger, and clung on . . .

Some minutes later she returned and completed the reading. She was left with two contradictory fates: The World at her feet, the Sword pointing at her heart.

She reached out to Call Girl, tried to find him in the dark, in the space and time he occupied, wherever that was. Stay with us, she urged him. We are coming to get you. She lit another cigarette, paced around for hours. She couldn't sleep. The clock stood still. In her mind's eye Call Girl's green italic hand wrote in the darkness like neon. The night held her prisoner.

The next morning she dressed for work, thinking about what they'd be doing at home. Colin would be in and out of cupboards, scouring the place for breakfast treats, and Jamie would be doing his floppy-legged early-morning walk. If she were there, she'd try and hug him and he wouldn't want it.

She had to walk, actually put one foot in front of the other, do things with her hands, get ready. Sweat was already beginning to spoil her blouse. She was having an anxiety attack, she realised. Colin phoned. He was on the warpath; he was jealous of the money she was spending on the motel. An unspecified threat had entered their marriage, and her behaviour was the weather system carrying it in.

She found herself drinking the useless glass of last night's water that she had meant to pour away. She was breathing too heavily. She went back into the bathroom and washed again, cleaned her teeth for the third time, re-touched her make-up. Her eyes were better – the antibiotics had worked – but they were still raw and bloodshot from tiredness and smoking too much. She hunched her shoulders, wiped her hair back. Too big and dramatic a woman, she accused herself.

She was frightened. DanceMaster, Psycho-dog, Jetman, Honeycake, she said to the mirror, thank you for coming. She wouldn't be alone when the door to the Velvet Dungeon swung open.

It was nearly eight o'clock. She forced herself to behave normally.

Where would the others be now? Would DanceMaster have arrived in Brussels yet? Honeycake would be in the air. Jetman . . .

Eight o'clock. She took her coat off the peg, picked up her stuffed briefcase, which held the photographs and cellphone numbers of all the other Roomers. As soon as she hit the cold, fresh air she lit another cigarette, smoked it quickly between the room and the car.

At work she couldn't concentrate. The ticket was waiting for her at Logan airport. She had her passport. She had to take cash out of the shop, drive back for clean clothes and stuff.

Her mind wandered; she started making mistakes. She couldn't talk politely to anyone, customers or staff.

In the end she decided to go home and sit it out. She removed five hundred dollars from the safe without signing for it. She told Teresa she was feeling sick and drove back to the house. Colin was at work; Jamie was at school. She found a parking slot and walked up Winter Hill. How strange, to come back. It felt like someone else's life. The sidewalk was slushy. In the porch various of her husband and stepson's shoes and boots languished untidily. She realised how seldom – almost never – she had been here alone. As soon as she let herself in Jonathan rubbed against her legs. In the kitchen a drip clung to the tip of the mixer tap, as if time were frozen and didn't allow it to fall. A sharp knife lay on the work surface, its blade a flat sheen of grey light reflected from the window. A toy bear of Jamie's lay sideways in the snug; she picked it up. Rows of underwear and socks were decked on all the radiators; the drier had broken down and Colin still hadn't fixed it.

Jamie and his child-minder would be the first to come home: they were due at four. It was Thursday; they'd be in a hurry to make it to drama class. If she didn't want to see Jamie she'd have to leave before then.

She went to the kitchen and found her spot in the diner booth. She set herself to composing a rough draft of the letter to Colin. This moment had grown inexorably closer – a hundred times it had been on the tip of her tongue to tell him the truth, even ask him to go with her. She'd drawn breath, felt the confession ready to tumble out, but had always stopped because he'd have clamped down and made it impossible for her to go. So, by default, there was only one option left: to disappear without saying anything. To spare them the anxiety she'd leave a note saying she'd be back and not to worry – there was something she had to take care of. She would beg them not to try and find her or stop her. She'd ask for their trust. She'd promise to tell them everything on her return – and she would do exactly that. She rubbed her itching wrists against her sides. How to begin? 'Dear Colin . . .'

She took a break for a cigarette.

'When you read this letter,' she continued, 'you'll already be wondering where I am . . .'

She watched the clock eat away at the time, minute by minute. The letter was finished and sealed in its envelope. She thought of visiting the Velvet Rooms but decided against it. Soon she would meet the Roomers. Out of the millions using chat rooms at any given time they had found each other. These were her people, living the other side of an electronic membrane, as she liked to think of it. The two worlds were moving closer: more people were spending longer living on the other side of their screens. The voices were multiplying; the physical realities were becoming a more distant experience for most people. We are turning into creatures of the imagination, she thought, like ghosts. The only reality will be our voices calling to one another, silently. Among them had once been the voice of Call Girl, writing large and green in the sky. But no longer. She was going to punch through and find him.

She went upstairs and packed fresh clothes. She hung the art deco cigarette lighter round her neck. On how many flights had it accompanied her, she wondered, when she'd been travelling for work? She went down again, stood for a few minutes, bag at her feet. Car keys: yes. She reminded herself to continue on the new three-lane I-90 westbound, and stay right for the airport exit ramp . . . She looked down at the passport in her hand. Call Girl had never known her real name. She gathered all her courage and spoke to him out loud: 'Jonathan, I'm coming.'

Peach enters Velvet Ballroom

Peach: *hi, any1 there?*

Asshole1: Hi peach. I'm the only one, but hey I'll dance

Peach: *Hi Asshole, who r you?*

Asshole1: I'm one big hairy assole, if you wanna lick me haha

Peach: ☹ ☹ ☹ *Sorry I don't do that kind of talk* ☹

Asshole1: ~ scratching my hairy but sorry ass ~ ughghhh, I apologise. It's just with a name like Peach . . .

Peach: *it's ok*

Asshole1: You got anyone for real, Peach, a man or such?

Peach: *Yes I have a man ~ smile ~ ☺ ~ but he is away. All my friends are away. I am waiting for them to call in*

Asshole1: Ahhhh. Then you and me are both alone Peachy, at the moment. We are both **alone** and **without love** in this sorry-ass, hairy-ass world

Peach: *True ~ grin ~* ☺

Asshole1: Are you really a **peach**, is that a good description?

Peach: *A bit, yes ~ smile ~*

Asshole1: I like a *good peach*

Peach: *Are you really an asshole? ~ wink ~*

Asshole1: I HAVE one, but I am NOT one

Peach: *~lol~*

Asshole1: quiet in here

Peach: *It isn't normally*

Asshole1: just tonight

Peach: *A lot of people are away ~ all my friends*

Asshole1: where they gone?

Peach: *oh , you know, on holiday and work and so on*

Asshole1: I like it just you and me dancing quietly here

Peach: *Yes. It's fine. Are you in America?*

Asshole1: yeah, PA

Peach: *Oh, that's a good job*

Asshole1: Not the job the state

Peach: *oh I see*

Asshole1: Where are you

Peach: *in the Bahamas*

Asshole1: **wow**!

Peach: *I know it is wow*

Asshole1: on holiday?

Peach: *No I live here*

Asshole1: what right on the beach I bet

Peach: *The beach is a little walk on a dusty track*

Asshole1: Hey I'm *coming straight over*

Peach: *~lol~ sure, come*

Asshole1: for real?

Peach: *yeah, my folks have a factory here*

Asshole1: You work for your dad?

Peach: *My uncle*

Asshole1: I work for my Dad

Peach: *You get more time off when you work for your family business ~smile~*

Asshole1: oof, you wanna see my dad ~sigh~ **TIME and OFF** aren't words in his dictionary

Peach: *Hey it's nice being here just the two of us*

Asshole1: sure is

On 22 November, Thruster contrived to walk alongside DanceMaster as the latter exited Zaventem airport. He took half a dozen photographs, pretending to wave to someone behind the wheelchair. He tracked DanceMaster through the arrivals hall and out to a taxi. He could see the thin, expert fingers pushing the rims of the chair's wheels, the empty puff of jacket which hardly seemed to have any shoulder in it.

He spoke to Honeycake. Something in the way she chewed gum, looked only at the signs, at the floor, at her own bags, told him he could get away with it; she'd never remember. He waited until she'd wheeled her trolley past him and then he walked after her, meanwhile emptying his wallet of cards, receipts and photographs. He stooped, made a play of picking up the wallet from the ground, and trotted after her. He touched her shoulder, calling softly, 'Excuse me.' He offered her the wallet. 'I think you dropped this.'

Honeycake's jaw stopped moving. She looked at the wallet. 'No, that's not mine.'

'Oh. Sorry. Never mind. I'll hand it in.'

She'd already turned away. He doubted she'd even seen his face. He retreated quickly, burying the charade and heading outside. For some minutes he chastised himself for breaking the rules. His jaw clenched and he balled his fists in his overcoat pockets. But the next moment he was checking that the recording of their conversation had come out OK on his phone.

He went back in and loitered for hours, waiting for Psycho-dog, schooling himself not to talk, not to give himself away. The circumstances were too unpredictable.

He swapped from one bar or eaterie to the next, stringing out the time. The airport's CCTV was still out of action.

When Psycho-dog's flight came in, Thruster was in the same position: waiting at the end of the loops of rope where new arrivals filtered through. This was Psycho-dog. The beard was correct, the wounded eyes. Most of all he recognised that tug downwards on one side of his bottom lip which added to his air of injury, or complaint. He took three photographs.

An hour later he'd returned from the airport to his room at the St Etienne hotel on the outskirts of Brussels. Immediately he set about downloading pictures from the camera to the computer and copying text messages.

By ten in the evening he'd used all the teabags in the anonymous hotel room. He had to call down for more, and extra sachets of milk. He carried the Jetman phone with him from place to place. He watched it closely.

At five to eleven he was lying on the bed with his hands knitted behind his head, staring at the ceiling.

Jetman enters Velvet Shore

Peach enters Velvet Shore

Jetman: That's better. No traffic - hey great to find u peachy

Peach: *darling, can't stop thinkging about u all - scared and proud u r all so brave ~ *vbs* ~ its wierd isnt it*

Jetman: weird, yeah

Peach: *and I am here left behind like always the wife of a soldier ~ sigh~ what did u hear from them?*

Jetman: signals from DM and psyucho and honeycake ~ they are in the hotel and wait for Fatarms then me tomorrow

Peach: *~ shiver ~ I'm scared and pray 4 ur safety*

Jetman: we'll be OK

Peach: *keep safe my Jetman*

Jetman: I will

Peach *~looking at ur mouth, resting my strong hand on ur thigh~ all this danger makes me think of how much luck I have*

Jetman: Mmmmm… nice hand ~putting mine on top~ tell me

Peach: *tell u what? ~stroking your handsome face~ u mean about my luck?*

Jetman: Yes

Peach: *ok ~smile ~ but tell me something first*

Jetman: What

Peach: *u ever had a relationship in a chat room before? Ur quite a smooooooth operator ~winks~ *vbs**

Jetman: Ummm

Peach: *U can tell me*

Jetman: OK I tried before but nothing worked out

Peach: *Can't believe anyone turned u down ~stroke ur face~ U been so kind and patient with me*

Jetman: No one's turned me down buyt whenever I've got close 2 someone they have kidn of disappointed me. Except u

Peach: *Godddd ~holding u tight~ you are good 4 me. ~ squeezing ur face in* my hands~ Hmmm? Honey pie? But I say I have luck ~ ☺ ~ like u ~ but I have some bad luck as well

Jetman: what bad luck?

Peach: There's some things I haven't told, I think you guessed some but I have 2 b sure

Jetman: U can tell me

Peach: I don't live at the Bahamas, I'm Chinese, if that's ok

Jetman: Oh

Peach: I know maybe u don't know any but I hope u like Chinese girls, hnnn? ~sweet smile~ ☺

Jetman: that's OK. how come ur English is so good?

Peach: My father was American who owned hygiene ceramics factory here in Hebei province

Jetman: What is hygiene ceramics?

Peach: baths and toilets and like that

Jetman: OK

Peach: With my uncle and he met my mum but they never were married and my family didn't like my American dad because he was a foreigner and thinking he was the rapist because he didn't marry her, but where from he came it was ok 2 b not married, 2 have children and not b married, but it means now he was gone my family treats me like a bastard

Jetman: that's cool, that's OK

Peach: ~deep breath, put my hand on your arm~ There's another thing why we won't ever 2 meet 4 real ~serious pleading look~

Jetman: what is it

Peachy: I'm hiv positive

Peachy:

Jetman: oh that's ok u have the drungs I hope

Peach: no I don't

Jetman: why not? maybe I can send them to u

Peach: *My father and mother split up and my father took me with him and then my mother's family came to the factory and beat him up in this factory where I'm typing and threw him out and kidnapped me aged ten and took me away and I've been with them here in Hebei province and abused so much by my uncle and now without medical help with hiv*

Jetman: thats amazing. how much longer have u got to live?

Peach: *don't know but my aunt and cousin are dead, my mother is ill and lost all her weight, both my sisters are prostitute because they don't have the disease yet*

Jetman: I'm sorry

Peach: *I shouldn't tell this 2 u*

Jetman: u need help or medicines or something?

Peach: *That's not why... I mean I don't want u 2 think that's why I'm in the Velvet Rooms trying 2 find help because it's not it's hopeless. I've tried 2 run away twice, no one can help me and I don't expect them*

Jetman: how old r u 4 real?

Peach: *I'm 18*

Jetman: really 18?

Peach: *16*

Jetman: And how do uhave a computer and interenet?

Peach: *My uncle's one fo the owners of the factory and I'm hiding the screen from him in this office when I'm on line so he thinks it takes me hours 2 translate all his stuff because it looks like I'm always working. I'm sorry that just all came out I didn't want 2 tell u because I'm afraid u have 2 go away and face danger now ... oh ~weeping now, sorry sorry~ I shouldn't tell u, not as quickly. Will u forgive and stay 4 me a small bit?*

Jetman: it's OK

Peach: *It was mistake with Green Eyed Man ... but going with him, you know, b4 I tell him. And when I say it, poof, he went very quickly, and I never saw him again, it made me feel dirty and so bad because I'd tricked him*

252

and he ran off, so I tell u b4, u see? B4 we start. When we r getting on so good but b4 the sex part. It was really really important, please please I don't want u 2 think about drugs or money or help 4 me or anything from u, I am only here with friendship and contact 4 the outside world and knowing u and finding u is the best that happens so please don't think about I needing help or wanting u 4 anything. I am in China and u r wherever you r far away and we r only two spirits that meet in cyberspace with nothing 2 holds us down, nothing stops us ~ soft smile~ we can do which we want, go where we want ~I kiss ur face~ sorry 4 my tears and that I am fifteen years old and have had a baby son also who died of Aids and I hope u forgive me I am the very same person u have been talking to. Do u forgive me? Do you promise not 2 tell anyone else, my darling darling darling love? My twin spirit in the skies, as u said? Like kites together we will fly, I promise.

Jetman: **~gone~poof!~**

Peach:

Peach:

Thruster blinked. He would in all likelihood never visit the Velvet Rooms again. He felt the blood settle in his veins. He showered in the little cubicle in the corner, the water drumming hollowly. Naked in the overheated room, he sat and watched pornographic films on the twelve-inch television screen. His mind went blank. Within the compass of his sturdy human frame – the strong neck, the inside of his clever, dull head – lived all mankind and its hungers and desires.

He rose early, washed and brushed his teeth. He unwrapped the new clothes – of a style and type foreign to him: a suit and tie. She wouldn't be close enough to notice that it was a velvet tie. He fastened it round his neck in front of the bathroom mirror. It didn't suit him; it made him look like a nightclub bouncer.

He consulted once again the photographs of Fat-armed Wife, the one she'd emailed and the one he'd printed from the members' gallery of the Velvet Rooms. She was not the only person he'd come across who used her own photograph as her icon, but it was rare.

The heavy beige overcoat was the last item of dress; then he left the hotel room. He checked his watch: 7.30 a.m. One hour until her flight arrived. It was still dark.

A few minutes' walk took him to the multistorey car park. There was a light scattering of snow, but it wasn't serious. His breath clouded eerily in front of him. Early traffic moved freely, although slowly. When he reached the Granada he checked it over: he opened all the locks, started the engine, checked fuel and oil. He pushed the spare tyre hard – yes, it had air in it. The jack and wheel-wrench were in place. He paid off the ticket and left, headed to the airport. At this time of the morning, when it was still before rush hour and he was heading out of town, he needn't use the ring road. He followed signs for Zaventem and headed directly through the centre. When he reached the airport complex he made for the short-term car park, closest to the terminal building. He booked the maximum four hours.

He locked the car and made sure he knew the direction of travel to the exit. He walked to the airport terminal.

Inside the arrivals hall he climbed the stairs to the balcony level and took a seat in the Caffè Nero franchise so he could look out over the rail and see the passengers coming through. He scrutinised the occupants of the other tables but there was nothing to trouble him. He was the only one sitting alone. He rested his elbows on the glass table and smelled on his hands the unfamiliar soap from the hotel. On the television monitor he watched as flight SN8002 silently changed, at 08.35, from 'due' to 'arrived'.

He listened to the words of the song playing softly in the background. He soaked up the emotion and enjoyed it as much as the sugary drink – an orange J2O sat in front of him. The minutes passed as blandly as he could wish, while he remembered envelopes 1 to 14.

He pictured the Granada in the car park. In his mind's eye vandals approached it, broke a window. He saw them off, caught one, pushed the youth to the ground. The youth begged for mercy.

Spam bought a ticket; he'd thrown aside his age, his fear of flying, the trauma of leaving the environs of the Sharland. After all,

DanceMaster, chief of the Velvet Rooms, had made a call to arms; an Englishman doesn't ignore a call to arms. He'd summoned a taxi to take him to Bristol airport and flown to Brussels on the early flight, surrounded by businessmen and women. His own mortality appeared doubly certain among all these wealth-creating types. He was not needed by anyone or anything; rather, he was excess baggage. And so, on the Baby flight from Bristol, he asked his neighbour for help in unpicking the croissant from its fierce cellophane wrapping, and sipped his coffee. It seemed as if only two minutes had passed before they started the descent to Brussels.

At the airport he switched terminals and looked for Fat-armed Wife's flight on the arrivals monitor. At the appointed time he joined the small throng of people waiting. She would be easy to pick out, all eighteen stone of her. Not many women looked like a monster from the deep.

Perhaps he wasn't used to the outside world, but everything was moving twice as fast as it used to. People hurried frantically. The little carts carrying disabled passengers drove as fast as Formula One cars, beeping away. The aeroplanes themselves streaked from one side of the world to the other in a flash. Even the advertising posters didn't have time just to sit and show you something you might buy; every few seconds they were shunted upwards so that a new one could be displayed.

There was no question that this creature was Fat-armed Wife. She was enormous, she had dark hair . . . the spectacles were a surprise. Spam ventured out and stood in the flow of people so he could interrupt her progress. He stepped forward, his heart filled with warmth at the extraordinary nature of the events that had come to pass. 'Fat-armed Wife?'

A frown settled on her face. Of course, she was not expecting to be met. She didn't even know that he, Spam, was among those who were coming.

'Fat-armed Wife?' he asked, more insistently. 'It's Spam.' He reached out to greet her with a handshake. 'Spam,' he repeated.

The woman's frown deepened. 'Honey, you head right on back to the funny-farm,' she said, and rolled onwards.

*

Thruster was caught short: Fat-armed Wife was much quicker through customs and immigration than he had expected, because she carried only one small piece of hand luggage and her handbag. He was just stirring from his balcony position when he saw the top of her head as she trod through quickly, heavily, on the heels of her flat shoes – the stride masculine in that way of American women. He was still trotting down the stairs from his vantage point in Caffè Nero when she went past. The dark glasses, of course, were because of the infection in her eyes.

The fact that he'd almost missed her caused a surge of adrenalin in his system. He switched on the camera as he went. She was heading straight outside, he realised. He buttoned his coat and matched her pace. As he got closer he judged her not to be unduly over-weight, just on the large side, but she had the same round curve to her shoulders as in the photograph, the same brown curly hair arranged untidily over her crown and neck. The famous fat arms were visible from the elbow downwards before she struggled into her fake fur coat. Her top was a smock affair; the dark slacks were ubiq-uitous travel wear.

Beyond the sliding doors the cold bit suddenly, fiercely. She stopped dead and dropped her bag. There was already a cigarette in her hand; she concentrated on lighting it. Thruster walked past close enough to see that she was shaking. A heavy smoker, then – and she was anxious, perhaps.

I have done this to you, he thought, lifting his camera. I have brought you here. I have given you the shakes. Can you see me? No, not even when I'm standing a few paces away.

It put him in a state of extreme excitement.

He mingled with other passengers waiting to be picked up by cars outside the terminal and took photographs from here. She oblig-ingly stood and smoked. He went a few steps closer and took more pictures. He wished she'd remove the dark glasses; it was important to see her eyes, what he'd done to them.

That's close enough, he told himself; remember the rules.

Then an idea occurred to him with such force that he couldn't resist; merey to think of it meant he was already folding out the mobile phone. His thumb was blunt on the keypad. As he tagged the buttons he heard the rational voice inside him telling him to keep safe, but he ignored it so he could photograph her reading the message. He pressed Send and waited. A moment later she started, reached in her handbag for her phone and read the text. He was entranced: she was posting an answer. He strolled a touch further off to wait for it.

Almost at once the phone vibrated in his hand: Message Received. 'Me also. Let's share a cab I'm standing outside by rank A smoking a cigarette wearing black.'

He stared. All caution left him. He circled further away, found another pair of automatic doors and re-entered the terminal. Briefly, as he made his way among the throng of people, that same internal voice came back and told him on no account to do this.

He ignored it again. He came back outside and without hesitation approached her.

'Hi. You must be . . . ' he began.

'Hi, yes. You're Jetman?'

'Pleased to meet you.'

'And you. And thanks so much for coming. Sorry, but d'you mind waiting just a tick? Are you a non-smoker?' She was fumbling with the packet in her handbag, starting to light another.

''Course not,' he said. 'Don't mind at all.'

Fat-armed Wife's first reaction on seeing Jetman was disbelief. He was nothing like she'd imagined. Her idea of a soldier was of an upright, crew-cut young man such as caroused in the bars of her home town; they all had a child-like simplicity and straightforward physical strength. This guy was short, had thick-framed glasses and looked like a door-to-door insurance salesman. The overcoat . . . and this slightly hysterical concern over the bag – they were at Brussels airport, not the subway into Harlem.

She was disappointed; she'd never trust a man shorter than herself. She told herself to give him the benefit of the doubt until after she'd had a cigarette; she couldn't rely on her judgement until she was properly stoked. She was far from home and an almost constant shivering crawled over her skin. What had Spam said? 'This is a chat room, not NYPD blue.' But if only it *could* be – in the absence of the real thing, she'd trust those actors, those script writers, to stem the flow of events, mend life so it came out right.

'Cold,' she said, shrugging deeper into her coat.

'Yes. It snowed earlier.' Chill grey sleet pricked the pavement where the cabs came and went.

'I have a hire car waiting for me,' he said. 'It'll be warmer and you can smoke in comfort while we find the hotel.'

'That is a great offer. Thank you.'

He led the way; she walked alongside him, her gait heavy and rolling next to his rather prim steps. 'Sorry,' she said, holding up the cigarette. 'I'm totally addicted, so a flight that long is hell for me.'

'Don't worry,' he said. 'How many years have you been smoking?'

'Since I was fifteen.'

'How many a day?'

'Recently . . . maybe forty.'

'Proper habit.'

'It sure is. I mean, I could use the money to take the family on holiday or pay off the car or buy my stepson a new computer but I just carry on smoking.' She realised she was burbling on out of nerves. She wanted to clutch someone's arm, but Jetman's square face with its slab sides and neat side parting was unapproachable. The thick spectacles were unflattering – hadn't he heard of contact lenses?

'Don't we take a bus to the hire-car place?' she asked.

'No, they park it in the terminal and give you the level and the number of the bay. I picked up the keys at the desk.'

'OK, great. And can I just say an enormous thank you for helping us out on this,' she said.

'It's nothing. I'm happy to do it for Peach.'

'And that makes Peach a lucky woman.'

'Well . . .'

'No, listen, there's not many who'd step up to the mark, believe me, and I appreciate it even if we don't get any kind of result.'

'It's fine.'

Waves of shivering continued to break over her, despite the fact she'd got to her cigarettes. She had an urge to run away, but she must stick to it, put one foot in front of the other. She longed with all her heart to reach Call Girl, hear his laughter, enjoy his eloquence and humour, his dwelling in misery but his self-knowledge in waiting for the floor to rise up, as he put it. Call Girl, she thought, we are going to find you, even if Jetman isn't much of a soldier after all. She dropped her cigarette end on the ground and stood on it and immediately pulled a third one from the packet. Anonymous travellers cut across their path. Yes, one foot in front of the other, thought Fat-armed Wife.

The sidewalk soon gave way to a crossing. They waited with half a dozen others. The signal for pedestrians turned from red to green and they crossed. Jetman put his hand under her elbow; it made her feel uncomfortable. She thought that she might buy him a gift to make it up to him. She'd visit a gentleman's outfitter's and replace that coat.

They gained the other side. To give herself courage she counted in time with her heavy footfalls: one, two, three . . .

Jetman pointed: that's where they were heading. The short-term car park looked like a helter-skelter with its looping, tilting, concrete driveways. It was a much older building than the terminal itself. Stains seeped through the joins in the concrete.

They ducked into the entrance and waited for the elevator, along with two or three others. Everyone walked in and turned to face outwards. Jetman pressed the button to take them to level 4. The doors remained obstinately open. A young couple pushing a covered baby buggy went by, dragging luggage. An old man stood and stared at them. A hunched teenager scurried past, cold. A dog lay in a recessed area as if it had chosen to live there some time ago.

The doors closed. Fat-armed Wife counted in her head again. When they stepped out Jetman guided her to the car. Their footsteps sounded sinister, solitary. The rows of vehicles waited for their drivers like frozen metal horses. The smell of old concrete and damp stuck in her throat.

A hundred and sixteen, a hundred and seventeen.

Jetman released her elbow and went a pace or two ahead of her to a vehicle which looked too old for a hire car. He put her bag down by the trunk and bent to the lock; it popped open.

Spam wandered around in the airport concourse. There were other flights coming through. No Fat-armed Wife! What did it mean, if she hadn't come?

He was tired on his feet. It was worth the laborious climb up the steps to be able to sit for a while in Caffè Nero, scanning the crowds below.

As time passed he felt steadily more foolish and out of sorts. He had come all this way and the world callously disregarded him. He had been seduced by the companionship of the Velvet Rooms and yet the minute he'd reached out to touch it, it had disappeared. He wanted to go home. He peered long and hard at the departures monitor, looking for a flight back to Bristol, but then remembered that he was in the wrong terminal and he must retrace his steps. He rose to his feet and pushed himself off. 'Fat-arms, where are you, hmm?' he mumbled. He still entertained a vain hope that she might suddenly approach and give a cry of welcome, and take him in those fat arms. They would travel together in a warm taxi to the hotel where everyone was due to meet.

At the bottom of the steps the incoming tide of travellers broke around him. Had the others arrived, he wondered? He turned in a circle, trying to remember what they looked like. DanceMaster, Psycho-dog, Honeycake, Jetman? He saw none of them.

At a snail's pace the Granada toured the car park. Only on the second go round did it take the exit ramp.

Thruster's mind worked overtime to put into position the defences that he usually would have planned in advance. The sweat from her skin soiled his hands; he was driving slowly enough to take the rag he used for condensation and wipe them thoroughly – and the steering wheel. There was a spray glass cleaner in the glove box. The scent filled the car. On level 1 he found what he wanted, a grille set into the side of the shaft containing the lift. He took the phone labelled Jetman and made sure it was on Silent. He rooted in her bag, found her phone and likewise switched it to Silent. Then he climbed from the car and pushed both phones through the vent. From here they would continue to signal the local receiver, giving their position in this quarter of the city. From hereon, they would both disappear into thin air.

The Granada continued its descent to ground level, slowly. At the barrier it stopped, the ticket was fed into the machine. The vehicle bounced over the speed bump and joined the slipway, entered the flow of traffic to the ring road.

The Granada's needle sat on the exact speed limit every inch of the way.

Sometime during the journey Fat-armed Wife recovered consciousness. Everything was black. The road and engine noise drummed in her ears. She called out, over and over. Pressure built behind her eyes as she tried to push free, in panic. Her vision blurred and became pinpricked with small bright stars which floated gracefully. She used all her strength to push the lid of the trunk. She tried to twist her head sideways and relieve the pain and restriction. It felt as if her head was going to dissolve in so much darkness and, despite all her conscious effort, it was like someone was slowly turning down the brightness control on a TV: by degrees her vision diminished, went. She lost consciousness again.

In the Hotel Intercontinental, a few miles from the airport, two of the Velvet Roomers sat on a pair of studded leather sofas, facing each other over a low, Moroccan coffee table. A third, DanceMaster, was hunched in his wheelchair, concentrating intently on what had happened – and not happened.

Fat-armed Wife hadn't turned up as expected, and the deadline for the Velvet Dungeon was drawing near.

Psycho-dog rose to his feet and booked some time in the hotel's business suite. It was only to play on-line poker. He wanted to get back to his normal life from this distant outpost. As his chips diminished he lost confidence. He'd seen the same confidence leaking out of the eyes of the others when Fat-armed Wife hadn't turned up, nor Jetman. The whole thing was a joke and they were the dupes. No wonder the police hadn't played ball: they had more sense.

When he'd finished in the business suite he returned to the others. They hadn't moved. The only difference was that a white china cup and saucer was in front of each of them and DanceMaster was on the phone.

Honeycake was leaning forward, uncomfortably plump and heavy on the sofa, which was too slippery, too deep. She picked at the buttons on the leather. She wanted to go home, too. The whole situation, brought out from the imaginary realm of the Velvet Rooms and into the harsh light of reality, had softened to nothing and slipped from her grasp. Their chat-room names had lost their charm. The people here, gathered in this hotel lobby in a foreign country, were the suckers who'd fallen for it.

'I'm sorry,' Psycho-dog said simply.

DanceMaster would try with the last ounce of his strength to hold them together. 'Wait,' he said. 'They are checking the flight register to see if she actually arrived. If she did, that changes everything.'

Psycho-dog shrugged. 'She didn't come.'

DanceMaster was suddenly, violently, disappointed. Did Psycho-dog not trust in his long voyage of the imagination in the Velvet Rooms? DanceMaster himself counted the intimacies of the Velvet Rooms more truthful, more deserving of trust, than anything that could be engineered in the real world. Everyone was losing faith. 'I understand,' he said to Psycho-dog. 'But can I ask you to wait until they come back with a result? It is simple. If she was on the plane they will have a record of it. They are checking the flight register.'

'Sorry, I'm outta here.'

'Would it not change everything if we could prove she'd landed?'

'Sorry,' mumbled Psycho-dog.

They watched him go. DanceMaster said, 'We will never see him again in the Velvet Rooms.'

There was silence round the table.

'Keep faith,' urged DanceMaster.

They waited. A half-hour later they became aware of an old gentleman, with a red, square face and a moustache, leaning towards them, his eye beady on first one, then the other. He lifted a crooked finger and pointed at them as if confused. His lip trembled and he shuffled on his feet to keep his balance. The overcoat looked too big for him. 'Is she here? Has she got here already?'

At DanceMaster's request, Spam gave a detailed account of what had happened: he'd taken a spur-of-the-moment decision to join them and knew Fat-armed Wife's arrival time from having bought her ticket. He knew her picture from her icon, which was the same as the photograph in the members' gallery. He'd approached a stranger who'd obviously not had a clue what he was talking about. He'd remembered the name of the hotel where they'd agreed to meet and had made his way here. Informed by everyone else, now, that she'd lost nearly six stone since that picture had been taken, he couldn't be sure whether anyone resembling her had got off the flight. He hadn't heard or seen anything of Jetman.

DanceMaster offered him Jetman's room, for now. Spam went up and soaked in the bath to bring himself up to room temperature; none the less he felt exhausted. It was enervating to have to concentrate on people with whom one had nothing in common. The casual intimacy and fun of the Velvet Rooms seemed impossible to achieve under these circumstances.

The Velvet Dungeon beckoned. They waited. Psycho-dog returned, apologetic.

An hour before the appointed time for the Dungeon, they heard from the airline: Fat-armed Wife had been on the flight. She'd had hand-luggage only. She had gone through passport control.

If she'd been delayed for any reason she would have called. DanceMaster called the police and the American embassy. Their last hope was that she'd turn up at the President Nord Hotel sometime before 8.30 p.m., but Jetman's continued absence took on a sinister aspect now. Where was Fat-armed Wife, what had happened? When they checked into the Ballroom on the laptop, they found Peach, in tears. Jetman . . .

When Fat-armed Wife opened her eyes there was a much greater constriction around her – she could hardly move. From the smell and the rough surface, she knew it was a wooden box of some sort. With a rush of panic she realised she might have been buried alive. The thought of six feet of earth weighing down on top of her magnified the claustrophobia; it was unbearable – she needed to faint. It was as if she were making a dash for unconsciousness, pushing open the door to save herself . . .

Everything went blank again.

Once more consciousness returned. The same darkness was around her; the same tightly encasing wooden surfaces were at her hips and elbows and knees and feet and head. The panic surfaced again, but this time she managed to make a sound. Her groan stayed close by, in the box. She couldn't imagine it would penetrate the dense earth and reach the surface . . .

The memory of what had happened came back to her: the car, the clean interior of the trunk neatly lined with a tartan blanket, the blur of movement at the periphery of her vision and then immediate, utter darkness, as if a light had been switched off. The drumming noise of the journey, the surfaces around her cold and hard as iron.

A headache banged in her crown. She was tightly contained – if she tried to move, the box held her more tightly – and in silence, stillness. She closed her eyes and steered her thoughts, tried to find something that might help her. Mentally, she summoned her allies, DanceMaster, Psycho-dog, Honeycake. They were somewhere close by; she brought them closer. They stood in a line; she could see their voices write in the darkness. She concentrated hard. Help me, she begged. Can you? In this black, closed-off place it seemed possible that the Velvet Rooms might be reached; its dream world was like a giant ship passing close by in the night. In the electronic ether her friends knew where she was, they had a godlike overview. She called out, as loudly as she could.

Her flesh melted and she was floating. Their hands were on her. She moved her fat arms and rose from the sea; 'a lion among women', Call Girl had called her. A sudden burst of grief caught her. What had happened? She was travelling the same road as Call Girl. She sobbed; tears leaked from her eyes. She remembered the card, The Fool. Folly, thoughtlessness. Jetman and Thruster were the same person.

She shouted to each Velvet Roomer who'd taken this trip with her. 'Help! find me!' She became hoarse from shouting. She pushed hard with her back and felt the resistance of the wood, solid, immoveable. The abrasive surface told her it was made of rough-sawn timber. She twisted violently, squirmed. When she wiped the tears from her eyes the backs of her hands touched the lid, it was only a couple of inches from her face. She pushed upwards, pushed hard, for a long time. Her muscles burned. She shouted. The sound tore her throat. Her ears rang – too loud. It was airless in here. She shouted again.

No answer came. She listened; her sense of hearing was free to travel, search for any small sound. After a few minutes there was something. She clung to it. She slowed her breathing and each time her lungs either filled or emptied, she paused, to gain a few precious seconds of silence . . . in which she found . . . yes, there it was, a faint movement. She tilted violently and shouted; the panic galloped afresh and she allowed it to carry her. She pushed outwards with all her strength, felt the wood refuse to move, and shouted again and again.

For what seemed like for ever she maintained this attack while the panic ran ragged through her. Lines of pain coursed like hot wires along her constricted limbs. She was panting too much; she was breathing in her own exhaled breath and she'd lose consciousness again. Suddenly a thin white line snapped into position in the air above her head. She blinked and realised it was light filtering between the planks. At the same time there had been the unmistakable sound of the light switch. Who was it? Whose footsteps, whose breathing, could she hear above her?

Fat-armed Wife cried again, 'Help!' Her fist had only a few inches of travel before it hit the wood.

There was the sound of footsteps and breathing. There came the scratching of a key in a padlock.

Abruptly the lid opened and light blinded her; she was aware only of the blurred outline of a figure, one arm outstretched to hold the lid open. She had to close her eyes. She couldn't move, yet at the same time she felt as if she'd burst upwards from underwater, gasping for air. She called out but her mouth was stiff with pain, like she'd been at the dentist. Her eyes were still squeezed tight shut. Cramps seized her limbs; she was in agony. She couldn't move, she couldn't even half sit up. She blinked, squinted; her eyesight adjusted to the painful whiteness and she could see the outline of the figure, but couldn't at first work out who it was. Details of his face and figure filled in the silhouette. As she knew it must be, this was Jetman. It was like a fearful plunge into freezing water. It changed everything she thought had happened in the Velvet Rooms.

'Jetman . . .?'

'Yes I am Jetman. I am also Thruster. You are Fat-armed Wife. And you are Blob. And you are Wet Lysette.'

A dull stupidity settled over Fat-armed Wife. Even as this internal, mental darkness descended, so did the lid slowly, with crushing disappointment, lower and by degrees shut out light. The clasp was fastened. There was a final click as the padlock was let go.

DanceMaster enters Velvet Sanctuary

Sweetpea: tell us everything

DanceMaster: we are in the lobby

Big Black Woman: is she there?

DanceMaster: No. Neither is Jetman

Sweetpea: are the police there?

DanceMaster: I have called them in UK and here but it's difficult to know if they will come. They know we are here

Peach: *oh* ☹

DanceMaster: Peach it is not your fault - hold your horses

Big Black Woman: hi Honeycake hi Spam

DanceMaster: They say hi

Sweetpea: What time is it there?

DanceMaster: 8.15

DanceMaster:

Big Black Woman: sorry, don't know what 2 post.

Peach: *I am sorry I am sorry sorry sorry*

DanceMaster: The police did a trace on their phones and say they are still nearby, somewhere here.

Sweetpea:

DanceMaster:

DanceMaster: hold on, we were talking to the reception of the hotel here

Peach: *what is happening?*

DanceMaster: she was nice at first but now she doesn't like us because we cannot give the name of the guest we are waiting for, only the room number. She is becoming agitated because why are we waiting for who shows up at room 19

Big Black Woman: what is the time?

DanceMaster: 8.21

Sweetpea: what have u told the hotel people?

DanceMaster: we said the person who is really waiting for the guest isn't here yet, we are with her.

Big Black Woman: Is there anyone coming into the hotel?

DanceMaster: No it is strange and silent, quite modern with white walls and purple carpet. We are waiting in small lobby which is part of the corridor leading to the stairs. We can see the steps to the front door and no one has come in since we arrived. Psycho-dog is going to stand near anyone who walks up to the desk to try and overhear if they ask for room 19. If we are not thrown out first

Sweetpea:

Peach: *oh ☹ what's happening? I hate this. Was it me, what I did?*

Big Black Woman: time now?

DanceMaster: 8.28

Sweetpea:

Big Black Woman:

Sweetpea: Anyone?

DanceMaster: Nothing. No one. 8.32

Thruster left the works; the steel shutter rolled down behind him. The Granada waited, a zone of comfort and pride, within his control. It was covered in a thin veil of condensation. He removed the blanket that had lined the boot and burned it. He climbed in and drove to the service station and for two hours he cleaned the car, inside and out. He wiped every seat and surface with alcohol. Later on, when he got back, he would put the vehicle up on the ramp and steam-clean the underside, especially the treads of the tyres and the wheel arches. Given the circumstances, this was only a temporary measure. He'd have to get rid of the Granada. He'd take it to the quarry, where it would join the Renault in a watery grave. He vowed never again to take such a risk: he had started work without thought, without the detailed planning that had kept him safe so far. Vanity and excitement had clouded the proceedings and brought him close to danger.

By the time he'd finished it was light and he'd grown hungry. He drove the six miles back to the barracks and showed his pass. He parked outside the Naafi. The unexpected work had left him febrile with the expectation of being caught for real. The adrenalin was flowing in his body. He had the weightlifter's ability to read the chemical and hormonal changes that affected his physical perform-ance, so he knew this would continue until it was all over, done with – maybe as long as two weeks. He must claw back his excite-ment, cover his tracks, continue his preparations: the large meals to build stamina, the car cleaned, the wait for silence.

He sat by himself with his double all-day breakfast, with extra tinned tomatoes on fried bread on a separate plate. There were a few nods he had to give, but no one bothered him. He could concentrate. He went and re-filled his plate, his mug. He ate enough for two.

The meal was done. There would be several like this over the next few days. He cleared his tray and went to take a shower under very hot water. He returned to the Granada, which gleamed in the early sunlight. Even the door lock seemed to work better.

David Bowie played on the Armed Forces Radio as he motored around the usual circuit, checking security on his rota of buildings. 'Ground Control to Major Tom'. A pop/military drumroll marched the song forwards. That's what he liked about the drums, how they were the engine to a good song, drove it.

He walked fences, checked locks. He rattled bolts and pushed doors and windows. The same boundaries, always.

Back at the works, he turned up the heater so he could be naked. There was utter silence. He went closer to the trunk, watched it for several minutes. He drew up a chair and planted himself on it, knees wide apart. He watched, listened carefully. There was no movement, no sound at all. He began to overflow with anticipation.

In his head each extra minute of stillness, of quiet, was like taking a step down, further into the blackness of what he had become. And perhaps he needn't have come down here; that seemed possible. There had been a gate at the top of these steps: that gate had been set in a section of broken wall. The trigger to open the gate he'd stumbled on by accident, at least that's how it had seemed. There was that tiled floor strewn with rubble, the appearance of the

enemy, unarmed and harmless, his own sudden, automatic clench of
the trigger and the barrel of the gun heating his hand all at once, the
puff of the uniform jacket as, only an arm's length away, the bullet
sought, discovered the man's chest. The disturbance created by the
bullet, that sharp tug inwards, as if a small animal had turned tail and
run into the man's heart. The barrel of the gun warmer in his hand.
The agony on the man's face. At that point the gate had swung open
and shown him this set of stairs, and he'd started down.

Now, here, he could prolong this for as long as ten days.

Fat-armed Wife was semi-conscious. She imagined herself on the
scales in the bathroom at home, weighing herself. She saw Colin
awkwardly pulling on his clothes; somehow they always ended up
crooked, his belt at a slant, however much he tugged up one side or
the other. She re-lived the sale of her first company – the woman
who bought it was surprised to be asked to be photographed with
her, shaking hands over the signed documents in the attorney's
office, but had gracefully agreed. Then, in her dream, she and Colin
rocketed up Space Mountain at Disneyland; over the top they shot
at dizzying speed. She could hear Colin shouting next to her. She
herself counted – one, two, three – her eyelids peeled back and her
teeth gritted. The counting was the only way of dealing with the
continual terror. As they were hurled around the darkened interior,
strange sights came at them: a moon hung, still as a pool of water;
stars flashed past in a bewildering array that tripled their sensation
of speed; the swoop downwards and sudden banking had her shouting the numbers as loudly as the screams of other passengers. When
they coasted into the finishing area and the capsule released them,
she dreamed that Colin had become mentally retarded. He was hol-
lering and whooping but his mouth had slipped sideways and his
eyes stared. He leaned over to kiss her but missed her mouth and
instead slobbered over her chin and nose. There was the squirm of
his tongue against her face. His mouth was cold from the ice-cream.
It felt obscene; she was scared. She wanted to leave the dream.

She nosed along, the darkness of her mind illuminated by flashes of memory. When she bumped against the membrane between reality and the Velvet Rooms, sexual excitement took root in her. There was no pain or unhappiness. She was looking for a gap through which she might reach Call Girl. I'm coming, she told him.

He arrived then; her beloved was next to her. The light in his eyes was so tempting. She moved towards him. He took her hand – and it was such a dead simple thing but it was all she'd ever wanted: their fingers to be entwined as their eyes met, held fast. Then she watched as their fingers separated in a reverse sequence; it was like the dream rolled backwards. 'Treasure,' came his voice, from far off.

'Please,' she begged as darkness descended. 'Don't go.' Her own voice sounded hollow, empty. When she tried to reach him there was only thin air, the darkness of her dream. All the times that she'd missed him were bunched together like a clot at the top of her throat; she was frightened to speak in case her own voice floated further away. She tried to school herself in grief. She wished to find some acceptance of the gap between them, but couldn't. He'd gone, even though his voice was writing its green sky-writing in her head closer than ever. She ached for him. She called again and again. It was as if she'd been handed everything – and then all at once, the next moment, it had been taken away and she was alone. It was a cold, cheerless place. She felt terrible anguish and hurt. She would need every ounce of strength. There was the sensation of falling back to earth, and of burning, but then she realised it wasn't heat but pain, which she was suffering as the sides of the box moved quickly towards her, fastened themselves against her, very tight, close. She could hear her own breath, loud; the warmth blew back against her face. It wasn't the box pressing in on her but the opposite: her hands were pushing against the surface a few inches over her face. She kept pushing, not merely hard, but with a wild passion that hammered in her chest, and the panic drove her mad . . .

It was no good. She lay there, breathing hard, exhausted, her hands against her chest.

It almost gave her a jump: she realised her fingers were touching the art deco cigarette lighter round her neck, the real thing.

*

DanceMaster stared at his fellow Velvet Roomers. Who were they? What were they? He didn't know. They had confirmation that Fat-armed Wife had arrived on the plane, that her phone was still signalling the aerial that covered the airport, but that no one was answering it. Jetman's phone was in the same area; no one answered that, either. Yet everyone waited here, paralysed. There was nothing they could do – they'd been expressly instructed to stay put. They were like refugees. If they were in the Velvet Rooms, thought DanceMaster, they would be acting together, the flow would be OK, but in the clumsier, quicker-moving parade of reality, they couldn't join forces. Anyone who made a suggestion was immediately cut down. Their separateness seemed cruel. Honeycake talked the most. She rambled wildly and speculated on plotlines from a hundred TV programmes that might offer some insight into what had happened. Psycho-dog came and went, always on the verge of leaving but sticking with it for now. Spam rested frequently in his room. DanceMaster led the way in the rounds of phone calls – to the police, to the embassy, to the friends and family of Call Girl in England, to Colin, currently in transit from Boston. He also organised refreshments. It was ridiculous that people needed sandwiches. He summoned his assistant and had her catch a flight over here. He called the press and gave a full account of the story so far to three separate journalists. More sandwiches. Reality, he thought, was a laughable machine. Mostly, he stared at the faces of the other Roomers and tried to read them. He prayed audibly.

There was a half-inch gap now on the hinged side of the box – Fat-armed Wife could feel its looseness signal her; it gave her hope and drove her to try harder, for longer. She scraped at the burned wood with the sharp edge of one of her rings, then held the flame of the cigarette lighter against that spot, burning deeper into where the hinge was fixed. Then she scraped again. She was in a cold sweat at the idea of setting the box and herself ablaze.

When the screws holding one hinge gave way, she managed to push sufficiently hard against the corner of the lid to apply leverage:

the second hinge twisted. Some minutes later she could sit up. She rolled clumsily out of the box, crying with pain as her big, over-weight limbs straightened. Pins and needles attacked. She could see the box now, an old wooden trunk, painted pale blue. The hinges had burst but the hasp had held good, so the lid had swung over onto that side. She couldn't stop crying at the sight and the smell and the mess. She rolled, crawled in a circle on her hands and knees. She wanted to see in every direction; she had to be ready for Thruster to come at her. Under her was carpet, full of dust, gritty and threadbare. The walls were a distance away, made of blockwork, except for one side which was of glass, which she couldn't see through. A televison rested on a broken garden seat. Facing it was a green armchair, its arms stained with oily residue. A long, thick door had been fashioned into a trestle table: on it were a Mac and a laptop. Printers and other bits of equipment rested on a shelf above it. A small camping fridge stood at the end of a squiggle of cable. There was a small metal window, but it was set too high up in the wall. It showed a blank grey sky, nothing else. The ceiling contained panels of fluorescent light, currently switched off. Probably these were – or had been – offices. The scent of engine oil and metal filled her nostrils. While she glanced around, took in these details, she was listening for *him*; but there was silence. Nothing.

It took some time to stand. One of her shoes was missing. Her whole body ached; her nerves sang. She took tentative steps – anx-ious to find a phone, a way out of here, someone who would help. She went first to the desk. An idea occurred to her; she checked behind the Mac. A familiar thin grey cable ran to a small white socket screwed to the wall underneath the makeshift table. She looked at the keyboard. The green On/Off button glowed conspicu-ously. She touched it and the screen sprang to life. 'Logged off. Please enter password.' She could have cried with frustration. It meant she couldn't email home, or DanceMaster, or anyone . . . Was there no phone, at all, anywhere? She stared at the little white plug in despair. She wanted to shout at it, in the vain hope that her voice would somehow get through.

There was no way round that password, not that she knew of.

Her eyes moved over the Mac, the laptop, a scanner, the printers, piles of stuff, litter.

Her right foot nudged a cardboard box. It was full of old cell phones. Clumsily she emptied the box onto the table and pawed through them, checking each one for power. None had a sim card, even; they were useless. She looked up, saw this desperate, big, brown-haired, fat-armed woman reflected in the glass wall. Seeing how pale and ill she looked, she felt a lunge of thirst and hunger.

The fridge: she went and looked. Inside was only one bottle of beer. She took it out, saw the label was in German. Maybe she was in Germany, or it was imported from there . . . There was no way of opening it unless she broke off the top – it depended on what else she could find. She carried it with her, limping painfully towards the door through the glass partition. On the way she passed the television. She tagged the On/Off button. More German – or what she thought was German – poured from the speaker. The picture caught up, popped onto the screen to show a nondescript mall and a young man indicating something behind him and talking. She switched it off and went and stood by the glass door. There was no sign of anyone. She pushed through and found herself in what had once been another office, presumably. The walls were white-painted brick and there was the same threadbare, gritty carpet underfoot. Her eye was caught by a tray balanced across a chair in the corner: on it stood a kettle. She limped over and touched the side. It was cold, half full. She dropped the beer bottle, tugged the cord from the base, took off the lid and drank deeply and quickly, spilling the stale water down the sides of her mouth, uncoordinated, her hands trembling.

Afterwards she stood dead still and listened intently. The water swarmed through her stomach: she could feel its life-giving power like never before.

There was nothing to be heard except her own breath.

Also on the tray was a clear plastic bag containing individual portions of long-life milk such as are served in hotels and restaurants. One by one, using her teeth, she peeled open every one and drank them – a sip each. Milk was food, energy. This took some minutes: there were more than fifty. She didn't stop to check if they were in date but noticed the word 'milch' – German. She was sure she was in Germany.

A Baby Belling cooker stood on a side table, its gas canister underneath. It meant there would be food somewhere but she couldn't see any. She went and pulled out the grill. She pinched up crumbs of grease and ate them; they tasted of bacon. She dropped the wire grate to one side and lifted the pan, licked it clean. Inside the little oven was a hard, dried out pastry of some sort. She ate it.

She walked the room, thinking, 'Find a way out, find a phone.' Terror was firmly lodged in her breast. She returned through the glass door and found a metal staircase. She hadn't known she was upstairs. As she descended she wished she had her other shoe. The metal was cold on the bare sole of her right foot as she limped down, one step at time, listening to make sure.

At the bottom a smell of burned wood filled her nostrils. There had been a fire down here and the charred room to her left had inches of water standing in it; she could see through the broken window that gave onto this corridor. There was no window letting out the other side, no daylight. She paused for a moment, registering the broken glass that stood around the edges of the interior window frame.

Further on there was another room: she peered in and saw, incongruously, a drum kit standing on a linoleum-tiled patch of floor. Beyond, in a little room to the side, there had obviously been a sink, a kitchen; it had all been ripped out. Pipes tracked across the wall and then ended for no reason. A drain gaped at her. She checked each inch of wall and surface for a phone. There was none. But, in here was a window, although it was caged in a wire grille. She went and looked out. She could see a landscaped bank with newly planted grass. It looked like it might be shoring up a new road. She grabbed the grille, pulled and pushed for several minutes until her fingers were raw. She could have cried with frustration. It was screwed tightly into the frame.

Among the dirt and cobwebs and debris on the window sill were three rings. She picked them up. There was a plain wedding band, a beautiful amber stone held in a gold clasp shaped like a fist, and an aquamarine cluster set in silver – this last one she'd given to Call

Girl. She put all three rings on. What it meant, their lying here, was too awful to think about; it begged such questions that she couldn't stop. It felt as if they'd been left to her as a sign – carry on this way.

She heard the sound of an engine starting up somewhere in the building. She was shocked. It wasn't a car engine; it had a steady tone. She recognised the sound from driving past highway repair teams using tools driven by compressed air. She didn't know whether to head towards it or run away. Either this was *him*, or it was someone who would help her, a rescuer. She was shaking, couldn't decide. She prayed and edged out of the room, nosing towards the sound, aiming to catch sight of whoever it was, before she herself was seen.

She pushed open another door: a toilet. Her bowels clenched. She retraced her steps and made her way towards where daylight flared in the corridor. The sound of the compressor was louder here. She turned towards it, kept going. As she drew closer she could hear more: the chink of some metal object. The regular, even sound of the engine was much louder.

She inched along until she was at the corner. The daylight was brighter, the noise louder. She came into a big, airy space. On the right was a roller door, made of grey aluminium slats, wide and tall enough to drive huge vehicles through. It was shut. She imagined that such a big door would have to be motorised; there was no way you could just lift it up, like a garage door.

The broken-up remnants of an oversize vehicle, an armoured troop carrier or suchlike, stood abandoned against the far wall, and the smell of oil and metal was stronger. This was a repair shop for military vehicles, she'd guess. High above, along the top of the roof, was a glass section such as might be found in a railway station. Parts of the floor had bolts sunk into the concrete like broken teeth. They marked the places where heavy machinery had been taken away. She trod forwards softly. Now she could see that in a bay at the other end was a hydraulic hoist and on it, lifted in the air, was the car – *that* car. She stared. The noise was, yes, a compressor, driving a high-pressure water jet. A shadow moved in a cloud of water vapour, visible only from the waist up because he was standing in a well, set underneath the vehicle.

There must be another door, apart from the big roller ... She realised she could walk safely – he couldn't hear or see her because he was engrossed in cleaning. She limped on, but only for a pace or two. It was obvious: there was no way out. The workshop had four square, high walls, interrupted only by the grey serrations of the roller door. She would have to find a switch ... there was none obvious. She tried to lift the shutters, touching the wall like a blind woman.

Nothing. She hobbled back to where she'd come from, and hid.

This had been done on purpose, she realised; it was impossible to escape. There was no door, no window, that wasn't barred or blocked up. There was no phone. It had been deliberately adapted by this man as a prison. She turned in circles, breathing heavily. Soon he'd finish cleaning the underside of the car ... She peered around and watched the shadowy figure moving, swaying as he directed the jet of vapour.

Round the sides of the bay, tools were leaning against the wall. There was an all-purpose toolbox, a socket set, various tool rolls, a wheel brace. Her eye was caught by a tyre lever – if she could take that back to the window, there was a chance she might prise the grille away from the frame and break the glass.

The breath hissed through her teeth. Her large frame wobbled, uncertain on its one shoe. He was working on the front wheel arches and the underside of the engine block; she didn't have long. She stepped into the open, faced him, eyes switching from the tyre lever to the man working underneath the car. She kicked off her other shoe. Under her breath – inaudibly – she counted, 'One, two, three ...' and set off across the broken concrete surface.

The compressor switched off and there was silence. She froze, only halfway. There came the sound of Thruster's footsteps as he shuffled around in the well beneath the raised vehicle. He was only a short distance away – she was by the rear axle, he was up front.

An intense fearfulness broke over her. Then she did this without thinking: she stepped forward and slapped down the row of hydraulic levers that stood out horizontally from the upright beam of the hoist. The car immediately started to drop – but slowly. She ducked to look underneath and for a fraction of a second she met Thruster's blank, uncaring eye as he turned. He put both hands on the low wall in front of him, levered himself up and rolled sideways, out from under the vehicle. The hoist settled the car back to ground level. She heard a shout – a release of anger – from the other side. He'd escaped.

For a while, all the Velvet Roomers were dead still, listening for the same truth to arrive – what had happened, what was going to happen.

DanceMaster stared sightlessly out of the rain-streaked window of the Intercontinental Hotel in Brussels. There were only so many times he could make the same calls to the same people without something new to report. And they would call him, if they . . .

Spam blinked and leaned on the back of the leather sofa they'd commandeered as their centre of operations, in the lobby. He was old in years and far from home, out of his comfort zone. None the less he would stick with it. He wished his brother and sister-in-law would stop calling DanceMaster's phone to check on him. It made him feel like an escaped lunatic. He missed the Sharland, all his things. The bath ran a whole lot quicker and hotter here, though.

Honeycake rested face down on the bed in her room. Like all of them, she was disappointed at the way their physical bodies acted as a barrier; the intimacy they'd had in the Velvet Rooms was stifled, killed by the overload of sensory material – the sight and sound of each other, the social and sexual faculties. The pecking order. She'd never been top dog, far from it, she'd always been somewhere near the bottom. She knew she talked too much but couldn't stop herself.

Psycho-dog paused for a while in his aimless wandering of the hotel corridors. He was hungry and not drunk enough. His thoughts turned again and again from on-line poker to Fat-armed Wife and back again.

All of them waited, connected, but utterly separate.

*

Fat-armed Wife was rooted to the spot, listening to Thruster's breathing – the sound was effortful. Why hadn't he appeared? She waited some more, but nothing. She was too afraid to move.

Maybe ten minutes later she took a cautious few steps and peered round the end of the car. He was up near the fender, sitting down.

He turned his head and stared at her. After a while he went back to looking at his foot: it was as if it belonged to someone else and he was trying to help. The hydraulic hoist had come down and trapped him.

He was utterly still now. It was uncanny, like a painting of someone. His breathing sounded as if he was trying to lift a heavy weight.

A feverish energy invaded her: she could reach the tyre lever and break the glass in that window. She hobbled over the pitted concrete and fetched it, then headed back the way she had come. She could not spare one glance at Thruster; even the act of looking might release him.

When she reached the window she tried to insert the end of the bar behind the grille to lever it off. It wouldn't fit. She tried banging it against the frame but there was no way it would break. She dropped the bar and headed back to the metal stairs – she could maybe climb up to the other window in the raised, office part of the building. She might see someone and call out.

Before she even reached the top floor she heard a faint scraping noise behind her: metal on concrete, down on the workshop floor. She listened hard. She turned towards the metal staircase to hear better.

She had no shoes on, now. The metal was hard, cold against the soles of her feet as she went down, one step at time, listening.

At the bottom of the stairs was the same smell of burned wood. As before, daylight flared where the corridor turned. As she drew closer she could hear more: yes, the chink of some metal object and that low groan.

She turned the corner and again the daylight was much stronger. The same big, airy space invited her. He must still be trapped, she hoped – begged – as she walked forwards.

She stopped when she heard a slight sawing sound. She took more steps, and could see as far as the driver's door. A corner of his shoulder was in view. It was moving: a methodical back and forth, in time with the sawing. He was sitting. His squat neck was bent over. She could see his knee pointing up. He was holding a flap of leather, pulling it back while he cut the leather of his boot with a little penknife – that was the sound and the movement of his shoulder.

She stood stock still.

He was cutting away his boot so he could pull himself free. Bitterly cold, she rocked from foot to foot. Her toes were aching harshly. She looked around for something to hit him with. The tyre lever was in the other room – but to use it would mean she'd have to get close to him.

A sudden vision came back to her: his hopping out from under the car, rolling sideways, his look, when she saw he was trapped.

She scouted for a weapon. There was a length of pipe but it was too long and thin, electrical conduit, stretching halfway up the wall before falling back crazily – even if she managed to break off a section it wouldn't be strong enough. She might check around the abandoned vehicle. Their eyes met – he was twisted round, watching her closely. His face was blank of expression. But she could move closer if she didn't look at his eyes. She walked slowly until she was level with the back of the car. Now she could see that blood had leaked from his boot, staining it a darker brown. The leather was cut from the eyelets down to the sole. He'd removed the bootlace and tied it in a single loose circle round his ankle. The penknife was in his clenched hand, and he was leaning on that hand to support his weight as he skewed round to see what she was doing; the knife was a tiny blade pointing out of the top of his fist.

Maybe she'd just wait like this, and outlast him. He'd lose consciousness. Help would come, wouldn't it? If everything stayed exactly like this, the stalemate would work in her favour.

For a full five seconds she met his eye. It was blank, as if nothing were happening. Yet his lips were compressed and there was that breathless noise coming from his throat. Then he turned back and continued with the knife: he sawed steadily at the leather. She took a step closer. He stopped sawing and turned again to watch her. She risked another step. He dropped his weight on to his elbow so that, although he was uncomfortably twisted, he had both hands free – one holding the knife, the other to grab her if she got close. She wavered. Again their eyes met. She went a step closer. He blinked, grunted. The car waited, inert, its weight – plus that of the rig – on his foot.

She couldn't do it. She couldn't hurt him even if she could think of a way of doing so. It was impossible, obscene. To be near him at all terrified her. She felt hopeless; she turned and ran as fast as she could between the bolts sprouting from the broken floor. She must find a way out. She needed help, someone who was willing, able, to hurt him, stop him. Her limping run took her back to the metal stairs, up, round and down again, trying every door she came across. She shivered with cold and fear. She stood underneath any window and shouted as loud as she could, over and over, for minutes at a time: 'Help!'

Silence. Nothing came back.

For half an hour she sat at the computer and tried the most popular passwords she could think of. Elvis. Jesus. All the signs of the Zodiac. None worked.

Fear overtook her again: she was alone. What was happening downstairs? She wound her courage to the highest pitch and again walked down to that enormous, light-filled space.

The top half of Thruster's body was naked. Next to him lay his vest and the heavy fleece shirt. His shoulder moved rhythmically as before; there was the same smell of concrete and oil and water and the long-ago fire. The movement of his shoulders was different: he wasn't sawing at the boot leather any more. There was this rhythmical twisting of his elbows, as if he were performing Tai Chi. The movement was repeated. Something . . . She went closer. He was turning a large spanner in a circle next to his calf muscle; end over end it went. The wrench was threaded through the bootlace to make a tourniquet.

He paused, looked at her over his shoulder. He was like an animal, occupying some other world from hers. The dull, instinctive expression, the lack of care. She looked at his ankle. The boot and the sock had been cut away to expose bare skin. Blood soiled the whole area. He gazed at her. It was all she could do, under that gaze, even to try to think of a way of stopping him. He turned away as if she were of little interest and continued with the tourniquet. Then he picked up his discarded shirt and used it to bind the spanner to his calf, so it would not untwist. She stood a short distance away and rocked from foot to foot, praying for the mental strength, the courage, to hurt him badly.

He leaned over and picked up the penknife. He pressed his thumb into his ankle joint, as if looking for something. He touched the inch-long blade against the skin and drew it round his ankle – the line wrote in red as blood welled from the cut. The knife went back to the start, wrote the line again, deeper . . . She could hear the same urgent noise from his throat, yes, as if he had been holding up that same heavy weight all this time. She wished she could use all the strength in her famously heavy, fat arms and strangle him, but she couldn't.

She turned and walked unsteadily away. She went back to the computer and for a further hour she guessed at passwords. None worked. She walked the outside skin of the building, cupping her hands to her mouth and shouting for help as loudly as she could.

Nothing came back. For the umpteenth time she walked either side of the roll-up shutter, looking for where the control might be to open it. Nothing.

She could picture Thruster's shoulder moving, the knife writing on the skin. Was what he was intending to do humanly possible? She doubted it. The silence was ominous; it was like a terrible weight, of supernatural density. She returned upstairs, searched again for a phone, for a way out. The computer – its telephone line a tenuous, fibre-thin connection to the outside and to the Velvet Rooms – mocked her with its demand for a password.

In a frenzy, she searched again.

There was nothing that might help her.

An hour later, standing near the desk, she heard the car start. She walked the walls like a trapped animal. She strained to listen again –

yes, it was the car engine. There was an unmistakeable clank as the wheels came off the ramp. The tick-over of the engine increased briefly, before dropping back again. Then, a minute or two later, came a low, churning, rattle of metal on metal. It went on for a number of seconds. She was at the top of the stairs, shivering with cold and fear. As she made her way down the darkened corridor a new breath of chill, fresh air moved against her face. She could hear the steady burble of the car's engine. When she turned the corner she saw the nose of the car pointing at the big roller door, which was fully retracted, open.

Where was he? Presumably struggling into the driver's seat, and then he would drive away? Any minute now she would hear the clunk of the car door, the selection of first gear; the car would move forwards – and she certainly wasn't going to stop him. She could only pray that he'd leave the shutter raised and she could escape. She waited, dead still, frozen with nerves. Would he come for her before he went? Why was nothing happening? The car was motionless. There was no sound other than the engine. She saw that a tyre was deflated. She edged closer, step by step. Now she could see that he wasn't in the driving seat. Sudden panic gripped her. She turned in a complete circle. Eerily, there was no sign of him. She waited silently. The clean, cold air moved through, washing out the scent of hydraulic oil, blood and burned wood. The engine burbled on. The giant steel shutter stood open. She summoned the courage to walk on.

The shortened leg was incongruous, wrong. In the same blink of an eye that she saw him – inert, incapable, lying face down – she rushed her hand to her mouth and turned and ran outside. The cold hit her even more forcefully. She made for the bank and scrambled up it, the ground freezing and wet but the freedom making her drunk with hope. She reached the top – a road. She began to wave at passing cars.

A translation of the police report was made for her some hours later, and it was only then that Fat-armed Wife discovered that she had at first been arrested for 'deliberate endangerment of the traffic'. The first Polizei at the scene didn't speak English and she didn't know a word of German. Only when she was taken to the police headquarters in Koblenz could she make herself understood. The Senior Public Prosecutor, Hans Almeier, immediately took her under his wing. It was his own wife who lent her clothes and soothed her distress. He arranged for the immediate transport by helicopter of the Velvet Roomers from Brussels. A message was sent to Colin in mid-flight.

She was struck by how, in the English version of the report, Thruster had become 'the author'. It stated, 'The author lay dead from blood lack. The determination of the kriminalpolizei persist: in the context of the immediate discovery the police attained at first a crucial witness with reference to the presumed author.'

And they found Call Girl.

The Velvet Roomers were asked which of them would be prepared to identify him; they chose to go all together. During the journey Hans Almeier told them that Thruster's fingertips were disfigured with perfect circles of scar tissue. In his opinion Thruster had deliberately burned them on the hotplate of an electric cooker to avoid identification by finger-printing. It implied that there was a criminal record attached to those prints somewhere in the world but they would probably never find it. They had unearthed several sets of false identity papers on the premises, one of a soldier who had died in '94, another a German scientist who had emigrated to Russia, another the identity of a child who had died aged only two days in 1970. They had taken a DNA sample but it hadn't matched anyone on the Europol database. Thruster remained anonymous, unknown. Their only hope of finding out who he really was, would be for someone to come forward when pictures were released to the press.

They climbed out of the police cars and walked self-consciously across the derelict car park in the wake of DanceMaster's chair. They were aware of photographers shouting. A helicopter blatted the air above them. Honeycake linked arms with Fat-armed Wife; now there was someone to look after, she felt better; that was her role.

They were taken to a separate building, a bunker which might formerly have housed fuel tanks or coal. DanceMaster rolled in first. There was the smell of wet diesel and cement. A grimy window was the only source of illumination. In the centre of the cramped space Call Girl hung on a chain, a little above head height. He was light and dry as cardboard, still and silent and curled in a foetal position, whitened by lime, fixed by rigor mortis. The strange, leaping figure could be seen in every detail as it hung there, the chain a set of hard, cold iron loops issuing from his neck. The thin, acne-scarred face showed like a dull, switched-off mask, bowed against the chest; the tattooed flesh had withered on the bone and become powdery, the eyes dull, dried-out pellets devoid of life and the black hair stiff and dry like a wig in a second-hand shop. His hands were white gloves, like those of a mime artist except limp and unusable, folded close against his chest. His legs were doubled under his chin. It gave the impression, thought Fat-armed Wife as they all fumbled to hold hands and silently prayed for him, yes, that he'd been frozen in time just at the moment he'd leapt – from standstill – as high as possible. And that was suitable somehow: Call Girl had always wanted, above all, to be in flight, not to crash to the ground, not to die.

She stepped forward, shaking like a leaf, to look at his tattoos. They'd lost some of their colour and had shrunk and condensed a little, like the writing on a balloon when you let the air out. She found her initials, FAW, in dense fat letters written on top of the dragon over his left breast. That signal, that writing on his body, reached her, finally.

For real, she touched him; she laid her hand against his face and told him out loud that she loved him. She was overcome; she couldn't say any more.